I0764580

SUN BOAT

THE ODYSSEY DECIPHERED

Michael MacRae

C-FAR BOOKS

COPYRIGHT © 2014 by Michael MacRae

Michael MacRae has asserted his right under the Copyright Designs and Patterns Act 1988 to be identified as the author of this work. This work is sold subject to the conditions that it shall not by way of trade or otherwise, be lent, resold, hired out, or otherwise circulated without the publisher's prior consent in any form of binding or cover other than that in which it is published and without a similar condition including this condition being imposed on the subsequent purchaser.

ISBN 978-0-646-91773-3

Cover design: Jacqueline Houghton

C-FAR BOOKS

Penelope (Vatican Collection, Rome)

'Odysseus wrought no wrong in deed or word to any man in the land, as the wont is of divine kings – one man they hate and another they love. Yet he never wrought iniquity at all to any man.'

Penelope to the herald Medon *The Odyssey,* Book 4: 690

CONTENTS

ACKNOWLEDGEMENTS

My deepest gratitude extends to Jacqueline Houghton who accompanied me throughout the creation of this book. Her encouragement and multiple edits of the evolving manuscript have been invaluable.

Many thanks also to Alastair O'Brien for his patient technical support.

PREFACE

The Iliad and *The Odyssey* are the oldest complete books in the western world. They are twin aspects of a single theme, the Trojan War and its aftermath. Together they constitute the first expression of the western mind in literary form. *The Iliad* means 'the poem about Ilium or 'Ilios', which was the early place name for Troy. *The Odyssey* recounts the adventures experienced by the Greek prince Odysseus during the years that followed the sacking of Troy. Odysseus is more readily known by his popular Roman title, Ulysses.

Both *The Iliad* and *The Odyssey* were composed in the style of ancient oral poetry. As such, the language is direct and dramatic, maintaining a dignity of expression. The translations existent today cannot be identified with the language of any particular people or place, for the texts have been derived from traditional dialects, mostly Ionic Greek, although a few Aeolic forms can be recognized, as well as an element of extremely old Greek. Certain scholars consider the epics to be imperfectly unified accounts derived from the joining of several 'remembered' ancient ballads or as mythic embellishments added to a short original manuscript. Because of the stylistic variations, the poems have been held to be neither of the same period nor by the same author.

Homer

It is known that Homer, the supposed original author/editor of the works, had collected various myths and legends which he then collated into two seemingly coherent sagas.

Homer was renowned as a 'divinely-inspired' poet who, although old and blind, still managed to make a living as an itinerant bard or singer. His year and place of birth remain a mystery, as no definitive record of his life exists.

Quotations from Homer's epics made in the fourth and third centuries B.C. show the texts then current to have been widely divergent. These disagreements do not appear to have been resolved until about 250 B.C. when the scholar Aristarchus of Somothrace (220 - 143 B.C.) published editions that were regarded as authoritative. It is not known whether Aristarchus prepared his edition from several different manuscripts or if he had recourse to an impressive single text from earlier times.

Homer's geographical detail of the Mycenaean world was so accurate that it enabled the amateur archaeologist Heinrich Schliemann (A.D. 1822 - 1890) to locate the long lost citadels of Troy and Mycenae. Actual place names including Egypt, Ethiopia, Crete, Phoenicia and Libya have all been identified within the texts of Homer's *Iliad* and *The Odyssey*, However, when Odysseus comes to relate his travels to the Phaeacian elders, the imagery he uses is essentially mythopoeic. He tells of visiting a land wherein dwelt the one-eyed Cyclops, of another that was inhabited by cannibalistic giants and of a faraway paradisiacal island that was the abode of the sweet-singing goddess, Calypso. Despite this mythic camouflage, scholars throughout the ages have generally accepted that *The Odyssey* is based upon historical facts. Very few however, are in agreement as to the actual location of these various, mysterious lands.

Before introducing the reader to this present interpretation of *The Odyssey*, a brief description of *The Iliad's* storyline is necessary.

The Iliad

Paris, son of the Trojan king, Priam, has abducted Helen, a beautiful Greek queen. The princes of Greece plot a rescue mission and under the leadership of King Agamemnon, they launch an armada of ships and sail northwards. Landing upon the coast of Troy, the Greeks beach their ships and set camp beside them. Bitter skirmishes and a siege lasting ten long years take place on the Scamander Plain, a barren stretch of land that lies between the coast and the walls of the Trojan citadel.

During this time, the legendary Greek hero Achilles argues bitterly with King Agamemnon and departs the battlefield. He later returns to slay the

Trojan champion, Hector. A final victory for the Greeks seems elusive and it is not until the Greek prince Odysseus devises the idea of a giant wooden horse that the Greek army is finally able to enter the city and sack it. In the aftermath of Troy's destruction the Greek chieftains agree to divide the spoils of war. Having loaded their ships with ***'stores of gold'*** and ***'fair girdled women'*** they quickly set sail for Greece. Among the last to leave the shores of Troy, a forlorn Odysseus complained that apart from a sculpted figurine called the Palladium, he had received no share of Troy's stolen treasures. Having stood in Troy's central temple, the Palladium was a sacred image of the virgin goddess, Pallas Athena. In her role as the patroness of Troy, Pallas Athena had been beseeched by the Trojans to protect their beleaguered city.

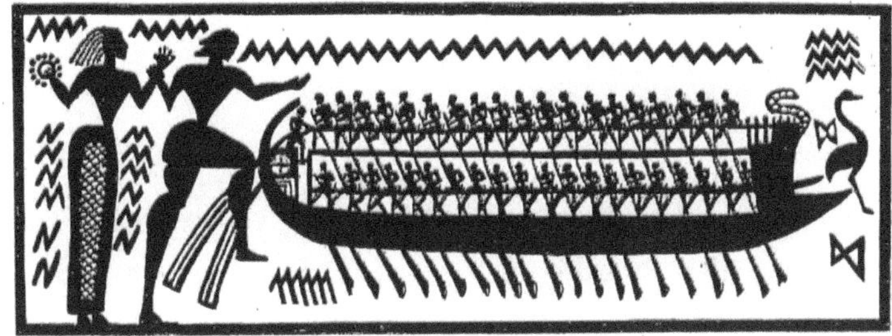

A stylized vase painting from Thebes depicts Paris abducting Helen

The Odyssey

Immediately after he departs from the shores of Troy, Odysseus is waylaid by a terrible storm and becomes totally disoriented. The storm is the first in a series of ill-fated events that befall him as he endeavors to find his way home. The general consensus is that Odysseus went 'missing' for ten to twenty years but it is also possible that Odysseus took as long as forty years to complete his Odyssey. A majority of scholars believe that Homer's version was enacted within the limits of the Aegean and Adriatic Seas. Contrary to this belief, other historical authors have suggested that the events described in *The Odyssey* occurred far from the shores of the Mediterranean region. An example of this is found in Odysseus' description of what appears to be icebergs.

> ***'... wandering rocks that no man could scale even if he had twenty hands and twenty feet... for they run sheer up, as though they had been polished'***

From the time they inherited the lucrative Minoan sea-trading routes (c.1600 B.C.) the Mycenaeans prided themselves on their seamanship. It is highly unlikely that Odysseus would have been extolled as a great hero and revered thereafter as 'god-like' if he was unable to navigate a simple course from Turkey to Greece c.1160 B.C. It has been estimated that an ancient Greek warship could have been rowed across the Aegean in about three days; a small sailboat could accomplish the journey in about the same period of time.

The Odyssey is comprised of a number of separate voyages, each of which took between nine to nineteen days to complete. Considering how Homer makes casual mention of places as far afield as Phoenicia, Egypt, Libya and Ethiopia, it makes little sense that a commander of ships could be 'lost' within the Mediterranean for a period of twenty years. Ancient Greek and Latin writers such as Polybius (200 - 118 B.C.), Apollodorus of Athens (165 - 115 B.C.), and Strabo (c.64 B.C. - c.24 A.D.) have all speculated on how Odysseus may have sailed into the Atlantic Ocean while others including Plutarch (60 A.D. - 119 A.D.) and Tacitus (55 A.D. - 120 A.D.) remained resolute in their belief that *The Odyssey* was enacted in regions far distant from the recognizably familiar lands of the Mediterranean. It is naive to underestimate the navigational skills and courageous attitudes of ancient peoples. Writing two hundred years after the event, the Greek traveller and geographer Herodotus (490 - 425 B.C.) reported that Phoenicians in the employ of Pharaoh Necho had circumnavigated the continent of Africa c.610 - 595 B.C.

> *The Phoenicians sailed from the Arabian Gulf into the Southern Ocean and every autumn put in at some convenient spot on the Libyan coast, sowed a patch of ground and waited for next year's harvest. Then having got in their grain they put to sea again. After two years they rounded the Pillars of Hercules and in the course of the third they returned to Egypt.* **(i)**

Even more astonishing is Strabo's claim that immediately after the sacking of Troy, King Menelaus had sailed across the Mediterranean to the Atlantic Ocean, navigated his way southward along the Africa coast, doubled Capo di Buona Speranza and thence into the Indian Ocean before returning to Egypt:

> *They who assert that Menelaus went by sea to Ethiopia, tell us he directed his course past Cadiz into the Indian Ocean; with which say they, the long duration of his wanderings agrees, since he did not*

(i) Herodotus, *Histories* 4:42

arrive there till the eighth year; others that he passed through the isthmus which enters the Arabian Gulf; and others again, through one of the canals. At the same time the idea of this circumnavigation, which owes its origin to Crates, is not necessary; we do not mean it was impossible, (for the wanderings of Odysseus are not impossible) [p. 61] but neither the mathematical hypothesis, not yet the duration of the wandering, require such an explanation; for he was both retarded against his will by accidents in the voyage, as by [the tempest] which he narrates five only of his sixty ships survived; and also by voluntary delays for the sake of amassing wealth Nestor says [of him]. Thus he, provision gathering as he went, and with gold abundant, roamed to distant lands. **(ii)**

The Stranded Greek King

Because of the eclectic nature of Homer's source material, many anomalies occur in his seemingly historical work. One of the most obvious examples concerns the stranding in Egypt of the above-mentioned Menelaus, King of Sparta. The modern translator of *The Odyssey*, E.V. Rieu, believed that among the myriad of myths at Homer's disposal there existed two separate stories of a marooned Greek prince. One he assigned to King Menelaus (Book IV, Line 290), while the other he accredited to Odysseus (Book XIV, Line 277).

A Stranded Menelaus

We should have run clean out of provisions and my men would have starved if a goddess had not taken pity upon me and saved me in the person of Idothea, daughter of Proteus, the old man of the sea, for she had taken a great fancy to me. She came to me one day when I was by myself, as I often was, for the men used to go with their barbed hooks all over the island in the hope of catching a fish or two to save them from the pangs of hunger. "Stranger", said she, "it seems to me that you like starving in this way, at any rate it does not greatly trouble you, for you stick here day after day, without even trying to get away though your men are dying by inches."

(ii) Strabo, *Geography* Book 1 Chapter 2:31

A Stranded Odysseus

> ***For a whole month the wind blew steadily from the South and there was no other wind, but only South and East. As long as corn and wine held out the men did not touch the cattle when they were hungry; when, however, they had eaten all there was in the ship, they were forced to go further afield with hook and line, catching birds and taking whatever they could lay their hands on; for they were starving. One day, therefore, I went up inland that I might pray heaven to show me some means of getting away.***

In the Menelaus version, the wandering nobleman is destitute in Egypt and unable to return home. To ward off starvation he and his crew are forced to scavenge amidst the rocky shoreline. This scenario seems totally out of context as the final chapters of the *Iliad* inform us that King Menelaus was reunited with his wife, Queen Helen and together they had departed Troy in a treasure-laden ship. It was customary for Mycenaean plunderers to sail directly to Egypt's Nile Delta; for it was there that they could conveniently dispose of captured slaves and pillaged treasure in exchange for prized Egyptian commodities. Far from being destitute, Menelaus would surely have traded some of his booty for food, as the Isle of Pharos was at that time the largest commercial port in the Mediterranean.

Homer is adamant in his claim that King Menelaus and Queen Helen had sailed to Egypt after the fall of Troy. In Book IV: Line 106 of *The Odyssey,* Homer reports that whilst they were in Egypt, Menelaus and Helen were presented with royal gifts including ten talents of gold and two baths of silver **(Note 1)**. A further 245 lines on (line 351), Homer reports that Menelaus and his crew have become stranded on Egypt's Isle of Pharos. Their plight is so desperate that they are forced to scavenge along the shoreline for food. No mention is made of Helen's whereabouts nor is it explained why Menelaus' ship was not amply supplied with food for its return voyage to Sparta. If Menelaus had stowed his ship with Egyptian gifts of silver and gold, it surely follows that he would have also stocked the holds with enough rations to survive the unpredictable events of ancient sea journeying.

It seems improbable that King Menelaus was the Greek personage left stranded on the Egyptian Isle of Pharos. A more likely scenario identifies Odysseus as the marooned prince. For all his cunning and heroic efforts at Troy, Odysseus had failed to acquire any of the stolen treasures. With the exception of the sacred Palladium (a small statue of the goddess Athena), Odysseus had departed from Troy impoverished and it is doubtful that he would have returned home in such a state. In setting a course for Egypt, Odysseus might have intended to reunite with his fellow Greek sea captains and thereby receive his fair share of Troy's pillaged booty. This however was not to be, for Odysseus and his comrades had aroused the ire of the goddess Athena. Nestor, a seafaring compatriot of Odysseus, reports:

> ***When, however, we had sacked the city of Priam*** (Troy) ***and were setting sail in our ships as heaven had dispersed us, then Jupiter saw fit to vex the Argives on their homeward voyage; for they had not all been either wise or understanding, and hence many came to a bad end through the displeasure of Jupiter's daughter Athena, who brought about a quarrel between the two sons of Atreus*** (Agamemnon and Menelaus).

Odysseus steals the Palladium from Troy

It seems evident that having departed from Troy the various Greek fleets had been subjected to unfavorable winds and driven off course. As a result, Odysseus failed to rendezvous with his comrades in Egypt and probably found himself stranded in the Port of Pharos (Rhakotis) where he subsequently became destitute.

The Vagabond Adventurer

Odysseus was well acquainted with playing the role of a destitute beggar. Queen Helen describes him entering the citadel of Troy as follows:

> ***... he covered himself with wounds and bruises, dressed himself in rags and entered the enemy's city looking like a menial or a beggar,***

and quite different from what he did when he was among his own people.

In Book XIV, wily Odysseus again assumes the role of a lowly beggar. Invited to spend the night in the hut of the pig-herder Emunaeus, he relates an apparently fictitious account of the events that befell him after his departure from Troy:

On the fifth day we reached the river Aegyptus (Egypt)***; there I stationed my ships in the river, bidding my men stay by them and keep guard over them while I sent out scouts to reconnoitre from every point of vantage. But the men disobeyed my orders, took to their own devices and ravaged the land of the Egyptians, killing the men and taking their wives and children captive... and I wish I had died then and there in Egypt for there was much sorrow in store for me.***

In Book XVII we read how Odysseus, once more in the guise of a ragged beggar, finally enters his palatial home. When Antinous hurls a stool at him, Odysseus defends his disheveled appearance by reiterating the tale of his unfortunate voyage to Egypt:

I had a number of servants, and all the other things that people have who live well and are accounted wealthy, but it pleased Jupiter to take it all away from me. He sent me with a band of roving robbers to Egypt. It was a long voyage and I was undone by it.

Odysseus' account of his misfortunes in Egypt presents a clear indication that he, rather than Menelaus, became stranded there.

Helen's Presence in Egypt

Other Greek authors such as Stesichorus (c.600 B.C.), Herodotus (c.490 - 425 B.C.) and Euripides (c.420 B.C.) contradict Homer's writings. Their accounts state that Helen was never abducted to Troy, nor did she spend ten years of her life there. According to their sources, the eloping couple was swept by storm to Egypt whereupon Paris fell foul of the local authorities and was deported. Having been separated from her lover, Helen was stranded in Egypt. She remained there for at least eight years, patiently awaiting the return of her seafaring husband. Visiting Egypt in the fifth century B.C., the Greek historian and geographer Herodotus was granted an opportunity to converse with the priests of Heliopolis. With exclusive access to records that were stored in the Temple of Ra, the priests were able to confirm the tradition that Helen had abode in Egypt for a good many years. Based upon what the priests told him, Herodotus wrote:

> *When I inquired of the priests, they told me that this was the story of Helen. After carrying off Helen from Sparta, Alexandrus* (Paris) *sailed away for his own country; violent winds caught him in the Aegean and drove him into the Egyptian sea; and from there (as the wind did not let up) he came to Egypt, to the mouth of the Nile called the Canopic mouth, and to the Salters.*

Herodotus claimed that Homer knew of this legend *'but seeing that it was not as well suited to epic poetry as the tale of which he made use, Homer rejected it but showing that he knew of it.'* **(Note 2)**

In Book 17 of his *Geography*, Strabo provides not only a detailed description of the Nile Delta but also confirms that the beautiful Helen had resided there for a time:

> *After the canal that leads to Schedia, one's next voyage to Canobus is parallel to that part of the coastline which extends from Pharos to the Canobic mouth. A narrow ribbon-like strip of land extends between the sea and the canal and on this, after Nicopolis, lies the little Taposeiris, as also the Zephyrium, a promontory which contains a shrine of Aphrodite Arsinoe. In ancient times, it is said, there was a city called Thronis here, which was named after the king who received Menelaus and Helen with hospitality. At any rate, the poet* (Homer) *speaks of Helen's drugs as follows: "goodly drugs which Polydamna, the wife of Thon, had given her."* **(iii)**

These so-called 'goodly drugs' were probably opiates as Homer further suggests in Book 4 of *The Odyssey:*

> ***Helen drugged the wine with a herb that banishes all care, sorrow and ill-humour. Whoever drinks wine thus drugged cannot shed a single tear all the rest of the day, not even though his father and mother both of them drop down dead, or he sees a brother or a son hewn in pieces before his very eyes.*** **(iv)**

(iii) Strabo, *Geography* Book 17: Chapter 1 Section 16
(iv) Homer, *The Odyssey* Book 4: lines 227 - 30

PREFACE

The Lost City of Thronis (Herakleion)

Engulfed by the sea about 1200 years ago, the Egyptian cities of Herakleion and Eastern Canopus had once stood at the mouth of the now extinct Canopic branch of the Nile. References to the cities are found in Greek mythology and the writings of ancient historians. Herodotus, who visited the cities in the year 450 B.C., reported that *'a temple to Heracles* (Hercules) *at the mouth of the Nile known as the Canopic mouth'* had existed there from the time of the Trojan War. Another Greek historian, Diodorus Siculus (90 - 30 B.C.), reports that Herakleion was *'the former emporium of the Egyptians'* and that it was named in honour of the same Greek god Heracles, who according to legend had once saved the city from a severe flooding of the Nile. Strabo, who lived at the time of Christ, described the location and immense wealth of Herakleion. His contemporary Seneca condemned the cities for their decadent and corrupt lifestyles.

Despite the numerous references to these two cities, the first real evidence of Herakleion's existence was not discovered until the year A.D. 2000, when French archaeologist Frank Goddio reported that he had found ruins lying on the seafloor about six kilometres off the coast of the Nile Delta. Concentrating on an area 1,000 metres long and 8,000 metres wide, Goddio located the remains of several significant temples as well as statues of gods and goddesses, bronze coins and pottery. Among the remarkable artifacts recovered by Goddio and his fellow marine archaeologists was a large greywacke stele that commemorates Herakleion by its Egyptian name Thronis. In October 2004, divers recovered a gold plaque that dates to the third century B.C. Inscriptions on the plaque confirm that the submerged city found by Goddio four years earlier was indeed the fabled Herakleion.

Jean-Daniel Stanley, a geoarchaeologist with the Smithsonian Institution in Washington D.C. reports *'there are no written documents on how, when, or why these two cities went down'*. He and his colleagues at the European Institute of Marine Archaeology firmly believe that the destruction of Herakleion and the Eastern Canopus was sudden and catastrophic *'because in both places gold and jewellry were found. Had there been time, the people would surely have taken these with them when fleeing'*. An analysis of cores taken from the seafloor, as well as high-resolution seismic profiles, suggest a severe flooding of the Nile had caused the land to suddenly liquefy into mud. The recovery of two Arabic coins dated A.D. 724 and A.D. 743, as well as written records documenting a major flooding of the Nile between A.D. 741 to A.D. 742

provides further evidence that the disaster had most likely occurred at this time.

Having reviewed the claims of Helen's onetime presence in the now submerged city of Thronis (Herakleion), let us now turn our attention to the nearby island of Pharos. Lying a mere twenty eight kilometres to the west of Thronis, the Isle of Pharos may well have served as the initial departure place for Odysseus' mysterious sea voyages.

Egypt's Isle of Pharos

The priests of Heliopolis proclaimed the Sun God Atum to be the 'sum of all existence'. According to their teachings, Atum by 'means of his own will' had risen up from the bosom of the cosmic ocean. Adopting the name Ra, the Sun God then soared to the heights of heaven and from this high vantage point he sighted the mound of a small island. Blazing in glory, Atum Ra beamed his spirit down upon the mound and so began the work of civilization. We might imagine that the site chosen by Atum Ra was the Nile's Isle of Pharos. From time immemorial, the Egyptians had respected the island as a sacred sanctuary. Alexander the Great in recognition of the island's ancient status had accordingly chosen the site to establish the great centre of worldly knowledge called Alexandria. Guarding the marine entrance to Egypt, the Isle of Pharos had long stood aloof from the mainland. Its proud isolation came to an end however, when the Royal Ptolemys built a causeway to the island and gradually the shoreline filled in to form a narrow land bridge.

From primordial times, the sea-caverns that lie beneath the Isle of Pharos were thought to be the domain of the Paleolithic seal-god Proteus (Phocus). Described as ***'an old man of the sea'*** Proteus was regarded as the ***'knower of all things'***. It seems appropriate that the sum of all the ancient world's knowledge had been housed in Alexandria's famous library, which was situated on the headland above Proteus' caverns.

Egyptian mythology also informs us that the indigenous inhabitants of the Lower Nile considered their womb-shaped, fertile Delta to be feminine in character. This region of Egypt was dedicated to the cobra snake-goddess Buto (*Wadjet*). The feminine wiles of the snake-goddess can perhaps be recognised in the persona of Proteus' daughter, Eidothee. The absence of prehistoric remains or artifacts on the Isle of Pharos itself suggests that apart from the shoreline, it had been kept as a wild and leafy sanctuary.

In about the year 2100 B.C., the island became the centre of a mighty transformation. With plans submitted to local authorities by Cretan or Phoenician marine architects, a vast Pre-Hellenic system of harbour works was established at Pharos. The extent of the now submerged harbour exceeded the size of the isle itself. The works consisted of an inner basin covering 150 acres and an outer basin of about half that area. The massive sea wall, jetties and quays were constructed of enormous stones, some of which weighed six tons.

At the time of the Trojan War, the Isle of Pharos was acknowledged as the maritime capital of the ancient world - a status it continued to celebrate up until and beyond the time of Alexander.

Alexander the Great (356- 323 B.C.)

Having liberated Egypt from the oppressive yoke of Persian rule, Alexander the Great was thereafter hailed as the legitimate heir of Egypt. In a tradition that dated back to 3200 B.C., Alexander was presented with the 'double crown' of Upper and Lower Egypt and like all the pharaohs who had preceded him, he was declared a divine god. Portrayed with the customary ram's horns of Amun Ra, Alexander's image was replicated throughout Egypt. Etched alongside his countenance a royal cartouche pronounced:

> *Horus, the strong ruler, he who seizes the lands of the foreigners, beloved of Amun and the chosen one of Ra - meryamun setepenra Aleksandros.*

Plutarch's *Life of Alexander* reports that Alexander's esteem for Egypt (and himself) became so great that he decided to build:

> ... *a large and populous Greek city which should bear his name and*

with the advice of his architects was on the point of measuring off and enclosing a certain site for it. Then in the night as he lay asleep he saw a wonderful vision. A man with very hoary locks and of a venerable aspect appeared to stand by his side and recite these verses: ***"Now there is an island in the much-dashing sea in front of Egypt; Pharos is what men call it."***

Alexander was familiar with the Homeric epics and apparently these lines were enough to call to mind the long passage from Book IV of *The Odyssey* where Pharos is described as offering:

> ***... a good harbour where one could pull ships up onto the shore and take on water.***

Plutarch continues on to tell us that Alexander:

> *... rose up at once and went to Pharos, which at that time was still an island, a little above the Canobic mouth of the Nile, but now it has been joined to the mainland by a causeway. And when he saw a site of surpassing natural advantages (for it is a strip of land like enough to a broad isthmus extending between a great lagoon and a stretch of sea which terminates in a large harbour), he said he saw now that Homer was not only admirable in other ways, but was also a very wise architect, and Alexander ordered the plan of the city to be drawn in conformity.* **(v)**

Alexander revering Horus

(v) Plutarch, *Life of Alexander* 26:1

Library of Alexandria

Shortly after the premature death of Alexander, Ptolemy I decided that a place of learning should be established within the model city of Alexandria. Originally called the Temple of Muses or *Musea*, Ptolemy's library complex continued to expand and eventually became renowned as the academic capital of the ancient world. With ready access to the library's extensive array of collected written works, scholars from the four corners of Alexander's empire were able to resolve scientific problems that had long puzzled previous great thinkers. A multitude of new disciplines such as grammar, manuscript preservation and trigonometry were established there. Mathematical and geometric theories were formulated, astronomical and geographical distances calculated and many breakthroughs in medical research achieved. (see POSTSCRIPT)

In 2004 a team of Polish-Egyptian archaeologists excavated a massive, ancient precinct dedicated to learning and research pursuits. Located in Alexandria's Bruchion district, the site revealed thirteen lecture halls each with a central podium. Classical writers who had visited Alexandria tell us that the university contained botanical gardens, courtyards, an astronomical observatory and a zoological park that housed animals from the far distant reaches of Alexander's empire.

The Pharos of Alexandria

Listed as one of the Seven Wonders of the Ancient World, an enormous lighthouse called the Pharos of Alexandria was completed in about 276 B.C. Its powerful beacon not only guided ships into the safety of its harbour but also served to symbolize the dispersion of illuminating knowledge.

A Spherical Earth

An intention of this current interpretation of *The Odyssey* is to illustrate the probability of Odysseus having sojourned in Egypt. Although Homer never places him directly in Egypt, he nonetheless suggests that the Greek prince did spend time in that land (albeit by means of having Odysseus give a supposedly fictitious account of his travels to Emaneus, the pig-herder):

> ***I stayed there for seven years and got together much money among the Egyptians, for they all gave me something.*** **(vi)**

If in fact Odysseus had spent seven years in the Land of the Pharaohs, it follows that he would have had plenty of time to absorb the tenets of ancient Egyptian sun worship. In a similar manner to the later Alexander the Great, Odysseus may have identified himself, or became identified, as a son of Amun Ra. In an essay entitled *The Naos of Heracleion*, Professor Jean Yoyotte states:

> *It is well known that the first Greeks settling in Egypt had assimilated Amun-Râ, king of the Egyptian gods and patron of famous Thebes, with their own Zeus, king of the Olympian gods. Also and more curiously, the young lunar god Khonsou, son of Amun of Thebes, had been assimilated with Herakles, son of Zeus and had even sited several stages and minor exploits of the famous hero traveller on the coast of the Delta. We know that from the 10th century onward, Khonsu had acquired great popularity as a saviour, healer and soothsayer. This would no doubt go a long way towards explaining that in the town of Canopus his cult had exceeded that of Amun to the extent that the foreigners there considered his temple as a sanctuary of Herakles* (Heracles).

Although Professor Yoyotte does not directly identify Khonsu (Heracles) with Odysseus, it is fascinating to consider that the minor exploits ascribed to a famous hero traveller on the coast of the Delta may well have been based on deeds enacted by Odysseus. Whether he was in the spirit of Heracles or merely in quest of adventure, Odysseus apparently set sail in the direction of the rising sun and in doing so he wittingly or unwittingly, became the first man to circumnavigate the world. Well-renowned for their remarkable sailing skills, the Phoenicians of Cadiz (c.900 B.C.) held a firm belief that the seafaring Heracles (Hercules) had completed a

(vi) *The Odyssey,* Book XIV

circumnavigation of the Earth c.1200 B.C. A temple to Heracles was erected in honour of this extraordinary feat and before venturing out into the sea the Phoenicians would customarily visit it to petition for a safe passage.

Coincidentally, the first accurate measurements of the Earth's circumference were calculated at Alexandria, as were the first proposed models of a heliocentric solar system. Alexandria's famous library also served as the place in which Aristarchus of Somathrace undertook the task of rewriting *The Odyssey.* Sifting his way through the various versions that had been accumulating on the library's shelves, Aristarchus completed what is thought to be an accurate interpretation of Homer's original work, or at least we would hope so as all of the subsequent translations of *The Odyssey* are based on the Aristarchus text. *Sun Boat* attempts to demystify *The Odyssey* by presenting the reader with both mythical and historical evidences of Odysseus' circumnavigation of the Earth c.1160 - 1132 B.C.

Samuel Butler's (A.D. 1900) translation of *The Odyssey* is referenced but in order to help clarify certain points, extracts from the Butcher and Lang translation have occasionally been used.

The hawk-god Horus seated upon the boat of Ra, Papyrus of Nu

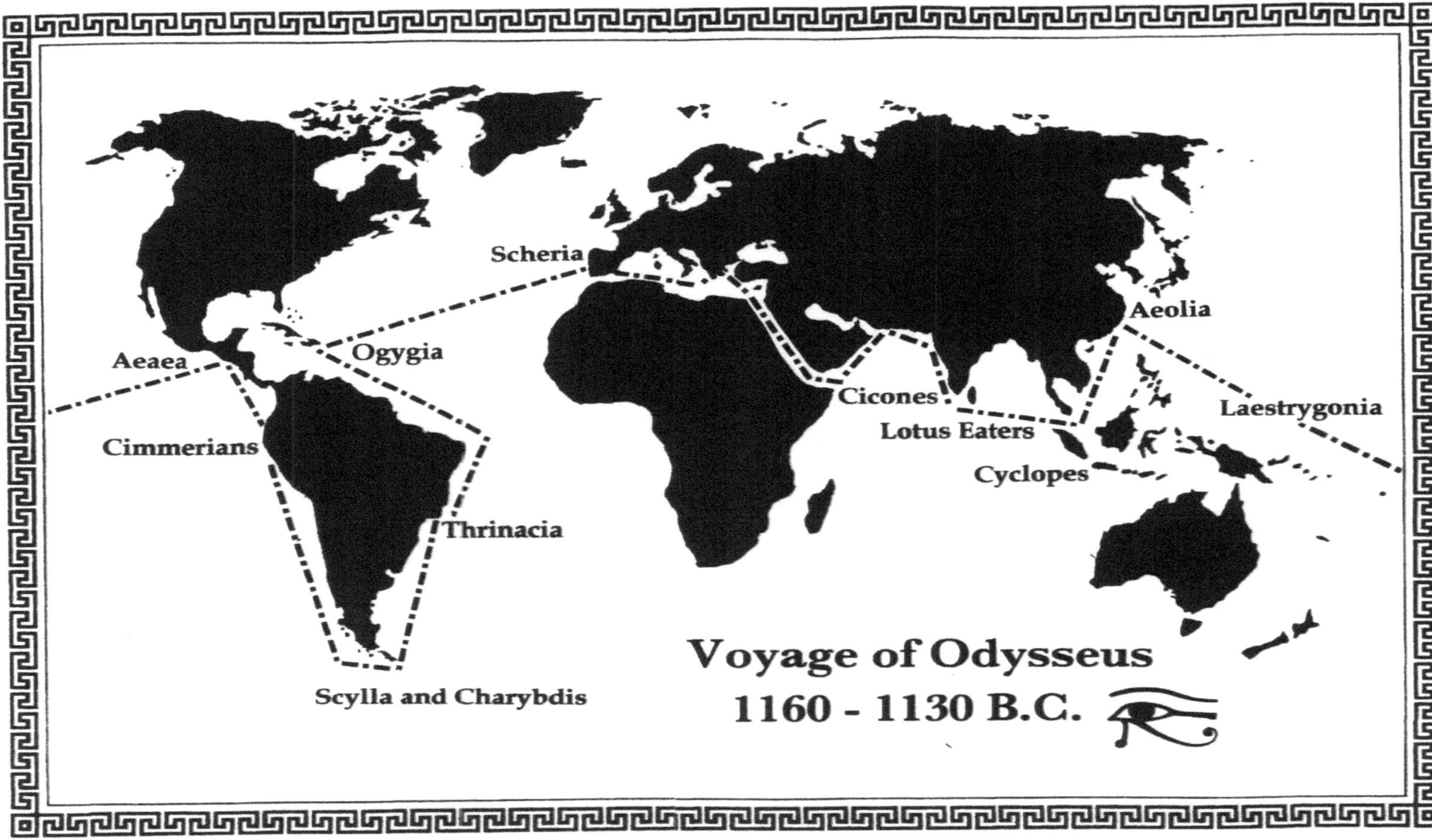
Scheria
Aeolia
Aeaea
Ogygia
Cicones
Laestrygonia
Lotus Eaters
Cimmerians
Cyclopes
Thrinacia
Voyage of Odysseus
1160 - 1130 B.C.
Scylla and Charybdis

INTRODUCTION

The Greek prince Odysseus was born into a world engulfed in immense social upheaval. During the years prior to his birth, nomadic peoples from the Black Sea region began to move in the direction of Asia Minor and Greece. These incursions led to a series of bloody battles, the most famous of which was the Trojan War. Charred remains from the archaeological site of Troy (V11A) indicate that the citadel was razed to the ground sometime between the years 1230 - 1180 B.C. These findings have led a majority of historians to assume that Homer's 'Trojan War' took place within this time frame. It is also important to note that a rebuilt Troy (V11B1) was destroyed yet again c.1180 - 1150 B.C.

Egyptian history confirms the extent of these 'northern struggles'. Their records reveal that the lands surrounding the Aegean Sea were at that time in the midst of a severe famine. In order to relieve the starving population and bolster alliances, Egypt sent shiploads of grain to the Hittite Empire in Asia Minor. Despite this strategy, masses of Aegean sea-peoples began streaming southwards towards Egypt in a desperate search of more fertile lands. Included among these seafaring tribes were Caucasians who migrated to Egypt's neighboring kingdom of Libya. It became imperative for Egypt to not only fortify its frontiers but take the offensive and strike the advancing hordes before they became invincible.

At eighty years of age, Ramses II (the Exodus Pharaoh) was too old and feeble to take the initiative and so he allocated the responsibility to his son, Merneptah, who launched an attack on Libya in the year 1227 B.C. Lured by the prospect of controlling the ever-fertile Nile Valley, the sea-peoples under the command of the Libyan king, Merai, prepared to invade Egypt along both its land and sea routes. In face of this threat Merneptah felt justified in taking whatever action was needed to defend his homeland. The events of this war were recorded upon the walls of Merneptah's temple tomb at Thebes. Presently called the 'Stele of Israel', these inscriptions give us a vivid account of Merneptah's success. The engagement took place at Per-Ir in the Delta region. The Egyptian fleet was positioned keel to stern along the sea routes of the Delta forming an impenetrable barrier that proved to be the key factor in the Egyptian victory. The battle lasted six hours and eventually the invaders retreated, leaving behind them nine thousand prisoners. Merneptah describes these captives as starving men who, prior to the battle had been:

... going about the land fighting to fill their bellies daily.

Battle of the Horns of the Earth (1221 B.C.)

Six years after their initial defeat the Sea Peoples reunited with the Libyans to attack the Delta but again the attempt to invade Egypt proved futile. To commemorate the occasion, the Egyptians etched victory inscriptions into Merneptah's memorial temple at Karnak. These describe the sea-people as being:

> ... *northern peoples coming from all lands.*

Wearing distinctive horned-helmets, the maritime warriors sailed in vessels with prows that terminated in the shape of a bird's head.

Relief sculpture from the temple of Ramses III depicts the Sea Peoples and Egyptians in battle (see Note 41)

The Karnak inscription also makes mention of the Lykians, Lukki or Lydians from coastal Turkey and the T-R-SH, which translates as Tursha-Tursenians-Terrhenians. Most interesting is the mention of the K-W-SH whom scholars believe to be the Achaeans because Akaiwasha was the Hittite name for Achaean. Assuming that this translation is correct, we might then place Odysseus' forebears (the Achaeans) at the site of this desperate battle. From a panel that describes the way in which the Egyptians counted the number of their dead enemies (6,500 Libyans and 2,500 sea-raiders), we learn that the Egyptian infantry hacked off a hand, or the genitals if uncircumcised, from each of their victims. They then presented their gruesome trophies to the scribes who conducted a census and dispensed rewards. It was recorded that because the Akaiwasha (Achaeans) had been circumcised they were thus spared the shame of castration.

1187 B.C. Thirty-four years after the Battle of the Horns, waves of Aegean sea-peoples came by land and sea to attack the southern extents of the declining Hittite Empire. Included among these invaders were the Minoan-Philistines, Teucrian, Sicilian, Weshesh and Danunian peoples who, accompanied by women and children, established themselves on the northern Syrian plain. In this same year Egyptian records report the capture of 100,000 of these desperate refugees.

1180 B.C. The proposed year of Odysseus' birth.

1177 - 1160 B.C. This was a decisive period in ancient Egyptian history. It marked the end of royal power and the beginning of a bureaucratic system. In 1164 B.C. the citadel of Troy was sacked by sea-peoples and in that same year the Minoan-Philistines and Teucrians secured the coastal plains of Palestine. Faced with the migration of hundreds of thousands of settlers onto their Northern Territories, Egypt decided to forsake its lucrative Palestinian mines and withdrew from these regions.

Due to its long-term policy of employing foreign mercenaries, Egypt gradually acquired a motley populace of Bedouins, Syrians, Cretans, Lydians, Canaanites and Phoenicians. Many of these immigrants chose to ignore the edicts and traditions of an empire to which they owed neither spiritual nor moral allegiance and as a consequence, Egypt's prosperity continued its downward spiral. This was an opportune time for a young adventurer such as Odysseus to sail his ship into Egypt's northern port of Pharos.

Being a royal prince, Odysseus would have been well aware that his cherished Mycenaean civilization was at that time in the throws of a serious decline. The deterioration is confirmed by excavations at Mycenae which revealed that vase painting during this period had become markedly unrefined and careless in craftsmanship. There is also less evidence of Mycenaean pottery found abroad, an indication that the formerly thriving sea empire was shrinking. Homer's heroes had once estimated their wealth in terms of how many generations their fortunes would last. By the time Odysseus appeared on the scene, it seemed that the only way a Mycenaean could maintain his wealth was to seize someone else's.

The Citadel of Mycenae

Pronunciations and meanings

Achaeans: ***a-kē'ans***
Achilles: ***a-kil'ez*** *(lipless)*
Agamemnon: ***ag-a-mem'non*** *(resolute)*
Aeaea: ***ē-ē'a*** *(mighty land of the eagle)*
Aeetes: ***ë-tes*** *(mighty or eagle)*
Aeolia: ***ē-ō'li-a***
Aeolus: ***ē-ō'lus*** *(earth destroyer)*
Alcinous: ***al-sin'-us*** *(mighty mind)*
Antiphates: ***an-tif'a-tēz*** *(spokesman)*
Aphrodite: ***af-rō-dī'tē*** *(foam-born)*
Arete: ***a-rē'te*** *(unspeakable)*
Argives: ***är'jīvz***
Artemis: ***är'te-mis*** *(high source of water)*
Calypso: ***ka-lip'sō*** *(hiden or hider)*
Charybidis: ***ka-rib'dis*** *(suckerdown)*
Ithaca: ***ith'a-ka***
Laertes: ***lā-er'tēz***
Ciconians: ***si-kō'ni-anz***
Cimmerians: ***si-mir'i-anz***
Circe: ***sēr'sē*** *(falcon)*
Clytemnestra: ***klī -tem-nes'tra*** *(praiseworthy)*
Cnossus: ***nos'us***
Cyclopes: ***sī-klō'pēz*** *(ring-eyed)*
Cythera: ***si-thir'a***
Danaans: ***dan'ānz*** *(judges)*
Dionysus: ***dī-ō-nī'sus*** *(lame god)*
Dorians: ***dō'ri-anz*** *(bountiful?)*
Elysian Fields: ***ē-lizh'an*** *(paradise)*
Eurylochus: ***ū-ril'ō-kus*** *(extensive ambush)*
Gaia: ***jē'a*** *(mother earth)*
Helios: ***hē'li-us*** *(the sun)*
Laestrygones: ***les-trig'ō-nēz***
Leucothea: ***lö-koth'-ēa*** *(white goddess)*
Malea: ***ma-lē'a***
Menelaus: ***men-e-lā'us*** *(mighty of the people)*
Mycenae: ***mī-sē'nē***
Nausicaa: ***nô-sik'ā-a*** *(burner of ships)*
Odysseus: ***ō-dis' ē-us*** *(angry)*
Ogygia: ***ō-jij'i-a***
Penelope: ***pē-nēl'ōpē*** *(with a web over her face)*
Persephone: ***per-sef'ō-nē*** *(bringer of destruction)*
Phaeacians: ***fē-ā'shanz***
Polyphemus: ***pol-i-f'mus*** *(famous)*
Scheria: ***shir'i-a*** *(land jutting into the sea))*
Scylla: ***sil'a*** *(she who rends)*
Telemachus: ***tē-lem'a-kus*** *(decisive battle)*
Teiresias: ***tī-rē'si-as***
Zeus: ***zös*** *(bright sky)*

Chapter 1

ODYSSEUS IN EGYPT

I was trying to sail home but the gods detained me in Egypt, for my hecatombs had not given them full satisfaction and the gods are very strict about having their dues. Now off Egypt, about as far as a ship can sail in a day with a good stiff breeze behind her, there is an island called Pharos. Here the gods becalmed me twenty days without so much as a breath of fair wind to help me forward. We should have starved, if a goddess had not taken pity on me and saved me in the person of Idothea, daughter to Proteus, the Old Man of the Sea, for she had taken a great fancy to me. She came to me one day when I was by myself, as I often was, for the men used to go with their barbed hooks, all over the island in the hope of catching a fish or two to save them from the pangs of hunger.

"Stranger," said she, "There is an old immortal who lives under the sea hereabouts whose name is Proteus. He is an Egyptian, and knows every inch of ground all over the bottom of the sea. If you can snare him and hold him tight, he will tell you about your voyage, what courses you are to take, and how you are to sail the sea so as to reach your home."

Meanwhile the goddess fetched up four seal pelts from the bottom of the sea, all of them just skinned, for she meant to play a trick on her father. Then she dug four pits for us to lie in. When we were close to him, she made us lie down in the pits one after the other, and threw a seal skin over each of us. We waited the whole morning and made the best of it, watching the seals come up in hundreds to bask upon the seashore, till at noon the old man of the sea came up too and when he had found his fat seals he went over them and counted them. We were among the first he counted, and he never suspected any guile, but laid himself down to sleep as soon as he had done counting. Then we rushed upon him with a shout and seized him; on which he began at once with his old tricks. He at first changed himself into a lion with a great mane; then all of a sudden he became a dragon, a leopard, a

wild boar; the next moment he was running water and then again directly he was a tree, but we stuck to him and never lost hold, till at last the cunning old creature became distressed, and said,

"Which of the gods was it, Son of Atreus that hatched this plot with you for snaring me and seizing me against my will? What do you want?"

"You know that yourself, old man," I answered. "Which of the immortals is it that is hindering me, and tell me also how I may sail the sea so as to reach my home?"

Proteus (the Seal God of Pharos)

The name Proteus is a Greek word meaning 'first' or 'early' man. I presume that primordial Proteus was originally associated with *Phocis* (seals) or *Phorcys* (pigs). The Egyptians regarded Proteus as their most ancient deity; a claim that may well be tenable for the cult of Proteus appears to have had its origin amid the coastal caves of Stone Age man. A Paleolithic drawing found within the Altamira Caves of Spain depicts a group of women in the guise of seals performing a ritual dance. This ancient pictograph is possibly an early illustration of Proteus worship.

Seal Dancers, Altamira Cave, Spain

In his book, *The Greek Myths* (Complete Edition p.274), Robert Graves reports that the ritual dance of the Seal Maidens occurs in the folklore of almost every European country:

... usually the hero sees a flock of seals swimming towards a deserted shore under a full moon and then stepping out of their skins reveal themselves as young women. The hero hides behind a rock while they dance naked on the sand, he then seizes one of the seals' skins, thus

winning over its owner whom he gets with child. Eventually they quarrel; she regains her skin and swims away.

I imagine that 'early man' would have esteemed certain coastal sites as a plentiful source of food during the seals' breeding season. Having feasted on seal flesh, the hunters would have utilised the pelts for making garments or to stretch over the frames of ocean-going canoes. It is likely that particular coastal caves were especially bountiful and after millennia of seasonal use became associated with spirits or deities who possessed the ancestral knowledge of the ancient seal hunters.

Depiction of Proteus by German artist Hoellischer A.D.1695

Those familiar with Arthurian legends would recognise the similarities that exist between Egyptian Proteus and the wizard Merlin. Like Proteus, Merlin was a sorcerer and shape-changer who was gifted with the ability to access mankind's past and future history. The name Merlin derives from an Old French form of the Welsh *Myrddhin*, whilst *Clas Myrddhin* (Myrddhin's enclosure) was an early name for Britain. The etymology of Merlin might be further traced to the Old Celtic *Mori-dunon*, literally 'of the sea-hill'. **(Note 3)**

Personified as the 'old man of the sea', Proteus is related to the moon and its effect on the ocean's moods. Mythologists generally consider the waxing and waning of the moon to be feminine in nature and therefore it is usually identified with female deities. There are exceptions of course, and one of these is the Akkadian moon god Sin/Enzu (Sumerian Nanna) who was venerated as the 'father of the gods' and 'creator of all things'. The 'wisdom' personified by Sin was expressed in the sciences of astronomy and astrology wherein the moon's phases were observed. The Egyptians probably revered Proteus in a similar manner. His connection with seals, 'tides of time' and the silver moon may be linked to the etymology of the word silver, which is derived from the Old English word *seol for* (seal fur).

Robert Graves' *The White Goddess* tells us of Pelasgian seafarers honoring the spirit of Proteus on several island locations. According to his research, Pelasgian seafarers had formulated a calendar system of 100 months or lunations, which equaled one Pelasgian year. It is also possible that these ancient seafarers understood the concept of the 'Great Luna Year': a 28-year cycle of time that consisted of 365 full moons or lunations.

28 days = **1 moon**
365 days = **1 year**
365 moons = **28 years**
28 years = **1 Luna Year Cycle**

Odysseus' metaphorical descriptions are a hallmark of his Odyssey. Time and time again he uses the language of allegorical myth to describe his adventures with the likes of the one-eyed Cyclops, giant cannibals and sea sirens. The episode concerning his alleged encounter with Proteus is typical of his parabolic style and convinces me further that Odysseus was the Greek king left stranded and starving in Egypt. The Egyptian deity Proteus was certainly revered for his great memory and knowledge, however I suspect that his mercurial ability to change shape at will may allude to altered states of consciouness. We note that those seeking to access Proteus' auguries were warned to keep a firm hold of him as he constantly changed form. This curious capability might hint at the various phases of a drug-induced experience. Homer and Strabo certainly make references to the 'goodly drugs' Helen was presented with during her time on the Delta though I rather consider that Odysseus' colorful recollection of his encounter with Proteus was due to the effects of near starvation.

> *... for the men used to go with their barbed hooks, all over the island in the hope of catching a fish or two to save them from the pangs of hunger.*

Proteus' Forecast

Securely held in check by Odysseus and his crewmen, Proteus defiantly utters:

> ***"If you would finish your voyage and get home quickly, you must offer sacrifices to Jove and the rest of the gods before embarking for it is decreed that you shall not get back to your friends and to your house until you have returned to the heaven-fed stream of Egypt and offered holy hecatombs to the immortal gods that reign in heaven. When you have done this they will let you finish your voyage."***

As the ***'knower of past and future events',*** Proteus would certainly have been aware that Odysseus' predicament was directly related to his theft of the sacred Pallas Athena Palladium. With this in mind, Proteus advised Odysseus that if he wished to return to his homeland he must first pay penitent homage to the eternal gods who dwelt in the ***'heaven-fed stream of Egypt'***. Most scholars would consider the heaven-fed stream to be the Nile River. However, in other Egyptian texts such as the *Book of Pylons*, the heaven-fed stream is equated with the River of Duat, a stream that ostensibly flowed on the opposite side of the world. Like the Nile whose source is located in 'darkest' Africa, the River of Duat was thought to flow through various forbidding zones. Before endeavoring to traverse such frightening realms it was prudent to ask protection from the hawk-god, Horus. As additional security, *utchats* (the symbolic hawk eyes of Horus) were painted onto the prows of Egyptian and Greek ships. Seated in his solar baque, Horus was deemed to be accompanying the sun as it sank into the West. Having traversed the nether regions of an underworld ocean Horus returned at dawn, basking in the glory of the risen sun.
(Note 4)

Enthroned upon his solar boat, Horus holds an *ankh*, the symbol of life

Amun Ra

Horus was not the only Egyptian god to be assigned the responsibility of navigating the Sun Boat's course. Depictions on royal tombs show the ram-headed god, Amun Ra, also enthroned upon a solar barque as it passed through the Underworld of night.

Proteus' directive to Odysseus that he must first sail to the regions of Egypt's ***'heaven-fed stream'*** might thus be interpreted as meaning that he should voyage towards either the most distant extents of the West or the East. We can discount the extreme West, as this region was assigned to Elysium, a paradisiacal realm forbidden to mortal Greeks. This leaves us to deduce that Odysseus' pilgrimage to the ***'heaven-fed stream'*** entailed a ***'long and terrible'*** voyage eastwards to a land the Egyptians called Punt or Utjenet. **(Note 5)**

The Land of Punt

The exact location of Punt has never been definitively identified. Also referred to as Utjenet (God's Land), this enigmatic region appears to have been originally associated with the East for the god Amun declared:

> *Turning my face to sunrise I created a wonder for you, I made the lands of Punt come here to you with all the fragrant flowers of their lands.*

According to ancient Egyptian writings, the god Amun instructed the 18th Dynasty Queen Hatshepsut (c.1500 B.C.) to organise a large-scale expedition to the land of Punt. Conversing with the queen by means of an oracle, Amun described the mysterious land as follows:

> *Punt is the sacred region of God's land; it is my place of distraction; I have made it for myself in order to cleanse my spirit, along with my mother, Hathor, the Lady of Punt.*

Amun's bestowal of the title 'Lady of Punt' upon his mother Hathor is a further indication that the Land of Punt might be located in India. As we know, the Egyptian goddess Hathor was revered in the form of a celestial cow and cows have been venerated in India from time immemorial.

Pronounced as '*oo*' the 'u' in Punt (Poont) is pronounced in the same way as the 'u' in the Indian/Sinhalese word *puna* (poona) which is used to describe a species of tree that is native to India and Sri Lanka. The timber of the puna tree was used to make masts for ships and its resin provided waterproofing for the hulls. From the very beginnings of its civilization, Egyptian commerce had relied upon cargo ships to transport goods back and forth along the Nile. It has been well documented that the ancient Egyptians were able mariners and as such, they likely made regular expeditions to the land of Punt so that they might collect not only the valuable puna timber but also ivory, ebony, gum (*kemy*) and incense (*antyu*).

Relief carvings from the 5th Dynasty (c.2400 B.C.) depict the people of Punt as having fine features, dark-reddish complexions and long hair. However by the 18th Dynasty (c.1500 B.C.), the natives of Punt are portrayed with closely cropped, Afro-styled hair which gave rise to the subsequent notion that Punt was located in Africa.

The oldest surviving record of an expedition to Punt is found on the Palermo Stone and dates to Egypt's 5th Dynasty. Later during the 11th Dynasty (c.2000 B.C.), it was recorded that Mentuhotep III ordered his captain Henenu to gather together three thousand men so that they might construct ships for a journey to Punt. The early expeditions to Punt were probably launched from the Gulf of Suez or the nearby Sinai coast. At the time of the Middle Kingdom the starting point was Coptos. During the period of the New Kingdom (c.1500.B.C.), and up until the time of Odysseus (c.1160 B.C.), the place of embarkation is thought to have been Nekheb (modern day Berenike).

The Voyage to Punt (Utjenet)

It is impossible to ascertain how sincere Odysseus was in his intentions to pay homage to the 'eternal gods'. To this day, India remains a place of pilgrimage and it would not be surprising to find that this custom was existent in Odysseus' time. What we do know about the late Mycenaean period is that it was quite a common practice for Greek mariners to enlist into the services of Egyptian pharaohs. Once in their employ, the Greeks may have had the option of having their ships towed through a series of narrow canals that then connected the Mediterranean to the Red Sea. Many *Odyssey* theorists are unaware that these canals existed or that Egypt, at this juncture of its history, had ships arriving from as far away as the Indus Valley (Pakistan), Insia (India), Arabia, Phoenicia, Crete, Greece, the Adriatic and even the Black Sea littoral. **(Note 5)**

The Egyptian black market in the 1160 B.C. era provided a ready exchange for all manner of pirated goods. Taking advantage of this lucrative trade, the wily Egyptian traders may have employed experienced sea-raiders, such as the Achaean Greeks, to plunder the small coastal ports of Arabia, the Persian Gulf and India. When the laden ships returned, the stolen booty would be divided up and shared with the Egyptians.

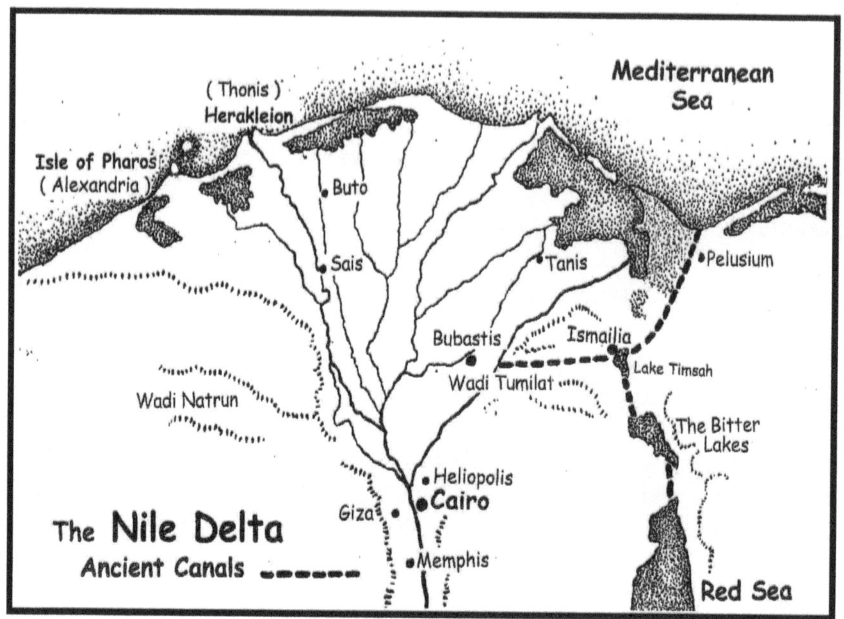

Map of the Nile Delta c.1160 B.C.

If Odysseus was still begrudging the fact that he was without treasure, he too may have decided to resort to piracy. Equipped with knowledge he had acquired in Egypt and guided by astute Egyptian or Phoenician navigators, Odysseus' would most likely have set a direct course for Ismarus, the port capital of the Cicone people.

Although certain scholars identify Ismarus as a place in northern Greece, I suggest that in the original text it reads as Ismenius, a word that infers 'knowledge of the River God' or to be more explicit, 'knowledge of the River of Life'.

In sailing to the eastern antipodes, Odysseus might have imagined himself to be venturing into the Underworld realms ruled by the Greek god Dis (Pluto). According to ancient Greek tradition, Dis dwelt among ramshackle temples wherein were hidden jewels and all manner of precious metals. Black ewes and black rams were the favoured sacrificial animals offered to Dis. To invoke this dread god, one had to strike the ground with bare hands all the while uttering terrible oaths and curses. Cunning and stealth would be paramount when seeking his fabled treasures for anyone caught attempting to steal them was summarily executed.

Chapter 2

LAND OF THE CICONES
(Indus Valley)

Book 9: Line 39 -

When I had set sail thence the wind took me first to Ismarus, which is the city of the Cicones. There I sacked the town and put the people to the sword. We took their wives and also much booty, which we divided equally amongst us, so that none might have reason to complain. I then said that we had better make off at once but my men very foolishly would not obey me. They stayed there drinking much wine and killing great numbers of sheep and oxen on the sea shore. Meanwhile the Cicones cried out for help to other Cicones who lived inland. These were more in number, stronger and they were more skilled in the art of war, for they could fight, either from chariots or on foot as the occasion served. In the morning they came as thick as leaves that bloom in summer and the hand of heaven was against us, so that we were hard pressed. They set the battle in array near the ships and the hosts aimed their bronze-shod spears at one and another. So long as the day waxed and it was still morning, we held our own against them, though they were more in number than we; but as the sun went down, (towards the time when men loose their oxen), the Cicones got the better of us and we lost half a dozen men from every ship we had; so we got away with those that were left.

The Indus Valley

Located in Pakistan's Indus Valley, the once flourishing metropolises of Harappa and Mahenjo-Daro resemble the mythological descriptions of the Dis realm. Today the Indus Valley is littered with the ghostly ruins of crumbling temples and palaces. The reason for the sudden abandonment of the formerly thriving cities of Mahenjo-Daro and Harappa remains a point of contention. While some archaeologists believe it was due to the recurrent earthquakes in this part of the world, others suggest that the inhabitants fell victim to the numerous incursions that occurred c.1550 - 1150 B.C. Early Vedic writings such as the *Rig Veda* made record of these invasions. They also tell of a dark-skinned people called the Dasas (the original Untouchables) who abode in the broken ruins (*armaka)* of buildings demolished by the great Aryan god Indra, acting in his role as Purandera 'the destroyer of cities'.

At the site of Mohenjo-Daro, excavators have uncovered ancient skeletons of men, women and children who had been stabbed or clubbed to death and apparently left to rot where they fell. Archaeologists also discovered remnants of other Indus Valley citadels that featured uniform streets and elaborate drainage systems. These ruins are scattered over an immense area that stretches from the foothills of the Himalayas in the Punjab to the coast of the Arabian Sea, and as far south as the Gulf of Cambay - a broad inlet just above the modern city of Mumbai (Bombay). A cohesive society of priests, merchants, artisans and farmers formed the nucleus of this great trading nation, which flourished for about 1,000 years, c.2500 – 1500 B.C.

Soapstone trading seals engraved with a script that is yet to be deciphered, as well as sculptures and various other artifacts from the Indus Valley regions have been unearthed in Mesopotamia. These discoveries reveal that an ancient trade link once existed between the two civilizations. Archaeologists have also ascertained that Mohenjo-Daro imported gold from southern India, silver, copper and lapis lazuli from Afghanistan and turquoise from Iran. In return, Indus Valley merchants are said to have exported stone, ivory, timber and certain exotic animals.

Odysseus' Raid on the Cicones

Having sailed to the Cicones' coastal city of Ismarus, Odysseus and his crewmen immediately set about sacking it. The wealth and vulnerability of Ismarus might identify it with the Indus Valley port of Lothal. Located on India's Gulf of Cambay, Lothal was once connected by a four-kilometre channel to the Narmada River. Its brick-lined dock would have been abundant with trade goods at the time of Odysseus. The recent discovery of very large anchor stones in this region has led archaeologists to make comparisons with similar stones found on the Mediterranean island of Crete.

Odysseus' raid had been swift and without warning. Past experience of such sudden attacks would likely have taught the Cicones to have at their ready a vast army to protect their territory. Homer's description of how the Cicones ***'gathered as thick as the leaves of summer'*** is perhaps another indication that the Land of the Cicones was situated in a densely populated India.

Vedic sources report that at various times when faced with the prospect of certain death from invaders, the ruling elite had fled to the relative safety of neighbouring kingdoms. On one occasion the entire populace is said to have sailed away to far distant lands.

Excavated from Lothal, soapstone seals similar to the one pictured above indicate that the port was in continual use c.2000 - 1100B.C. (Note 7)

Thor Heyerdahl

Renowned for his voyages aboard the ocean-going rafts called Kon-Tiki and Ra, the late anthropologist Thor Heyerdahl bravely demonstrated the possibilities of ancient, ocean migrations. In his book *Kon Tiki Man*, Heyerdahl states his belief in the former existence of an ancient race of Hindu mariners whom he describes as having elongated earlobes decorated with large disc-shaped earrings. According to Thor Heyerdahl, the intrepid

Hindu seafarers had fled from one of the Aryan invasions of the Indus Valley. Having made their way southwards to the Maldives, the refugees then set their course towards the rising sun and sailed into the Pacific Ocean. Evidence of their distinctive 'fingerprint' masonry can be found in places as far a field as the island of Bahrain in the Persian Gulf (an old trading ally), the Maldives, Nias, Easter Island and Peru.

Ismarus Sacked

With Ismarus (Lothal) in ruins and only a remnant of his fleet surviving the rout, Odysseus fled the carnage and escaped to the safety of the open sea. Adrift over deep ocean waters he implored the dreaded god Dis to release the souls of his fallen comrades. In an apparently disdainful response, the skies darkened and a terrifying ***'hurricane'*** lashed down upon Odysseus' vessel.

Book 9: line 66 -

> ***Then Jove raised the North Wind against us till it blew a hurricane, so that land and sky were hidden in thick clouds and night sprang forth out of the heavens. We let the ships run before the gale but the force of the wind tore our sails to tatters, so we took them down for fear of shipwreck and rowed our hardest towards the land. There we lay two days and two nights suffering much alike from toil and distress of mind but on the morning of the third day we again raised our masts, set sail and took our places, letting the wind and steersman direct our ship.***

Chapter 3

LAND OF THE LOTUS-EATERS
(Maldives, Sri Lanka)

Book 9: line 77 -

> ***I should have got home at that time unharmed had not the North wind and the currents been against me as I was doubling Cape Malea and set me off my course hard by the island of Kythera. I was driven thence by foul winds for a space of nine days upon the sea.***

The Maldives

The geographical locations described in *The Odyssey* are often sparing in detail and this is but one of the reasons why the actual route taken by Odysseus has long been a matter of conjecture. I am mindful of the general consensus that locates Malea at the southern-most point of the Greek Peloponnesus but I suspect that the Cape Malea Odysseus refers to was actually Male, the island capital of the Maldives archipelago. The word *malea* denotes maliciousness or danger, and this description is equally applicable to both the Greek Malea and the Maldives' Male.

A mythological double entendre may apply to Odysseus' account of his fleet being ***'driven hard by the island of Kythera'*** and thence over the open sea for a period of nine days to eventually beach on the island of the Lotus Eaters. This description bears a remarkable similarity to the legend of Aphrodite's birth. According to Greek mythology, the love-goddess Aphrodite had emerged from the foamy ocean whereupon she was carried swiftly atop white-capped waves past the island of Kythera and thence across a tumultuous sea to finally arrive on the shores of Cyprus. Perhaps Odysseus made use of this well-known myth to describe his experience of being borne by the waves to the sultry and dreamlike Land of the Lotus-eaters; a realm seemingly worthy of comparison to Aphrodite's Urania (Paradise). **(Note 7)**

The Island of Sri Lanka

Book 9: line 83 -

> ***On the tenth day we reached the Land of the Lotus-eaters, who live on food that comes from a kind of flower. Here we landed to take in fresh water and our crews ate their midday meal on the shore near the ships. When they had finished eating and drinking, I sent three of my company to see what manner of men the people of the place might be. They started at once and went among the Lotus-eaters who did them no hurt but gave them to eat of the lotus. The lotus was so delicious that those who ate it left off caring about home and did not even want to come back and say what was happening to them. They were for staying and munching lotus with the lotus-eaters without thinking further of their return.***

One of the ancient names for Sri Lanka is the Arabic word *Serendip* (a corruption of the Sanskrit *Simhaladypa).* Serendip was the source of the 18th century English word serendipity: the occurrence of happening upon fortunate discoveries when not actually in search of them. In this sense, serendipity certainly applies to Odysseus' chance discovery of the island.

Homer's description of Odysseus as being beset by a hurricane and subsequently driven to an exotic island finds parallel in a Roman story related eight hundred years later by the historian Pliny (*Natural History,* Book V1*).* Writing in the year 50 A.D., Pliny reports the tale of a fellow-Roman citizen named Annius Plocanus who *'having farmed the Red Sea revenues of the Roman Empire then set sail in a vessel'.* Meeting with a hurricane off the coast of Arabia, the Roman sailor had been driven by *'stress of weather'* for fifteen days until he arrived at Hiporos (modern Kuduramala), a small port on the island of Taprobane (Sri Lanka). Warmly greeted by the natives, the shipwrecked Roman was forthwith conducted to their king who offered him hospitality for a period of six months. **(Note 8)** Pliny also reported that a native ambassador from Taprobane while on a visit to Rome had boasted that his island hosted as many as 500 cities and supported a population of 200,000 citizens.

Taprobane

The aromatic spice Cinnamon (from the Greek *kinnámōmon*) is native to Sri Lanka (Taprobane) and evidence of its presence in Middle Kingdom

Egypt (c.2000 - 1500 B.C.) is an indication that Egyptian merchants had established trade links with the island's inhabitants. The earliest known documented information concerning Sri Lanka reached Europe c.336 B.C. This initial account is found in the writings of two admirals named Onesicritus and Nearchus. Dispatched by Alexander the Great to sail from the Indus to the Persian Gulf, the admirals reported that although they themselves had never ventured to the mysterious land, they had met and conversed with adventurers who described an island to the east of India called Taprobane. The origin of the name Taprobane is described in the following excerpt from an ancient Hindu book titled *Mahavansa* (Great Genealogy of Dynasty).

... exhausted by sea sickness and faint from weakness, the 700 men with the king at their head landed at the spot where the colour of their palms became copper-coloured (tamba-pannayo). From this circumstance the wilderness obtained the name TAMBAPANNA and became celebrated under that name.

The Helas

The ancient history of Sri Lanka is also preserved in 'stone writings' (*sel lipi*) and 'leaf-writings' (*hela atuva*). According to these respective works, Sri Lanka was once called Heladiva (Island of the Hela). The writings describe the Helas as a nation of master builders, capable of carving irrigation channels into solid bedrock and constructing water reservoirs that enabled them to harvest grain three times a year. Could the origin of this remarkable legend have been based on the advent of Odysseus and his crew of 'fair-skinned' Greeks? The ancient Greeks of Odysseus' time referred to their homeland as Hellas and hence they were called Hellenes. If certain members of Odysseus' fleet had decided to accept the '***Land of the Lotus Eaters***' as their new home, then it is quite possible that they also referred to themselves as Helas. **(Note 9)**

Odysseus' serendipitous arrival in Sri Lanka may have instigated a local legend that records the advent of a 'foreign god' to their southern shores. In his essay, *Kataragama - the Mystery Shrine*, Patrick Harrigan elaborates upon this fascinating legend:

Indeed, Ptolemy provides at least three references to Dionysus in his catalogue of Sri Lanka's coastal landmarks, all of them in the close vicinity of Kataragama which was already an ancient cult centre in Ptolemy's day. In most cases, he retains transcribed renderings of local names. Ptolemy records that Alexandrian mariners knew of the waters off the island's desolate southeastern coast as the Dionysi Mare (Latin: The Sea of Dionysus). Some versions of Ptolemy's 'Tarpobane' indicate that a coastal landmark near Kataragama was called Dionysi Promontorium, 'the Promontory of Dionysus'. Thirdly but not least, he attests that there was an important settlement near this coastline that his mariner-informants called Dionysi seu Bacchi Oppidum, 'The Town of Dionysus or Bacchus'.

This terse identification, based upon the supporting testimony of not one but many Alexandrian mariners who typically sojourned for weeks or even months at a time in Taprobane, bears the stamp of authenticity. As informed observers, some of these mariners must have been bacchantes or initiates into the still-flourishing mystery cult of Bacchus, for whom the fundamental identification of Dionysus with the local cult centre or deity was self-evident.

At the very least, there was a clear consensus among contemporary observers that here, far from Greece and Asia Minor, was an outpost realm of the god Dionysus. Extending even to the sea off Kataragama is a graveyard of wrecked trading vessels from ancient times. Furthermore, the association of an ever-youthful Dionysian god with a promontory extending into a restless sea is not without precedent. In the very opening verse of his Hymns to Dionysus (1: 1- 4), Homer evokes the god, saying:

"It is Dionysus, son of the most glorious Semele, that I speak of and I shall tell how he appeared on the shore of the untiring sea, on an outpost promontory with the aspect of a young man in his first adolescence."

Tempting it is to conclude that early Greco-Egyptian mariners who were familiar both with the cult of Dionysus and with Homer's 'Hymns to Dionysus' had this opening verse in mind when they spoke of the Kataragama region. Evidently, Alexandrian mariners and Ptolemy along with them, believed exotic Taprobane was the original home of Dionysus as described by Homer a thousand years earlier in the 9th century B.C. This identification would have further reinforced the prevailing opinion of the time that Sri Lanka or Taprobane was the Antipodes (Greek: literally, 'where feet are opposite'); a fabulous, topsy-turvy island realm where anything was possible, the natural abode of gods like Dionysus.

The account of a youthful Dionysus manifesting on the southern shores of Sri Lanka may seem fanciful but there are numerous references in ancient Greek legends that tell of Dionysus' travels to India. During his time there he is reported to have made war with its inhabitants (the Cicones) set up sacred pillars (esoteric knowledge) and introduced the 'art of viniculture' to its inhabitants.

Greek vase depicting Dionysus boarding a ship

The Lotus and the Buddha

Buddhism had held sway in Sri Lanka for well over a century before the first documented information concerning the island reached Europe c.336 B.C.

Sakamuni Guatama (the Buddha himself) is believed to have visited the island on three separate occasions during the 6th century B.C. On his third visit, it is said that the Buddha journeyed to the foot of the sacred mountain Sri Pada (Adam's Peak). Having related the 'Law of Dharma' to his followers, Guatama then trekked his way up to the peak of the 7,360 foot high mountain. To this very day, Buddhists maintain a traditional belief that an imprint of the Buddha's foot has been miraculously preserved at the mountain's summit. Currently protected by a stone slab, the footprint is purportedly embedded with a large blue diamond. The island's three other distinct religions also lay claim to the footprint: Christians believe it was created by Saint Thomas; Moslems declare it to be that of Adam while Hindus are adamant it was formed by the the ascetic god Shiva. Throughout the ages, the site has attracted a constant stream of pilgrims and mystics including such notable travellers as Marco Polo (A.D. 1292) and Ibn Battuta (A.D. 1344). One wonders if Odysseus too might have visited this sacred mountain which in his day was called Samanalakanda (abode of the god Samn). Apollonius of Tyana (2nd century A.D.) reports how Dionysus (Odysseus?) was 'thunderstruck' by sages (Brahmans) who inhapited the summit of a steep hill that rose 'straight up from the plain' of India.

High on the list of Buddhis pilgrimage is the now abandoned city of Polonnarwa. Once populated with over a million inhabitants, the ruined city features an enormous stone sculpture of the Reclining Buddha. Lying amidst hundreds of lotus-filled lakes that sparkle like jewels in the tropical sun, the Reclining Buddha emanates all the blissful serenity of an idle 'lotus-eater'. **(Note 10)**

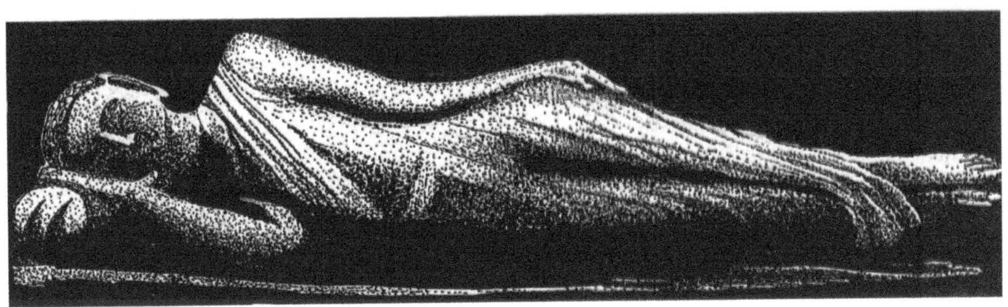

The Reclining Buddha at Polonnarwa, Sri Lanka

In Homeric times, the term 'lotus-eater' was in common usage and described someone 'prone to forgetfulness'. The habit of eating the lotus is thought to have originated in Egypt where numerous images depict its ingestion. The Greeks of Homer's time were unaware of the fact that the ancient peoples of Sri Lanka also partook in the eating of the lotus.

Besides the lotus, Sri Lanka's diverse tropical flora contained many other psychotropic plants, including the Kiribadu (*Ipomoea Mauritana*). Administered with honey and clarified butter, the flower of the Kiribadu plant is noted for its aphrodisiacal properties.

Book 9: line 97 -

> ***... nevertheless, though they wept bitterly I forced the men back to the ships and made them fast under the benches. Then I told the rest to go on board at once, lest any of them should taste of the Lotus and leave off wanting to get home, so they took their places and smote the grey sea with their oars.***

According to Sri Lankan folklore, a legendary 'Realm of Gold' known as *Savarnadvipata* once existed in a land to the east of Sri Lanka. I suspect that such tales may have inspired a covetous Odysseus to again point the prow of his ship in the direction of the rising sun. Assuming Odysseus did in fact set an easterly course, his fleet of ships would have ploughed their way across the immense Bay of Bengal to eventually make landfall on the western coast of Malaysia. Aided with the reliable winds of the South-West Monsoon, the voyage would have taken approximately four or five days. **(Note 11)**

It is not at all implausible that Odysseus's fleet would have been able to traverse the vast expanse of the Bay of Bengal. Recent excavations along the coast of Tuticorin in southern India indicate that the people of this region had established ancient trading links with other parts of Asia c.1800 - 1100 B.C.

The Adichanallur Civilization, Southern India c.1800 - 1100 B.C.

Lauded for their seamanship, the essentially agrarian inhabitants of the so-called Adichanallur civilization were also master blacksmiths who had the ability to forge a variety of iron implements. Mr. Arun Malik, an archaeologist with the Archaeological Survey of India, reports that the study of human morphological types based on the cranial evidences, suggests the existence of more than one particular ethnic group in that region. Adding his comments to the recent findings, Mr. P. Raghavan, a bio-anthropologist with A.S.I., said the discovery of Southeast and Far East Asian genetic traits in Indian skulls and bone morphology indicates that an ancient India-Asia sea trade had been in existence c.1800 B.C.

Although the premise of Odysseus sailing further eastward towards Malaysia may at first seem odd, we should take into consideration that Odysseus and his crew had left behind a Mediterranean world in which war and famine were constant predicaments. Having experienced the pleasures and idylls of a tropical lifestyle, Odysseus may have decided to continue venturing his way along the course of Oceanus, which at that time was thought to surround the known world.

Solar totem of the Redin Sea People

Rediscovered and presented in Thor Heyerdahl's *The Kon-Tiki Man*, the Redin solar symbol may illustrate an ancient method of sailing along the path of the Equator. I imagine the upper line represented the 'modern', northern Topic of Cancer, the middle the Equator, while the lower line represented the Topic of Capricorn. By aligning the ship's mast with the daily orbit of the tropical sun, a mariner could maintain a direct easterly course. In unwitting support of Heyerdahl's theory, Professor Joseph Campbell also proposed that an ancient sea route once extended across the equatorial Indian and Pacific oceans:

> *A single language family, the Malayo-Polynesian extends all the way from Madagascar (just off the coast of southeast Africa) eastward to Easter Island (off the coast of Peru) and from New Zealand north to Formosa, and northeast to Hawaii. Such linguistic affinities indicate not only cultural and historical relationship, but also psychological homologies – and to such a degree that not even the most passionate supporter of a theory of parallel development would presume (I should think) to explain according to his cherished principles such coincidence as that represented by the following ways of naming the numbers from one to ten.*

	MADAGASCAR	INDONESIA			POLYNESIA	
	MALAGASY	MALAY	JAVANESE	TAGAL	SAMOAN	MAORI
1	isa	sa	sa	isa	tasi	tahi
2	rua	dua	ru	dalawa	lua	rua
3	telu	tiga	telu	tatlo	tolu	toru
4	efatra	ampat	pat	apat	fa	wha
5	limi	lima	lima	lima	lima	rima
6	eni(na)	anam	(ne)nem	anim	ono	ono
7	fitu	tujuh	pitu	pito	fitu	whitu
8	valu	dulafan	wolu	walo	valu	waru
9	sivi	sambilan	sono	siyam	iva	iwha
10	fulu	puluh	puluh	polo	sefulu	nahuru

Joseph Campbell, *The Masks of God – Primitive Mythology* (pp. 201-202)

Chapter 4

LAND OF THE CYCLOPES
(Southeast Asia)

Book 9:

We sailed hence, always in much distress, till we came to the land of the lawless and inhuman Cyclopes. Now the Cyclopes neither plant nor plough, but trust in providence. They have neither laws nor assemblies of the people, but live in caves on the tops of high mountains; each is lord and master in his family and they take no account of their neighbours.

(116 -) Close to the land of the Cyclopes, but still not far, there lies a wooded fertile island with a good harbour where no cables or anchors are needed, as all one has to do is to beach one's vessel and stay there till the wind becomes fair for putting out to sea again.

(143 -) When we got to the land, which was not far, there on the face of a cliff near the sea, we saw a great cave overhung with laurels. This was the abode of a huge monster that was away from home shepherding his flocks. He would have nothing to do with other people, but led the life of an outlaw.

(287 -) The cruel wretch vouchsafed me not one word of answer but with a sudden clutch he gripped up two of my men at once and dashed them down upon the ground as though they had been puppies. Their brains were shed upon the ground and the earth was wet with their blood. Then he tore them limb from limb and supped upon them. He gobbled them up like a lion in the wilderness, flesh, bones, marrow and entrails, without leaving anything uneaten.

(304 -) Then I thrust the beam of wood far into the embers to heat it and encouraged my men lest any of them should turn faint-hearted. We drove the sharp end of the beam into the Cyclops' eye.

Greek vase depicting Odysseus and his crew blinding the Cyclops

Malaysian Coast

If a vessel sails directly eastwards from Sri Lanka and maintains a course at six degrees north of the Equator, it will with the aid of the West Monsoon, directly arrive in the Malaysian state of Kedah. Rising from the horizon to greet those who arrive from India is a 4,140 feet (1380m.) tall peak called Mount Kedah (*Gunung Jerai*). Forming part of a massive limestone outcrop, this majestic mountain dominates the surrounding terrain of the Malaccan landscape. Mariners approaching this ominous region are treated to the sight of bizarre rock formations and mysterious caves that are a feature of the nearby island of Langkawi. This rocky tropical region presents itself as an ideal, hypothetical habitat for the Cyclopes people who are said to ***'neither plant nor plough, but trust in providence'***. In other words, the Cyclopes were hunters and collectors whose diet consisted of game and fruits.

Raja Bersiong

Among the many legends that are attached to Mount Kedah is one that claims the mountain was once the domain of Raja Bersiong, 'the king with fangs'. This monstrous ogre is said to have held power over a neighbouring kingdom. Recent archaeological findings on the mountain have revealed the existence of the so-called 'Temple of the Ninth Pool'. Present-day, local indigenous people retain the belief that this site was Raja Bersiong's personal bathing pool.

Odysseus' blinding of the Cyclops monster is obviously narrated in terms of allegorical mythology. Contemporary readers would be reticent in accepting as literal, Odysseus' escape by means of thrusting a fiery beam of wood into the Cyclops' single eye.

Odysseus offers the Cyclops wine

The Cyclops

The one-eyed Cyclops encountered in *The Odyssey* may be considered as synonymous with the three-eyed Hindu god, Bali. Both creatures were fearsome, ancient giants who were revered by cruel, primitive peoples. Odysseus describes the Cyclops as being:

> ***… a horrid creature, not like a human at all but resembling rather some crag that stands out boldly against the sky on the top of a high mountain.***

Animism - the practice of venerating spirits that were believed to dwell in natural landforms - was integral to the indigenous cultures of South East Asia.

Located about 70 kilometres south of Odysseus' proposed landing site, Gua Harimau (Tiger Cave) presents an excellent example of animistic practices c.3000 - 1000 B.C. Archaeological diggings at Gua Harimau have unearthed seven skeletons, numerous bronze axes and various articles of jewellry including bangles, chains and earrings. The bronze axes verify the existence of an early bronze tradition in Malaysia.

Filipino Cyclops

Tribal folklore in the neighbouring Philippines recounts how one-eyed giants once roamed the plains of central and northern Mindanao. The most legendary of these ogres was Agyo, who is said to have fought against the first Spanish invaders. It is reported that Agyo's skeletal remains were retained as objects of ritual worship within a sacred cave near Bukidon. There are also unconfirmed reports of giant skeletons in Siargao and Agusan. According to Artemio Barbaosa, chief of the National Museum's anthropology department:

> *Tribal folklore, particularly in Mindanao, portrays the one-eyed giants as half men and half beasts with supernatural powers. Beliefs about giants (Kapre), as well as dwarfs (duwende), will always be alive in the hearts and minds of Filipinos.*

Balinese Cyclops

The island of Bali derives its name from ancient Indian tradition. Hindu scripture states that Bali was a demon-god who, in a time long passed, had contested with the hero-god Vishnu over possession of the demon's three realms: Heaven, Earth and the Underworld. The scripture relates how Vishnu, in the form of a dwarf, outwitted Bali with the simple request that he be granted all the land that he could encompass in three strides. When Bali confidently agreed, Vishnu suddenly reassumed his cosmic form and in three steps, strode across the demon's three realms. Although Vishnu allowed Bali to continue his rule in the Underworld, a final, battle later ensued during which Bali was killed and his body divided into separate pieces.

> *From his bones came diamonds, from his eyes sapphires, from his blood rubies, from his marrow emeralds, from his flesh crystals, from his tongue coral and from his teeth pearls.* The Pusanas

Throughout the island of Bali today, professional actors can still be seen re-enacting the scene of Bali's death. In these 'street plays' Vishnu is traditionally portrayed in the guise of a human archer named Rama. Mortally wounded by one of Rama's deadly arrows, the dying Bali complains that his demise will be an act of gross injustice because Rama slew him without revealing his true identity. Bali's peeved complaint of not being made aware of his slayer's real character is akin to that made by Homer's Cyclops:

> ***... and the strong Polyphemus*** (Cyclops) ***spoke to them again from out of the cave: "My friends, no-man*** (Odysseus) ***is slaying me by guile, not at all by force."***

On February 20th each year, the Balinese people celebrate the New Year Festival of Kunigan with a re-enactment of the battle fought against an oppressive giant called Sang Mayadenawa or Barong. Balinese legends tell of how their ancestors (the *Aga*) were once terrorized by a giant ogre who lived in a cave called Goa Gajah. The giant not only prevented them from performing their religious ceremonies but also demanded human sacrifice. To this day, the Balinese people periodically sacrifice one of every species of animal found on the island.

According to Balinese tradition, 'fair-skinned' Aryan warriors from India fought a great battle with this ogre and eventually they managed to kill it. Those Aryans who died fighting the giant are remembered as great heroes and their spirits continue to be venerated.

On the nearby island of Sulawesi, the native Torajans retain a tradition whereby they place their dead in caves that have been carved into cliff faces. The Torajans claim that their houses, which resemble large ships, had in the distant past been pulled ashore and converted into dwellings by ancestors who had sailed from India.

Greek Rituals in Indonesia

Having slain Polyphemus the heinous Cyclops, Odysseus might have endeavored to introduce more 'civilized' methods of placating the gods.

Professor Joseph Campbell relates that there is strong evidence to suggest that the present-day Indonesian pig sacrificing ceremonies are based on ancient Greek rituals. According to Professor Campbell an Indonesian myth concerning the three goddesses, Satine, Rabia and Hainuele, corresponds in theme and similarity of minute details with the ancient Greek Festival of Thesmophoria where sacrificial pig ceremonies honoured Persephone, Demeter and Hekate. **(Note 12)**

Asian Tsunamis

Odysseus relates how the enraged Cyclops broke off:

> ***... the peak of a great hill and threw it at us, and it fell in front of the dark-prowed ship. And the sea heaved beneath the fall of the rock and the backward flow of the wave bore the ship quickly to the dry land with the wash from the deep sea and drove it to the shore.***

South East Asia is a geologically unsound region. It hosts a great many active volcanoes and has long been susceptible to earthquakes and large tsunamis. As recently as 20,000 - 12,000 years ago, most of South East Asia existed as one single land mass called Sundaland. During that period and often times since, the ocean has suddenly inundated large tracts of coastal land. As a result of these floodings, the land bridge that once connected Australia to New Guinea is now submerged below the ocean and the once united landmasses of Indonesia and the Philippines have been reduced to a scattering of islands.

In A.D. 1555 a Portuguese scholar named Antonio Galvano produced a book entitled *Discoveries of the World.* Compiled from the various traditions he had gathered throughout the East, Galvano's writings agree with the contemporary view of a rapidly changing geographical Asian landscape:

> *Many writers affirm that in India and Malabar, which now abounds in people, the sea once reached the foot of the mountains; and that Cape Comorin and the island of Ceylon* (Sri Lanka) *were once united; also that Sumatra once joined with Malacca by the shoals of Caypasia; and not far from thence there is a small island which only a few years ago was joined to the opposite coast.* **(Note 13)**

When massive tsunamis struck this area of the world on December 26th 2004, we witnessed how hundreds of fishing boats were swept miles inland. Survivors who had found sanctuary on higher ground were left to placate the various gods of Hinduism, Buddhism, Islam and Christianity so that they might be spared further suffering. Perhaps Odysseus arrived in this region after a similarly devastating tsunami. This would explain why the Cyclopes natives did not have any ships to '***sail over the sea***'. Homer's one-eyed Cyclops, Polyphemus, was a son of the mighty sea-god Poseidon (Neptune) and so the practice of human and animal sacrifice in cliff-top caves might have been an endeavour to appease the powers of the destructive ocean.

Chinese-Malay Connections

Although the existence of a Malay-Chinese trade route is not historically noted until about A.D. 200, evidence of more ancient exchanges between the two cultures has recently been discovered in China. The excavation of several Shang Dynasty tombs c.1500 - 1160 B.C. have unearthed huge tortoise shells of a species unique to Malaysia. These same tombs also contained large quantities of cowry shells. Used as currency in ancient China, the rare cowry shells are found in abundance throughout the Indian Ocean regions. Reciprocally, Shang-styled bronze drums and distinctive forms of Chinese 'ancestral stones' have been discovered in diverse locations throughout South East Asia. The uncovering of these artifacts tells us that Shang ships travelled long and far in search of the valuable cowry.

As exponents of animistic beliefs and ritual slaughter, the cruel yet culturally advanced Shang Dynasty shared certain cultural affinities with the various trading centres that once thrived along the coastlines of Malaysia, Thailand, Cambodia and Vietnam. By the first century B.C., the trading ports of these lands became renowned for their participation in a sea trade route that transported silk from China to Rome. Historians are now of the opinion that Indian mariners probably met with their Chinese counterparts at Oc-eo in southern Cambodia. From there, the Indians shipped silk, spices and other cargoes via Takkaola (now Ta Kua Pa) on the Malay Peninsula to ports on the southern tip of India and thence to Europe.

If Odysseus had happened to come into contact with a more primitive form of this ancient trade route, he most likely would have been directed on towards the illustrious Shang Kingdom of China. Its capital city, An-yang, was at that time the capital of the legendary Shang civilization. Renowned for his sagacity, a Shang emperor would certainly be an appropriate person to inform the disoriented Odysseus of a homeward route.

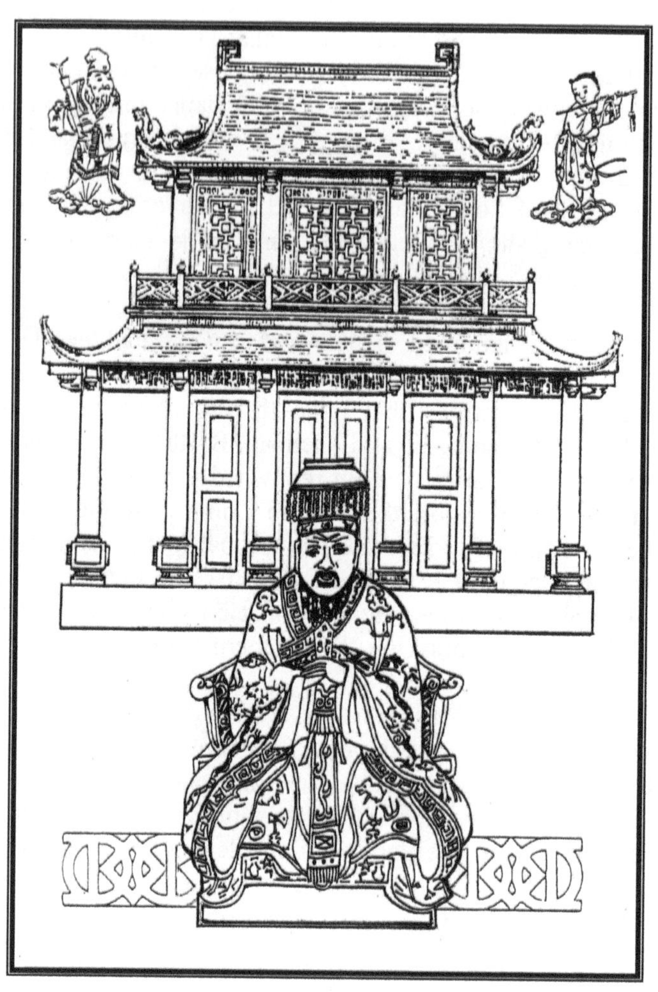

Chapter 5

KINGDOM OF AEOLUS
(Shang Dynasty, China)

Book 10: Line 1 -

> ***Thence we went on to the Aeolian island where lives Aeolus son of Hippotas, dear to the mortal gods. It is an island that floats (as it were) upon the sea, bronze bound with a wall that girds it. Now Aeolus has six daughters and six lusty sons, so he made the sons marry the daughters and they all live with their dear father and mother, feasting and enjoying every conceivable kind of luxury. All day long the atmosphere of the house is loaded with the savour of roasting meats till it groans again, yard and all; but by night they sleep on their well-made bedsteads, each with one's own wife between the blankets. These were the people among whom we had now come.***

Odysseus describes the Aeolian land as appearing to:

> ***...float above the sea with steep cliffs rising sheer from the lapping waters and all about it a great wall of bronze.***

This is an apt introduction to China's Shang Dynasty as its artisans are now considered the finest exponents of bronze making in the ancient world.

The Aeolus Kingdom

The ancient Chinese believed their world existed in three tiers: Heaven (T'ien) above, Earth in the middle and the Underworld below. With a mandate bestowed upon him from Heaven, the Emperor ruled the Earth's

Middle Kingdom from a central throne. As he was perceived to be the 'pivot' of earthly harmony, it was essential the Emperor be at all times correctly 'attuned' to his realm. It is fabled that in the glorious prehistoric period of Huang Ti the people had mastered their passions to such an extent that an accord between Heaven and Earth was created and thus the Middle Kingdom became an earthly paradise. The Huang Ti inhabitants found no necessity to eat; to merely sip dew sufficed for nourishment. Into this rarified atmosphere, the four benevolent animals (phoenix, unicorn, dragon and tortoise) manifested and took up their abodes in the gardens of the royal palace. The Emperor's understanding of the divine nature of all things enabled him to grant boons to those he considered worthy. The legendary Chinese emperors of this period are credited with conferring numerous gifts on their communities. These celebrated rulers formulated calendars, invented musical instruments, imparted knowledge of the arts of divination and mathematics, and also gave instruction as to the techniques of working in clay, metal and wood.

Emperor Aeolus

Greek mythology relates that Aeolus' consort was Eos (the Goddess of Dawn) and that she dwelt in the Far East. It seems Odysseus has indeed sailed into Oriental waters.

Odysseus tells us that King Aeolus was ***'the keeper and ruler of the four winds'*** and furthermore, he was the father of twelve children (six boys and six girls) whom he caused to wed each other. The title ***' keeper and ruler of the four winds'*** readily identifies King Aeolus as a ruler of Shang China. The Shang realm was divided into four main territories, each appointed to a lesser lord but protected by the Emperor. It is said that certain ritual temples of the Shang period had twelve outer walls that represented the twelve new moons in a year (the twelve children of Aeolus?). When the Shang Emperor worshipped inside such a temple, he accordingly changed rooms, robes and rituals with the advent of each new moon. As for Aeolus' palace, it is described as follows:

> ***... all day long the house is fragrant with the roasting of meat and the courtyard echoes to the sounds of banqueting within.***

In contrast to their ancient celestial ideals, Chinese culture maintains the custom of operating aromatic kitchens that operate well into the early hours of the morning. Chinese banquets today are acclaimed as lively gatherings where patrons feast upon a great number of exotic courses.

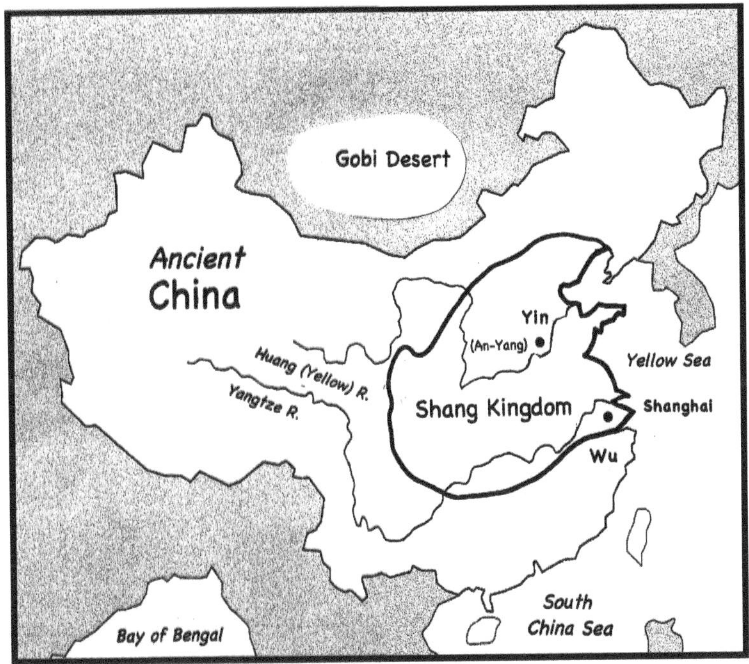

Extent of the Shang Kingdom, China c.1160 B.C.

Liangzhu Kingdom (Wu)

While it is possible for Shang Dynasty ships to have escorted Odysseus to their capital city of An-yang, it is more likely that he made contact with a coastal kingdom that is located in the vicinity of modern Shaghai. Referred to in ancient Chinese writings as Wu, this kingdom is also associated with the neolithic Liangzhu culture that spread across the present-day provinces of Zhejiang, Jiangsu, Anhui, Jiangxi and Shanghai. During the winter of 2006, archaeologists discovered the ruins of what was most likely the capital of the Lianghzhu kingdom. Situated in the province of Yuhang, the ruins of this city date to 2300 B.C. Its walls were 4 - 6 metres thick, extending 1500 - 1700 metres east to west, and 1800 - 1900 metres north to south. Covering an area of 2.9 million square metres, this ancient city was 200,000 square metres larger than Beijing's Forbidden City!

Under a patch of rice field, archaeologists found a 40 metre-wide ancient ditch built of hardened earth in which were large amounts of pottery shards. Liu Bin, a researcher at the Zhejiang Archaeological Institute, said when archaeologists dug a deep hole on the eastern bank of the north-south ditch, they were surprised to find a large area built of hammered soil and pebbles. Further excavations showed that the ancient ditch was a canal outside the city, and the area to its east was the remains of part of the city wall. **(vi)**

Yin (capital city of the Shang/Yin Dynasties)

In the year 1350 B.C., a warrior-king named Pangeng established the sixth and final Shang capital on the banks of the Huang (Yellow) River. The city that Pangeng established was called Yin and from that point on, the Shang dynasty would be known as the Yin Dynasty. The term Yin Dynasty has historically been synonymous with the Shang Dynasty, although it is now often used specifically in reference to the latter half of the Shang. The Japanese and Koreans still refer to the Shang Dynasty exclusively as the Yin Dynasty.

Although the Shang Dynasty had been mentioned in Sima Qian's *Records of the Grand Historian* (109 - 91 B.C.) it was regarded as a mythical fabrication until the year A.D. 1899. The then Director of the Chinese Imperial College, Wang Yirong, had been prescribed certain 'dragon bones' from a traditional pharmacist. He noticed they were engraved with strange markings that he thought might be samples of China's earliest writings and traced the source of the bones to the ruins of the ancient city of Yin. However the site remained unexcavated until 1928 and during the following nine years archaeologists from the National Government's Academia Sinica uncovered the remains of a royal palace, eleven royal tombs and ritual precincts that contained weapons of war. There was evidence of human and animal sacrifices, as well as tens of thousands of bronze, jade, stone and ceramic artifacts. To date, the Yin site has yielded over 100,000 inscribed oracular bones and turtle shells. These inscriptions form the first significant corpus of recorded Chinese characters and the earliest body of Chinese writing.

A number of excellent literary works are now ascribed to the Shang Dynasty. During this time Taoism held sway and the world's first dictionary was compiled. Significant advances in medicine occurred and the practice of acupuncture was introduced. Astronomers observed the movements of planets and produced an accurate calendar that included the addition of seven extra lunar months over a period of nineteen solar years. Shang artists also created highly decorative yet practical maps that were used by the captains of their ocean-voyaging vessels.

(vi) *Asian News International*

China's maritime explorations may have begun as early as 2250 B.C. Written during the legendary Hsia Dynasty, a scroll entitled *The Shan Hai King* (The Classic of Mountains and Seas) recounts the tale of a nautical expedition that crossed 'the great ocean' (Pacific Ocean?) to arrive upon a foreign shore. The ensuing southward exploration of this wondrous land included an inland trek to the foot of a 'great, luminous rock-wall valley' that some scholars assume to be Arizona's Grand Canyon. During this same Hsia Dynasty, the intricate art of jade carving was mastered (c.2000 B.C.) and from that period on, dragons as well as other animals were meticulously sculpted. The distinctively Chinese custom of carving jade has led certain archaeologists to compare Chinese figurines with similar objects found within the man-made mounds of Mexico's Olmec civilization c.1200 – 800 B.C. (see Chapter 7)

Mexican Olmec statues (c.1000 B.C.) portray oriental facial features

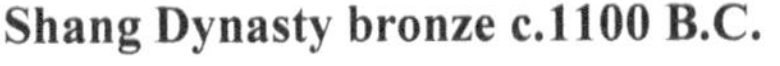

Shang Dynasty bronze c.1100 B.C.

Olmec mask c.900 B.C

Book 10: Line 14 -

> ***Aeolus entertained me for a whole month, asking me questions all the time about Troy, the Argive fleet and the return of the Achaeans. I told him exactly how everything had happened. When I said I must go and asked him to further me on my way, he made no sort of difficulty but set about doing so at once. Moreover, he flayed me a prime ox-hide to hold the ways of the roaring winds, which he shut up in the hide as in a sack. Jove*** (Zeus) ***had made him captain over the winds and he could stir or still each one of them according to his own pleasure. He put the sack in the ship and bound the mouth so tightly with a silver thread that not even a breath of a side-wind could blow from any quarter. The West Wind, which was fair for us, did he alone let blow as it chose; but it all came to nothing, for we were lost through our own folly.***

Chinese emperors were considered to be the living embodiment of the celestial emperor Shang Di, written 上帝 or simply 帝. According to Dr. Chen Wei-Zhong's book *Our Common God*, there are literally hundreds of oracle bone-inscriptions on which the symbol for Shang Di appears: for example, 'Shang Di orders rain'; 'Shang Di orders wind'; 'Shang Di gives his blessing' and so on. In the classic *Shang Shu* (Book of Annals), Shang Di appears 45 times, in the *Shi Jing* (Book of Poems) it appears 42 times and in the *Li Ji* (Book of Rituals) it appears 35 times.

Emperor Zu Jia (also known as Di Jia 帝甲: Divine Jia)

Assuming Odysseus had in fact arrived in Shang China c.1159 B.C., he may have conversed with Emperor Zu Jia who was then in the latter stages of his thirty-three year long reign. Oracle bones from that period record how he had won wars and quelled rebellions. While Emperor Zu Jia discontinued the practice of sacrificing to mythical ancestors, mountains and rivers, he purportedly made his government more judicious by increasingly offering sacrifices to historical figures such as his illustrious forefather, Wu Ding. Also known as Di Jia, meaning 'divine' emperor, Zu Jia was figuratively endowed with the attributes of righteousness and benevolence. Most importantly, Zu Jia equates to Aeolus in that both were regarded as being 'arbiters of human destiny'. It was in the capacity of divine arbiter that the 'Emperor' Aeolus consistently asked Odysseus quite probing questions regarding the military exploits of the Greeks. Naturally, Aeolus would have been curious about the existence of any foreign civilization that might pose a threat to his magnificent kingdom. Despite those concerns, Aeolus had no intention of further delaying Odysseus and generously provided him with what appears to be an early form of the compass. To protect the magnetic needle, Aeolus may have had the primitive compass bound in ***'a purse of ox-hide'*** so that:

> ***... not even a breath of side wind could blow from any quarter.***

The Compass

'Emperor' Aeolus' presentation of an early version of the magnetic compass to Odysseus finds correlation in Chinese history. Ancient texts report that the Chinese Minister of State, Tcheou-Koung (Ki-tan), c.1150 B.C. had instructed envoys from Youa-tchang in the applications of the needle and compass. The Chinese words *you ā zhǎng* translate as 'friends a long' or possibly, 'friends from a long way'.

> *As the ambassadors were about to take their departure (which was in the twenty-second cycle, more than 1040 years B.C.), Tcheou-Koung gave them an instrument which upon one side always turned towards the north and on the opposite side to the south, the better to direct them upon their homeward voyage. This instrument was called tchi-nan (chariot of the south), and it is still the name given to the compass, which leads to the belief that Tcheou-Koung invented the latter. In his chapter on 'the magnetic needle,' Humboldt says the apparatus was called fse-nan (indicator of the south).* **(vii)**

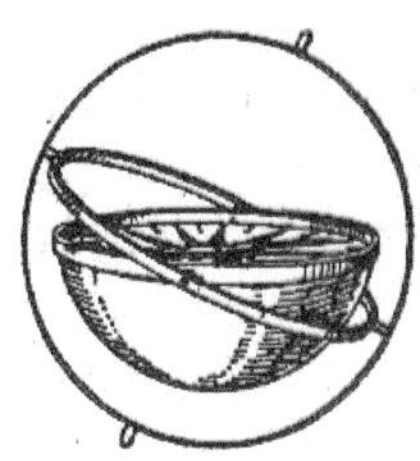

(vii) Ennemoser, Joseph *The History of Magic* 1854; Bohn, Henry G. London; Du Halde *Description de la Chine* 1736 Vol. I p. 312; *Klaproth Boussole* p. 81; Azuni *Bous-sole* pp. 190 - 191; Humboldt, *Cosmos* London 1849 Vol. II p. 628, and Vol. V. p. 52

During his long discussions with Aeolus, Odysseus undoubtedly exchanged views on the subject of world topography. Besides an obvious grounding in Hesiod-styled theology, an educated Odysseus would have believed that Europe and Asia were part of one huge landmass that was surrounded by a boundless ocean. Drawn in the 6th century B.C., Hecataeus' map of the world clearly illustrates this ancient concept. In his map the region of Scythue (Asia) is represented as bordering Europe's eastern and northern extents.

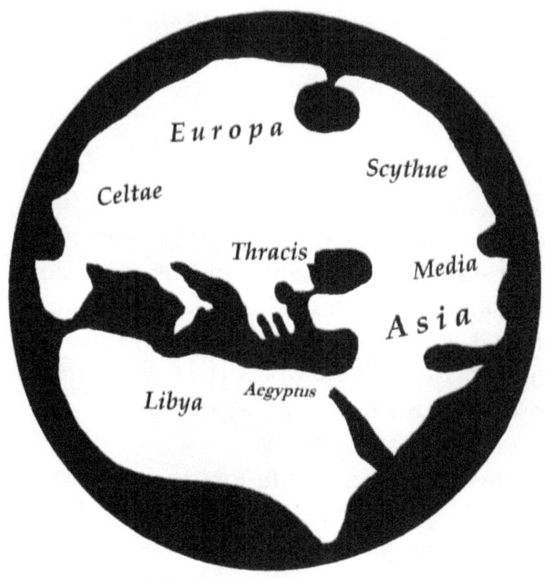

Hecataeus' map of the world c.500 B.C.

At this stage of his journeying, Odysseus may have erroneously concluded that he had almost completed a circumnavigation of the European-Asian landmass. With an understanding of such notions, he probably believed that if he continued sailing along the coast in a counter clockwise direction, he would theoretically arrive back to the familiar waters of Caucasian Europe. To attempt such a voyage is of course impractical but not incredulous. We should take into account that the aspiration of Mycenaean Greeks was to emulate the feats of mythic heroes. As in the example of Jason and the Argonauts c.1500 B.C., to be fearless in the face of overwhelming odds and danger was an expectation. The same courageousness was demonstrated by the later sea explorers of the 16th and 17th centuries A.D., particularly those who sailed the North Pacific in an attempt to find a northern passage back to Europe. **(Note 14)**

The return home via the North East Passage?

We might also take into account the fact that *The Odyssey* was undertaken during a period of extreme global warming. Ice core samples have revealed the Earth's temperature at the time of Odysseus was two degrees warmer than average. The shrinking of the Polar Ice Caps would hypothetically have provided a clear passage for adventurers to sail from the Orient to Europe or vice versa. Taking advantage of the Earth's present period of global warming, the French yachtsman, Eric Brossier, successfully completed a sailing voyage by way of the North East passage in the summer of 2002.

Emperor Zhou

The last of the Shang rulers was the notoriously cruel Emperor Zhou. Noted as being the inventor of chopsticks, Zhou was also infamous for coming up with novel ways to torture his enemies. Considering himself an equal of the gods, he mocked the ancestral deities and it is recorded that he severed all connections with the rites and rituals of his forebears. Zhou's bizarre behaviour occasioned a civil war and in the midst of despair he ultimately committed suicide. Whenever a 'divine Emperor' passed away, it was customary for his loyal subjects to sacrifice their lives so that they might rejoin their esteemed leader in Paradise. Upon the news of Zhou's death, ten thousand of his subjects are said to have 'disappeared' into the 'Eastern Sea'. It appears that in order to avoid suicide, many of Zhou's less devout subjects elected to cast their 'fate to the wind' and set sail upon the swift flowing Kurashio current ('the Way of the Divine Wind'). If this is actually what transpired, then it follows that the very powerful Kurashio current would have rapidly transported the Shang refugees to the shores of Central America. The survivors of such a momentous journey across the sea may have subsequently introduced comparable sacrificial practices to the indigenous peoples of Mesoamerica. Ironically, the slaughtering of royal servants all but ceased during the following Ch'ou Dynasty, c.1160 - 260 B.C. **(Note 15)**

Shang Dynasty bronze axe used in ceremonial sacrifices c.1200 B.C.

Having departed China, Odysseus sailed for nine days and on the tenth rejoiced that he was at last approaching the home shores of a familiar Aegean Sea. It was a logical enough supposition for since his departure from Egypt, Odysseus had been travelling through warm, sub-tropical and tropical regions. Sailing northward from China, the climate becomes cooler and the geographical features appear somewhat similar to those of the Mediterranean. Odysseus' mistaken claim that his '***native land lay on the horizon'*** is understandable in that the offshore islands of Japan do bear an amazing resemblance to those dotting the Greek Aegean Sea. Assuming that his ship was safely sailing into ***'home waters'***, Odysseus relaxed and soon drifted into a deep slumber. As he slept, his crew began to mutter about the 'Chinese' treasures they thought Odysseus had concealed from them. They decided to unfasten the mysterious ox-hide pouch that contained the ***'four winds of divinity'***. Immediately a great tempest was unleashed and the precious divine winds escaped up into the atmosphere. Amidst the ensuing commotion, the hapless vessel was cast back onto the recently departed shores of China. Odysseus found himself in the humiliating position of having to present himself once again to Emperor Aeolus and declare his inability to find his way home.

In returning to China after even such a short period of absence, Odysseus may have found that the Emperor had already changed his monthly abode and was now ensconced in a new chamber that emitted different harmonic energies. The rotation of the Emperor's residence might explain the sudden change in Aeolus' attitude toward Odysseus. Chinese philosophy at that particular time preached the view that man has the power to control his own destiny. Heaven (*T'ien*) rewarded virtue and therefore, if a man remained righteous he would consequently be blessed. Because Odysseus had proven himself incapable of making his way homeward after accepting hospitality and every assistance, the Emperor deemed him contemptible. The sons of Aeolus said nothing as their father denounced Odysseus:

> ***"How do you come to be here? What evil power is to blame for this? Surely, when we sent you off we had thought of all you could possibly need to get you home or to any port you might choose. Be gone from this land instantly! The world holds no greater sinner than you and I am not one to entertain and equip a man detested by the blessed gods. Your very presence here is proof of their enmity. Be off!"***

Having departed China a second time, and now without succour, it is difficult to ascertain whether Odysseus decided to launch out upon the Kurashio Current (Way of the Divine Winds) or to resume his original course by sailing the equatorial route towards the rising sun. Either way, his intention would be to continue voyaging eastward in the hope of returning to recognizable landscapes.

Trans-Pacific Migrations

To illustrate his theory of Asian influence upon the ancient cultures of Mesoamerica and Ecuador, Professor Joseph Campbell writes:

Asian influences in the cultures of Middle America received dramatic support in December 1960 when pottery sherds and stone figurines in a style identified as Japanese, c.3000 B.C. were discovered. Cord-marked, Middle Joman ware was unearthed on the coast of Ecuador at a site known as Valdivia, these were the earliest signs either of pottery or of works of art yet discovered in the New World.

About 2000 B.C. a second landing along the Ecuadorian coast, a few miles north of the first, at Machalilla, brought a second ceramic style, together with a curious Asian custom of intentional skull deformation that became in time the hallmark of the most highly developed Amerindian civilizations; the Incas, Maya and Aztec.

A third trans-Pacific company seems to have arrived about 1500 B.C. on the west coast of Guatemala, there to leave sherds of a later Japanese Jomon style known as Horinouchi ware soon after which, in the words of one leading authority, "the American cultures received quite a shock, one that was to change their character profoundly; the sudden introduction of a religio-political system that demanded great public works". **(vii)**

Professor Joseph Campbell's dating of trans-Pacific migrations accord with those presented in James Guthrie's book, *Lymphocyte Antigens Pre Columbiana,* 2001:

By the third millennium B.C., certain tropical Asian parasites, Jomon-like pottery, monumental architecture and various Oceanic traits had appeared in western South America. It is not unreasonable to attribute each transmitted trait as specifically Indonesian, Japanese, Melanesian, Micronesian or Polynesian in order to recognize an explosion of Pacific mobility that affected America to some degree. Dates given by Ibarra Grasso (1982) for trans-pacific influences, (based on decades of study) are a little before 3000 B.C. Various waves from Indonesia to Ecuador and Mexico from various Asian sources are dated at 1800 - 1500 B.C. McLean (1979) listed 38 musical traits shared by Asia, Oceania and Mesoamerica c.1000 - 700 B.C. Tolstoy (1974) compiled an extensive list of traits that seem to have been

(vii) Joseph Campbell, *The Mythic Image*

> *transmitted from America, including the musical bow, pan-pipes and the slit drum. Many others have compiled comparative trait lists, including Nordenskiold (1924, 1933), MacLeod (1929) and Campbell (1983 - 89).*

If Odysseus had opted for a resumption of his original equatorial course he would have instructed his fleet of ships to sail in a southwesterly direction. This route would have taken him past the northern Philippines and thence onwards to the Solomon, Fijian and Samoan islands. It was also the way of an ancient sea trade passage. Rectangular-shaped adze blades used in the northern Philippines c.1750 - 1250 B.C. are almost identical with those utilised at a much later date throughout Polynesia. (Beyer, *Philippine and East Asian Archaeology.*)

Odysseus' Swift Black Ship

As previously mentioned, it is difficult to identify the exact location of the exotic places Odysseus visited because they are so often described metaphorically. We encounter the same vagueness of detail in regards to Odysseus' precise route. The number of days it took to sail from one land to another is given but these time spans may have been trimmed in later versions to suit the geographical extents of the Mediterranean.

In his essay, *Where Did Odysseus Go?* Edward Furlong suggests to his readers that Odysseus' ***'swift black ship'*** was capable of travelling at a very fast rate of knots indeed and could continue on a direct course with winds that blew at right angles to the ship. By a careful scrutiny of *The Odyssey* text, Furlong was able to discern that Odysseus captained a crew of fifty-seven men and that this was a very significant number:

> *... for it tells us that Odysseus had a penteconter, the top of the line and fastest capital warship of his day. The penteconter had fifty rowers and at least one square sail. Each rower needs about 40 inches; that's 25 x 40 inches or about ten to twelve feet, with probably some decking to keep things dry under it, and a poop deck, say 10 - 15 feet at the stern where the helmsman stood to steer. That's about 105 - 110 feet in length. The speed of a boat is affected by the bow wave. At slow speeds the small bow wave will have little effect. As speed increases the bow wave will lengthen, this raises the bow of a ship. Then the stern drops. Now the ship is trying to climb uphill and more power is needed to drive it. The greater the length of the ship the faster it will go before trying to climb uphill. This may sound theoretical but what it means in practice is very startling: the fastest penteconters had an estimated*

speed under oars of 9.5 knots, or 17.6 kilometers per hour, close to that amidship) of about 12 - 14 feet and a draft (depth in water) of only two feet. It had an elastic hull that could give with the action of wind and waves. This is a very important speed factor.

Penteconters were not clicker-built with overlapping planks like the later Viking ships. Apparently each piece of timber was cut on the curve with an adze (or axe), and mortise-and-tenoned into place. This carvel-built system gives a smoother, faster hull. The crew could easily pull these lightweight craft up on shore overnight when they wanted to. **(viii)**

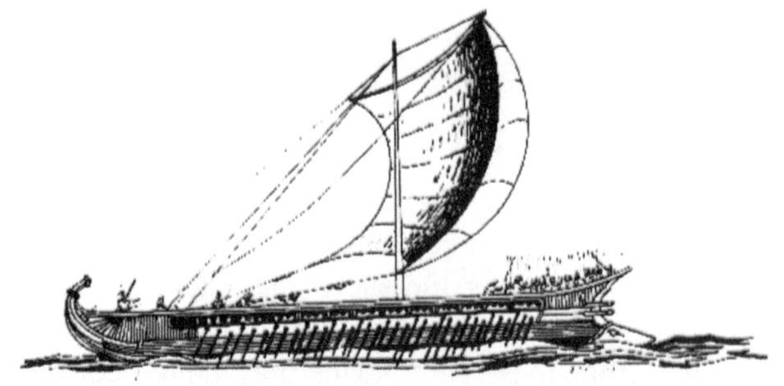

Greek Penteconter c.1160 B.C.

Relief sculpture depicting Greek oarsmen c.400 B.C., Athens

(viii) *http://cumulus.planetess.com/Odysseus/Ch2.ht*

Chapter 6

ISLE OF THE LAESTRYGONIANS
(Polynesia)

Book 14: Line 77 -

> ***Thence we sailed sadly on till the men were worn out with long and fruitless rowing, for there was no longer any wind to help them. For six days, night and day did we toil and on the seventh day we reached the rocky stronghold of Lamus-Telepylus, the city of the Laestrygonians.***

After six days of ceaseless rowing, Odysseus notices clouds of smoke billowing up from the horizon. Directing his fleet towards these rising clouds, his exhausted crews are greatly relieved when what might be a habitable island comes into view. Pressing stalwartly on, they sight a seemingly ideal harbour surrounded with high cliffs. Eleven of the ships in Odysseus' fleet anchor within the actual harbour while Odysseus opts for fastening '***his ship to a rock at the very end of the point***'. A small reconnaisance party is forthwith dispatched to investigate the source of the strangely spiralling clouds. As they are scaling a high hill for better vantage, '***a daughter of the Laestrygonians***' greets the group. The men ask her who the king of her isle might be. The woman announces that she is the daughter of the king and escorts them back to her father's house. When they arrive there the men are introduced to the maiden's mother whom they describe as being '***huge as a mountain***'. The massively large woman calls her husband Antiphates (Greek: spokesman) from the place of assembly. Upon his arrival, Antiphates at once begins preparations for a feast with the intention of eating the newly arrived visitors. Horrified, the scouts flee for their lives with a host of spear-toting Laestrygonians in hot pursuit. Odysseus had barely enough time to loosen the moorings of his ship before the Laestrygonians began to:

> ***... throw vast rocks at us from the cliffs as though they had been mere stones and I heard the horrid sound of the ships crunching up against one another and the death cries of my men.***

Odysseus manages to steer his ship ***'into the open water and out of reach of the rocks they hurled'*** but the men from the other ships are left floundering in the water as the huge Laestrygonians ***'speared them like fish'***.

Polynesian Origins

Sometime during the period of the Shang Dynasty (c.1600 - 1160 B.C.), a distinctive reddish pottery called Lapita appeared in the Melanesian islands of the Pacific Ocean. The carefully incised designs on Lapita pottery display geometric shapes, eyes, concentric circles and shields. Anthropologists generally agree that the people who introduced Lapita pottery into the Pacific were maritime traders from South East Asia. These people are believed to have arrived in the Melanesian islands around 1500 B.C. From there they sailed to Fiji c.1300 B.C. and soon after, settled in Tonga and Samoa. **(Note 16)**

Lapita pottery sherd displaying a Greek-like fret design

The Samoans

Although the Samoan island of Savaii is the third largest in Polynesia, it has very few residents. This is predominantly due to its active volcano that erupts regularly, spewing massive boulders into the surrounding seascape. While it is possible that hefty Polynesians hurled rocks down upon Odysseus' fleet of ships, it is also possible that the entire episode is an allegorical portrayal of an unfortunate encounter with Samoa's active Savaii volcano.

From the earliest of times, people have preferred to live on the neighboring island of Upolu. It was from Upolu that they made further migratory expeditions to various islands throughout the Pacific region.

The ability of the Samoans to construct very large outrigger canoes and competently sail them over vast distances led 18th century European explorers to refer to the Samoan Islands as the 'Navigator Islands'.

One of the navigational methods employed by the Samoans was to observe the natural phenomenon of clouds forming over islands that were not within visual range. As these cloud formations rise to a height of over 3,000 metres, a skilled eye could calculate landfall from a distance of 192 kilometres (120 miles). The large, Samoan double-hulled canoes called *'pirogues'* could skim so swiftly across the ocean that it was possible for them to travel 180 kilometres in a 10 or 12-hour day. To phrase this remarkable feat in another way, it would be possible for one of these boats to cover the distance between Hawaii and California, or from Easter Island to South America, in only 20 days. Anthropologists now claim that Polynesians regularly made trips of 4,000 kilometres, and sometimes even 9,000 kilometres, without ever having to put ashore!

Homer's description of the Laestrygonian inhabitants being ***'as huge asmountains'*** characterizes many of the peoples who live in the islands of this region. To be endowed with great weight symbolises the gods' favour and coveys both prestige and power. The present-day royal rulers of the Fijian and Tongan islands are renowned for their enormous, rotund bodies. It is a well-known fact that the peoples of Micronesia, Melanesia and Polynesia had also, in the not so distant past, participated in cannibalistic rituals, a practice that appears to have been flourishing at the time of Odysseus. The Laestrygonians' island is described as being the ***'rocky stronghold of Lamus-Telepylus'***. According to Robert Graves' *Greek Myths*, the word *lamus* translates as 'glutton', while *telepylus* translates as 'far distant port'.

An etching made during Captain Cook's visit to the islands of Hawaii depicts a Greek-style crested helmet

Hawaiian and Greek Language Similarities

We may never know exactly where Odysseus might have come into contact with the race I am loosely terming 'the Polynesians'. However, a list of common words compiled by Arnold Wadler in his book *One Language,* suggests that Polynesian islanders had at some time in their history, encountered seafarers who spoke in ancient Greek.

HAWAIIAN	**ANCIENT GREEK**
Aeto (Eagle)	**Aetos (Eagle)**
Noo-Noo (Thought)	**Nous (Intelligence)**
Manao (Think)	**Manthano (Learn)**
Mele (Sing)	**Melodhia (Melody)**
Lahui (People)	**Laos (People)**
Hiki (Come)	**Hikano (Arrive)**
Noko (Live, sit)	**Naio (Dwell)**

Wakea (Wah-kay-ah)

One-time curator at Hawaii's Bishop Museum and author of *Vikings of the Sunrise*, the late Dr. Peter Buck believed that Wakea ('the white god of Polynesia') was:

> ... *evidently a human being who arrived in the Pacific with three 'Roman-type ships' coming from the direction of the Red Sea.*

A full-blood Polynesian, Dr. Buck states that his theories had been compounded when Hawaiians of Chinese and Indian heritage relayed to him similar ancient legends concerning a 'white' teacher who in the remote past had arrived by ship to their respective ancestral lands. **(ix)**

In Japan, a mysterious Caucasian teacher named Wako is said to have taught in the vicinity of the 'sacred mountains' (*Yama*) and thenceforth that particular region became known as Wakayama. The Japanese word *wako* means 'to translate the Japanese spirit into Western learning'.

(ix) Buck, P. *Vikings of the Sunrise* Whitcombe & Tombs, Christchurch 1975

The same word, most interestingly, can also be interpreted to denote 'the son of a person of high social standing' or 'a marauding pirate'. Odysseus might aptly be dubbed with either of these titles. Located on the southern tip of Japan's Honshu Kii peninsula, the rugged Wakayama region continues to be a destination of spiritual pilgrimage.

It was Dr. Buck's belief that the Wakea/Wako personage had heard of the Polynesians' great navigational skills and had utilized them in order to journey further eastwards. Although Buck concluded that Wakea's voyage had originated in the Mediterranean and then continued into the Pacific via the Orient, he never proposed that the fair-skinned seafarer, Wakea, could have been Odysseus.

Lono

Throughout his long odyssey, Odysseus described many of the lands he had visited in terms of their agricultural potential. His knowledge and interest in horticultural endeavors may have earned him the Polynesian title, *Lono*. According to Hawaiian folklore, the agricultural god Lono was a white man whose honour was celebrated at harvest festivals. One day Lono (who was also the patron of singing and music) sailed away but promised to return laden with gifts. The following extract from Thor Heyerdahl's *Early Man and the Ocean*, further informs us that:

> *Amongst the chiefly families of New Zealand, Easter Island and the Chatham Island there is a different group who are tall, pale-skinned, bearded and long-headed with a distinctly Semitic nose, narrow lips and occasionally reddish-brown hair with a wavy texture. The Polynesian name for families carrying this racial type are called 'Urukehu' and are said to be descended from an earlier population of blonde and fair-skinned people.* **(x)**

In his book, *Migration, Myth and Magic from the Gilbert Islands*, Sir Arthur Grimble also recorded Pacific Islander legends that tell of a pale-skinned, red-haired people who referred to themselves as 'Children of the Sun.'

(x) Heyerdahl, Thor *Early Man and the Ocean (The beginning of navigation and sea-born civilization)* Allen and Unwin London 1978

Genetic Evidence

Recent studies of genetic blood groups indicate that mariners from the Eastern Mediterranean migrated across the Pacific and into Central and South America c.1200 B.C. In his paper entitled *Human Lymphocyte Antigens Pre-Columbiana,* 2001, James L Guthrie informs us that:

> *Human lymphocyte antigens (HLAs) are part of the compatibility system, whose main function is to produce antibodies. They are proteins on white blood cells that play a role in tissue and organ transplantation similar to that of the more familiar blood groups in transfusion. HLA distributions differ among world populations to such a degree that careful typing and matching must be done at transplant centres in order to minimize adverse reactions. This diversity gives population geneticists a powerful tool for tracing ancient migrations, and, at present, HLA distributions are more informative in this regard than any other genetic system except DNA.*

Antigen B*18

Guthrie's extensive research material notes how one particular antigen called B*18, is indicative of a genetic link between Ancient Greeks and the natives of Mexico and Ecuador:

> *B*18 appears to be an ancient Caucasoid antigen, linking Basques, Berbers, Sardinians, Greeks, and Southern Europeans. It also went along the Asian coast, especially to Indonesia, then apparently to Ecuador and Mexico. The overall distribution suggests involvement of Mediterranean seafarers. In America, it appears above the 1% level only among the Nahua, Quechua, and eastern Maya, with traces among the Araucano, northwest Canadian Eskimos, and the Greenland Eskimo. I suggest it came to the Pacific coast by way of Indonesia.*

Guthrie also nominates other scholars who share this opinion:

> *Some scholars see South America and Central America as endpoints in a process that carried elements of Mesopotamia and Near-Eastern culture throughout the Pacific: Heras 1953; Ibarra Grasso 1954, 1969, 1982; Heine-Geldern 1956; Kirchhoff 1964; Grieder 1982. Two main routes are postulated: one by way of India and Indonesia and another through China.*

In light of Guthrie's analysis, I might further suggest that those Medi terranean seafarers who entered the Pacific Ocean c.1200 B.C. were none other than Odysseus and his comrades.

Odysseus sails clear of the rock-hurling Laestrygonians

Chapter 7

CIRCE'S REALM OF AEAEA
(Central America)

Book 10: Line 133 -

> ***Thence we sailed sadly on; glad to have escaped death, though we had lost our comrades and came to the Aeaean island. There, Circe lives - a great and cunning goddess who is own sister to the magician Aeetes. They are both Children of the Sun by Perse, who is daughter to Oceanus. We brought our ship into a safe harbor without a word; for some god had guided us thither, and having landed, we lay there for two days and two nights, worn out in body and mind.***

Aeaea (Land of the Eagle)

We are not told how long it took Odysseus to voyage to Circe's realm of Aeaea but we can safely assume that it was located in an equatorial region for Circe and her wizard brother, Aeetes, are referred to as ***'Children of the Sun'***, or to be more specific, children of the sun god Helios.

In his initial description of Circe's realm, Homer reports the ***'fierce heat of sun'*** **(Note 17)** had caused an ***'antlered stag'*** to venture down to a stream. With a ***'well-aimed spear'*** Odysseus slew the stag and hauled its carcass back to his ship. As he and his starving crew feasted upon the stag, Odysseus declared:

> ***My friends, we are in very great difficulties; listen therefore to me. We have no idea where the sun either sets or rises, so that we do not even know East from West. I see no way out of it; nevertheless, we must try and find one.***

Odysseus' strategy of attempting to circumnavigate the Earth by way of an easterly equatorial route had come to grief when he found his passage blocked by yet another strange land. If this present landfall occurred in Central America, then indeed, Odysseus would ***'have been in very great difficulties'***. **(Note 18)** Upon realizing their predicament, Odysseus relates that his crewmen:

> ***... wept bitterly in their dismay, but there was nothing to be got by crying, so I divided them into two companies and set a captain over each; I gave one company to Eurylochus, while I took command of the other myself.***

Eurylochus' company was dispatched to reconnoiter the hinterland while Odysseus and the second group remained behind to keep watch over the ship. Some days later, Eurylochus returned alone to the moored vessel and declared:

> ***"We went as you told us, through the forest and in the middle of it there was a fine house built with cut stones in a place that could be seen from afar. There we found a woman, or perhaps she was a goddess, working at her loom and singing sweetly; so the men shouted to her and called her, whereupon she at once came down, opened the door, and invited us in. The others did not suspect any mischief so they followed her into the house, but I stayed where I was, for I thought there might be some treachery. From that moment I saw them no more, for not one of them ever came out, though I sat a long time watching for them."***

On hearing this news, Odysseus ordered Eurylochus to show him the way to Circe's home but the distressed captain pleaded with Odysseus to forsake these men and instead make good their escape while they were still able to do so. Ignoring Eurylochus' advice, Odysseus armed himself with both a ***'sword and bow'*** and set off alone to investigate the disappearance of his crewmen. As he made his way inland, Odysseus encountered the Greek god Hermes (Mercury). In the guise of a young native, Hermes cautions Odysseus:

> ***"My poor unhappy man, whither are you going over this mountaintop, alone without knowing the way? Your men are shut up in Circe's pigsties, like so many wild boars in their lairs. You surely do not fancy that you can set them free? I can tell you that you will never get back and will have to stay there with the rest of them.***

> ***But never mind, I will protect you and get you out of your difficulty. Take this herb which is one of great virtue and keep it about you when you go to Circe's house, it will be a talisman to you against every kind of mischief."***

Hermes tells Odysseus that Circe is skilled in the ways of witchcraft and will drug his food and drink but the special herb he has provided will protect him from her spells. Hermes offers further counsel:

> ***"When Circe strikes you with her wand, draw your sword and spring upon her as though you were going to kill her. She will thus be frightened and will then desire you to go to bed with her; on this you must not point blank refuse her, for you want her to set your companions free, and to take good care also of yourself. You must make her swear solemnly by all the blessed gods that she will not plot against you, otherwise, when she has got you naked she will unman you and make you fit for nothing."***

The herb Hermes had casually plucked from the ground revealed a long black root while its flowers were ***'white as milk'***. He informed Odysseus that the gods called the herb Moly and that no mortal man could ever uproot it. After handing the herb to Odysseus, Hermes transformed and flew up over the wooded land to return to ***'high Olympus'***. Odysseus proceeded to Circe's house. At the gates he called out to the goddess and she came down and invited him in:

> ***So I followed her - much troubled in mind. She set me on a richly decorated seat inlaid with silver, there was a footstool also under my feet and she mixed a mess in a golden goblet for me to drink; and she drugged it, for she meant me mischief. When she had given it to me and I had drunk it without its charming me, she struck me with her wand. "There now," she cried, "be off to the pigsty and make your lair with the rest of them."***

Having been forewarned, Odysseus rushed at her with his sword drawn. Circe screamed and sliding to the ground, clasped her arms about his knees. She beseeched him to divulge his identity for no man had ever before been able to resist her charm or potions:

> ***"You must be spell-proof; surely you can be none other than the bold hero Odysseus, who Hermes always said would sail here some day while on his way home from Troy; so be it then: sheath your sword***

> ***and let us go to bed that we may be friends and learn to trust each other"***

Heeding Hermes' advice, Odysseus declined Circes' offer until she had made a solemn oath to plot no further harm against him. She agreed at once and so he went to bed with her.

Despite its tendency to describe events in terms of mythic imagery, *The Odyssey* nevertheless provides us with vital clues as to where certain episodes may have taken place. Close scrutiny of the following excerpts reveals southern Mexico to be the most likely location for Circe's realm of Aeaea. We are told that Circe and her brother Aeetes were ***'Children of the Sun'*** and that in order to arrive at Circe's abode, Odysseus had to traverse a mountain. Circe's palace was ***'constructed of polished stones'*** and located ***'on a site that could be seen from afar'***. Circe's ***'home'*** is further described as being surrounded with a ***'forest',*** inhabited by ***'wild mountain wolves and lions'.*** As the Hindu word 'jungle' did not come into common usage until around A.D. 1600, we might presume that the word ***'forest'*** was meant to imply a jungle. Odysseus' description of Circe's island being the haunt of 'mountain lions' and 'wolves' is also curious, as I know of no island on Earth (let alone the Mediterranean) that supports both these species. Mountain lions and wolves however, are both native to Central America.

If Odysseus had in fact trekked his way up to a ***'palace'*** that existed somewhere within the jungles of Central America c.1160 B.C., it stands to reason that a community of temple builders must have already established themselves in the region prior to his arrival.

Circe's Palace

> ***We brought our ship into a safe harbour without a word, for some god guided us thither.***

It would be all too convenient to suggest that Odysseus' first point of contact in Mexico occurred on the beaches of beguiling Acapulco Bay. **(Note 19)** We know that the region of Acapulco was inhabited at the time of Odysseus because pictographs and cave paintings at nearby Pie de la Cuesta have been dated to 1200 B.C. Sir Francis Drake had also utilized Acapulco's idyllic harbour in the year A.D. 1579.

In the case of Odysseus, we must locate his mooring to a place that was within walking distance of Circe's 'community'. The present-day border region of southern Mexico and Guatemala seems the most likely setting for Odysseus' initial landfall. Named the Soconusco coastal region, this area is now considered by some archeologists to be the 'cradle' of both the Olmec and Maya civilizations. Eighty kilometres inland and running parallel to the coast, the Sierra Madre mountain chain includes twenty-four active volcanoes and many of these volcanoes are noted for their persistent emissions. It is feasible that Odysseus sighted from afar the plumes of smoke billowing from one of the volcanoes and was thereby able to navigate his ship to land. Standing like an angry sentinel over the Soconusco coast, the 4,220-metre high Mount Tajumulco may have been discharging at the time of Odysseus. Even when dormant, its majestic twin peaks can be seen from a distance of seventy or so kilometres out to sea.

The Soconusco Coastal Culture

At the time of Odysseus the Soconusco coastline was part of the principal travel route along the Isthmus of Tehuantepec. The narrow Isthmus connected mainland Mexico to the Yucatan Peninsula and Central America. Had Odysseus come ashore near the present border region of Mexico and Guatemala, he doubtlessly would have come in contact with coastal communities such as those located at La Blanca, Canton Corralito, Ocós, El Mesak, Paso de la Amada and Ujuxte. Each of these ancient sites contained architecturally designed ceremonial centres. Although a wide range of animals were hunted throughout the occupational phases of the Soconusco locales, evidence of deer hunting predominates. We may recall that Odysseus' first deed upon his arrival in Circe's Aeaea was to spear ***'an antlered stag'***. Pottery unearthed at the Ocós site is considered to be the most sophisticated ever found in southern Mesoamerica. When archaeologists excavated the ruins of Paso de la Amada they discovered a ball-court structure which they believe was constructed around 1400 B.C.

Situated between two parallel mounds, the ball court measures approximately 80 metres (262 feet) long and 8 metres (26 feet) wide. Uncharacteristically, the ball court was not located in the ceremonial centre but instead stood nearer to the high-status residences. This suggests that the ball court was reserved for the elite members of society.

'Fat Boy' sculpture

From as early as 1800 B.C., monumental stone heads and 'potbellies' or 'Fat Boys' were being crafted at nearby Monte Alto. These quite unique sculptures were carved from magnetic stone and deliberately shaped so that either the north or south magnetic pole was located in the head of the figure. In their decidedly corpulent appearance, the 'potbellies' might represent the adherents of a drug cult that rendered participants obese and slovenly. The transformation of Odysseus' crewmen into pigs under the command of Circe may be a metaphorical reference to the outcome of such practices.

Canton Corralito

The most viable location for a Circe 'palace' is the coastal settlement of Canton Corralito. Destroyed by a flood in about 1000 B.C., the site has been recently excavated by archaeologist David Cheetam who states:

> *What makes Canton Corralito so intriguing is the incredible quantity and quality of foreign 'Olmec-style' objects and its location in the centre of a territory occupied for centuries by the Mokaya people, a culture with its own distinctive traditions and styles.*

During his 2005 excavations of Canton Corralito, Cheetam discovered a 3,000 year-old burial site that contained the skeleton of an adolescent male surrounded by fifteen jade axes arranged in the shape of one giant axe. A decapitated adult male was found approximately two metres to the south. The ritualistic, close positioning of the bodies signify that the two burials were linked to some important event.

Map of Southern Mexico

An indication that Pre-classical temples existed at the time of Odysseus may be perceived in his account of the demise of the youngest crewman, Elpenor. According to Odysseus, the intoxicated Elpenor had fallen to his death because he failed to negotiate a certain ***'stairway'*** that led down from the ***'roof'*** of an Aeaean ***'house'***. The Mayan temples that we are familiar with today (albeit they date from a later period) are readily identified by their incredibly steep stairways.

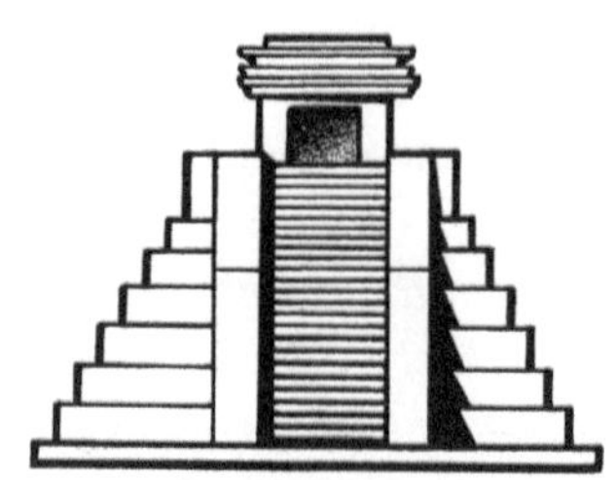

Odysseus reports how he dutifully took the body of young Elpenor back to where the ship was moored to bury him. The grave was then covered cairn-like, with a pile of stones and on top of the mound Odysseus set an upright oar. The discovery and excavation of Elpenor's seaside grave would undoubtedly provide irrefutable proof of Odysseus' presence in ancient Mexico.

Pre-Columbian statues displaying Phoenician-Caucasian features and pointed beards have been found in Mexico and Guatemala

We can only guess as to how far Odysseus may have ventured inland. His Mycenaean crewmen were battle-hardened warriors so the prospect of a hundred kilometres or so walk would not have perturbed them. It might also be presumed that during the year-long stay with Circe, Odysseus or members of his scouting parties were escorted along one or more of the many trade routes then prevalent throughout the Central American region. It is also possible that, when on one of these expeditions Odysseus either sighted or was informed that other seas existed further westward across the mountains. This may explain Odysseus' description of Circe's realm being surrounded by water.

The premise that Odysseus was capable of making overland journeys across the landscape of Pre-Columbian Mexico is vindicated by the fact that in the summer of A.D. 1619, the Spanish adventurer Hernán Cortéz, along with an army of 400 men, 15 horsemen and 15 cannons, marched over three hundred kilometres from Vera Cruz in the Gulf of Mexico to the elevated heights of Mexico City. We might also recall Francisco Pizarro's incredible conquest of Peru. Having subdued the Inca city of Caxamalca (modern Caxamarca), Pizarro and his small band of just 170 conquistadors took only two months to complete a 1,500 kilometres trek to the alpine citadel of Cuzco. Travelling along the famous Royal Inca Road, the intrepid Spaniards braved swollen rivers, precipitous mountain passes and ferocious Inca attacks to finally enter the forbidding Inca capital on November 3rd, 1532.

Cortés with mistress Doña Marina (*History of Tlaxcala Codex* c. A.D. 1590)

There is every reason to suppose that Odysseus had likewise utilized the well-trodden paths in Circe's realm. His claim that he had traversed a mountain in order to arrive at Circe's inland citadel may well be literal, but for now it is suffice to suggest that Odysseus' sojourn with the goddess Circe was confined to the coastal regions of Guatemala. His presence there would naturally have attracted native dignitaries from various other parts of Central America. Misinterpreted geographical information perhaps led Odysseus to believe that Circe's realm was surrounded by water. **(Note 20)**

Archaeologist Richard Diehi is of the belief that Olmec merchants from the Gulf of Mexico first appeared on Guatemala's Pacific Coast around 1150 B.C. According to Diehi, these visits led to a certain 'Olmecization' of society and gave rise to Canton Corralito becoming a regional centre. Diehi's opinion is intriguing because 1150 B.C. is the exact time of Odysseus' proposed presence in Canton Corralito.

The Olmecs

Prior to the recent discoveries on the Pacific Coast, Olmec culture was thought to have originated within the lowland coastal regions of Vera Cruz and Western Tabasco. Located on the Gulf of Mexico, this area is acknowledged as the heartland of Olmec culture. Archaeologists inform us that the Olmec culture had flourished there from approximately 1250 - 500 B.C. This time frame is further divided into three distinct periods.

Initial Olmec Period (1250 - 1150 B.C.): Contact increased between the various regions and Olmec ideology began to be depicted on pottery and other artifacts.

Early Olmec Period (1150 - 1000 B.C.): This epoch coincides with the proposed arrival of Odysseus to Mesoamerica.

Late Olmec Period (900 - 500B.C.): A definite Mayan influence begins to dominate Olmec culture.

Olmec monument #13 from La Venta displays the image of a bearded male figure with a distinctively Caucasian appearance. As the Mayan word for serpent also means a pole, we might deduce that the male figure is a representation of Quezalcoatl in his guise of Ehecatl (Lord of the Winds).

Although it is generally agreed that the Olmec culture evolved from within the confines of Mesoamerica, other schools of scholarship claim that an African or Chinese influence can be discerned. According to Weiner (1922), Lawrence (1962), Winters (1986) and Soustelle (1989), a seafaring African people called Manding arrived on the East Coast of Mexico c.1200 B.C. These black-skinned mariners are reported to have introduced into Mesoamerica their language (*Malinke-Bambara*), as well as a primitive form of writing called Libyco-Berber. Apparently the earliest depictions of this script can be traced to a place called Oued Mertoutek in the Sahara.

Commenting on Afro-Asiatic similitudes, James Guthrie writes:

> *Ethnological evidence for African presence in America includes: tooth alteration that began at about 1400-1200 B.C. (Stewart 1974); details of Yucatan log-beehive construction (Crane 1983); distinctive uses of stilts and masks (Lindblom 1927); the Nilotic one-legged resting posture of Venezuela (Lindblom 1949; DuPouy 1957); distinctive watercraft; fishing techniques, including the use of poisons and two-toned log signalling gongs (Lathrap 1977). Especially convincing to me are the hundreds of Mexican ceramic portrait heads collected by von Wuthenau (1975 and other publications) that clearly depict African and other non-Indian physiognomies. They are considered authentic, many being found in archaeological context dating before 500 B.C. and as early as 1200 B.C. Jairazbhoy, in numerous controversial treatises (as in 1974), claimed that extensive Egyptian influences in Mesoamerica began during the period of Rameses III (1186-1070 B.C.).*

Jairazbhoy's claim that Mesoamerica culture had been affected by certain Egyptian influences c.1186 - 1070 B.C. is most interesting in that it approximates with the proposed date of Odysseus' arrival in Central America c.1158 B.C.

Chinese Influence

Anthropologists similarly present a case for the existence of an Oriental connection with Olmec culture. The use of jade in fashioning artifacts, along with figurines displaying Chinese features, ornate mirrors and certain written symbols are cited as evidence pointing to an influence from Shang Dynasty China into Olmec Mexico. Among the accredited scholars who have recognized Chinese forms and iconographical motifs in the Olmec artifacts are Professors Heine-Geldern (1958), Ford (1969),

Campbell (1974) and more recently, Michael Xu (2001). **(Note 15)**

La Venta Figurines

The premise of foreign influences having been exerted upon early Olmec culture is possibly exemplified by a group of sixteen figurines that are on display in Mexico's National Museum. Dated to 1200 - 800 B.C., the miniature statues were unearthed from beneath the pavement of a La Venta temple. The figurines appear to have been involved in a ritual scenario as they were found placed in a circular arrangement amid six, long, polished jade celts. A white-coloured figure constructed from an unusual material stands at centre stage. Two green jade figurines and thirteen others made of black serpentine stone surround the white central figure. The Olmec's use of three differently coloured materials (white, green and black) has an obvious symbolic intent and may connote a representation of Caucasian, Chinese and African visitors.

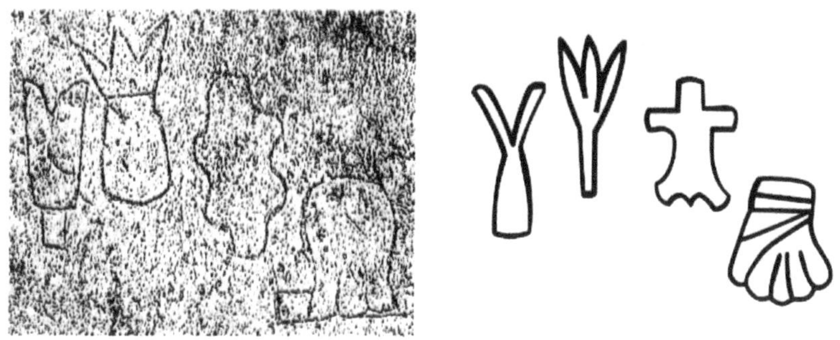

Casajal symbols (left) compare with Phaistos Disc glyphs (right)

Olmec Writing c.900 B.C.

In the year A.D. 1999 a small block of stone incised with 62 symbols was unearthed from a rock quarry in Vera Cruz. Referred to today as the Casajal Block, the carved stone is thought to display the oldest form of a written language yet discovered in the Americas. Made from native serpentine stone, the tablet is 15 inches long, 5 inches thick, and weighs a hefty 25 pounds. Arranged in horizontal rows, the tablet's 62 symbols are unlike the usual Mesoamerican scripts which are typically written in vertical rows. Similar symbols dating to 1000 B.C. have been found on figurines unearthed from the Pacific coastal site of Canton Corralito and this has led some researchers to consider the possibility that the script may have originated there. Representing ears of corn, clam shells, pelts, knives and bees, the symbolic glyphs are comparable to the Mycenaean Linear-B logograms and as well as those incised on ancient Crete's famous Phaistos Disc.

The Maya Civilization

The Maya civilization shares many features with other Mesoamerican civilizations due to the considerable social interaction and cultural diffusion that characterised the region. Although advances such as writing, epigraphy and the calendar did not originate with the Maya, they nevertheless developed them to a greater degree of sophistication. Many outside influences are found in Maya art and architecture and this is thought to have resulted from trade and cultural exchange rather than direct external conquest. According to the most widely held view, the first clearly 'Maya' settlements were established in the Soconusco region of the Pacific Coast c.1800 B.C. Known as the Early Pre-Classic, this period is typified by sedentary communities and the introduction of pottery and fired clay figures. Archaeological evidence indicates the construction of ceremonial architecture began in the Maya regions approximately 1000 B.C. The earliest configurations of such architecture consisted of simple burial mounds that were the precursors to the stepped-pyramids subsequently erected in the Late Pre-Classic period.

Maya Calendars

The most extensively used calendars in ancient Mesoamerica were the 365-day solar calendar (*Haab'*) and the 260-day ceremonial calendar (*Tzolk'in*). The Maya, or perhaps their predecessors, the Olmecs, came closest of all ancient peoples to calculating the exact length of the solar year, a measurement unknown to the West until comparatively recent times. The Maya estimated their solar year to be 365.2420 days, which is only fractionally different from the modern scientific measurement of 365.2422 days. As these two calendars are based on cycles of 365 days and 260 days respectively, they corresponded with each other every 52 years.

Tzolk'in Calendar

The Tzolk'in calendar served as an astrological almanac for all the peoples of Mesoamerica and is still in use today in some parts of Mexico and Guatemala. Utilized as a guide to the daily rituals and cultural achievements of the people, the Tzolk'in calendar also formed the basis for interconnecting the various measurements of cyclical time.

Long Count Calendar

A different form of calendar was used to track longer periods of time and for events that occurred in relation to each other. Known as the Long Count, this type of calendar begins at a mythological starting point and then counts the number of days that have elapsed since. The starting point of the Long Count calendar is August 11th, 3114 B.C. (equivalent to September 6th, 3114 B.C. in the Gregorian calendar). The completion of significant calendar cycles ('period endings'), such as a *B'ak'tun*-cycle (394 years), was often marked by the erection and dedication of specific monuments. **(Note 21)**

Mycenaean warrior c.1150 B.C. **Huastec statue of Quezalcoatl**

King Quetzalcoatl

When Eurylochus' initial scouting party failed to return to the ship, Odysseus took ***'both sword and bow'*** and charged off by himself in search of his missing men. The sight of a plume-helmeted Odysseus storming alone across the landscape may have caused the local natives to identify him as an incarnation of Quetzalcoatl, the feathered-serpent god.

The name Quetzalcoatl is a combination of *quetzal,* a brightly colored Mesoamerican bird and *coatl*, meaning serpent. The cult of the serpent in Mesoamerica is extremely old; the earliest representations of snakes with bird-like characteristics are dated to 1150 B.C. The origin of the temporal Quetzalcoatl is variously given. In one cycle of legends it is claimed that he was not born in any country known to the natives of Mesoamerica and another cycle gives his birthplace as Tollan (Tula).

Not to be confused with any earthly city in ancient Mexico, the original Tollan/Tula was instead a mythical City of Light. The Toltecs who claimed to have originated from Tollan revered Quetzalcoatl as a 'divine white god', the teacher of arts, inventor of the calendar and the provider of maize. He was regarded as being both 'Son of the Lord of the High Heavens' and 'Son of the Lord of the Seven Caves'. It is said that at birth he was endowed with an all-knowing wisdom and because he displayed a great purity of character, his realm flourished gloriously. Juan de Torquemada's *Monarquia Indiana* (1723) informs us that:

> *This Quetzalcoatl, according to true histories, was the Great Priest of the City of Tula (bountiful). They say of him that he was a 'White Man', large of body, wide forehead, large eyes, long black hair and large round beard. In all spiritual and ecclesiastical matters this Quetzalcoatl was supreme and as a Great Priest he never wanted nor permitted sacrifices of blood from dead men, nor animals, but only of bread and roses and flowers. He very efficiently prohibited and forbade wars, robberies, death and other harm they inflicted on each other. It is said that whenever they mentioned deaths or wars or other evils in front of him, he would turn his head and stop his ears in order not to see or hear them.* **(xi)**

(xi) Torquemada, Juan de *Monarquia Indiana* Madrid, Spain 1723 vol. 2

Compiled in the late 19th century, Daniel Brinton's *American Hero Myths* tells of the Toltec belief that their ancestors had been the subjects of Quetzalcoatl:

> *They were astrologers, necromancers, marvelous poets, philosophers, and painters as were not to be found elsewhere in the world, and such builders that for a thousand leagues the remains of their cities, temples and fortresses strewed the land. "When it has happened to me," says Father Duran, "to ask an Indian who cut this pass through the mountains, or who opened that spring of water, or who built that old ruin, the answer was, "The Toltecs, the disciples of Papa". The original home of the Toltecs was said to have been in Tlapallan - the very same Red Land to which Quetzalcoatl was fabled to have returned; Old Tlapallan (Hue Tlapallan), is distinguished as being that from which he and the Toltecs had emerged. Other myths called it the Place of Sand, Xalac, an evident reference to the sandy seastrand, the same spot where it was said that Quetzalcoatl was last seen, beyond which the sun rises and below which he sinks.* **(xii)**

The following extract from *The Odyssey,* Book 10: Line 348 - describes the 'god-like' treatment Odysseus experienced during his stay in Aeaea:

> ***Meanwhile her four servants, who are her housemaids, set about their work. They are the children of the groves and fountains and of the holy waters that run down into the sea. One of them spread a fair purple cloth over a seat and laid a carpet underneath it. Another brought tables of silver up to the seats and set them with baskets of gold. A third mixed some sweet wine with water in a silver bowl and put golden cups upon the tables, while a fourth brought in water and set it to boil in a large cauldron over a good fire which she had lighted. When the water in the cauldron was boiling, she poured cold into it till it was just as I like it and then she set me in a bath and began washing me and anointing me with oil, she arrayed me in a good cloak and shirt and led me to a richly decorated seat inlaid with silver; there was a footstool also under my feet. Circe then bade me eat but I would not and sat without heeding what was before me, still moody and suspicious.***

In his book *Primitive Mythology,* Professor Joseph Campbell recounts an ancient description of Quetzalcoatl's apartments. Homer's references

(xii) Brinton, Daniel H. *American Hero Myths* Philadelphia 1882

to Circe's four servants (Quetzalcoatl's four apartments), the lavishness ofher palace and the ceremony of 'Royal Bathing' are all recognized in the following extract:

Quetzalcoatl's temple-palace was composed of four most radiant apartments: one toward the east, yellow with gold; one toward the west, blue with turquoise and jade; one toward the south, white with pearls and shells; one toward the north, red with blood-stones, symbolising the cardinal quarters of the world over which the light of the sun holds sway. And it was set wonderfully above a mighty river that passed through the midst of the city of Tula; so that every night, precisely at midnight, the king descended into the river to bathe; and the place of his bath was called 'In the Painted Vase' or 'In the Precious Waters'.

Joseph Campbell continues:

Quetzalcoatl had taught a philosophy of gentleness and austere asceticism, offering blood from his ears and limbs daily to the gods who abode in the outer heavens. When the revolutions of time brought the stars (astrologically speaking) into the pattern that meant that his planet was setting, Quetzalcoatl fell under temptation. The black god, Tezcatlipoca, presented him with a potent drink - an alcoholic plaque prepared from the agave heart - but Quetzalcoatl refused it, saying he was ill. Urged then to taste it from the tip of Tezcatlipoca's finger, Quetzalcoatl did thus and was immediately overpowered by its magic. He lifted the bowl and was drunk. That night, neither Quetzalcoatl nor his sister, Quetzalpetlatl, said prayers nor went to the bath but instead, slept together. In the morning, Quetzalcoatl cried out in shame,

"I have sinned; the stain on my name cannot be erased."

The king remained four days in an underground tomb and when he came forth he wept and told his people that the time had come for his departure to the Red Land, the Dark Land, the Land of Fire.

Having burned his palace of the four fair world colours, buried his treasures in the neighbouring mountains, turned his chocolate trees to mesquite and told his multi-coloured birds to fly on ahead, in deepest sorrow Quetzalcoatl, the Feathered Serpent, departed. At a certain place along the way he rested and looking back at his City of the Sun, he wept. His tears went through the rock and he left in that place the mark of his sitting and the impress of his palms. Further on, he was challenged by necromancers who would not let him pass until he had given them the arts of working silver and wood, of feather-crafting and of painting. When he crossed the mountains, many of his attendant dwarfs and humpbacks died of cold.

At another place Quetzalcoatl met Tezcatlipoca and was challenged to a ball game - which he lost. And at another he aimed an arrow at a large pochotl tree; the arrow, too, was a pochotl tree and when it penetrated the first, the two together formed his sign - a cross.

The ability to release 'miraculous' arrows is also attributed to Odysseus. In the final climatic chapter of *The Odyssey*, Odysseus shoots an arrow through the rings of twelve, crescent-shaped Cretan axes.

And so Quetzalcoatl passed along, leaving many signs and place-names behind him, until coming at last to where the sky, land and water come together. There he departed and sailed away on a 'raft of serpents' into the sun.

The Quetzalcoatl myth has many variants, but all agree that he would return with a 'fair-faced' retinue from the East and resume sway over his people. The native priests and astrologers of the 16th century A.D. did not know in what particular cycle Quetzalcoatl was to reappear. They did know however, that Quetzalcoatl himself had predicted the name of the year. It was the year of 'One Reed' (*Ce Acatl*), which in the Mexican calendar is a year that occurs only every fifty-two years. Because the 'One Reed' cycle recurred in the year 1519 A.D., the astrologer-priests of the Aztec kingdom mistakenly identified the Spanish conquistador Cortéz as the reincarnation of the god Quetzalcoatl. The great banner emblazoned with a cross that Cortéz held aloft when he appeared on Mexico's eastern shores had definitively marked him as the returning Quetzalcoatl.

On November 8th 1519, Cortéz and his army entered the Aztec capital (Mexico city) and were peaceably received by Montezuma who presented them with lavish gifts and various gold artifacts. In his correspondence with King Charles V of Spain, Cortéz claimed from thence on he was considered by the Aztecs to be either an emissary of their feathered-serpent god Quetzalcoatl or Quetzalcoatl himself. In one of his letters back to Spain, Cortéz relates the momentous speech orated by Montezuma. Dated30th October 1520, the original letter was reprinted in the year 1770 by order of Don Francisco Antonio Lorenzana, Archbishop of Mexico.

Montezuma's Speech

> *It is now many days since our historians have informed us that neither my ancestors nor myself, nor any of the people who now inhabit this country, are natives of it; we are strangers and came hither from very distant parts: they also tell us, that a lord to whom all were vassals brought our race to this land and returned to his native place. Also, that after a long time, he came here again and found that those whom he had left were married to the women of this land, had large families and had built towns in which they dwelt. He wished to take them away but they would not consent to accompany him, nor permit him to remain here again as their chief; therefore he went away. We have been assured his descendants would return to conquer our country and reduce us again to his obedience. You say you come from the part where the sun rises; we believe and hold to be true the things which you tell us of this great lord or king who sent you hither; that he is our natural lord, particularly as you say that it is very many days since he has had notice of us. Be therefore sure we will obey you and take you for our lord in the place of the good lord of whom you tell us. In this there shall be neither failure nor deception; therefore, command according to your will in all the country, that is, in every part I have under my dominions; your will shall be obeyed and done; all that we have is subject to whatever you may please to command. You are therefore in your own country, in your own house; rejoice and rest from the fatigues of your journey and the wars you have been engaged in.*

In elaborating upon ancient oral traditions, Montezuma has clearly stated his knowledge of previous ancient contacts between European mariners and Mexican natives.

Circe's Spell

Circe's spellbinding liquor may well have been *Sinicuichi*, a local brew that is extracted from the foliage of the attractive shrub, *Heimia Salicifolia*. Although the plant grows all over Central America, it was used exclusively as a narcotic in Mexico. *Sinicuichi* is prepared by crushing its wilted leaves in water and allowing the juice to ferment in the sun for about three days. A cup of this intoxicating beverage induces a vision that is typically overcast in yellow and for this reason, *Sinicuichi* is sometimes known by the name 'plant of the yellow vision'. A mild euphoria overcomes the participant and an ability to discern microscopic detail accompanies the visionary state. Auditory hallucinations are common and they may consist of sound displacement or the total exclusion of sound. It is believed that while under the influence of this drug, a psychic regression to past events may occur.

Sculpted image of the Maya pulque-god whose adherents drank a concoction of liquor that induced visions of 'Underworld deities'

The Dionysus/Tlaloc Drug Culture

The initial sighting of fair-complexioned Greek warriors would certainly have been an awe-inspiring experience for the Mexican natives. With his face masked inside a bronze helmet that was crowned with a bright horsehair plume, Odysseus' appearance would no doubt have been most intimidating, even godlike. In order to test Odysseus' true mettle, Circe's magician-brother Aeetes had invited Odysseus to participate in the local drug-taking rituals. Raised as a Greek prince, Odysseus was likely to have had some prior experience through the drug-fuelled rites of Dionysus. These ancient Greek rites included the consumption of hallucinogenic toadstools and alcoholic beverages. Robert Graves, a foremost authority on Greek mythology, informs us that:

> *The pre-Colombian 'toadstool-god' Tlaloc, represented as a toad with a serpent headdress, has for thousands of years presided over the communal eating of the hallucinogenic toadstool, Psilocybe - a feast that gives visions of transcendental beauty. Tlaloc's European counterpart, Dionysus, shares too many of his mythical attributes for coincidence; they must be versions of the same deity.*

In his forward to *The Greek Myths,* Robert Graves elaborates upon this subject:

> *I have myself eaten the hallucinogenic mushroom psilocybe, divine ambrosia in immemorial use among the Masatec Indians of Oaxaca province, Mexico; heard the priestess invoke Tlaloc, the Mushroom God, and seen transcendental visions. Thus I wholeheartedly agree with R. Gordon Wasson, the American discoverer of this ancient rite, that the European ideas of heaven and hell may well have derived from similar mysteries. Tlaloc was engendered by lightning; so was Dionysus; and in Greek folklore, as in Masatec, so are all mushrooms proverbially called 'food of the gods' in both languages. Tlaloc wore a serpent-crown; so did Dionysus; Tlaloc had an underwater retreat; so had Dionysus. The Maenads' savage custom of tearing off the victims' heads may refer allegorically to tearing off the sacred mushroom's head since in Mexico its stalk is never eaten. We read that Perseus, a sacred King of Argos, converted to Dionysus worship, named Mycenae after a toad-stool which he found growing on the site and which gave forth a stream of water. Tlaloc's emblem was a toad; so was that of Argos; and from the head of Tlaloc's toad in the Tepentitla fresco issues a stream of water. Yet at what epoch were the European and Central American cultures in contact?*

In Chapter 3; The Land of the Lotus Eaters, it was proposed that Odysseus and his crew had visited Sri Lanka and that during their stay they may have introduced certain Dionysian rituals. Ancient maps show that a town, a promontory and a sea in Sri Lanka were named in honor of Dionysus. According to the island's mythology, Dionysus had arrived upon their shores 'aboard a stone raft of snakes'. In Mexican folklore, the god Quetzalcoatl departs his realm aboard a remarkably similar 'raft of snakes'. Both Sri Lankan and Mexican mythologies recount the deeds of the mysterious 'Nagas', a mischievous 'snake-like' people, gifted with arcane knowledge.

Miniature 'mushroom statues' from Guatemala c.1000 B.C.

The late Maya archaeologist, Dr. Stephan de Borhegyi, published several articles in which he proposed the existence of a mushroom cult in the Guatemalan highlands as early as 1000 B.C. According to Dr Borhegyi, this cult had its origins along the Pacific Coast piedmont.

Messengers Are Dispatched

Another interesting coincidence concerning both Odysseus and Quetzalcoatl is that they are both recorded to have dispatched emissaries who failed to return. The failure of Odysseus' crewmen to return to their moored ship is comparable to the following extract taken from the 16th century *Florentine Codex*, which explains the origin of the Maya word *moxoolotitlani.*

> *Moxoolotitlani: a page is sent. This is said about someone who is sent with a message and fails to return with an answer, or else does not go where he was sent. It is said for this reason. They say that when Quetzalcoatl was King of Tollan, two women were bathing in his pool. When he saw them he sent two messengers to see who they were. And the messengers just stayed there watching the women bathing and did not take him the information. From that time on they began saying; 'a page is sent'.*

The Mesoamerican Wheel

When Pizzaro and his Spanish conquistadors arrived in Peru A.D. 1532, they discovered an elobrate system of paved roads and pathways. Winding through high mountain passes, over long suspension bridges and by a system of causeways over lakes, these roads evidenced that quite an advanced transportation system was in place.

Curator and author, Dr. J. Manson Valentine furthers:

> *But there were no wheels; everything was transported by safari-like human caravans or, in the Andes, on the backs of llamas as well as human beings. In Inca times, human runners ('chasquis') became almost a selective breed, being able to cover ground so quickly in relays that the Inca, in his mountain capital, received and ate fresh fish from the coast, fresher, be it said in passing, than the fish now available in Cuzco, the former Inca capital. But in spite of all the organization, building culture, technical advancement, transportation of goods and food in the Indian empires, the lack of wheels has usually been accepted as proof that the Pre-Columbian inhabitants of America had never graduated from the Stone Age.*

The recent discovery of Pre-Columbian wheeled artifacts in Mexico has caused many researchers to reassess a long held belief that the ancient peoples of Mesoamerica were unaware of the wheel. Attributed to the Olmec culture c.1160 B.C., wheeled artifacts have been found at various sites throughout Mexico including Cholula, Tres Zapotes, Oaxaca, El Tajin near Vera Cruz and also in the Republic of Panama.

Pre-Columbian horse on wheels excavated near Vera Cruz (left) resembles the traditional Trojan horse (right)

One artifact in particular is comparable in design to the Homeric 'Trojan Horse'. We might recall that wily Odysseus was credited as being the architect of the Trojan Horse. Odysseus would have been well aware of the terrible carnage wrought by the wheeled chariot. In Book XXII of Homer's *Iliad* we read how Odysseus' compatriot, Achilles, had attached the body of his enemy Hector to the rear of his chariot. With the body trailing behind him, Achilles then drove the chariot continually around the perimeters of Troy. Odysseus' witnessing of this very macabre event would surely have served as a grim reminder of wheeled warfare. In the jungles of Central America, Odysseus was apparently revered and honored as a manifestation of the 'benevolent god' Quezalcoatl. It would have been inappropriate for him to introduce such a potentially destructive device as the wheeled chariot.

The Greek Language in Central America

When the Spanish conquistadors first came into contact with the Indians of Mexico c.1530 A.D., they addressed them in Latin. However, because many of the Mayan syllables sounded so very much like those used in the ancient Greek language, the Spanish decided to try to communicate with the natives in that tongue.

In his book, *Mysteries of Forgotten Worlds*, author Charles Berlitz elaborates upon the many similarities that exist between the languages of ancient Mexico and Greece.

> *The Nahuatl (Aztec) word or word-prefix for god or gods is 'Teotl'; shortened to 'Téo' in compound words. 'Theos' means god in Greek and often occurs in combinations such as 'Teocalli' - 'House of the God' ('kalía' is 'small dwelling' in Greek), 'Teotl' or 'Teo' is also used in many place names in Central America, such as the famous pyramids of Teotihuacan (literally 'the place of those who have the gods'). A Mayan exorcism was found to resemble almost exactly a phrase used in the ancient secret celebration of the Greek mysteries. The name of Tlaloc, the Mexican rain and water god, has been compared with the Greek word for sea – 'thalassa,' not only for the sound of the name but for the element which he rules.*

Named after the Greek letter it resembles, the Tau cross is a most ancient and potent totem. It was a symbol for the Roman God Mithras, the Greek Attis as well as their predecessor, Tammuz - the Sumerian solar god of death and resurrection.

Attired in Greek-style togas, Mayan natives make offerings to a Tau-style cross in Palenque

The above illustration of natives revering the Tau-style cross is found in Ricardo Almendariz's *Collection of Stamps,* 1797. In the 1787 edition of *Description of the Ruins of an Ancient City Discovered Near Palenque, in the Kingdom of Guatemala, in Spanish America*, the Spanish writer Antonio Del Ri reports a Greek influence within Maya culture:

> *Among the embellishments are some enamelled stuccos. The Grecian-like heads represent sacred objects to which the natives addressed their devotions and made offerings, probably consisting of strings of jewels. Father Jacito Garrido, who was a Dominican friar and native of Hueste in Spain, visited this province in 1638. There he taught theology and was well versed in the Hebrew, Greek and Latin languages together with three of the native dialects, as well as arithmetic, cosmography and music. He left a Latin manuscript in which he states that in his opinion, the northern parts of America had been discovered by the Greeks, English and certain other nations; a supposition he deduces from the variety of their idioms, as well as some monuments existing in the village of Ocojingo, situated twenty-four leagues from Palenque.*

Fair-skinned 'Teacher-gods'

Among the more culturally advanced nations of ancient Mexico and South America, there existed persistent legends of visits by pale-skinned, bearded godlike teachers. Traditionally the Mayas remembered such fair-skinned teachers as coming from and returning to 'a land where the sun rises'. The Guatemalian Maya called their teacher-god Gucumatz; in Oajaca he was Wixepechocha, while in the Yucatan the voyaging 'white god' Zamna was depicted with a flowing beard and was acknowledged as the patron of writing and scholarship. Another fair-skinned teacher to visit the Yucatan area was Culkulcan. Having arrived from the west with nineteen companions, Culkulcan had been revered as a bird-snake god while others in his party were venerated as gods of fish, agriculture and thunder. After formulating wise laws Culkulcan and his men set sail in the direction of the rising sun.

It has been suggested that the legends of visiting Caucasian teachers may have originated through contact with either Phoenicians, Romans, Carthaginians or even Irish monks. Although the possibility of such contacts cannot be ruled out, various legends associated with another fair-skinned teacher called Votan, indicate that his arrival in Mexico occurred at about the same time as Odysseus' proposed visit. **(Note 22)**

Votan

Compiled by Daniel G. Brinton in 1882, his *American Hero-Myths* comments on the ancient legend of a 'white' teacher named Votan:

> *Few of our hero-myths have given occasion for wilder speculation than that of Votan. He was the culture hero of the Tzendals, a branch of the Maya race, whose home was in Chiapas and Tabasco. The Votan myth appears to have been written down some time in the seventeenth century, by a Christianized native. His manuscript of five or six folios, in the Tzendal tongue, came into the possession of Nuñez de la Vega, Bishop of Chiapas, about 1690, and later into the hands of Don Ramon Ondonez y Aguiar, where it was seen by Dr. Paul Felix Cabrera, about 1790. What has become of it is not known. No complete translation of it was made; and the extracts or abstracts given by the authors just named are most unsatisfactory and disfigured by ignorance and prejudice. None of them, probably, was familiar with the Tzendal tongue, especially in its ancient form. What they tell us runs as follows:*

At some indefinitely remote epoch, Votan came from the Far East. He was sent by God to divide out and assign to the different races of men the earth on which they dwell, and to give to each its own language. The land whence he came was vaguely called 'ualum uotan', the land of Votan. His message was especially to the Tzendals. Previous to his arrival they were ignorant, barbarous and without fixed habitations. He collected them into villages, taught them how to cultivate the maize and cotton and invented the hieroglyphic signs, which they learned to carve on the walls of their temples. It is even said that he wrote his own history in them. He instituted civil laws for their government and imparted to them the proper ceremonials of religious worship. For this reason he was also called 'Master of the Sacred Drum,' the instrument with which they summoned the votaries to the ritual dances.

They especially remembered him as the inventor of their calendar. His name stood third in the week of twenty days and was the first dominical sign, according to which they counted their year, corresponding to the Kan of the Mayas. As a city-builder, he was spoken of as the founder of Palenque, Nachan, Huehuetlan and in fact, any ancient place the origin of which had been forgotten. Near the last mentioned locality, Huehuetlan in Soconusco, he was reported to have constructed an underground temple by merely blowing with his breath. In this gloomy mansion he deposited his treasures and appointed a priestess to guard it, for whose assistance he created the tapirs.

Votan brought with him, or, according to another statement, was followed from his native land by certain attendants and subordinates. They were called in the myth, Tzequil (petticoated), from the long and flowing robes they wore. These aided him in the work of civilization. On four occasions he returned to his former home, dividing the country when he was about to leave, into four districts, over which he placed these attendants. **(xiii)**

When at last the time came for his final departure, Votan did not pass through the 'valley of death', as must all mortals, but instead penetrated through a cave into the Underworld and found his way to the 'root of

(xiii) Nuñez de la Vega, *Constituciones Diocesanas, Prologo* Rome 1702; Boturini, *Idea de unaNueva Historia de la America Septentrional*; Dr. Paul Felix Cabrera *Teatro Critico American* translated London 1822; Brasseur de Bourbourg *Histoires des Nations Civilisées de Mexique* Vol. 1 Chap. II; and H. de Charencey *Le Mythe de Votan; Etude sur les Origines Asiatiques de la Civilization Américaine* Alencon 1871

heaven'. With this particularly odd idiom, the native myth closes its account of Votan.

Commenting on the loss of the original manuscript, Mexican scholar Felix Cabrera c.1794, wrote:

> *It is to be regretted that the place is unknown where these precious documents of history were deposited; but still more is it to be lamented that the great treasure should have been destroyed. This treasure, according to Indian tradition, was placed by Votan himself as a proof of his origin and a memorial for future ages in the casa lobrega (house of darkness) that he had built in a breath (a metaphorical expression intended to imply the very short space of time employed in its construction). He committed this deposit to a distinguished female and a certain number of plebian Indians appointed annually for the purpose of its safe custody.* ***His mandate was scrupulously observed for many ages by the people of Tacoaloya, in the province of Soconusco****, where it was guarded with extraordinary care until being discovered by the prelate before mentioned, who obtained and destroyed it. Let me give his own words from no. 34, section 30 of his preface:*
>
> *"This treasure consisted of some large earthen vases of one piece and closed with covers of the same material on which were represented in stone, the figures of the ancient Indian pagans, whose names are in the calendar, with some calchihuites, which are solid hard stones of a green colour and other superstitious figures. These were taken from a cave by the Indian lady herself and the Tapienes or guardian of them and given up; when they were publicly burnt in the square at Huehuetan on our visits to that province in 1691."*

The cave into which Votan placed his 'records' was located somewhere near Huehuetan, the place where they were publicly burnt in A.D. 1691. Huehuetan itself lies in very close proximity (25 - 35 kilometres) to the proposed site of Odysseus' landing, so it maybe postulated that the 'distinguished female' with whom the sacred treasures were originally entrusted, was none other than Odysseus' royal consort, Circe.

Book 10: Line 466 -

We stayed with Circe for a whole twelve months. But when the year had passed in the waning of moons and the long days had come around, my men called me apart and said, "Sir, it is time you began to think about going home, if so you are to be spared to see your house and native country at all."

Thus did they speak and I assented. Thereupon through the live long day to the going down of the sun we feasted our fill on meat and wine, but when the sun went down and it came on dark the men laid themselves down to sleep in the covered cloisters. I, however, after I had got into bed with Circe, besought her by her knees and the goddess listened to what I had got to say.

"Circe!" said I. "Please keep the promise you made to me about furthering me on my homeward voyage. I want to get back and so do my men; they are always pestering me with their complaints as soon as ever your back is turned."

And the goddess answered, "Odysseus, noble son of Laertes, you shall none of you stay here any longer if you do not want to, but there is another journey which you have got to take before you can sail homewards. You must go to the house of Hades and of his consort the dread Persephone to consult the ghost of the blind Theban prophet, Teiresias, whose reason is still unshaken. To him alone has Persephone left her understanding even in death, but the other ghosts flit about aimlessly."

I was dismayed when I heard this. I sat up in bed and wept and would gladly have lived no longer to see the light of the sun, but presently when I was tired of weeping and tossing myself about, I said, "And who shall guide me upon this voyage - for the house of Hades is a port that no ship can reach."

"You will want no guide," she answered, "raise your mast, set your white sails, sit quite still and the North wind will blow you there of itself."

Although a Central American 'Sun Goddess' would be unfamiliar with the character of the blind Theban prophet, Teiresias, she nevertheless would be well aware of the nether-realms of Hades. According to Circe, the land of Hades could only be reached with the assistance of the North Wind. If the goddess's words have been translated accurately throughout the ages, we can surmise that 'Hades' lay on the Pacific coast of South America.

In later Aztec cosmology, the Lord of the Underworld is recognized in the character of Huitzilopochtli. This fearsome god is said to have inspired the ancestors of the Aztecs to make the long and dangerous journey from their original homeland in Northern Mexico. This same Huitzilopochtli is also credited with annihilating his rivals, the peoples of the south. I venture that these 'southern rivals' were the 'civilized' coastal communities of Peru. **(Note 23)**

Odysseus bids Circe farewell,
Greek ivory carving, Athens Museum

Chapter 8

LAND OF THE CIMMERIANS
(Peruvian Coast)

Aided by a stiff northerly wind that ***'blew dead aft'***, Odysseus' vessel skimmed across the ***'deep waters of the ocean'*** (the Peruvian Trench) to arrive in ***'the land and city of the Cimmerians who live enshrouded in mist'***. We can safely presume that Odysseus' southerly voyage to the Land of the Cimmerians took place during the winter as heavy mists mantle the coast of Peru at that time of year. Laden with moisture these mists bring welcome relief to the parched interior, which in some areas receive rainfall barely once in a decade. The dryness of the coastal plain is due to the Punt winds that drift across the open terrain during the summer. The use of the word 'Punt' to describe these warm winds may owe its origin to the arrival of Odysseus or even earlier expeditions from Egypt and Sumer. Modern researchers now realize that Peru's ancient pyramids (c.2000 B.C.) were constructed at about the same time as a unique Middle Eastern strain of cotton was introduced. **(Note 24)** This and other discoveries such as an inscribed Sumerian bowl near Bolivia's Lake Titicaca has influenced certain anthropologists to speculate the possibility of ancient contacts between the Middle East and the western seaboard of South America. **(Note 25)**

When Odysseus initially departed from Egypt he sailed directly to the Land of the Cicones (Punt/India?). At that relatively early stage of his odyssey, Odysseus probably thought that he had already voyaged to the Earth's most distant extents. In those forbidding regions Odysseus had entreated the god Dis to release the souls of his fallen comrades. Now having sailed to the opposite side of the world, Odysseus is still none the wiser as to where on earth he actually is. In the hope of receiving some guidance as to a direction homewards, Odysseus has to once again summon the spirit of Dis. Considering the magnitude of their impending plight, it is little wonder that Odysseus' crew is described as ***'weeping and in great distress'*** when they depart the shores of western Mexico.

Circe's instructions to Odysseus had been clear and direct. After sailing southwards to the Lands of the Cimmerians, he was to dig a trench a cubit deep and about a cubit in length and breadth. He should then offer sacrifice and prayers to Dis and his consort Persephone (the rulers of Hades). Only when this dark and dread duo had been appeased would the ***'glorious fellowship of the dead'*** begin to parade before him.

Book 11: Line 1-

> ***Then, when we had got down to the seashore we drew our ship into the water and got her mast and sails into her; we also put sheep on board and took our places, weeping and in great distress of mind. Circe, that great and cunning goddess, sent us a fair wind that blew dead aft and stayed steadily with us keeping our sails all the time well filled; so we did whatever wanted doing to the ship's gear and let her go as the wind and helmsman headed her. All day long her sails were filled as she held her course over the sea but when the sun went down and darkness was all the Earth, we reached the deep waters of the River Oceanus. Here lies the land and city of the Cimmerians who live enshrouded in mist and darkness. The sun never pierces, either at his rising nor as he goes down again out of the heavens. The poor wretches live in one long melancholy night. When we got there we beached the ship, took the sheep out of her, and went along by the waters of Oceanus till we came to the place of which Circe had told us.***

Upon arriving at the place to which Circe had directed him, Odysseus drew his sword and carved out a deep trench. He swiftly slaughtered two black rams and sprayed their blood into the ditch as a sacrificial offering to Dis and Persephone, all the while his sword held firmly so as to ward off the unwelcome spirits who began to hover about. Presently, the spectre of the famed hermaphrodite, Teiresias, materialised.

> ***Then came also the ghost of Theban Teiresias, with his golden sceptre in his hand. He knew me and said,***
>
> ***"Odysseus, noble son of Laertes, why, poor man, have you left the light of day and come down to visit the dead in this sad place? Stand back from the trench and withdraw your sword that I may drink the blood and answer your questions truly."***
>
> ***So I drew back and sheathed my sword, whereon when he had drank of the blood, he began with his prophecy.***
>
> ***"You want to know," he said, "about your return home, but heaven***

will make this hard for you. I do not think that you will escape the eye of Neptune who still nurses his bitter grudge against you for having blinded his son. Still after much suffering you may get home if you can restrain yourself and your companions when your ship reaches the Thrinacian land, where you will find the sheep and cattle belonging to the Sun, who sees and gives ear to everything. If you leave these flocks unharmed and think of nothing but of getting home, you may yet after much hardship reach Ithaca; but if you harm them, then I forewarn you of the destruction of both your ship and of your men."

Ayahuasca (Vine of the Dead)

Odysseus' encounter with the spirit world was undoubtedly induced with the aid of some form of hallucinogenic potion. Most likely it would have been a concoction brewed from the plants *Psychotria virridis* and *Banisteriopsis caapi*, or perhaps *Datura.* The Incas called this sacred brew *ayahuasca*, a word that translates as 'Vine of the Dead' or 'Vine of the Soul'.

Cover illustration: A Pictorial Chronicle of the Incas, 1615 A.D.

According to William Emboden's *Narcotic Plants*

> *The datura plant of the Andes region differs from its relatives of Central America in both morphology and the usual modes of use. Most often, the seeds of the white trumpet flowers are ground into a meal and put into beverages of various sorts. The result is a narcotic so violent that the participant often has to be physically restrained or placed in a small trench to protect himself and others. Eventually, the user will be overtaken by an extended sleep interspersed with waking fits, hallucinations and colorful visions that are understood to be communication with the spirit world and souls of the departed.* **(xiv)**

The above description of the visions that can accompany the ingestion of hallucinogenic plants and the need to sometimes be physically restrained within a protective trench concurs with that of Odysseus' experience in encountering the ancestral heroes whose ***'ghosts flocked in from every side with wondrous cry'***.

Coastal Peruvian Temples c.2600 B.C. - 1000 B.C.

If Odysseus had been directed to a location on the Peruvian coast, it is reasonable to assume that it was to one of several metropolises that once existed there. The region is known for its ancient temple complexes and any one of them could have operated as a gateway to 'the Underworld realm of Hades'. The largest and oldest of these temple settlements is referred to today as the Caral complex. Located in the Supe Valley, 120 miles north of Lima, the Caral complex covers an area of 160 acres and incorporates the temple sites of Aspero, Sechin Alto, Huaca de las Reyes and Garagay, all of which were occupied c.2600 - 1000 B.C.

Aspero

The coastal site of Aspero hosts some of Peru's most impressive ancient temples. During the second millennium B.C., well-organised teams of laborers shifted thousands of tons of earth and stone to erect six great ziggurat-styled constructions, some of which stood 10 metres in height. Masonry structures decorated with adobe friezes stood atop the tiered platforms. Dedicatory caches unearthed from the temple altars of these buildings included: clay figurines, feathers, cotton, cane objects, carved wooden sticks and a ceremonial bowl with two symbolic 'toad' handles.

(xiv) Emboden, William *Narcotic Plants* London

The bowl's 'toad' handles indicate that it once held a hallucinogenic concoction called the 'hundred-clawed toad'. In his book *The White Goddess,* Robert Graves states that the partaking of this powerful 'toad' intoxicant had empowered the ancient Mediterranean Titans (Centaurs) to row sea-going boats (canoes?) over prolonged distances.

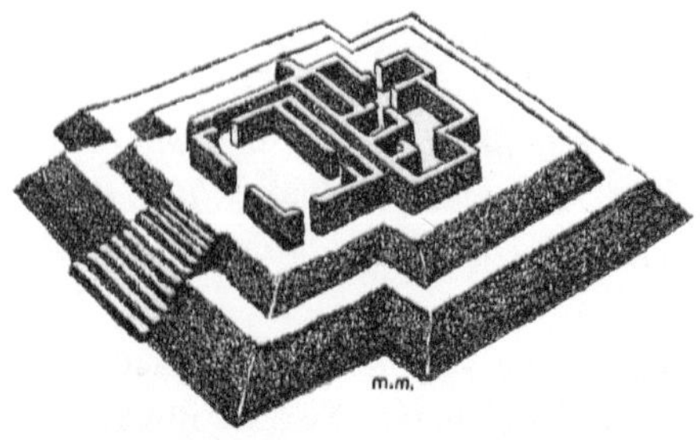

Peruvian temple, Aspero c. 2600 B.C.

Graves further informs us that the wild and warlike tribes of Titan/Centaurs are also identified as the *Hecatontocheiroi* ('hundred-handed ones'). I suspect that their 'fifty-oared' boats were similar to those depicted on artifacts from ancient Greece c.2800 - 2300 B.C.

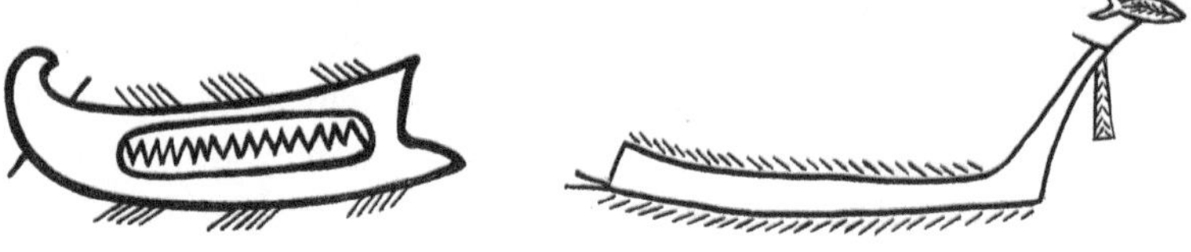

Ancient Peru-Mexico Sea Trade Link

Archaeologists confirm that a long-distance, sea trade route between the cultural capitals of Central America and Peru had existed from as early as the third millennium B.C. 'Circe' and her Mesoamerican compatriots, having exchanged goods via this seaway, would have been well aware of the many temple metropolises along the Peruvian coast. It is plausible that native South American seafarers had also explored the coastal lands to the south; perhaps even as far as the infamous Horn that separates the Pacific and Atlantic Oceans. **(Note 26)** Excavations of Peru's Caral complex have unearthed brilliant feathers and hallucinogenic snuffs that had been imported from the Amazon jungles, so it can be assumed that the 'Cimmerians' of Caral were acquainted with the geographical extents of the immense South American continent. A traditional knowledge of those inhospitable realms through sea and overland trading routes may have prompted his 'Cimmerian' hosts to forewarn Odysseus about the 'Land of Helios' (Brazil's equatorial Amazon region). **(Note 27)** Teiresias' spirit had sternly advised Odysseus to avoid this dangerous area, for ***'therein dwell the sacred kine of Helios'***. Despite living in a fog-bound environment that was often devoid of sunshine, the 'Cimmerians' of ancient Peru certainly practiced sun worship.

Casma Valley

Odysseus' initial contact with the natives of Peru possibly occurred in the Casma Valley. Situated about 198 miles (318 kilometers) north of Peru's capital city of Lima, the majority of Casma's temples are located at the confluence of the Sechin and Casma Rivers. The unification of these two snow-fed rivers forms the Rio Casma, which then flows into the Pacific Ocean. We might recall that Circe had directed Odysseus to venture to a place:

> ***... where the rivers Pyriphlegthon and Cacytus flow into Acheron and you will see a rock near it, just where the two roaring rivers run into one another.***

Cerro Sechin

Standing in the heart of the Casma Valley and dating to 1600 B.C., the site of Cerro Sechin was discovered by Peruvian archaeologists Julio C. Tello and Toribio Mejia on July 1st, 1937. Tello believed it was the capital of an entire culture that he termed Sechin. Located close to the Cerro Sechin site is Sechin Alto, which is considered to be the greatest architectural complex in Peru. Nearby Sechin Bajo has a circular plaza constructed of stone and mud and dates to 3,500 B.C.

In his book *The Representation of America in Roman Maps at the time of Christ*, South American archaeologist and author Dick Edgar Ibarra Grasso identified what he believed to be the image of two Phoenician ships etched onto the centre slabs of a Cerro Sechin temple. Julio C. Tello also noted that other monoliths in the area depicted what appeared to be a large ocean-going craft and a sextant. **(xv)**

(xv) Julio C. Tello *Arquelogia del valle de Casma* Lima 1956

Could the petroglyph etched onto a stone monolith at Sechin (left) be a depiction of an ancient sextant?

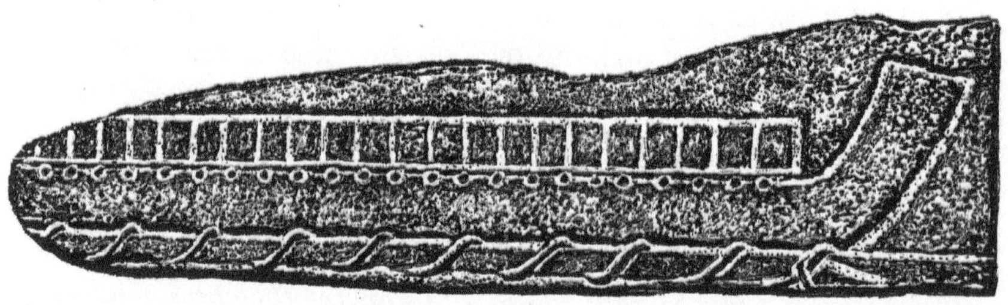

A stone slab found near the entrance of a Cerro Sechin temple displays an ocean-going ship with a detached mast lying alongside

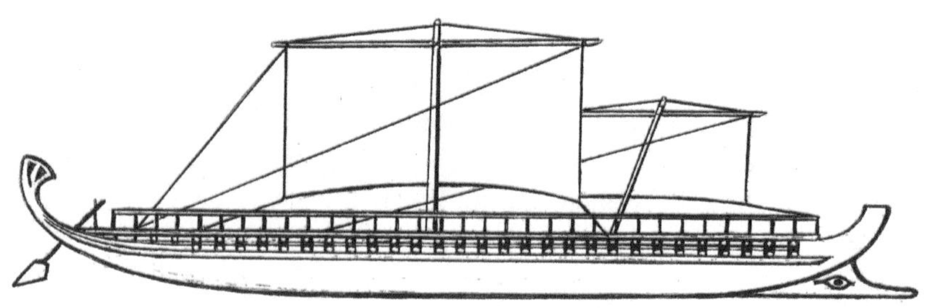

Greek Penteconter c. 1100 B.C.

The ocean-going vessel depicted on the centre slab of the Cerro Sechim temple appears to be a Greek Penteconter. The mast has been removed and is lying parallel to the ship. Odysseus attests to the practice of removing and replaying a ship's mast. When he departed from Circe's realm he had said:

> ***Then, when we had got down to the seashore we drew our ship into the water and got her mast and sails into her.***

During the time of Odysseus' proposed visit to Peru, the methods of weaving, fishing and horticulture improved significantly. The practice of funerary offerings was instigated and monumental temples displaying the very first examples of relief sculpture were constructed in the Casma Valley. Ceramic ware developed from crude, undecorated pots to highly sophisticated sculpted and incised, coloured vessels. Archeologically termed 'Chavin', this new cultural phase is considered to mark the 'true' beginning of civilization in the Andes.

Chavin Culture

The citadel of Chavin de Huantar was the religious centre of the Chavin people. It stands at an elevation of 3,150 metres and is located at the convergence of the Mosna River and the Huantsan River. The merging of two rivers is referred to as *tinkuy*, a word that defines the harmonious meeting of opposing forces. Like its earlier coastal counterpart at Casma, Chavin de Huantar served as the meeting place of the natural and cosmic forces. Archaeological findings suggest that the Chavin people did not partake in warfare. On the contrary, evidence of warfare is only found in the contemporaneous sites that were not under the influence of Chavin culture. The site of Chavin de Huantar was occupied and probably served as a religious centre at the time of Odysseus. Around 900 B.C., the Chavin people began to demonstrate their mastery of metallurgy and engineering and the practice of temple building.

Old Temple

The first known Chavin temple was an inward-facing U-shaped structure composed primarily of passageways built around a circular, sunken courtyard. A white granite totem pole called the Tello Obelisk is thought to have originally stood at the centre of the sunken courtyard. This obelisk features a central figure surrounded by various iconographies and is believed to represent the 'Tree of Life'. The central positioning of the obelisk served as a material manifestation of the *axis mundi*, a pivot linking the Heavens, Earth and Underworld. We might recall that Odysseus' sole intention for travelling to the land of the Cimmerians was to enter the underworld to regain an orientation for his journey home. Commenting on the Tello Obelisk, James Q. Jacobs writes:

> *Chavín is located at an important route from the Pacific Coast to the Amazon Basin. Travelling via the Santa and Monsa Valleys it is possible to traverse the Andes by crossing only one high pass. Chavín is located along this route and the Obelisk's iconography reflects the natural world in the tropical lowlands, the coast and the highlands.*

The Chavín's unique interregional synthesis is also reflected in the monumental architecture. The Old Temple combined the U-shaped pyramid and the sunken circular court with diverse coastal traditions, employing a stone masonry unique to the highlands. The antecedent for relief carvings also has many coastal antecedents, in both stone and plaster. Chavín's iconography and architecture is seen as an unprecedented unification of previously heterogeneous elements. This is particularly the case with the Obelisk. **(xvi)**

Located in an underground chamber of the U-shaped temple is a 4.5 metre-tall monolith called the Lanzon. Extending up through an entire floor and ceiling of the structure, the Lanzon is understood to represent the supreme

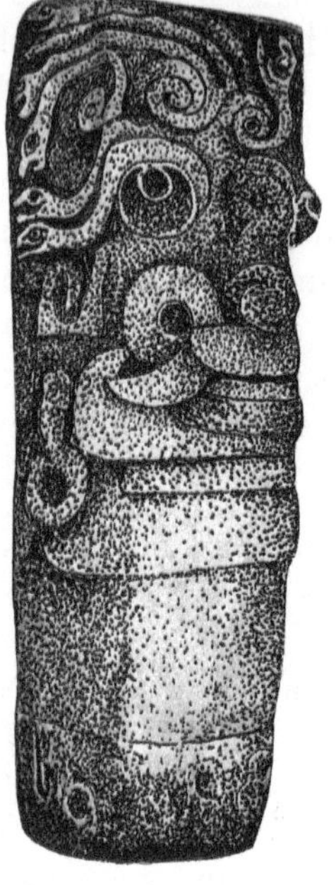

Lanzon Monolith

Greek Gorgon

Chavin deity. The sculpture displays an androgynous figure with large tusks, bulging eyes and a head of writhing snakes. Those versed in Greek mythology might recognize it as a representation of the Greek Gorgon, Medusa. Devotees at Chavin rituals were led through a maze of pitch-black tunnels to eventually come face to face with the giant sculpture's snarling mouth and upturned eyes. The participants' disorientation, no doubt compounded by the hallucinogenic effects of the San Pedro cactus

(xvi) Jacobs, James Q. http://www. Jqjacobs.net/andes/tello.html they had ingested before entering the maze, served to heighten the visual and psychological impact of the monolith.

> ***… and pale fear seized me, lest august Persephone might send forth upon me from out of the house of Hades the head of the Gorgon, that awful monster.***

Fair-skinned Natives (Children of the Sun)

The advent of Odysseus' arrival to their shores would have had a profound effect on the comparatively primitive natives of ancient Peru. Those tribes who came into direct contact with the 'white' harbingers of civilization may have considered themselves to be a 'blessed elite'. I imagine that in due time, these so-called 'blessed' tribes would have taught their successors to see themselves as the 'elite progeny' of 'white ancestors'. Such being the case, those more 'civilized' tribes who had adopted Mycenaean knowledge and customs would as a consequence, have experienced resentment from their less fortunate neighbouring tribes. The resulting hostilities may have forced the 'blessed elite' to escape to the mountains where they constructed protective fortresses such as those found near Cajamarca. The premise of an ancient division of Peruvian society is supported by current archeological evidence which suggests that the integration of coastal settlements ceased c. 900 B.C., whereupon a period of fortress construction began, particularly in the mountains.

Cajamarca

Cajamarca is renowned for being the place where the Spanish conqueror Pizarro first encountered the Inca emperor, Atahualpa. It was here that he accepted the first offerings of Inca gold and it was here that the Spanish began their massacre of the Inca peoples. Did fate decree that these historic events should occur in exactly the same region as the fair-skinned 'blessed elite' had established their roots?

The Cumbe Mayo

Located a mere 12 kilometres to the east of the Cajamarca site is a quite remarkable aqueduct called the Cumbe Mayo. Constructed around 1100 B.C., the aqueduct's purpose was to redirect water towards the coast. The name Cumbe Mayo is derived from the native Quechua words *Kumpi* and *mayu*, meaning 'well-made water channel', or *humoi mayo*, meaning 'thin river'. The numerous ancient petroglyphs etched onto the aqueduct and surrounding caverns are yet to be deciphered.

The Ventanillas de Otuzco

Only 8 kilometres from Cajamarca in the district of Los Banos del Inca, is the Ventanillas de Otuzco, a pre-Inca catacomb-like cemetery that dates from 1000 B.C. Here hundreds of galleries and individual alcoves resembling windows were hewn into the volcanic cliff face. Rectangular or quadrangular in shape, the alcoves are 8 - 10 metres deep and 50 - 60 centimetres high. Judging from fragments found nearby, the alcoves had originally been sealed with gravestones depicting figures in haute relief. Legend has it that the successive Incas cleared out the funerary alcoves and utilized them as grain silos (Quechua: *collca*), redirecting their entrances towards the cooling wind. The alcoves lead into a remarkable network of dark and mysterious galleries. These seemingly endless galleries gave rise to the myth of a secret tunnel that linked Cajamarca to Cuzco.

Kuntur Wasi (Quechua: House of the Condor)

The fortress-site of Kantur Wasi is located on the outskirts of Cajamarca at the headwaters of the Jequetepeque River. The Jequetepeque Valley provided a ready transportation corridor between the coastal regions and the highlands. Thought to have been constructed during the initial period of its occupation, c.1000 - 700 B.C., the Kantur Wasi fortress consists of a hilltop temple, several quadrangular platforms, a sunken courtyard and a series of rooms. In 1989, scientists from the University of Tokyo excavated the site's burial area. Valuable items, such as pectoral necklaces (decorative breastplates), a number of gold crowns, ornamental stone beads, earrings and various iconographies were discovered in four separate tombs. A further eight tombs have since been discovered.

Kuelap

Erected around 800 A.D. by the Chachapoyan 'Cloud People', Kuelap was then the largest structure in the Americas. It is estimated to contain three times more building material than Egypt's Pyramid of Cheops. Protected on one side by a sheer drop, the Kuelap complex stands at an elevation of

2,895 metres (9,500 feet) and is surrounded by extremely dense forests. An enormous wall of pale yellow boulders encompasses over 400 houses and ceremonial structures, many of which are now lying buried beneath tangled vegetation. Reminiscent of a Mycenaean citadel, Kuelap was capable of accommodating 3,500 people. Although the Incas eventually conquered this massive fortress and enslaved its occupants, small remnants of the fair-skinned 'Cloud People' are thought to have escaped into the nearby mountainous jungles where vestiges of their refugee settlements continue to be discovered.

Utcubamba

Armed with machetes, local people have recently opened a path into what appears to be the final Chachapoyan outpost. Perched high on a mountainside in the Jamaica district of Peru's remote Utcubamba region, the 12-acre settlement is believed to be about 1,000 years old. The main encampment is comprised of circular stone houses and next to these dwellings are platforms that were used to grind seeds and plants for food and medicine. This high fortress overlooks a breath-taking panorama of mountains and a waterfall dropping 500 metres to the valley below. It is one of the longest waterfalls in Peru. Archaeologist Benedicto Perez Goicochea believes the ancient inhabitants may have valued the site as a lookout point from which they could espy potential enemies.

Inca Invasion

At sometime during the period 1475 - 1480 A.D., the Inca king Tupac Yupanqui began to extend his empire up into the northeast of Peru. Leading an army of around 6,000 warriors, Tupac traversed the Maranon River and began to assail the Chachapoyan nation. Their 'Seven Great Cities' were soon overcome and in the following extract the Inca king describes the realm his warriors had conquered:

> *I shall never forget their round houses built in tiers, their fortresses well-situated against the rock and sometimes commanded by a tower... monuments built on high cliffs which appear inaccessible... tombs where they enclose the mummified bodies of their chiefs and priests. Their dead have no company but the wind and the condor.*

In the period before their conquest, the Chachapoyas ('Cloud People') had enjoyed a distinctly civilized lifestyle. Under the direction of a strict priesthood, an advanced culture flourished. There were vast agricultural works, cities, ceremonial centres and monuments, as well as schooling in the arts of music and dance. The language the 'Cloud People' spoke was not Quechua, as spoken by the Inca, but some other unknown language. The Chachapoyas, whom the Incas called 'cousins', were reputed to be fierce warriors. They were tall and fair-skinned, with light hair and blue eyes. Following their subjugation, the Chachapoyan women were greatly prized and the Chachapoyas men, being masterful stonemasons, were resettled in faraway regions to build cities and administration centres for the ever-expanding Inca Empire. When the Spanish reached Peru, they noted with surprise that the hereditary aristocracy of the Inca nation was extremely fair-skinned, with sometimes brown, red or blonde hair. The conquering Spaniards also observed that the girls who served as 'Virgins of the Sun' in the temples had by far the lightest skin coloring of all. Describing the Chachapoyas, chronicler Pedro Cieza de Leon wrote:

> *They are the whitest and most handsome of all the people I have seen and their wives were so beautiful that because of their gentleness, many of them deserved to be Incas' wives or to be taken to the Sun Temple. The women and their husbands always dressed in woollen clothes and on their heads they wear their llautos (woollen turban), which are a sign they wear to be known everywhere.*

Less then 60 years after they had destroyed the Chachapoyan kingdom, the Incas themselves suffered overthrow by the Spanish conquistadors at Cajamarca (A.D. 1532). The devastating routing of the Inca armies and subsequent surrender of their emperor may have been facilitated by the Incas' perception of the fair-skinned Spanish conquistadors as being the 'ghosts' of the Chachapoyan 'Cloud People'. It is not surprising to learn that the remnants of the Chachapoya became willing allies of the Spanish in their war against the Incas.

Chachapoyan Tombs

The Chachapoyan 'Cloud People' were renowned for entombing their dead in cliffside tombs called *chullpas*. Painted in bright hues of red and cream, many of the chullpas have gabled roofs and are emblazoned with cross-shaped niches. Local farmers call the red target-like rings *ojoys*, meaning 'eyes of the ancestors'. The Chachapoyan tomb-houses are somewhat similar in appearance to the small megaras of ancient Greece. According to Charles Picard, they are:

> *"Oval or rectangular in shape and, as a general rule, very elongated. They had wall ledges, inside and out, in the Minoan style. Akin to those sites where sacred objects were kept (treasuries) and usually*

> *close by, they had rather the same kind of decoration, possibly a little less splendid; the holy statue, by sacred prerogative, was set at the far end. The vital, major change in architecture was that these holy places became completely independent of the palaces that had fallen into disrepute. They were moved from the acropolis-citadels and were built apart in the pasturelands of the plains, either within or outside the cities. But they were set, we should remember, in the holiest spots of the countryside.* **(xvii)**

Karajia

Imposing 'white' figurative statues standing over 2 metres tall, guard a burial site located near the town of Karajia, 37 kilometres northwest of Chachapoya. Perched high on a cliff ledge that faces the west, the giant helmeted warrior-figures display very prominent noses and beards that are comparable to the *moia* statues of Easter Island. The tall Karajia figures are called *Purunmachus*, from the Quechua *purun* (wild) and *machu* (old or old men).

Con Tiki Viracocha

The full title, Con Tiki Viracocha, translates as 'god of the foamy ocean who brings fire or light'. The peoples of the Andes believed that during a time of primeval darkness the life-giving sun had arisen from Lake Titicaca. When the fair-skinned Viracocha suddenly appeared and began instructing the natives in the arts of civilization he was perceived to be a manifestation of the very Sun itself. Other references tell of a group of Caucasians named the *Suncasapa* or 'bearded ones'. They were the mythic soldiers who accompanied Viracocha, the 'angelic warriors of Viracocha'. **(Note 28)** Documenting the legends of the Aymara Indians, Spanish chronicler Pedro Cieza de Leon reports how Viracocha:

> *... had great power in-as-much that he could change plains into mountains, great hills into valleys and make water out of stones. In most parts he is generally called Tikiviracocha, but in the province of Collao they call him Tuapaca and in other places, Arnauan. In many they built temples in which they put blocks of stone in likeness of him and offered up sacrifices before them. It is held that the great blocks at Tiahuanacu were from that time.* **(xviii)**

(xvii) Picard, Charles *Larousse Encyclopedia of Prehistory and Ancient Art*
(xviii) De Leon, Pedro Gieza *Chronicles of Peru* 1553

Image of Pre-Columbian Viracocha found in Chile

The Sun Gate at Tiahuanaco portrays Viracocha with an aureole around his head and a snake staff in either hand. Similar depictions are found at the almost 1,000 years older site of Chavin de Huantar in northern Peru. The Chavin images have led some researchers to suggest that the origin of a human Viracocha might be traced to northern Peru rather than Titicaca. In the year A.D. 1638, an Augustine monk named Antonio de la Calancha, reported that Thunupas/Viracocha:

> *...appeared on the Altiplano in ancient times, coming from the north with five disciples. He was a man of august presence, blue-eyed, bearded, without headgear and wearing a cusma, a jerkin or sleeveless shirt reaching to the knees. He was sober, puritanical and preached against drunkenness, polygamy and war.* **(xix)**

(xix) de la Calancha, Antonio Corónica moralizada de la orden de N.S.P.S. Agustín en el Peru 1638

In A.D. 1608, a Catholic priest named Francisco de Avila collected the following Indian legend from one of the natives in his diocese:

> *They say that in most ancient times the Coniraya Viracocha appeared in the form and dress of a very poor Indian clothed in rags, insomuch that those who knew not who he was reviled him and called him a lousy wretch. But by his word of command, he caused the terraces and fields to be formed on the steep sides of ravines and the sustaining walls to rise up and support them. He also made the irrigating channels to flow, by merely hurling a hollow cane, such as we call a cane in Spain; and he went in various directions, arranging many things.* **(Note 29)**

Grahame Hancock's book, *Fingerprints of the Gods* presents a summary of Viracocha's achievements:

> *Above all else, Viracocha was remembered in the legends as a teacher. Before his coming, it was said, 'men lived in a condition of disorder, many went naked like savages; they had no houses or other dwellings than caves and from these they went forth to gather whatever they could find to eat in the countryside.' Viracocha was credited with changing all this and with initiating the long-lost golden age that later generations looked back on with nostalgia. All the legends agreed, furthermore, that he had carried out his civilizing mission with great kindness and as far as possible had abjured the use of force: careful instruction and personal example had been the main methods used to equip the people with the techniques and knowledge necessary for a cultured and productive life. In particular, he was remembered for bringing to Peru such varied skills as medicine, metallurgy, farming, animal husbandry, the art of writing (said by the Incas to have been introduced by Viracocha but later forgotten) and a sophisticated understanding of the principles of engineering and architecture.*

Lake Titicaca

Archaeologists now realize that Lake Titicaca once supported two separate societies. The oldest was the Pukara culture, which emerged from the northeastern region of the lake 200 B.C.; the other was the Tiwanaku civilization that began to flourish along the lake's southeastern shores around A.D. 400. Stone tunnels and underground tombs are a common feature of both the Pukara and Tiwanaku cultures. White-skinned natives (Greek offspring?) are reported to have once lived along the shores of Lake Titicaca. In the year A.D. 1553, an ex-conquistador by the name of Cieza de Leon, compiled a chronicle of Peru's Pre-Columbian history. Commenting on the spectacular megalithic ruins of Tiahuanaco, de Leon wrote:

> *Two great warlords, one called Sapana and the other Cari caused the destruction of Tiahuanaco. One of these chiefs entered the large island in the Lake of Titicaca and found there a white people who had beards; they fought with them in such a manner that all were killed.*

Archaic references to 'giant white visitors' are reputedly engraved onto certain Hieratic Tablets. Fashioned from gold, silver or copper, these mysterious tablets are supposedly hidden somewhere on one of Lake Titicaca's two sacred islands (respectively Isle of the Sun and Isle of the Moon). Other legends declare the existence of a submerged city called Wanaku.

The narrow Strait of Tiquina connects Lake Titicaca's two almost separate sub-basins. The larger sub-basin, Lago Grande (also called Lago Chucuito), has a mean depth of 135 metres and a maximum depth of 284 metres. The smaller sub-basin, Lago Huinaimarca (also called Lago Pequeno) has a mean depth of 9 metres and a maximum depth of 40 metres. Recent paleo-climate studies indicate that around 3100 B.C. the waterline of Lake Titicaca would have been as much as 85 metres lower then the present-day level. In other words, the majority of Humaimarca's lakebed was above the surface in the year 3,100 B.C., a date that happens to coincide with the beginning of the Inca calendar.

We might also note that the Incas regarded the lake to be the birthplace of their civilization. In Inca myth, the 'Children of the Sun' (fair-skinned peoples) are said to have emerged from these very same waters. A number of sub-aquatic expeditions have explored the waters of Lake Titicaca. In A.D. 1961, the famed French diver, Jacques Cousteau, investigated the remains of a town that was located only five metres below the lake's surface. Then in A.D. 2000 an international, thirty-man scientific group also discovered submerged ruins. By following a road that led down into the lake, a team of divers came upon an area that featured crop terraces, an 800 metre long wall and a large temple site that measured 200 metres by 50 metres. The ruins have been attributed to the Tiwanaku or Tiahuanaco peoples who are believed to have inhabited the region A.D. 300 - 1000. **(Note 30)**

Tiwanaku (Tiahuanaco)

The ruins of the ancient city-state of Tiwanaku are located 24 kilometres from the southeastern shores of Lake Titicaca. It has been proposed that Tiwanaku's name is related to the local Aymara Indian term *taypiqala*, meaning, 'stone in the centre' and alludes to the belief that their kingdom lay at the centre of the world.

The roots of the Tiwanaku Empire can be traced back to a small agricultural settlement that came into existence c.1500 B.C. During the period from A.D. 600 - 800 the Tiwanaku state expanded to become the regional power in the southern Andes. At its maximum extent the city covered approximately 6.5 square kilometres. Recent satellite imaging of fossilised *suka kollus* (raised terraces) across the three primary Tiwanaku valleys led researchers to conclude that the region had once been capable of sustaining a population of between 285,000 and one million people.

El Frayle (the brother) stands at Tiwanaku

Tiwanaku nobility dwelt within the confines of a square-walled compound. Surrounded by a moat, their sanctuary is thought to have been representative of a sacred island. Within the compound was imagery depicting the origin of humanity, however its viewing was reserved exclusively for a privileged elect although commoners may have been granted entry to the sacred precinct during ceremonial occasions.

In contrast to the masonry style of the later Inca, Tiwanaku stone architecture usually employed rectangular ashlar blocks that were laid out in regular courses. Some of the huge stone blocks used in the construction of Tiwanaku weigh as much as 131 tons and were hauled from a quarry 10 kilometres away. The Tiwanaku site contains massive platforms, large courtyards and sunken temples embellished with monolithic statues and impressive gateways.

The Gateway of the Sun

Sculpted from a one huge 10-ton block of stone, Tiwanaku's renowned Gateway of the Sun is four metres wide and stands three metres tall. At the centre of the gate's lintel is a carved depiction of the 'white' creator-god Virachoca. As mentioned previously, the Sun Gate figure (c.A.D. 700?) compares to a Chavin deity that dates to 900 B.C. The Sun Gate image of Viracocha can also be compared to the later Aztec god Tlaloc. Revered as the god of rain and fertility, Tlaloc was for the most part a benevolent deity who bestowed life and sustenance. Depicted with forked snakes in his hands, Tlaloc ruled all aspects associated with the powerful element of water and so as Lord of the Waters, he was also feared for his ability to send potentially destructive hail, thunder and lightning.

Greek and Peruvian Parallels

Commenting on the origins of Peruvian culture, James L Guthrie writes:

> *In South America, Greek inspiration has been claimed for such items as Peruvian jointed figurines of about 1200 B.C. (Lathrap 1973), European–style tweezers and the Greek form of metal masonry cramps used at Tiahuanaco during the first or second century A.D. (Ibarra Grasso 1969). Bosch-Gimpera (1970) suggested that gold and copper working techniques originating in Anatolia were introduced both to the Chavin culture of Peru and the Dongson culture of Vietnam about 500 B.C. It could be argued that Aegean sailors explored South America sporadically over a period of more than a thousand years, explaining the apparent Proto-Anatolian elements in Quechua, Aymara, and Uru-Chipaya as pointed out by Key (1994) and others such as Sauvageot (1930), Ferrario (1933) and Dumezil (1955).* **(xx)**

(xx) Guthrie, James L. *Human Lymphocyte Antigens Pre-Columbian* 2001

Sisyphus

According to ancient Greek mythology, Sisyphus was a most cunning individual who foolishly attempted to outwit the almighty Zeus. As punishment, Zeus cast Sisyphus down into Hades and sentenced him to the endless task of pushing huge boulders up a steep hillside. Whenever Sisyphus managed to manoeuvre a boulder to the top of the slope it would simply slide back to its original position. Odysseus' recognition of Sisyphus toiling in the Land of the Cimmerians (Hades) was possibly made in reference to him witnessing the seemingly endless labors of the native workforce.

Black-figured Greek vase depicting Sisyphus in Hades

The indomitable perseverance of ancient Peru's native labour force is described by Spanish chronicler Garcilaso de la Vega A.D.1539 – 1616:

> *More than 20,000 Indians brought this stone up, dragging it with great cables. Their progress was very slow, for the road up which they came is rough and has many steep slopes to climb and descend. Half the labourers pulled at the ropes in front while the rest kept the rock steady with other cables attached to it, least it should roll back downhill. On one of these slopes, as a result of carelessness on the part of those who failed to pull evenly, the weight of the rock proved too much for the strength of those controlling it and it rolled back down the slope, killing more than three thousand Indians. Despite this disaster, the rock was again dragged up and deposited on site.*

The image of a Spartan warrior (left) bears an uncanny resemblance to the Peruvian deity, Veracocha

The gold death mask from Mycenae (left) is similar to an Inca gold mask

Andean 'Pan Pipe'

The Pan Pipe is a musical instrument of aligned tubes or reeds played by Pan and the shepherds of ancient Greece. Virtually identical pipes are still played in the highlands of the Andes by shepherds who serenade their llamas and sheep. Besides an obvious structural resemblance, the pitch of these instruments has been discovered to be identical.

Sun Gate, Isle of Naxos, Greece **Sun Gate, Tiahuanaco, Bolivia**

Sun Gates

The Tiahuanaco Sun Gate stands on a 4,053-metre high plateau in Bolivia. Carved into its lava-stone surface is a system of designs that are thought to relate to astronomical events such as equinoxes and solstices. The discovery of a similar Sun Gate on the Greek Island of Naxos has led certain archaeologists to concede that the principles of astronomy as practiced in Egypt and Greece, were almost certainly employed by the ancient, high cultures of Peru and Bolivia.

The tradition of weaving classical Greek patterns into Mexican and Peruvian textiles continues to the present day. Greek-style sandals were once worn by the Pre-Columbian Incas.

(For further Greek and Peruvian comparisons see **Notes 31 - 35**)

The Pictorial Chronicle of the Incas

Although the Incas left no written records, a gifted priesthood called 'Rememberers' employed a unique method to record past events. Aided by data stored in an arrangement of stringed knots called *quipus*, the 'Remembers' were able to relate the various chapters of their long history. In the aftermath of the Spanish conquest these 'Rememberers' abandoned their practices and the *quipus* became lifeless strings. The ardent Spanish campaign against idolatry all but obliterated the Inca culture. Fortunately, a few chroniclers wrote down accounts culled from the dying oral tradition. Around the year A.D. 1615, Felipe Guamán Poma, a minor Spanish official, completed an immense 1,179-page treatise on Inca culture. Written in 'abominable' Spanish and Quechua, his work included a wealth of detailed drawings. Lost for three centuries, Poma's drawings, entitled *A Pictorial Chronicle of the Incas*, resurfaced in Copenhagen A.D. 1908. The book's illustrations depict certain Inca customs that are comparable to those of ancient Greece, for example, the 'reading' of entrails to predict the future.

The Return From Hades

We are informed that Odysseus' main objective in sailing to the Land of the Cimmerians had been to invoke the advice of the ghostly prophet, Teiresias. This is somewhat illogical as Teiresias, or any other such spirit, could have been summoned from within the bounds of Circe's realm of Aeaea. A possible explanation might be that Circe was cognizant of Peru's massive temple complexes. She may have reasoned that as the Cimmerian priests of these coastal metropolises were well versed in both celestial and geographical knowledge, they would be better qualified to reorient the lost Odysseus and set a course for his homeward journey.

The entire episode of Odysseus and his crews' experiences in the land of the Cimmerians is related in the very surreal imagery of a Hades made manifest. According to the ancient Greeks, Hades was the Underworld realm of death ***'wherein was housed vast stores of treasure'***. Whether Peru had a prior reputation for being 'a realm of Hades' or alternatively, Odysseus had introduced this notion is a matter of conjecture. However, the concept of this land containing a significant 'Underworld treasure-realm' is integral to Peruvian mythology. The mythological concept of a Peruvian Underworld continues to this day with rumors of subterranean tunnels that supposedly run throughout the Andes Mountains and into reaches far beyond the Pacific coastline. The quite recent discovery of underground passageways below the streets of La Paz has reignited legends of hidden Inca gold. According to popular folklore, the Incas at the time of the Spanish conquest had buried enormous hordes of golden artifacts deep within subterranean caves. An association with underworld deities persists among the miners of modern Peru. At the beginning of every shift before descending underground, the miners make offerings to a sculpted figurine that resembles Dis, the ancient Greek god of Hades.

Of his formidable Peruvian/Hadean sojourn, Odysseus confessed:

> ***... so many thousands of ghosts came round me and uttered such appalling cries that I was panic-stricken lest Persephone should send up from the house of Hades the head of that awful monster Gorgon. On this I hastened back to my ship and ordered my men to go on board at once and loose the hawsers; so they embarked and took their places, whereon the ship went down the stream of the river Oceanus.***

Odysseus' 'god-like' presence in the vicinity of the later Moche and Chimu cultures possibly attracted tribes from as far away as the Amazon. It should be noted that even in the early stages of its history, this coastal region was uniquely connected to the Amazon Basin by means of a direct pass over the Andes Mountains. Passing through Cajamarca and the mighty citadel of Kuelap, this mountain trail is thought to be the original 'gold and feather route' that connected the coast to the Moyobambas jungle zone. The arrival of curious and extremely primitive tribesmen from the Amazon jungle may have prompted Odysseus to describe them as ***'myriad tribes of the dead thronging up from Hades with wonderful clamor'***.

The reason Odysseus had given for hastening back to his ship and abruptly departing from Hades was that he was ***'in dread fear of being presented with the head of Medusa'*** (the snake-haired gorgon of Hades). The custom of shrinking heads and presenting them as gifts was once a common practice among Ecuador's Jivaro Indians. It is quite possible that Odysseus may have witnessed this grotesque custom and in an effort to avoid being the recipient of one of these trophies, fled from the region ***'panic stricken'***. As soon as he had sailed clear of the Cimmerian coast, Odysseus returned to the ***'deep stream of Oceanus'*** and soon found his way back to Circe's realm, ***'where there is dawn and sunrise as in other places'***.

The Moche custom of offering human heads is depicted on both tapestry (left) and stone artifact (right)

Pedro Sarmiento de Gamboa's 6th century *History of the Incas* tells of Viracocha departing from Peru in a northerly direction. Gamboa's report concurs with our present premise in that having completed his Peruvian mission, Odysseus had rejoined his crew and sailed off northwards and back to Mexico.

> *... Viracocha continued his journey, working his miracles until he reached the territory on the equinoctial line, where are now Puerto Viejo and Manta (Equador). Intending to leave the Land of Peru, he made a speech to those he had created, apprising them of the things that would happen. He told them that people would come who would say that they were Viracocha but that they were not to believe them, for in the time to come he would send his messengers who would protect and teach them. Having said that he went to sea with his two servants and went travelling over the water as if it was land, without sinking. For they appeared like foam over the water and the people therefore gave them the name Viracocha, which is the same as to say grease or foam of the sea.* **(xxi)**

Viracocha

(xxi) de Gamboa, Pedro Sarmiento *History of the Incas*

Teiresias' Prophesy Recounted

Upon hearing of Odysseus' return, Circe and her maidservants hastened to the shore where his ship had landed. She congratulated them all for their bravery and then took Odysseus aside so that she might hear of his experiences in the Land of the Cimmerians. Odysseus related to Circe all the events that had occurred in the Underworld realm of Hades. He told how the ghost of the blind eunuch Teiresias had predicted that 'heaven' would make it difficult for him to voyage homeward, but it would still be possible to reach home safely as long as he and his crew remembered to refrain from eating any ***'cattle of the sun'*** that thrived in the land of Thrinacia.

The prophet Teiresias had made it clear that Odysseus and his crew were not to put ashore on the 'Land of the Sun' and especially, were not to kill any of Thrinacia's creatures. If they disregarded this edict then the wrath of the sun god Helios would swiftly descend upon them all.

The goddess Circe must have understood Teiresias' grim forebodings. Not only did she agree that Odysseus' intended voyage along the coast of Thrinacia would be fraught with dangers, but she also cautioned that it was very far away and he would first have to navigate his way past an eerie coastline that was haunted by malevolent, sweet-singing Sirens. Greek mythology describes the Sirens as being bird-like creatures whose heads and busts are in the form of beautiful women. **(Note 36)** Circe warned Odysseus that even if he sailed clear of the Sirens, he would then have to negotiate the tumultuous waters at ***'the limits of the world'***, wherein dwelt the sea monsters Scylla and Charybdis.

Approaching the Horn of South America

Book 12: Line 132 -

> ***"Pay attention to what I am about to tell you - heaven itself indeed will recall it to your recollection. First you will come to the Sirens who enchant all who come near them. If anyone draws in too close and hears the singing of the Sirens, his wife and children will never welcome him home again, for they sit in a green field and warble him to death with the sweetness of their song. There is a great heap of dead men's bones lying all around, with the flesh still rotting on them. Therefore, pass these Sirens by, and stop your men's ears with***

wax that none of them may hear; but if you like you can get the men to bind you as you stand upright on a cross piece half way up the mast and they must lash rope's ends to the mast itself, so that you might have the pleasure of listening. If you beg and pray the men to unloose you, then they must bind you faster."

By the time Circe concluded her solemn advice, morning had begun to dawn over the horizon. A thoughtful Circe returned inland and Odysseus went aboard his ship, ordering his men to loosen her from the moorings:

... they at once got into her, took their places and began to smite the grey sea with their oars. Presently, the great and cunning goddess Circe befriended us with a fair wind that blew strongly aft and stayed steadily with us ensuring our sails were well-filled, so we did whatever wanted doing to the ship's gear and let her go as wind and helmsman headed her.

If Odysseus' ship was aided with a favourable wind that blew aft, we can safely assume he had once again set a course towards Peru. I suggest that on this second occasion, he continued voyaging past the coast of Peru and eventually arrived in the vicinity of southern Chile, where:

... there was not a breath of wind or ripple upon the water, so the men furled the sails and stowed them; then taking to their oars they whitened the water with the foam they raised in rowing. Meanwhile I took a large wheel of wax and cut it up small with my sword. Then I kneaded the wax in my strong hands till it became soft, which it soon did between the kneading and the rays of the sun god, son of Hyperion. Then I stopped the ears of all my men and they bound me hands and feet to the mast as I stood up on the cross piece; but they went on rowing themselves. When we had got within earshot of the land, and the ship was going at a good rate, the sirens saw that we were getting in shore and began their singing,

"Come here renowned Odysseus, honour to the Achaeans' name, and listen to our voices. No-one has ever sailed past us without staying to hear the enchanting sweetness of our song, He who listens will go on his way not only charmed but wiser, for we know all the ills that the gods laid upon the Argives and Trojans before Troy and can tell you everything that is going to happen in the whole world."

They sang these words most musically and as I longed to hear them further I made signs by frowning to my men that they should set me

free; but they quickened their stroke as Eurylochus and Perimedes bound me with still stronger bonds till we had got out of hearing of the Sirens' voices. Only then did my men take the wax from their ears and unbound me.

Depiction of Odysseus and the Sirens from a Greek vase

In voyaging down the west coast of South America towards Cape Horn, Odysseus' ship would have been carried along by the fierce currents that sweep through the narrow passages between the islands. Odysseus and his crewmen had to vanquish any thought of going ashore as this region has vast, swampy expanses of sphagnum moss. Mounds of slippery moss block the entranceway into the valleys, making overland transit almost impossible. Apart from one particular fungus that grows on tree trunks and has the appearance of an exotic orange fruit, there is no plant food and little game to be found in the gloomy interior of this region.

Odysseus and his brave crew eventually came to the ***'limits of the wide sea... where lies the dwelling place of early Dawn'***. Portside was a mountain whose sharp peak was ***'lost in dense cloud that never streams away, not even in summer'*** and on the starboard side were the horizon and the rocks that ***'the gods called The Wanderers'***.

Homer describes these wandering rocks in great detail:

No mortal man may scale these rocks. Even if he had twenty hands and twenty feet, he could not get a foothold to climb them, for they

> ***run sheer upwards as though they had been polished smooth. Not even a bird passes by here as these polished rocks are forever carried off from the sheer cliffs and Father Jove sends in others to make up their number.***

The above passage is an unmistakable description of floating icebergs! Odysseus had sailed into Antarctic waters and was about to round the Horn of South America. Interestingly, the word Antarctic is derived from the Greek words *anti* (in opposition) and *arktikos* (the Bear). Therefore, Antarctic means 'opposite the northern constellation of the Bear'.

Having navigated his way along the seemingly never-ending coastline of southern Chile, Odysseus had finally arrived in the vicinity of the infamous Horn of South America. According to the goddess Circe, this foreboding region marked the extent of her knowledge and power:

> ***"You will then have reached a point beyond which I cannot fully guide you. Two ways will now lie before you and you must choose between them as you see fit."***

Odysseus was confronted with a great dilemma, for he believed he had encountered:

> ***... the river Styx whose waters united round a pinnacle of rock, pouring their thundering streams into Acheron.***

Homer's words vividly describe a transit of the South American Horn. Long-since feared by mariners, it is here that the mighty currents of the Pacific and Atlantic Oceans meet in catastrophic confusion. Just as Circe had foretold, Odysseus now had to make the choice between braving the treacherous waters of the open sea, which is known today as 'Drake's Passage', or to row his ship through the narrow Straits of Magellan.

As Odysseus began to steer his vessel into ***'the strait that guards her entrance'*** the crew had ***'paled with fear'***. It was immediately apparent that this seaward passage was none other than the abode of the vicious creatures Circe had warned him about. On the portside loomed the evil Scylla and on the starboard lurked her sister, the terrible Charybdis ***'who sucked up and down the salt water from within her troubled deeps.'***

Magellan A.D. 1520

The Portuguese explorer Ferdinand Magellan made the first historically recorded voyage through these 'uncharted waters'. Sailing aboard the Vittoria, Magellan took 37 days to navigate his way along the narrow strait which now bears his name. Magellan described this strait as having *'icy mountains either side, stretching up to the heavens and all covered in cloud.'*

During his passage, Magellan saw numerous smoke plumes rising from the south and so he called this land Tierra Del Fuegos, the 'Land of Fires'. The myriad smoke plumes he had witnessed were from the constantly burning campfires of the local Ona Indians. Another hardy tribe, the Yahgan, lived along the most southerly beaches and although they occasionally wore fur cloaks, they usually wandered about naked.

On his voyage through this same inhospitable region, an anxious and exhausted Odysseus may have glimpsed a small band of Yahgan women fossicking amidst the eerie, lichen-covered rocks. In this quite forbidding atmosphere he might easily have imagined that these naked women were akin to the Sirens of Greek mythology.

In A.D. 1578 the British explorer and buccaneer, Sir Francis Drake also navigated his way around the Horn. For sixteen days he sailed between mountains whose *'snowy tops reached into the clouds.'* In reading excerpts from Drake's account of his voyage, one gets the distinct impression that he was conversant with the works of Homer. As Drake rounded the horn, one of his ships, the Marigold, went down with all hands. Drake relates that the crew aboard his ship, the Golden Hind, heard the *'despairing cries'* as the Marigold was *'overwhelmed by the mountainous seas'*. It seems incredible to contemplate the possibility that a very similar scenario had occurred 2,600 years previously as Odysseus reports:

> ***But meanwhile Scylla caught six of my company from our hollow ship. They were all lifted high and cried aloud in agony.***

Despite the loss of his crewmen's lives, Odysseus finally succeeded in rounding the perilous Horn. Turning the prow of his ship now northwards, he then set a course for the sun-drenched shores of the sun god, Hyperion (Brazil).

Chapter 9

THRINACIA: THE LAND OF HELIOS
(Coasts of Argentina and Brazil)

Book 12: Line 260 -

> ***When we had passed the Wandering Rocks, with Scylla and Charybdis, we reached the noble island of the Sun God.***

Determined to heed Teiresias and Circe's warning that he should ***'shun the island of the sun god'***, Odysseus continued to maintain a steady course along the coast of Thrinacia. The strain of the constant voyaging caused Eurylochus to approach Odysseus and complain:

> ***"You are very strong yourself and never get worn out; you seem to be made of iron, and now, though your men are exhausted with toil and want of sleep, you will not let them land and cook themselves a good supper upon this land, but go faring fruitlessly on through the watches of the flying night. It is by night that the winds blow hardest and do so much damage."***

First imploring his crew to swear a solemn oath that they would refrain from killing the ***'sun god's kine'***, Odysseus reluctantly headed his ship towards the nearest shore.

> ***When they had completed their oath we made the ship fast in a harbour that was near a stream of fresh water and the men went ashore and cooked their suppers.***

During the ***'third watch'*** (12 - 3 a.m.) of their first night ashore in the land of Thrinacia, Odysseus and his sleeping crew were struck by a strong '***hurricane***' that covered all the land and sea with raging winds and thick clouds. At the break of ***'rosy-fingered'*** dawn they returned to their moored ship and hauled it onto land, drawing '***her into a cave wherein the sea-nymphs hold their courts and dances***'. Odysseus then called his '***men together in council***':

> ***"My friends," said I, "we have meat and drink in the ship, let us mind, therefore, and not touch the cattle, or we shall suffer for it; for these cattle and sheep belong to the mighty sun, who sees and gives ear to everything." And again they promised that they would obey. For a whole month the wind blew steadily from the South, and there was no other wind, but only South and East. As long as corn and wine held out the men did not touch the cattle when they were hungry; when, however, they had eaten all there was in the ship, they were forced to go further afield, fishing with hook and line, catching birds, and taking whatever they could lay their hands on; for they were starving.***

The parallels between Odysseus' experience in Thrinacia and Sir Francis Drake's personal account of 'Rounding the Horn' are remarkable.

Odysseus' account:
'Then for a whole month the south wind blew without ceasing…'

Drake's account:
'For over a month a gale continued to blow… ' (The gale had shielded the sun, preventing Drake from taking bearings.)

Odysseus' account:
With no food left to eat, Odysseus accused Eurylochus of ***'broaching a wicked scheme'*** and having ***'set forth an evil counsel to my Company'***.

Drake's account:
When the food rations were depleted and his crew had begun hunting penguins, Drake accused one of his crewmen of treason, declaring: *'Thomas Doughty is a conjuror, a seditious fellow… '* **(xxii)**

The Slaughter of Hyperion's Sacred Cattle

Once they had exhausted their stores of wine and corn, Odysseus' crew soon became despondent and began muttering amongst themselves about their dire predicament. The ceaseless wind and his crew's constant grumbling provoked Odysseus to seek shelter and solitude further inland. Having found a quiet, secluded place, Odysseus washed his hands and began to placate the gods of Olympus so that they might grant him a safe passage home. Exhausted and famished, he then fell into a deep sleep. Taking advantage of Odysseus' absence, Eurylochus went about giving

(xxii) Lloyd, Christopher *Sir Francis Drake* London Faber and Faber 1957 'evil counsel' to his fellow comrades:

> ***"All deaths are bad enough but there is none so bad as famine. Why should we not drive in the best of these cows and offer them in sacrifice to the immortal gods? If we ever get back to Ithaca, we can build a fine temple to the sun god and enrich it with every kind of ornament; if however, he is determined to sink our ship out of revenge for these horned cattle and the other gods are of the same mind, I for one would rather drink salt water and have done with it, rather than be starved to death by inches in such a desert land as this is."***

The starving crewmen eagerly approved of Eurylochus' proposal and immediately began to stalk and slaughter the ***'sacred kine of the sun'***. Having no wine to make drink-offerings over the sacrifice, they instead poured a little water over the inner meats as they were being grilled.

When Odysseus awoke from his deep sleep and returned to his ship he could only lament over his crew's mutinous disobedience. For almost a week the crewmen continued to feast on the forbidden meats, then on the seventh day, the 'gods' began to visit them with evil portents.

> ***The hides of the skinned herd began to crawl across the ground; the meat, roast and raw, groaned upon the fires and a sound as though of lowing cattle could be heard.***

Meanwhile, the sun god's daughter Lampetie (sunlight) had hurried to her father Hyperion and informed him about the slaughter of his cattle. Hyperion flew into a great rage and pleaded with Zeus to punish the insolent mortals. Zeus replied:

> ***"Sun," said Zeus, "go on shining upon us gods and upon mankind over the fruitful earth. I will shiver their ship into little pieces with a bolt of white lightning as soon as they get out to sea."***

Hyperion and Helios

Hyperion was a primordial Titan god. His name means 'dweller on high' and he is said to have sired Helios (the Sun), Selene (the Moon) and Eos (the Dawn). On account of their almost identical natures, Hyperion is often confused with his son Helios who according to Homer, stood guard over the land of Aeaea where his children Circe and Aeetes dwelt.
(Note 37)

The Sun God Helios

The more ancient Hyperion appears to have been originally associated with the tropical regions such as Brazil.

Brazil

The Greek word for Brazil is Brazilia and it is derived from two verbs, *brazei* and *leiaino*. The word *brazei* translates as 'to boil' while *leiaino* means 'to polish, shine, flatten or level'. Together they characterize a flat land where the sun is so hot it might be described as 'boiling'. Being gods of light, both Hyperion and Helios perceived and had knowledge of everything. During Classical times (c.500 B.C.) many of the attributes originally associated with Hyperion and Helios were assimilated into the persona of Apollo. In his *Olympian Odes,* Pindar writes of Apollo:

> *He is the god who plumbs all hearts, the infallible, whom neither mortals nor immortals can deceive either by action or in their most secret thoughts.*

Helios' sister was the moon goddess Selene and many of her ancient traits may be recognized in the description of the virgin huntress, Artemis, who is Apollo's sister.

Artemis (Roman: Diana)

The protector of wild animals, Artemis also presided over the growth of all vegetable life. Born on the 'Isle of Quail' she, like her sister-Sirens, is thought to have, at times, taken the form of a bird. In her dual roles as 'Patron of Virgins' and 'Goddess of the Wild', Artemis was notorious for her vengefulness. Armed with a great golden bow and 'rejoicing in her chase', Artemis extracted a merciless revenge upon any man who dared to commit a crime against the weak or defenseless. Homer paid homage to Artemis with the following poem:

> *Of Artemis I sing whose shafts are of Gold, the wild pure maiden, the terror of the stags who delight in her bow.*
> *Over the shadowy hills and windy peaks she draws her Golden Bow, rejoicing in her chase and sends forth the grievous shafts.*
> *But then she slackens her Bow and hurries away to order the lovely dance of the charities and muses.*

Image from *The Pictorial Chronicle of the Incas* (top) is analogous with the Greek goddesses Athena (left) and Artemis (right)

Rio de Janeiro

Aided by the swift Falkland Current, as well as the persistent winds that his crew continually complained about, Odysseus may have continued sailing along the coasts of Argentina and Brazil until he arrived in the vicinity of present-day Rio de Janeiro. The renowned clippers of the 19th century A.D. were reported to have travelled up to 350 miles in a single day as they swept along this very same coastline. Ideally situated, Rio de Janeiro's beautiful harbour aptly fulfils the following description of Odysseus' reluctant anchorage.

Guanabara Bay

When the Portuguese first entered Rio de Janeiro's Guanabara Bay in A.D. 1502 they were guided ashore by a massive 842-metre tall monolith they named Pedra da Gávea, (rock of the topsail). One wonders if Odysseus and other Pre-Columbian expeditions might also have been 'lured' ashore by the eerie Pedra da Gávea. In a certain light, the massive monolith does resemble the head of a bearded giant staring out to sea. Although it has been asserted that Pedra da Gávea is partly sculpted by mortal hands, geologists assure us that the human resemblance is merely pareidolia.

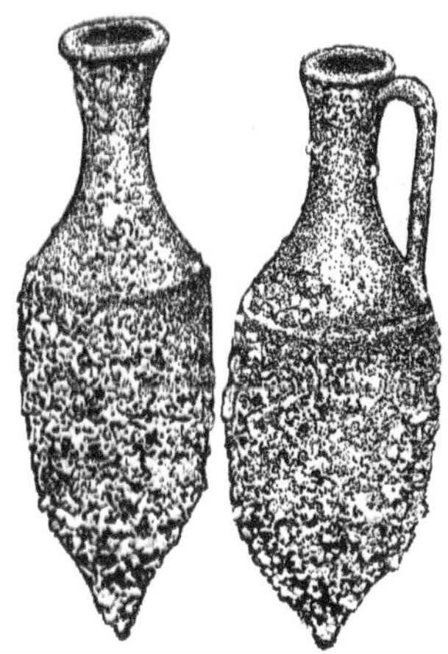

Recovered amphorae dated to 2nd century B.C.

Rio's Guanabara Bay may have provided safe anchorage for Odysseus and his crew but other mariners were not so fortunate. It is estimated that more than one hundred English, French and Portuguese shipwrecks remain unexplored on the sea floor of the immense bay. In 1976, a local Brazilian diver, Jose Texeira, salvaged three Roman-style amphorae from the bay.

Six years later, specialist diver and archaeologist, Robert Marx, used sonar technology to discover two wrecks at a site that is located offshore from Ilea de Gobernador. Marx subsequently recovered numerous Roman-style amphorae shards that he dated to the 2nd century B.C., as well as some marble objects and a bronze fibula (cloak clasp). In order to protect the reputation of Pedro Álvares Cabral, the official Portuguese discoverer of Brazil, the government has since banned any further investigation of the site.

Petroglyphs

Petroglyphs and pictographic inscriptions have been discovered at various places along the coastlines of Agentina, Brazil, French Guiana and Surinam. Author and the president of the Manaus Geographical Institute, Bernardo Silva Ramos spent over twenty years in the Amazon region uncovering and photographing some 2,800 stone inscriptions. Published in 1930, Ramos' book *Inscricoes e tyradecoes da America pre-historica, especialmente da Brasi,* identifies the majority of the inscriptions as Phoenician and Greek. The National Museum of Brazil also displays various photographs of foreign inscriptions that have been found throughout the coastal regions of the Amazon. **(Note 38)**

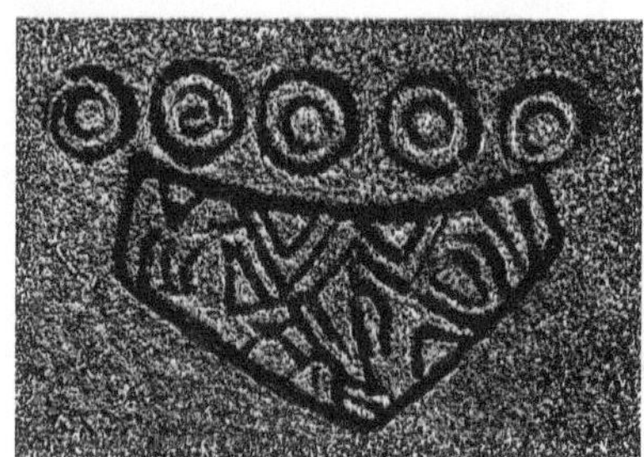

Boat-shaped petroglyphs discovered in Brazil indicate the possibility of Pre-Columbian visitors

Brazilian Legends of a 'White-skinned' Teacher

Legends retained by the natives of southern Brazil tell of Zume, a fair-skinned teacher who had visited them in the remote past. Zume is said to have had power over the elements and tempests. The trees of the forest would recede for his passing and the animals crouch before him.

Lakes and rivers became solid at Zume's bidding and he instructed the method of agriculture and the magical arts. When the early Portuguese settlers first came into contact with the natives of Brazil and Paraguay they were astonished to hear the legends of an ancestral 'fair-skinned' teacher. Citing early Portuguese chronicles, Daniel G. Brinton's book *American-Hero-Myths* presents the following account:

> *Wherever the widespread Tupi-Guaranay race extended from the mouth of the Rio de la Plata and the boundless plains of the Pampas, north to the northernmost islands of the West Indian Archipelago, the early explorers found the natives piously attributing their knowledge of the arts of life to a venerable and benevolent old man whom they called 'Our Ancestor', Tamu, or Tume, or Zume.*
>
> *The early Jesuit missionaries to the Guaranis and affiliated tribes of Paraguay and southern Brazil, have much to say of this personage, and some of them were convinced that he could have been no other than the Apostle St. Thomas on his proselytizing journey around the world. The legend was that Pay Zume, as he was called in Paraguay, (Pay: magician, diviner, priest) came from the East, from the Sun-rising, in years long gone by. He instructed the people in the arts of hunting and agriculture, especially in the culture and preparation of the manioca plant, their chief source of vegetable food. Near the city of Assumption is situated a lofty rock, around which, says the myth, he was accustomed to gather the people, while he stood above them on its summit, and delivered his instructions and his laws, just as did Quetzalcoatl from the top of the mountain Tzatzitepec, the Hill of Shouting.*
>
> *The spot where he stood is still marked by the impress of his feet, which the pious natives venerate. The story was that wherever this hero-god walked, he left behind him a well-marked path, which was permanent. As the Muyscas of New Granada pointed out the path of Bochica, so did the Guaranays that of Zume, which the missionaries regarded 'not without astonishment.' He lived a certain length of time with his people and then left them, going back over the ocean toward the East, according to some accounts. But according to others, he was driven away by his stiff-necked and unwilling auditors, who had become tired of his advice.* **(xxiii)**

(xxiii) Piedrahitas, Lucas Fernandez *Historia General* (1688); Simon, Padre Pedro *Noticias Historiales de las Conquistas de Tierra Firme en el Nuevo Reyno de Granada*; Kingsborough *Mexican Antiquities*

Odysseus Departs Thrinacia

On the seventh day of his Thrinacian stopover, Odysseus decided it was time to depart and so he ordered his crew to relaunch their sleek ship into the sea. As soon as they were well away from the Thrinacian coastline and nothing was to be seen but an expanse of sea and sky, a sudden darkness descended.

> ***From the East came a shrilling zephyr followed by a squalling blast of wind that snapped the forestays of the mast so that it crashed aft towards the stern. Then Zeus let fly with his thunderbolts and the ship went round and round and was filled with fire and brimstone as the lightning struck it. The men all fell into the sea; they were carried about in the water round the ship, looking like so many sea-gulls but the god presently deprived them of all chance of getting home again.*** **(Note 39)**

Homer's description of a sudden tempest manifesting out of a calm, clear day is typical of a tropical cyclone. The tropical waters of the Atlantic, particularly those at longitude 10 - 15 degrees north of the Equator, are infamous for their ability to generate hurricanes. Although the paths of hurricanes have only been registered in relatively recent times, it is now known that every year, an average of ten tropical storms and eight hurricanes rage their way westwards towards the Gulf of Mexico. **(xxiv)**

Despite the turbulence and carnage Odysseus ***'stuck to the ship till the sea knocked her sides from her keel'***. With a length of strong ox-thong that he had somehow managed to salvage, Odysseus bound part of the broken mast to the dislodged keel and ***'getting astride of them was carried wherever the winds chose'***.

(xxiv) *www.wunderground.com/hurricane/hurrarchive.asp*

Chapter 10

CALYPSO'S ISLE OF OGYGIA
(The Caribbean)

> ***The gale from the west had now spent its force and the wind got into the south again, which frightened me lest I should be taken back to the terrible whirlpool of Charybdis.***

Unaccustomed to the swirling violence of a tropical cyclone, Odysseus uses analogies to describe his dilemma. He explains how his makeshift raft was sucked down into the spinning waters:

> ***… then I was carried aloft toward the fig tree, which I caught hold of and clung onto like a bat…***

Odysseus relates that he was suspended precariously over a swirling whirlpool for an interminable period:

> ***… a very long while it seemed. A jury-man is not more glad to get home to supper, after having been long detained in court by troublesome cases, than I was to see my raft beginning to work its way out of the whirlpool again.***

The raft was eventually ***'spewed'*** out from the spiralling maelstrom whereupon Odysseus ***'fell heavily into the sea'***. Managing to straddle a massive beam, he then drifted numb and aimlessly for nine days until:

> ***… during the night of the tenth, the gods washed me up on the Isle of Ogygia, the home of the fair Calypso, that formidable goddess with a woman's voice; she received me kindly and looked after me.***

Odysseus, the once ambitious fleet commander and proud ***'sacker of cities'*** has been reduced to a humble castaway on the shores of Ogygia. Scholars are at variance as to the exact number of years he spent on Ogygia. Some say five or seven, while others have suggested eight, as eight is the number of notes in an octave and this would correlate with

Calypso's role as the 'goddess of the song'. Although we can only surmise as to the length of time Odysseus was marooned on Ogygia, we do know that during his sojourn there he resided ***'in the cave where Calypso lived'***. We can thus assume that the living conditions on Calypso's island were somewhat primitive.

The Odyssey is an account of a journey into unknown realms. The average citizen of ancient Greece would never have heard nor even dreamt of the exotic places described by Odysseus. The only meaningful way for him to relate the various experiences of his epic voyage was to couch them within the context of the mythologies they were familiar with. The lands visited by Odysseus are invariably portrayed as the realms of gods and goddesses. Certainly, the Cyclops never had just one central eye; nor did Aelous command a supernatural control over the four winds. The intention is to kindle an understanding that these lands lay far beyond the civilized bounds of the Mediterranean region. Odysseus' experience with the goddess Calypso is the last in the series of adventures that are related in terms of purely mythopoeic imagery. When Odysseus finally departs Calypso's island and eventually arrives in the land of the Phaeacians, his descriptions at once become identifiable with the everyday world of the ancient Mediterranean. Bearing in mind that we are now analysing the last and perhaps the most intriguing of these mythologized episodes, let us now endeavor to unravel the mystical weavings of Calypso's loom.

Land of Ogygia

(Pronounced, o-jij i-a: meaning primeval)

The word 'Atlantic' is an English translation of the Greek '*Atlantikos*', which in turn, was derived from the name of the ancient Titan god, Atlas. In the opening paragraphs of *The Odyssey*, Homer declared that Calypso was ***'a child of malevolent Atlas'***. Mythology states that Atlas and his fellow Titans had their origins in the far distant West. We may therefore deduce that Calypso's primeval island of Ogygia lay somewhere in the remote reaches of the Atlantic Ocean. This vital clue might also explain why, despite his ability to ***'travel as fast as the wind'***, it took the god Mercury so long to arrive in Ogygia:

> ***He flew and flew over many a weary wave, but then at last he got to the island... an island covered with forest in the middle of the sea.***

The Caribbean (West Indies)

The Caribbean Sea is host to more than 7,000 islands, islets, reefs and cays. Also referred to as the West Indies, the islands of the Caribbean are divided into three main groups: the Greater Antilles, the Lesser Antilles and the Bahamas. The Greater Antilles includes the large islands of Cuba, Jamaica, Hispaniola (modern Haiti and Dominican Republic) and Puerto Rico. The Bahamas are a cluster of low-lying islands located in the northeast of the Caribbean Sea while the Lesser Antilles are a chain of mostly young volcanic and coral islands that arch out eastwards towards the Atlantic.

The Lesser Antilles

The Lesser Antilles is further divided into two separate geographical groups, the 'southern' Windward Islands and the 'northern' Leeward Islands. The prevailing trade winds in this region blow from east to west, therefore sailing ships approaching the New World sailed windward towards them. Hence the islands that lay in the south became known as the Windward Islands, whilst those in the north were referred to as the Leeward Islands.

Island of Nevis (Ogygia?)

Almost any of the Caribbean's habitable islands could be considered a possible location for Calypso's beautiful realm. We should bear in mind that Odysseus' ship was wrecked in a tropical cyclone and therefore we can discard any of the Windward Islands as they lie too far south of the hurricane belt. However, the island of Nevis does qualify as a likely 'Ogygia'. Not only is it prone to hurricanes but it also fulfills the geographical landscape described by Odysseus.

Nevis is conical in shape with a volcanic peak rising at its centre. Protected by coral reefs, long strands of golden beaches fringe the island. The distinctive colour of the sand results from the mixture of coral and volcanic elements. In the lush interior are rivers and seasonal ponds, while the gently sloping coastal plain contains natural, fresh water springs, especially along the west coast. The native Caribs called the island *Oualie* (Land of Beautiful Waters). The name Nevis is derived from the Spanish, *Nuestra Se de las Nieves* ('Our Lady of the Snows').

The island was so named by Christopher Columbus because he thought the clouds over Nevis Peak gave the impression of a snow-capped mountain.

During the last Ice Age when the sea level was 200 feet lower, Saint Kitts and Nevis, together with Saint Eustatius and Saba, formed one single island. In its early history this large, single island hosted at least thirteen volcanoes, including the now dormant Nevis Peak. Its last eruption took place in 1692, but active fumaroles and hot springs are still to be found on the island, the most recent formed in 1953.

Mild, northeasterly breezes called the *aliz* or trade winds, temper the island from December through February and these are followed by a somewhat hotter and rainier season from May to November. Nevis lies in the track of tropical hurricanes that usually develop between August and October. This period also records the heaviest rainfalls of the year.

Calypso

The portrayal of Calypso being a goddess who ***'sings beautifully'***, wears her hair in ***'braided tresses'*** and is ***'busy at her loom'*** is a fitting description for the natives of the Caribbean. On the West Indian island of Trinidad, the expression *calypso* is used to describe improvised love songs. The origin of the word is uncertain but it is improbable that it was derived from a source other than *The Odyssey*. The Greek word *calypso* means 'hidden' or to be more exact, 'the hidden ones of Ca'. The Indians who originally migrated onto the Caribbean Islands venerated a 'life-energy' called '*Ca*', which they associated with their mother-goddess. An adjunct to this veneration can be observed in the many Caribbean tribal names with the prefix 'Ca', such as Carib, Calusa, Caracas and Karakawa. It appears that Odysseus may have associated the Caribbean Ca 'cave-goddess' with one of her primitive Mediterranean counterparts: Callisto, Cardea, Carmel or Carmenta, to name but a few. The antiquity of Ogygia's primitive culture may explain why Odysseus had referred to his cave-dwelling companion as Calypso ('the hidden goddess of Ca'). **(Note 40)**

Taino Indians (Men of Good)

Although the Caribbean tribe called the Taino does not have the prefix 'Ca' attached to its name, the tribe's spiritual precepts are centered on the fertility mother-goddess, Ca-guana and her sacred *Caciba* (cave). During the 15th century, a Catalan friar recorded many of the Taino legends. According to these accounts, the Taino revered a primal mountain they called Ca-ute. Located in the Ca-onao region of the Hispaniola island, this mountain has two caves: the Cacibajagua (Cave of the Jagua) and the Amayauna (Cave of No Importance). The Taino believed that the Cacibajagua was the place of their particular origin and that everyone else in the world came from the Amayauna.

Regarded to have been the most advanced of the Caribbean tribes, the Taino population at the time of Christopher Columbus' arrival was estimated to have been between 100,000 and 1,000,000. It did not take long for the effects of disease, war and slavery to take their toll on the Taino population and they soon faced extinction. As a result, not a great deal is known about the Taino culture.

> *They (the Taino) were rarely taller than five feet six inches, which would make them rather small to modern North American eyes. They painted their bodies with earth dyes and adorned themselves with shells and metals. Men and women chiefs often wore gold in the ears and nose, or as pendants around the neck. Some had tattoos. From all early descriptions the Tainos were a healthy people who showed no signs of distress from hunger or want. The Tainos, whose color was olive-brown to copper, reminded Columbus of the people of the Canary Islands, who were neither white nor black. He noted their thick black hair, short in front and long in back, and that it fell over muscular shoulders. On some islands, the women wore short cotton skirts after taking a permanent man but in others all the people went naked. In parts of Cuba and Santo Domingo, some of the caciques, village or nation chiefs, wore a certain type of tunic on ceremonial occasions, but they saw no apparent need to cover their breasts or genitals and they were totally natural about it. The Taino islands provided a vast array of edible fruits. The Arawaks made specific use of many types of trees and plants from an estimated floral and faunal range of 5,800 species. The jagua tree they used for dyeing cotton, the jocuma and the guama for making rope, the jucaro for underwater construction, the royal palm for buildings and specific other trees for boats, spears, digging tools, chairs, bowls, baskets and woven mats (in this art they flourished), cotton cloth (for hammocks), large fishing nets and good hooks made of large fish bones. Inspecting deserted seashore camps, Spanish sailors found what they judged to be excellent nets and small fishing canoes stored in watertight sheds. Further upriver in the villages, they saw large fields of corn, yucca, beans and fruit orchards covering whole valleys. They walked through the squares of villages,*

with grains and herbs drying, and sunlight-tight storage sheds with shelves packed with thousands of dried cassava torts. In one village, sailors found large cakes of fine wax, a local product. (Rivero, 1966)

The Taino were a sea-going people and took pride in their courage on the high ocean as well as their skill in finding their way around their world. They visited one another constantly. Columbus was often astonished at finding lone Indian fishermen sailing in the open ocean as he made his way among the islands. Among Tainos, the women and some of the men harvested corn, nuts, cassava, and other roots. They appear to have practiced a rotation method in their agriculture. Tainos along the coasts of Española and southern Cuba kept large circular corrals made of reeds that they filled with fish and turtles by the thousands.

Contrary to popular imagination, the Tainos were a disciplined people. Particularly during their spiritual and healing ceremonies, natural impulses were limited. In those important instances, strong abstinence over sexual activity and eating were demanded, even under penalty of death. **(xxiv)**

The Four Streams

The Caribbean Islands do not support a large variety of fauna, there is however an abundance of bird species and this concurs with Homer's description of Ogygia as being a ***'roosting place of long-feathered birds***' including owls, hawks (cara-caras) and sea-crows which '***swooped down daily to the sea***'. Like the Biblical Eden, Calypso's realm is portrayed as being blessed with four streams of water that irrigated beds of flowers and luscious herbage. These four streams are obviously symbolic, representing the four directions of the compass. The sacred number four was and remains integral to all the native cultures of Mesoamerica. This concept is

(xxiv) Barreiro, José *Island of Hispaniola* Northeast Indian Quarterly, 1990 recognised in Taino society where four cosmological beings, namely Deminan and his three sky-dwelling brothers, were believed to have walked amidst the clouds and blue-sky heavens of the Caribbean spirit world.

In the early Spanish annals, Española (Hispaniola) is described as the most advanced of the Greater Antilles islands. The Taino called the island *Bohio* (home) and it was from there that their culture travelled to Cuba and the outer islands. Gardens, ball courts and huge *areitos* with speaking forums were a feature of the Taino society. Their realm was confederated into five main *cacicasgos* or kinship nations, the Taino of Jaragua being a principal nation where, according to José Barreiro:

> *... they had a particularly good agriculture, with efficient irrigation systems that regularly watered thousands of acres of all manner of tubers, vegetables and grains.*

Father Bartolomé de las Casas, the Spanish friar who arrived on Columbus' heels and lived to denounce Spanish cruelty toward Indians, wrote (exaggeratedly but impressively) about '*vineyards that ran for three hundred leagues*', '*game birds taken by the tens of thousands*', '*great circular fields of yucca and greater stores of cassava bread, dried fish, corn fields and vast gardens of sweet yams*'. We might compare the above excerpts with Homer's description of Calypso's bounteous island:

> ***A vine loaded with grapes was trained and grew luxuriantly about the mouth of the cave; there were also four running rills of water in channels cut pretty close together, and turned hither and thither so as to irrigate the beds of violets and luscious herbage over which they flowed.***

Sacred Caves of the Caribbean

Located on the island of Hispaniola, the Chicho Cave is one of four spring-fed caves that make up the Padre Nuestro group. The adjacent subterranean springs are known as Papa Miguel, El Toro and Padre Nuestro. Taino artifacts recently retrieved from the depths of Chico Cave are now leading archaeologists to focus attention on this site. Although Chicho Cave resembles Calypso's cave in that it is ***'spring-fed'*** and surrounded by ***'thick wood'***, it is but one of many that fit this description.
American archaeologists, Charles Beeker, Geoffrey Conrad and John Foster have been investigating the Taino caves since August 1996.

In the *Journal of Caribbean Archaeology* we are informed that:

> *The caves were intimately associated with the spirits of the ancestors, whose veneration was a central element of Taino religion. The Taino conceived of a universe consisting of three layers united by a vertical axis mundi. The Earth's surface lay in the middle, with the celestial vault above. The bottom layer was a watery world known as Coaybay, 'the house and dwelling place of the dead'. Access between the Earth's surface and the Underworld was by way of sacred caves that served as portals to Coaybay and the ancestors. There is another connection between the caves and the ancestors. Caves are homes to colonies of bats. The Taino believed that the spirits of the dead (the opias) remained hidden during the day but came out at night to eat the fruits of the guava tree. To do this the spirits transformed themselves into bats - one of the most frequently depicted animals in Taino art.* **(xxv)**

Odysseus clinging 'like a bat'

Taino bowl with bat design

We may recall that during his shipwreck ordeal, Odysseus described himself as clinging ***'like a bat'*** to a symbolic fig tree (*axis mundi*?). Could this particular analogy have arisen from his experiences among the Taino?

(xxv) Beeker, Conrad, Foster *Journal of Caribbean Archaeology 3*, 2002

Fountain Cave, Anguilla

Having spent many years as the 'consort of Calypso', Odysseus may have come to be acknowledged by the Taino as the 'god-like' co-ruler of her realm. In this capacity, Odysseus might be identified with the bearded 'king' whose image is etched upon a stalagmite column located in the Fountain Cave on the Island of Anguilla.

Petroglyph of bearded king

Creator-god Jochu

Set above a crystal-clear stream of water, the petroglyph of a 'bearded king' features a four-quartered crown, signifying I presume, the four rivers of Calypso's Ogygia. Fountain Cave also displays other excellent examples of stalagmite sculpture. A twelve-foot high statue of the creator-god Jochu dominates the cave while petroglyphs of the Rainbow God and the Fertility Goddess also demand attention.

Islands of Antigua and Barbuda

In researching the prehistoric history of the Caribbean I was astonished to discover that the island of Antigua has megalithic stone circles and 'owl-eyed' petroglyphs that are similar to those found at Newgrange in Ireland and Carnac in France (c.2800 - 2000 B.C.). Images of the Taino goddess Atebey are also comparable to the Irish goddess Shilla na Gig. Local Taino histories refer to an ancient race called the 'Siboney' (stone people) who, according to folklore, once inhabited the eastern most islands of Antigua and Barbuda.

Mediterranean-style pictograph

Taino goddess Atebey

Scholars such as Kennedy (1971), Chadwick (1971), Franch (1985) and Guthrie (2001) are of the opinion that Beaker sea-peoples from Atlantic Europe and North Africa found their way to the Caribbean c.3000 - 1500 B.C. Could Calypso herself have been a surviving remnant of seafaring Beaker peoples? She certainly knew in which direction Odysseus should sail if he was to find his way home.

Island of Saba (Amonhana)

Lying close by the islands of Antigua and Barbuda is the island of Saba. In the year A.D. 1629, a Frenchmen named Guillaume Coppier visited the island. In his book titled *Histoire et Voyages des Indes Occidentales et de plusiersautres regions,* Coppier describes the inhabitants of Saba as follows:

> *A group of 'wild people' live there, that are named Igniris; they go with their body completely naked and they have beards, which is different from all other Indians, who pull out the hair as soon as it comes. They are idolatrous and they live in caves (litt: their retreat is in cave-like places), living like wild animals.*

Is it possible that the bearded Igniri were a remnant of the ancient 'stone people' called the 'Siboney'? Like Calypso, the Igniri were troglodytes and archaeological evidence indicates that their forefathers had been living on the island since the time of Odysseus. In the year 1978, Mr. Roobol and Mr. A. L. Smith of the University of Puerto unearthed shell tools at Fort Bay. Radiocarbon analysis of these tools dated their use to 1200 B.C. In recent years carved stone tools have also been discovered across the island and these are on display in the Harry L. Johnson Museum in Windward Side. **(Note 41)**

The Council of Gods

It is both interesting and humorous to observe that four Taino words have survived into modern usage. These words are hurricane, hammock, barbecue and tobacco, all of which might apply to Odysseus' activities, or lack of, during his long sojourn upon the island of Ogygia. Despite his peaceful existence, Odysseus is described as spending many hours staring wistfully out to the ocean's horizon. Having noticed Odysseus' melancholy, the goddess Athena ascended to Mount Olympus and addressed the pantheon of gods. She '***began to tell them of the many sufferings of Odysseus, for she pitied him away there in the house of the***

nymph Calypso'. Acknowledging Athena's request, Zeus, the 'father of the gods', summoned the god Mercury and said:

> ***"Mercury, you are our messenger, go therefore and tell Calypso we have decreed that poor Odysseus is to return home. He is to be convoyed neither by the gods nor men but after a perilous voyage of twenty days upon a raft he is to reach fertile Scheria, the land of the Phaeacians, who are near of kin to the gods and will honor him as though he were one of ourselves."***

Mercury

Obeying Zeus' command, Mercury:

> ***... flew and flew over many a weary wave, but when at last he got to the island which was his journey's end, he left the sea and went on by land till he came to the cave where the nymph Calypso lived. Even a god could not help being charmed with such a lovely spot, so Mercury stood still and looked at it; but when he had admired it sufficiently he went inside the cave. Calypso knew him at once, for the gods know each other, no matter how far they live from one another.***

Calypso trembled with rage when she heard' Zeus' decree.

> ***"You gods," she exclaimed, "ought to be ashamed of yourselves. I found the poor creature sitting all alone astride of a keel, for Zeus had struck his ship with lightning and sunk it in mid ocean. His crew all drowned, while he himself was driven by wind and waves onto my island. I got fond of him and cherished him and had set my heart***

> ***on making him immortal so that he should never grow old all his days; still, I cannot cross Zeus."***
>
> ***"Then send him away," said Mercury, "or Zeus will be angry with you and punish you." On this he took his leave, and Calypso went out to look for Odysseus, for she had heard Zeus' message.***

The Final Ocean

During his extended stay on Ogygia, Odysseus had ample time to reflect on the advice given to him by Circe and the blind seer Tieresias. He was probably aware that he was north of the coast of Thrinacia (Land of Helios) and that his homeland lay somewhere over the eastern horizon. Unfortunately, the prevailing winds in the Caribbean blow from the East and this would have made it very difficult for Odysseus to attempt a voyage in that direction. The irony of his situation is that he had almost completed a circumnavigation of the globe but was fated to bide his time on Ogygia for year after year, contemplating the feasibility of crossing yet another ocean.

The imagery of Odysseus ***'sitting upon the beach with his eyes ever filled with tears and dying of sheer homesickness'*** finds a parallel in the Caribbean legend of Deminian. In primordial times, Deminian is said to have mated with a female turtle and of their union the Taino people came into being. The name Deminian compares to the Latin words *deminutio* (deprived of citizenship) and *demitto* (cast down or down-hearted).

Mindful of Zeus' resolute decree, Calypso in sorrowful resignation bids Odysseus to construct a sailing craft so that he might now return to his homeland.

> ***So as soon as early, rosy-fingered Dawn shone forth, Odysseus put on a mantle and doublet and Calypso clad herself in a great shining robe, light of woof and gracious. About her waist she cast a fair golden girdle and a veil withal upon her head. Then she considered of the sending of Odysseus, the great-hearted.***
>
> ***She gave him a great axe of bronze, double-edged, and fitted to his grasp with a goodly handle of olive wood fastened well. Next she gave him a polished adze and she led the way to the border of the isle where tall trees grew, alder and poplar and pine that reacheth unto***

heaven, seasoned long since and sere, that might lightly float for him. Now after she had shown him where the tall trees grew, Calypso departed homeward. Odysseus set about busily cutting timber. He felled twenty trees and then trimmed them with the bronze axe. Meanwhile Calypso, the fair goddess, brought him augers so he bored each piece and jointed them together and then fastened them with trenails and dowels.

He wrought and set up the deckings, fitting them to the close-set uprights and finished them off with long gunwales and there he set a mast and fitted a yardarm thereto. Moreover, he made a rudder to guide the craft and fenced it with wattled osier withies from stem to stern, to be a bulwark against the wave.

Calypso then brought him web of cloth to make sails, which he fashioned very skillfully. He made fast therein braces and halyards and sheets and at last he pushed the raft with levers down to the fair salt sea.

It was the fourth day when he had accomplished all. On the fifth, the fair Calypso prepared to send him on his way from the island. She bathed him and clad him in fragrant attire. Moreover, the goddess placed on board the ship two skins, one of dark wine and another of water, corn too in a wallet and she set therein a store of dainties to his heart's desire. Finally, she sent forth a warm and gentle wind to blow.

Although Odysseus was apparently unassisted in his ship-building task, he perhaps gained inspiration from the Taino's ability to construct ocean-going canoes called *piraguas*. These canoes were large enough to hold 70 men and were used to ferry tribes from island to island, as well as to the mainland of North America.

In a previous chapter, it was proposed that Odysseus had come into contact with the Polynesians (Laestrygonians?). Using only the natural materials available to them, the Polynesians were able to construct massive twin-hulled canoes that enabled them to explore and colonize the Pacific Ocean. As an experienced mariner, Odysseus would have observed the skills involved in both Polynesian and Taino shipbuilding methods. He may well have employed some of these techniques when constructing his own vessel on Ogygia.

Written during his 1769 exploration of the Pacific Ocean, Captain James Cook's journals record the Polynesians' remarkable ability to build seaworthy vessels from the very limited resources at hand. According to Cook, Polynesian sails consisted of a *'coarse thick cloth which was made from the bark of the breadfruit tree and sometimes from the bark of other trees while the rope they use in rigging their canoes came from two or three sorts of plants'*. Cook continues on to describe the native vessels:

> ... *the two largest were each 76 feet long and when they had been in use were fasten'd together. They are built of several pieces of thick plank and have high, curved sterns. The head also curves a little and both are ornamented with the image of a man carved in wood. When one considers the tools these people have to work with one cannot help but admire their workmanship; these are adzes and small hatchets made of a hard stone and chisels or gouges made of human bones, generally the bone of the forearm. With these ordinary tools that a European workman would expect to break at the first stroke, I have seen them work surprisingly fast. To plane or polish their work they rub upon it with a smooth stone over coral beaten small and mixed with water. Most of their small woodwork is performed with shells. Their Proes or Canoes, large and small, are rowed and steer'd with paddles and notwithstanding the large ones appear to be very unwieldy, they manage them very dexterously and I believe perform long and distant voyages in them, otherwise they could not have the knowledge of the islands in these seas they seem to have.* **(xxvi)**

Homer states that it took Odysseus a mere four days to complete the construction of his vessel. The short time period may indicate that he converted an existing Taino canoe into an even more seaworthy, twin-hulled vessel. When all was in readiness, Calypso reminded Odysseus to

(xxvi) Captain James Cook, *Voyage of the Endeavour* (pp. 130 - 133)

carefully observe the various constellations of the night sky overhead as he journeyed homeward across the broad ocean.

Voyage Across the Atlantic

We cannot determine the exact course Odysseus took in sailing across the Atlantic Ocean. He may have set a course due east or alternatively; he may have unwittingly cast his fate to the swift Gulf Stream that flows along the east coast of America. Regardless of the route chosen, we do know that he utilized the constellations of the night sky to navigate his way homeward.

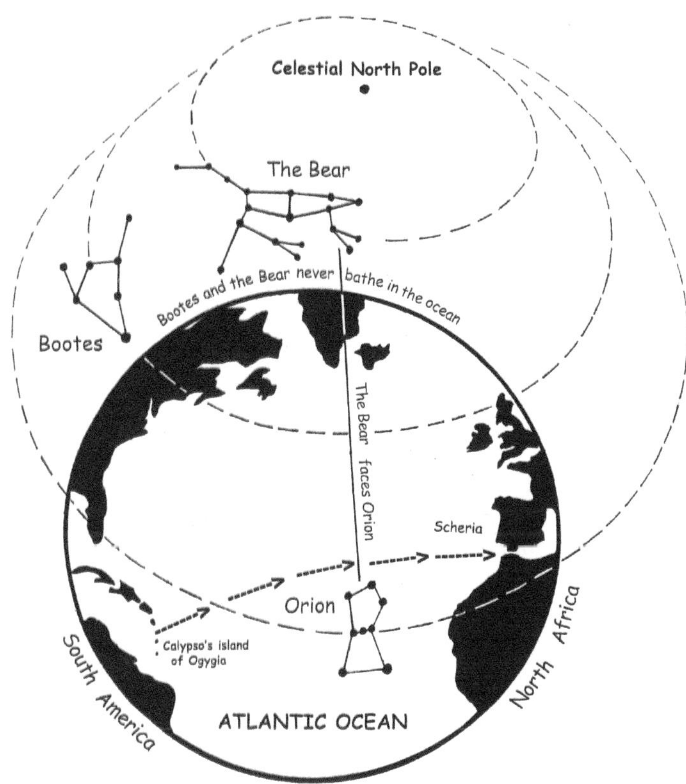

He never closed his eyes, but kept them fixed on the Pleiades, on late-setting Bootes and on the Bear, which men call the Wain and which turns round and round where it is, facing Orion and alone never dipping into the stream of Oceanus – for Calypso had told him to keep this to his left.

Calypso's advice was absolutely correct, for as we know, any mariner who intends to sail from America's east coast to Europe must at all times keep the constellation of the Bear to his left. In September the Bear reaches its nadir and near 'dips' into the ocean. The Greek historian Strabo (64 B.C. - A.D. 24) wrote the following commentary concerning this particular chapter of *The Odyssey*:

> *By 'the Bear', which he also calls 'the Wain' and describes as keeping watch upon Orion, Homer means the Arctic Circle, and by Oceanus he means the horizon into which he makes the stars to set and from which he makes them to rise. And when he says that the Bear makes its revolution in that region without having a part in Oceanus, he knows that the Arctic Circle touches the most northerly point of the horizon. If we construe the poet's verse in this way then we should interpret the terrestrial horizon as closely corresponding to Oceanus, and the Arctic Circle as touching the earth - if we may believe the evidence of our senses - as it is the most northerly inhabited point. And so, in the opinion of Homer, this part of the Earth is also washed by Oceanus.*
>
> *The Geography of Strabo,* Book 1: Chapter 1.

In his ground-breaking book *America B.C.*, Professor Barry Fell remarks that the constellation of the Great Bear was called 'Arctos' by the ancient Greeks and 'Ursa Major' by the Romans, both names signifying the bear. The Natick Indians of Boston referred to the same group of stars as *Paukunnawaw*, which means bear. In the Algonquian Micmac dialect, the word for bear is *mooeen,* which is also their name for this particular constellation. Professor Fell concludes:

> *To my mind the facts show that ancient mariners brought to the New World a knowledge of old Mediterranean beliefs about constellations, and in particular, about the mariners' direction-finder and clock, Ursa Major.*

The Gulf Stream

As it flows into the Caribbean, the South Equatorial Current reinforces the warm waters of the North Equatorial Current. These now combined equatorial currents then drift through the narrow Yucatan Channel and the Straits of Florida to emerge as the Gulf Stream. Maintaining a flow that is about fifty miles wide and 3,000 feet deep, the Gulf Stream then sweeps along the Atlantic Coast of America. From the Newfoundland coast, the massive current moves eastwards towards Europe. As it approaches Europe it divides into two separate streams, one stream flows towards North Africa, the other towards the British Isles. The Gulf Stream moves as fast as 138 miles a day and its rate of flow is 1,000 times greater than the Mississippi River. Modern-day oil tankers and ore carriers ride the Gulf Stream to save valuable shipping time. With the added aid of a sail, it would have been possible for Odysseus to traverse the Atlantic Ocean within a period of three weeks.

Evidence of Early Gulf Stream Voyages

In another remarkable book, *Mysteries of Forgotten Worlds*, Charles Berlitz documents the most incredible voyage of some American Indians almost 2,000 years ago:

> *The Gulf Stream transported a group of American Indians to Europe in the first century A.D. It is on record that a long canoe with copper-skinned occupants from parts unknown, washed ashore in Northern Europe from the North Sea. They were taken into custody and presented as slaves to the Roman Pro-Consul, Publius Metellus Cellar. There is even a Roman bust made of one of these Atlantic travellers whose features, in the representational style of Roman art, definitely show the characteristics of an American Indian.*

It is also recorded that before his epic voyage, Christopher Columbus had viewed the corpses of two 'natives' whose canoe had been washed ashore in Galway, Ireland. Christopher Columbus' son, Ferdinand, wrote that his father had also:

> *... learned from pilots who were experienced in the voyages to Madeira and the Azores, facts and signs which convinced him that an unknown land lay to the West. Martin Vincente, a pilot of the king of Portugal, told him how he had taken from the water an artistically carved piece of wood, 450 leagues from Cape St. Vincent. This wood had been driven across the ocean by the west wind – a fact which led the sailors to believe that there were certainly other islands in that direction that had not yet been discovered.*

Other evidences indicating the presence of an unmapped land in the western Atlantic had also been discovered on the islands of Madeira and the Azores. Large canes, an unknown species of pine and pieces of carved wood had been picked up on the westernmost beaches of these islands. The Portuguese colonists who inhabited the Azores reported that the bodies of two men had been washed ashore on Flores (the westernmost island of the Azores). The broad faces of the men showed that they were not European. Although the Portuguese of that time had no way of identifying these bodies with the Americas, it has since been conjectured that they might have been Carib Indians who, having been swept out to sea perished of either exposure or starvation. Not all those who have dared to cross the Atlantic in very small boats have met with the same fate as the unfortunate natives. The *Guinness Book of Records* reports that 'crossings of the Atlantic' have often been made in boats as small as two metres in length. In light of such voyages, the suggestion that Odysseus may have traversed the Atlantic in a makeshift vessel is not incredulous.

Scheria, 'rising like a shield on the horizon'

For seventeen days Odysseus steadily maintained his ocean course and upon the eighteenth day, the shadowy hills of the Phaeacians' country appeared ***'rising like a shield on the horizon'***.

The Ancient Greek's 'known world' was conceived of as shield-shaped and surrounded by ocean

At the beginning of this chapter we noted that Odysseus' experience with the goddess Calypso was the last in a series of adventures that are related in terms of mythic imagery. Once Odysseus departs her island and arrives in the land of the Phaeacians, the descriptions immediately become identifiable with the everyday world of the ancient Mediterranean. Evidence of Odysseus sailing from far distant Ogygia and arriving at the 'known' world of Europe is found in his description of Scheria ***'rising like a shield on the horizon'***. The ancient Greeks perceived their known and habitable earth as being shield-shaped and surrounded by water. Homer states that the Greek warrior Achilles had a map of the 'known' world emblazoned upon his shield, hence Odysseus' reference to it.

Shipwrecked Again

But Poseidon (Neptune), ***who was returning from the Ethiopians, caught sight of Odysseus from a long way off. He could see him sailing upon the sea and it made him very angry.***

Homer has informed us that the Ethiopians lived '***at the farthest limits of mankind'***. According to Homer the Ethiopians were a ***'people split in two'***. One group lived ***'where the Sun-god sets'*** and the other ***'where the Sun-god rises'***. Strabo's *Geography,* Book 1: Chapter 2 confirms this concept:

... we must conceive that on the other side of Oceanus also there are certain Ethiopians, the most remote of the other group of peoples in the temperate zone, since they dwell on the shores of this same Oceanus; and that they are in two groups and are 'sundered in twain' by Oceanus.

As Odysseus was approaching the relative safety of 'civilized' shores the vengeful sea-god Poseidon marshalled ***'the clouds and great squalls from each of the four directions so that a great darkness swooped down from the sky'***. The agitated ocean generated huge mountainous waves, one of which thundered down and snapped the mast of Odysseus' vessel.

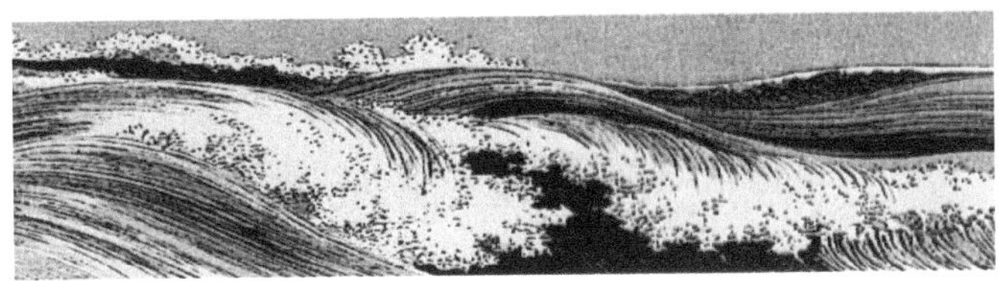

Leucothea (Ino)

But there was a witness to Odysseus' plight. This was Ino, who was once a woman speaking like ourselves but now lives in the salt depths of the sea and as Leucothoe, has been acknowledged by the gods. She took pity on the forlorn and woebegone Odysseus, rose from the water like a seamew on the wing and settled on his boat.

"My poor good man," said she, "why is Neptune so furiously angry with you? He is giving you a great deal of trouble but for all his bluster he will not kill you. You seem to be sensible person, do then as I bid you, strip, leave your raft to drive before the wind and swim to the Phaeacian coast where better luck awaits you. Here, take my veil and put it round your chest; it is enchanted and you will come to no harm so long as you wear it. As soon as you touch land take it off, throw it back as far as you can into the sea and then go away again."

Leucothea appears to Odysseus

With these words she took off her veil and gave it to him. Then she dived down like a seagull and vanished beneath the dark blue waters.

This is a most informative passage for it introduces us to the legend of the sea-goddess Leucothea. Greek mythology instructs us that Leucothea was originally a mortal women named Ino. The goddess Hera had cursed Ino's husband Athamas, causing him to become insane and begin killing his children. In order to escape her husband's murderous rampage, Ino gathered up her last remaining infant son Melicertes and frantically leapt from a clifftop into the Aegean Sea. Despite her desperate efforts both she and her son were drowned. A compassionate Zeus deified Ino, making her a 'goddess of the ocean' with the new name of Leucothea. He also deified her son Melicertes as the god Palemon, dispatching him on the back of a dolphin to the Isthmus of Corinth. Blessed with an ability to change her shape at will, Leuothea was famed for her power to save vessels from shipwreck. Whenever mariners were in peril they would invoke Leucothea and her son to deliver them safely to shore. (**Note 42)**

Odysseus is Cast Ashore

Odysseus initially chooses to disregard Leucothea's suggestion that he abandon his boat and swim for shore; he instead decides to ***'stick to the raft as long as her timbers hold together'***. However, it was not long before Neptune sent another terrible wave that '***broke right over the raft, which then went to pieces as though it were a heap of dried chaff tossed about by a whirlwind'***.

When this fatal wave struck, Odysseus stripped off the clothes that Calypso had presented to him and immediately bound Leucothea's veil about his chest in preparation for the long swim to shore. After battling against the exceedingly heavy swell for two days and nights, the wind suddenly dropped and Odysseus was indeed thankful:

> ***... when he again saw land and trees and swam on with all his strength that he might once more set foot on dry land.***

Odysseus' trials however, were not yet over for there was no place where he could come ashore:

> ***Everything was enveloped in spray; there were no harbours nor shelter of any kind, but only mountain tops, headlands and low-lying rocks.***

The surging waves repeatedly pounded him against the steep cliffs and jagged rocks but Odysseus' fervent prayers were finally answered and he was swept along into the mouth of a river and safety.

> ***... the sea had completely broken him. His body was all swollen, and his mouth and nostrils ran like a river with seawater so that he could***

neither breathe nor speak and lay swooning from sheer exhaustion. When Odysseus regained consciousness and his breath returned, he took off the scarf that Leucothea had given him and threw it back into the salt stream of the river, whereupon Ino received it into her hands from the wave that bore it towards her. Then he left the river, laid himself down among the rushes and kissed the bountiful earth.

Chapter 11

SCHERIA: THE LAND OF THE PHAEACIANS
(Coast of Southern Spain)

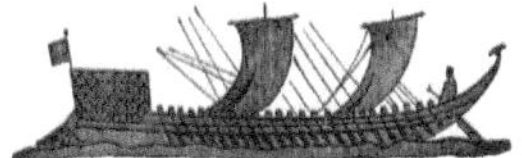

Having survived the pounding surf, Odysseus is washed ashore near the mouth of a river. He spends his first night on dry land in the open, so we might assume that Scheria was blessed with a mild climate. The regions of Southern Spain and Morocco experience mild climates and this is due to the warm Gulf Stream Current and the prevailing westerly winds that sweep across the Atlantic Ocean. A consideration of these geographical clues together with other evidences, indicates that Odysseus came ashore somewhere in the vicinity of the Pillars of Hercules. It might be surmised that Odysseus' encounter with the Phaeacians occurred upon a now submerged peninsula that once ***'jutted into the surrounding sea'*** where, according to Homer, the opulent Phaeacians lived in luxury ***'far from their fellow man'*** **(Note 43)**

Coastal Region of Southern Spain

Commenting on the people and landscape of southern Spain, the Greek geographer Strabo (c.30 B.C.) expresses his belief that Homer was quite familiar with Spain and that he knew of the ***'wealth and luxury'*** of its people who had become:

> *... so entirely under the dominion of the Phoenicians, that at the present day almost the whole of the cities of Turdetania and the neighbouring places are inhabited by them.*

Strabo continues to say he thought that certain events of *The Odyssey* had been enacted in Spain:

> *Even in Iberia is a city named Ulyssea* (Lisbon), *also a temple of Athena and a myriad other traces both of the wandering of Ulysses*

(Odysseus) *and also of other survivors of the Trojan War, which was equally fatal to the vanquished and those who took Troy.* **(xxvii)**

Comparisons Between Scheria and Atlantis

Regardless of where Scheria was located it no longer exists. According to Homer, the land of Scheria sank below the waves shortly after Odysseus' departure from its shores. Homer (c.750 B.C.) wrote of Scheria's tragic fate approximately four hundred years prior to Plato's account of the sinking of Atlantis (see *Timaeus* and *Critias*). Scholars have often made note of the numerous similarities that exist between these two legendary lands.

Both the Atlanteans and the Phaeacians had twin harbours filled with swift ships; magnificent turreted palaces; enormous mineral wealth; splendid orchards that provided every variety of fruit; a central temple dedicated to their 'father-god' Poseidon and the custom of sacrificing bulls to appease him. The only major point of difference between Plato's Atlantis and Homer's Scheria is that Plato dates the sinking of Atlantis to 9000 B.C., while Homer suggests that Scheria was in existence at the time of Odysseus c.1140 B.C. **(Note 44)**

Modern scholars who study Plato's *Timaeus* and *Critias* are in accord in their belief that the Azores, Madeira and Canary Islands are all visible remnants of the once vast continent of Atlantis. If modern scholars are correct in this assumption then it follows that these same island groups also qualify as being remnants of Homer's Scheria. If in fact Scheria had once existed somewhere off the coast of Portugal, it is quite likely that its submergence was due to a massive underwater earthquake. Recent geological studies of the Azores-Gibraltar Fault Line have revealed that it has a long history of violent eruptions, the most recent occurring in A.D. 1755. **(Note 45)**

The southern coasts of Portugal and Spain have long been susceptible to earthquakes and tsunamis. On the morning of 1st November A.D. 1755, a massive earthquake destroyed the Portuguese city of Lisbon. Measuring a magnitude of 9 on the Richter scale, the quake and its subsequent tsunami killed well over 100,000 people. Contemporary reports stated that within a period of three-and-a-half to six minutes, gigantic fissures five

(xxvii) Strabo, *Geography* III: 12-13

metres wide had torn the city centre apart. Survivors who had rushed to the open space of the docks for safety witnessed the water receding to reveal a seafloor littered with lost cargo and old shipwrecks. Thirty minutes after the earthquake, an enormous tsunami engulfed the harbor and downtown area. Tsunamis up to 20 metres in height also swept the coast of North Africa, killing 10,000 people. A three-metre tsunami hit the coast of Britain and on the other side of the Atlantic, the islands of the Caribbean experienced tidal waves. Lisbon was certainly not the only Portuguese city affected by the catastrophe. Throughout the southern part of the country, in particular the Algarve, there was general destruction. The shock waves of the earthquake were felt throughout Europe extending even to Finland and North Africa.

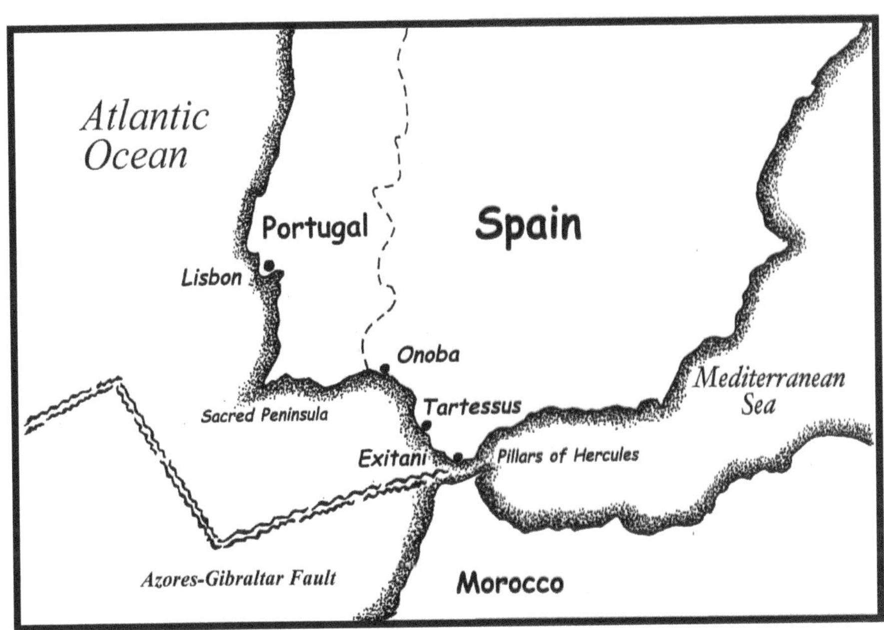

Map of Azores-Gibraltar Fault Line

The epicentre of the Lisbon quake was in the Atlantic Ocean about 200 kilometres off Portugal's Cape Saint Vincent. Referred to by the ancients as the Sacred Promontory, Cape Saint Vincent has over the millennia endured a series of violent earthquakes and tsunamis. Various evidences suggest that the entire coast of southern Spain, and particularly the shallow region of the Guadalquiver Delta, was struck by an enormous earthquake and tsunami c.1130 B.C. This quake would have destroyed the legendary city of Tartessus as well as two or three other port cities that probably existed along the coast of southern Spain.

If the Etruscans/Phaeacians had been among the survivors of the 1130 B.C. tsunami then I suggest that they would have subsequently migrated to the seemingly safer waters of the Mediterranean. It is known that the Etruscan (Villanova) culture began to take root in the Italian province of Tuscany c.1100 B.C. (Plato asserted that the ancient Atlanteans once held a sway of influence over Tuscany). It would be quite natural for the Etruscans/Phaeacians to migrate to the northern coast of Italy as this region was originally settled by the Ibero-Ligurians who had come up from the Iberian Peninsula (southern Spain) c.2500 B.C. The apparent ease with which the Etruscans took control of the western Mediterranean sea-trade c.700 B.C, as well as their connection to Gades (Cadiz) convinces me further that their ancestors had been familiar with these regions.

Odysseus Meets Nausicaa

Witnessing how Odysseus had fallen asleep on a bed of leaves, the goddess Athena took pity on him and began to plan how she might hasten his return to home shores. Like a gentle breeze, Athena wafted into the royal dwelling of Alcinous, king of the Phaeacians. There she found Nausicaa, the king's daughter, sleeping in her chamber. Athena caused the princess to dream that her marriage day was nearing and that it was her duty to arise and hasten to the place by the river where she and her handmaidens could do their washing.

The following morning a wagon is summonsed and loaded with laundry, a basket of provisions and a goatskin full of wine. Nausicaa's mother also provides her with ***'a golden cruse of oil, that she and her women might anoint themselves'***. The donkey-drawn wagon is then driven to a remote riverside where the clothes are scrubbed and spread out to dry. After they had eaten, the girls play a game of ball and it is their shrieks of laughter and excitement that rouse Odysseus from his exhausted sleep:

> ***... he crept from under his bush and broke off a bough covered with thick leaves to hide his nakedness. He looked like some lion of the wilderness that stalks about exulting in his strength and defying both wind and rain.***

Odysseus' gruesome appearance causes the handmaidens to flee along the beach but Nausicaa stands firm, for wise Athena:

> ***'had put courage into her heart and took away all fear'***.

Thinking he had awoken in the realms of heavenly Elysium, Odysseus addresses Nausicaa:

> ***"O Queen," he said, "I implore your aid - but tell me, are you a goddess or are you a mortal woman? I dare not clasp your knees, but I am in great distress; yesterday made the twentieth day that I had been tossing about upon the sea. The winds and waves have taken me all the way from the Ogygian Island and now fate has flung me upon this coast that I may endure still further suffering."***

To this Nausicaa answered:

> ***"Stranger, you appear to be a sensible, well-disposed person. There is no accounting for luck; Jove gives prosperity to rich and poor just as he chooses, so you must take what he has seen fit to send you and make the best of it. Now, however, that you have come to this our country, you shall not want for clothes nor for anything else that a foreigner in distress may reasonably look for. I will show you the way to the town and will tell you the name of our people; we are called Phaeacians and I am daughter to Alcinous, in whom the whole power of the state is vested."***
>
> ***Then she called her maids and said, "Stay where you are, you girls. Can you not see a man without running away from him? Do you take him for a robber or a murderer? Neither he nor any one else can come here to do us Phaeacians any harm, for we are dear to the gods and live apart on a land's end that juts into the sounding sea and have nothing to do with any other people."***
>
> ***"This is only some poor man who has lost his way and we must be kind to him, for strangers and foreigners in distress are under Jove's protection. So, girls, give the poor fellow something to eat and drink and wash him in the stream at some place that is sheltered from the wind."***

The maids present Odysseus with olive oil and bid him to bathe. He replies that he cannot do so in front of them and so they leave him to his privacy. When he returns from the stream, Nausicaa is amazed at his now noble appearance and counsels her hand-maidens:

> ***"Hush my dears, for I want to say something. I believe the gods who***

live in heaven have sent this man to the Phaeacians. When I first saw him I thought him plain, but now his appearance is like that of the gods who dwell in heaven. I should like my future husband to be just such a one as he is, if only he would stay here and not want to go away. Give him something to eat and drink."

They did as they were told and set food before Odysseus, who ate and drank ravenously for it was long since he had eaten food of any kind.

"Stranger," said Nausicaa, "rise and let us be going back to the town; I will introduce you at the house of my excellent father, where I can tell you that you will meet all the best people among the Phaeacians. But be sure and do as I bid you, for you seem to be a sensible person. As long as we are going past the fields and farm lands, follow briskly behind the wagon along with the maids and I will lead the way myself. Presently we shall come to the town where you will find a high wall running all round it and a good harbour on either side with a narrow entrance into the city. Everyone has a place where his own ship can lie. You will see the market place paved with large stones bedded in the earth and a temple of Neptune in the middle of it. Here people deal in ships' gear of all kinds, such as cables and sails and here too, are the places where oars are made, for the Phaeacians are not a nation of archers; they know nothing about bows and arrows, but are a sea-faring folk and pride themselves on their masts, oars, and ships, with which they travel far over the sea."

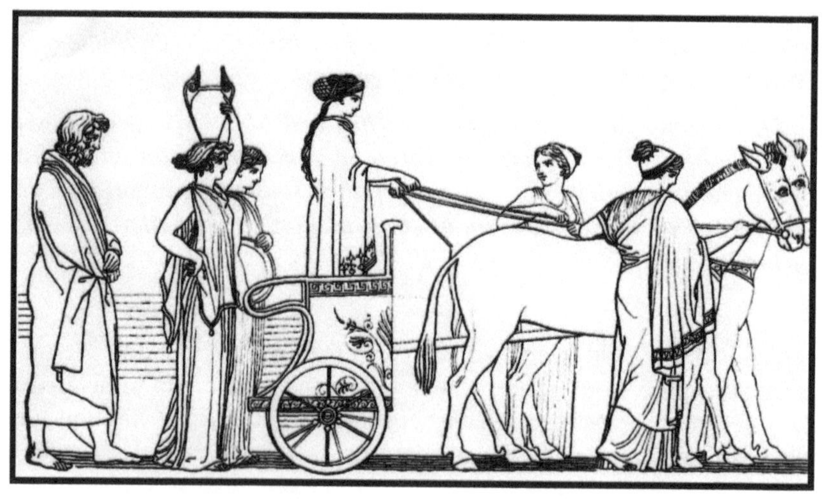

Nausicaa escorts Odysseus to her father's palace

Nausicaa further advises Odysseus that in order to avoid ***'gossip and scandal'*** he should follow behind her entourage until they arrive at a shrine dedicated to Athena. Odysseus is then to depart their company and pray at the shrine for a time before he enters the port town.

The Palace of King Alcinous

Thus then did Odysseus wait and pray and the girl drove on into the town. Presently, Odysseus rose and proceeded towards the town. Athena caused a thick mist all round him to hide him in case any of the proud Phaeacians he might meet should be rude to him or ask who he was. Then, just as he was entering the town, Athena came towards him in the likeness of a little girl carrying a pitcher. She stood directly in front of him and Odysseus said,

"My dear, will you be so kind as to show me the house of King Alcinous? I am an unfortunate foreigner in distress and do not know anyone in your town and country." Athena replied,

"Yes, father stranger, I will show you the house you want, for Alcinous lives quite close to my own father. I will go before you and show the way, but say not a word as you go and do not look at any man, nor ask him questions, for the people here cannot abide strangers and do not like men who come from some other place. They are a sea-faring folk and sail the seas by the grace of Poseidon (Neptune) ***in ships that glide along like thought, or as a bird in the air."***

On this she led the way and Odysseus followed in her steps; but not one of the Phaeacians could see him as he passed through the city in the midst of them, for the great goddess Athena in her good will towards him had hidden him in a thick cloud of darkness. He admired their harbours, ships, places of assembly and the lofty walls of the city, which with the palisade on top of them, were very striking. When they reached the king's house Athena said:

"This is the house stranger, which you would have me show you. You will find a number of great people sitting at table but do not be afraid; go straight in, for the bolder a man is the more likely he is to carry his point, even though he is a stranger. First you must find the queen. Her name is Arete and she comes of the same family as her

husband Alcinous. They both descend originally from Poseidon (Neptune)***, who was father to Nausithous by Periboea, a woman of great beauty. Periboea was the youngest daughter of Eurymedon who at one time reigned over the giants, but he ruined his ill-fated people and lost his own life to boot.***

Poseidon, however, lay with Eurymedon's daughter and she had a son by him, the great Nausithous who reigned over the Phaeacians. Nausithous had two sons Rhexenor and Alcinous; Apollo killed the first of them while he was still a bridegroom and without male issue; but he left a daughter Arete, whom Alcinous married and honours as no other woman is honoured of all those that keep house along with their husbands.

Thus she both was, and still is, respected beyond measure by her children, by Alcinous himself and by the whole people, who look upon her as a goddess and greet her whenever she goes about the city, for she is a thoroughly good woman both in head and heart. When any women are friends of hers, she will help their husbands also to settle their disputes. If you can gain her good will, you may have every hope of seeing your friends again and getting safely back to your home and country."

Phaeacian Heritage

In her guise of a young girl, Athena had advised Odysseus that his plea for a passage homeward should be directed to the revered Queen Arête.

Queen Arête is synonymous with the mythic Arethusae (Old English: virtuous sea queen). According to Greek legend, Arethusae and her sisters Aegle (dazzling light), Hesperia (night), and Erytheis (red), abode on a mystical island that lay in the distant west, far beyond 'the river of Oceanous'. Athena had given Odysseus a detailed account of Queen Arête's heritage, revealing that the Phaeacians were the descendants of Eurymedon ***'who at one time reigned over the giants'***. The Phaeacians' claim that their ancestors were giants leads me to presume that their original place of habitat was located somewhere along the Atlantic seaboard of Europe. Why? Because the early Greek writers, such as Hesiod, associated giants with the Atlantic seaboard of megalithic Europe. Hesiod's *Theogony* (c. 700 B.C.) relates how the original Titan giants were born from the blood of their father Ouranos' castration.

When they attempted to usurp Zeus' rule on Mount Olympus, the so-called Battle of the Titans erupted. Three Titan giants, namely Briareus, Gyes and Cottus, fought on the side of Zeus and eventually defeated their fellow Titans who were unceremoniously cast into the far reaches of Tartaurus. Envied for '*their looks, size and overwhelming masculinity*' and renowned for their '*insatiable love of war*', the three giants Briareus, Gyes and Cottus are said to have later returned to their homeland, which was located at the Ocean's source (the Pillars of Hercules). There, at the western limits of the Mediterranean, they stood guard over a fellow race of giants called the Cyclopes. Robert Graves' book, *The White Goddess* informs us that the Cyclopes were a tribe of Celtic people, so named, because of the large blue rings they tattooed around their eyes. Homer further reports that the Phaeacians once abode:

> ... ***near the lawless Cyclopes. Now the Cyclopes were stronger than they and plundered them, so their king, Nausithous, moved them thence and settled them in Scheria, far from all other people.***

The Pillars of Hercules

The Pillars of Hercules not only marked the gateway into the vast Atlantic Ocean, they also guarded access to the British Isles. The Greeks referred to those who lived on the Atlantic side of the Pillars as being Atlanteans, Cyclopes or Titan giants. **(Note 46)** The Greeks also believed that the distant reaches of Oceanus contained the sacred isles of Elysium, the dwelling place of the blessed dead.

> *The Pillars of Hercules were generally regarded to be twin rocks that stood opposite each other at the Ocean's source. On the European side stood Calpe (Gibraltar) and on the African side stood Abyla. Certain writers of ancient Greece assert that it was not Hercules who set up the Pillars but Briareus, a giant whose power extended to this region.*

> *When the memory of Briarus (also called Aegaeon) had faded, they renamed the entrance in honour of Heracles because he had founded the city of Tartessus (Heracleia) which was located only five miles from Calpe. Although vast ancient walls and ship-sheds can still be seen there, it must be remembered that the earliest Heracles had also been called Briareus.* **(xxviii)**

Composed by Hesiod (c.700 B.C.), *Theogony* describes Briareus as a monster who had fifty heads and one hundred arms. When modern mythographers analyse Hesiod's metaphoric descriptions, they should realise that Hesiod was merely alluding to Briareus as being the captain of a ship that was manned with a crew of fifty oarsmen; a one hundred-armed warship. The Phaeacians' heritage of Titan customs is illustrated when King Alcinous orders his fellow Phaeacians to:

> .... ***draw a ship into the sea, one that has never yet made a voyage and man her with two and fifty of our smartest young sailors. Then when you have made fast your oars each by his own seat, leave the ship and come to my house to prepare a feast.***

Hesiod's allegorical reference to Briareus and his brother-giants as *Hecatontocheires* (hundred-handed ones) might also identify them, or their descendants, with the giant Centaurs (*centaurus*: one hundred strong). The name the Greeks gave to the Centaurs' mother-goddess was Leucothea (the White Goddess). This is the very same Leucothea who had rescued Odysseus from drowning and delivered him safely to Scheria. In Plato's *Critias,* it is stated that Poseidon (Neptune) took his daughter Leucippe (Leucothea) for wife and that the offspring from this union were the Atlanteans who are credited with the construction of the legendary port city of Atlantis. According to Plato the extremity of Atlantis stretched from:

> ... *near the Pillars of Heracles up to that part of the country now called Gadeira* (Gades).

Plato further informs us that the descendants of the giants, Atlas and his twin brother Gadeira (Hu Gadarn?) had: (**Note 47)**

> ... *dwelt for many generations bearing rule over many other islands throughout the sea and holding sway besides, as was previously stated,*

(xxviii) Eustrathius on Dionysius's *Description of the Earth* 64 ff.; Scholiast on Pinder's *Nemean Odes* iii, 37; Aristotle, quoted by Aelian *Varia Historia* v. 3

over the Mediterranean peoples as far as Egypt and Tuscany (the Etruscans). *It was the eldest who, as king, always passed on the sceptre to the eldest of his sons and thus they preserved the sovereignty for many generations. The wealth they possessed was so immense that the like had never been seen before in any royal house nor will ever easily be seen again; they were provided with everything of which provision was needed either in the city or throughout the rest of the country. For because of their headship they had a large supply of imports from abroad. But at a later time there occurred portentous earthquakes and floods and one grievous day, night befell them, when the whole body of your warriors* (Greeks) *was swallowed up by the earth and the island of Atlantis in like manner was swallowed up by the sea and vanished; wherefore also the ocean at that spot has now become impassable and unsearchable, being blocked up by the shoal mud which the island created as it settled down.*

Plato's *'extremity of Atlantis'* stretched from the Pillars of Heracles up to Gadeira (Gades), hence it lay somewhere within the modern Gulf of Cadiz. The Greek geographer Strabo (64 B.C. - A.D. 8), relates that the Gulf of Cadiz had long been inhabited by a mysterious people called the Turduli who:

... are esteemed to be the most intelligent of all the Iberians; they have an alphabet and possess ancient writings, poems and metrical laws that are six thousand years old, as they say. The other Iberians are likewise furnished with an alphabet although not of the same form, nor do they speak the same language. **(Note 48)**

The Turduli not only enjoy a salubrious climate, but their manners are polished and urbane, as also those of the people of Keltica, by reason of their vicinity, or according to Polybuis (203 - 120 B.C.) *on their being of the same stock but not to a great degree.*

Strabo and Polybuis' claim that the Tuduli and the Celts were of similar stock has been recently enhanced by John T. Koch's 2010 publication, *Celtic from the West.* Koch's work reports how the ancient Tartessian (Turduli?) language spoken in southern Spain demonstrates the characteristic sound inflections that define Celtic languages.

Returning to Polybuis' account of southern Spain we read:

One of the Iberian kings had such a magnificent and richly furnished palace that he rivaled the luxury of the Phaeacians, except that the vessels in the interior of the house, though made of gold and silver, were full of barley wine.

Like the Phaeacians, the Turduli (Tursa/Tyhenians?) were renowned not only for the size and number of their ships but also for the respect they offered to the aged, whose wisdom they valued.

Tartessus

According to Strabo's writings, the Turduli's legendary port city of Tartessus was located at the mouth of the Guadalquiver River:

It appears the ancients knew the Guadalquiver [river] under the name of the Tartessus. They say that on the piece of land enclosed between the two outlets of this river there formerly stood a city named, like the river, Tartessus and that the district was called Tartessis, which the Turduli now inhabit... words cannot convey their excellence. Gold, silver, copper, and iron, equal in amount and of similar quality, not having been hitherto discovered in any other part of the world.

Homer's description of the Phaeacian royal palace makes it abundantly clear that the Phaeacians were very similar to the Turduli in that they had access to, or traded in Spain's immense mineral wealth:

... a kind of radiance, like that of the sun or moon, lit up the high roofed halls of the great king. Walls of bronze, topped with blue enamel tiles ran round to left and right from the threshold to the back of the court. The interior of the well-built mansion was guarded by golden doors hung on posts of silver that sprang from the bronze threshold.

Disappearance of Tartessus

Although the city of Tartessus had disappeared from history, the Romans continued to refer to the wide bay of southern Spain as Tartessius Sinus. The ancient port of Tartessos is apparently buried in the shifting wetlands and dunes that presently lie adjacent to the mouth of the Guadalquiver River. A huge sandbar stretching from the mouth of the Rio Tinto near Palos de la Frontera, to the riverbank opposite Sanlúcar de Barrameda, gradually has blocked off the former estuaries that once formed the river delta. Satellite photographs of this region have revealed two rectangular temple structures that appear to be surrounded by a series of large concentric-ringed canals. Archaeologists such as Marisa de Hinojosbut are of course eager to excavate this site but unfortunately it lies within the ecologically protected Parque Nacional de Donana. **(Note 48)**

The Arrival of the Phoenicians

Not long after Tartessus had been submerged, the Phoenicians sailed through the Pillars of Hercules and established the port city of Gades (c.1110 B.C.). Strabo's *Geography* recounts the following legend of Gades' colonization:

> *According to the people of Gades themselves, the King of Tyre* (capital of Phoenicia) *was ordered by an oracle to found a colony near the Pillars of Heracles. In accordance to the oracle he sent out three successive parties of exploration. The first party, thinking that the oracle had referred to Abyle* (Morocco) *and Calpe* (Gibraltar), *landed inside the straits where the city of Exitani now stands; the second sailed about two hundred miles beyond the straits to a place opposite the Spanish city of Onoba; but both parties were discouraged by unfavorable omens when they offered sacrifices and so returned home. The third party reached Gades, where they raised a temple to Heracles on the Eastern Cape and successfully founded the city of Gades on the Western.* **(xxix)**

It appears that the Phoenicians had knowledge of the devastating tsunami that had destroyed three coastal cities on the southern coast of Spain. One of these cities had existed near Gibraltar; a second lay 200 miles beyond the straits and a third was the legendary city of Tartessus. The cunning Phoenicians were also aware of the rich mineral treasures that had long been exported from these coastal cities, hence they referred to the region as Sapan (Spain), which means 'well hidden'.

(xxxiii) Pliny, *Natural History* III; Proem, *Strabo* III 5.

The Current Search For Tartessus

Cuban-born Georgeos Diaz-Montexano's discovery and exploration of submerged islands lying in the waters off the Straits of Gibraltar have led him to conclude that they might at one time have been part of the fabled Atlantis. According to Diaz-Montexano, a plethora of pre-Christian writers including: Eutímenes de Massalia (c.500 B.C.); Anacreonte (570 B.C.); Hecateo de Mileto (560 - 480 B.C.); Ferécides (c.456 B.C.); Píndaro (518 - 438 B.C.); Eurípides (485 - 306 B.C.); Heródotus (484 - 430 B.C.); Isócrates (436 - 338 B.C.) and Euctemon (436 B.C.), had all made reference to an island or peninsula that had existed somewhere off the coast of southern Spain. The now vanished island or peninsula has been recorded under a variety of names such as Aliba, Etheria, Scheria, Erythea, Gadeira, Sarpedonia, Ogigia and Tartessós.

In the summer of 2003, Diaz-Montexano launched a deep-sea expedition called 'Atlantis Ibero-Moroccan'. In scouring the relatively shallow seabed that lies between southern Spain and Morocco, the diving team discovered the remains of submerged villages. Some of these immersed settlements still retained semi-circular walls, pillars, paving and mill stones as well as various Bronze Age artifacts. Although Diaz-Montexano was encouraged by these findings he continues to seek more substantial ruins and favors several other locations, including one near Huevela and another off the far southern coast of Spain. We might recall that these two sites were among the three favoured by the Phoenicians to rebuild the lost city of Tartessus.

Diaz-Montexano currently considers the 'submerged peninsula of Trafalgar' to be the most likely site of a lost maritime kingdom. Venturing out into the waters off the Trafalgar coast, Diaz-Montexano dived down to a submarine platform that lay at a depth of 9 -12 metres. There he located circular constructions that displayed curiously large round holes. He also discovered a series of walls, megalithic slabs, paving stones and pillars.

Similarities Between Phaeacians (Phaiakes) and Etruscans

Etruscan citizens of ancient Italy avidly attended public recitals of *The Odyssey*. Their fascination with Homer's great epic may have been due to the many affinities they shared with the Phaeacians. A comparison of Etruscan and Phaeacian cultural traits leaves little doubt that they were, if not one in the same people, very closely related.

Phaeacian Seafarers

Homer describes the Phaeacians as:

> ***... seafarers who spent their energy on masts and oars and on the graceful craft they love to sail across the foam-flecked seas.***

Etruscan Seafarers

The Etruscans were formidable sailors who soon took control of the Western Mediterranean, transporting silver from Spain and tin from the British Isles.

*

Phaeacian Purple

Queen Arête wove a yarn ***'stained with sea-purple'*** and Odysseus was given a purple cloak that he wore when seated at the Phaeacian banquet.

Etruscan Purple

The robes of the Etruscan rulers were dyed purple, a colour adopted by Roman rulers and which today, still signifies royalty.

*

Phaeacian Senate

According to King Alcinous, the Phaeacians were co-ruled by 12 chiefs.

Etruscan Senate

The Etruscans elected 12 kings to rule 12 principalities (see Livy, *History of Rome* Book I: VIII)

*

Phaeacian Luxury

> ***For a kind of radiance, like that of the sun or moon, lit up the high roofed halls of the great king, walls of bronze, topped with blue***

enamel tiles, ran round to left and right from the threshold to the back of the court. The interior of the well-built mansion was guarded by golden doors hung on posts of silver that sprang from the bronze threshold.

Etruscan Luxury

Ancient Greek writers made overt mention of the Etruscans' fondness for luxury. Scenes of uninhibited pleasure seeking were depicted on the walls of their tombs and reveal that the Etruscans 'were a life-loving people charged with such vigor as the Greeks had reason to complain of'. These people's unabashed taste for extravagance rather than the Greek dictum of moderation in all things, contradicts the claim that the Etruscans were of Greek origin.

*

Phaeacian Feasting

Homer described the house of a Phaeacian nobleman as a place of perpetual entertainment, where chieftains sat and enjoyed the food and wine that were always forthcoming.

The house keeps fifty maids employed. Some grind the apple-golden corn in the hand-mill; some weave at the loom or sit and twist yarn, their hands fluttering like the tall poplar's leaves, while the soft olive oil drips from the close-woven fabrics they have finished. For the Phaeacians' extraordinary skill in handling ships at sea is rivaled by the dexterity of their womenfolk at the loom, so expert has Athene made them in the finer crafts and so intelligent.

Etruscan Feasting

The Greek historian, Herodotus, describes Etruscan luxury:

Twice each day they spread costly tables and upon them everything that is appropriate to excessive luxury, providing gay-coloured couches and having ready at hand a multitude of silver drinking cups of every description and servants-in-waiting in no small number; and those attendants are some of them exceeding in comeliness and others are arrayed in clothing more costly than befits the station of a slave.

Herodotus' mention of richly attired slaves may explain the origin of the Gaelic word '*truscan*' which means 'clothing'.

Phaeacian Music and Dance

> ***But the things in which we take a perennial delight are the feast, the lyre, the dance, clean linen in plenty, a hot bath and our bed. So, forward now, my champion dancers and show us your steps, so that when he gets home our guest may be able to tell his friends how far we leave all other folk behind in seamanship, in speed of foot, in dancing, and in song.***

Etruscan Music and Dance

Throughout the ancient world the Etruscans were celebrated for their devotion to music. At festivals, religious ceremonies and 'funeral games', both male and female members of the guilds of dancers performed to the sound of stringed instruments and the shrill notes of the double flute. The Etruscan word for 'dancer' was '*hister*', from which the modern word 'histrionic' is derived.

*

Phaeacian Sports

> ***"Let us go out of doors now and try our hands at various sports, so that when our guest has reached his home he can tell his friends that***

at boxing, wrestling, jumping and running there is no-one who could beat us."

Etruscan Sports

The brutal gladiatorial contests that delighted the crowds of Imperial Rome were a heritage from the Etruscans. Scenes of wrestling, boxing and discus throwing are often depicted on Etruscan tombs.

*

Phaeacian Omens

With his land threatened by catastrophe, King Alcinous had cried out:

"My father's prophecy of long ago has indeed come home to me. He used to maintain that Poseidon resented our giving safe conduct to all and sundry and he foretold that one day he would wreck one of our excellent ships on the high seas as she was returning from such

The Phaeacians make sacrifice to Poseidon

a mission and would overshadow our city with a ring of high mountains. Now all these prophecies of the old king's are coming true! But listen: I have remedies to suggest, which I hope you will all accept. For the future, give up your custom of seeing home any

> ***traveller who comes to our city; and for the present let us sacrifice twelve picked bulls to Poseidon. He may take pity on us and refrain from hemming in our town with a long mountain range."***

The people were filled with consternation and immediately prepared their prize bulls for sacrifice.

Etruscan Omens

Etruscan priests, called '*Haruspices*' (diviners), were responsible for the appeasement of the gods. They studied omens and read portents to uncover the future's secrets. The correct interpretation of signs and the due observance of appropriate rites were of crucial importance. The Christian writer Arnobius, later described Etruria as the 'creator and mother of superstitions'. The Etruscans appear to have been locked within a rigid doctrine of protocol that, having been handed down by their ancestors, was considered immutable. This ancestral doctrine however, was not at all concerned with ethical issues or moral conduct.

The Origin of the Phaeacians/Etruscans

The origins of the Phaeacians and the Etruscans remain a mystery. The writers of ancient Greece and Rome offered conflicting views on the subject of Etruscan provenance and to this day the enigma remains unresolved. **(Note 49)** The Etruscans did not call themselves Tyrrhenians or Etruscans but rather Rasenna. The etymology of Rasenna is perhaps *Zena*, an ancient word used by the Ionians to describe the sun. Early Roman writers identified the Etruscans (Tyrrhenians) with the Pelasgians. The meaning of the word Pelasgian is also debatable, however it is generally used to describe the pre-Greek seafarers of the Aegean. The name Pelasgian supposedly derives from the word *pelasgos* meaning to branch out or flourish. In this sense, it might be suggested that certain clans of 'solar worshipping' Pelasgians branched out into and beyond the Mediterranean. These Pelasgians may have included the Telechines, the Tuatha de Danaan and the Phaeacians (shining ones), who according to Homer dwelt '***far from their fellow man***'.

The Etruscan's identification with *The Odyssey* is evidenced on one of their elaborately carved steles. Depicted in the centre of the relief sculpture one might recognize a near nude Odysseus running ahead of Nausicaa's mule-drawn chariot. On the upper part of the tombstone, a sea serpent and

Etruscan stele from Bologna

a fishtailed horse are entwined in close embrace (see illustration above). Together these totemic creatures probably represent an amalgamation of two distinct seafaring tribes who, if correctly identified, may help solve the mystery of Etruscan origins.

The Serpent and the Horse

The Etruscan depiction of a sea serpent embracing a horse is derived from Pelasgian mythology. The seafaring Pelasgians are thought to be among the earliest people to inhabit the coastal regions of Greece and the Aegean. Apollonius Rhodius's *Argonautica* provides a poetic description of how Eurynome, the 'Goddess of All Things', transformed herself into a mare so that she might mate with the serpent Ophion.

> *In the beginning Eurynome, the Goddess of All Things, rose naked from Chaos, but found nothing substantial for her feet to rest upon. She therefore divided the sea from the sky, dancing loosely upon its waves*

> *towards the south. This action set a wind motion behind her and it seemed something new with which to begin a work of creation. Wheeling about, she caught hold of the North Wind, rubbing it between her hands and behold! There appeared the great serpent Ophion. Eurynome danced to warm herself, wildly and more wildly until Ophion, grown lustful, coiled about those divine limbs and was moved to couple with her. Now, the North Wind, who is also Boreas, fertilized Eurynome; which is why mares often turn their hindquarters to the wind and breed foals without aid of a stallion. So Eurynome was likewise got with child.* **(xxx)**

Though recognised for being emblematic symbols of Etruscan origin, the sea serpent and the horse were originally two separate totems representing two distinct seafaring tribes. During the 2nd millennium B.C., the Greek mainland hosted a variety of seafaring tribes; the dominant two being the Danaans and Centaurs (*Heratontocheiroi*). The Danaans claimed to have descended from Eurynome's encounter with the North Wind serpent Ophion, whilst the Centaurs (half-men, half-horse) held Eurynome to be the mother of their ocean-goddess, Leucothea. **(Notes 50, 51)**

Odysseus Enters the Phaeacian Citadel

> ***Odysseus went on to the house of Alcinous and he pondered much as he paused a while before reaching the threshold of bronze, for the splendor of the palace was like that of the sun or moon.***

Massive gold and silver sculptures of dogs stood guard on each side of the entrance hall. A gift from the blacksmith-god Hephaestus (Vulcan), the dogs were so well crafted they seemed to be imbued with sentient life. Mounted on impressive pedestals, golden statues of boys held lighted torches, spreading light throughout the palace. The Phaeacian elders occupied two rows of splendid seats in the large banquet chamber.

> ***So here Odysseus stood for a while and looked about him, but when he had looked long enough he crossed the threshold and went within the precincts of the house.***

(xxx) Apollonius Rhodius *Argonautica*: Graves, Robert *The Greek Myths* (Complete Edition) 1955

Still hidden by the cloak of invisibility in which Athena had enveloped him, Odysseus continued through the court until he reached Queen Arête. He outstretched his hands upon the knees of the queen and at that exact moment he became visible. Every one was speechless with surprise at seeing a man there, but Odysseus began at once with his petition:

> ***"Queen Arête" he exclaimed, "daughter of great Rhexenor, in my distress I humbly pray you, as also your husband and these your guests (whom may heaven prosper with long life and happiness and may they leave their possessions to their children, and all the honours conferred upon them by the state) to help me home to my own country as soon as possible; for I have been long in trouble and away from my friends."***

Impressed with Odysseus' noble manner, Alcinous presented him the seat of his favourite son Laodamas and immediately instructed his maids to fetch him food. Once Odysseus had eaten his fill, Alcinous ordered a drink offering to Zeus. When those present had partaken of as much drink as he was minded, Alcinous said:

> ***"Aldermen and town councilors of the Phaeacians, hear my words. You have had your supper, so now go home to bed. Tomorrow morning I shall invite a still larger number of aldermen and will give a sacrificial banquet in honour of our guest; we can then discuss the question of his escort and consider how we may at once send him back rejoicing to his own country without trouble or inconvenience to himself, no matter how distant it maybe. We must see that he comes to no harm while on his homeward journey, but when he is once at home he will have to take the luck he was born with for better or worse like other people. It is possible, however, that the stranger is one of the immortals who has come down from heaven to visit us; but in this case the gods are departing from their usual practice, for hitherto they have made themselves perfectly clear to us when we have been offering them hecatombs. They come and sit at our feasts just like one of our selves and if any solitary wayfarer happens to stumble upon some one or other of them, they affect no concealment, for we are as near of kin to the gods as the Cyclopes and the savage giants are."***

Odysseus tells Alcinous that he is not a god but a mere mortal who despite his many misadventures, is still endeavouring to find his way home. Everyone present in the court agrees that Odysseus is indeed a noble man and should therefore be provided with an escort to his home shores.

Once the court attendants had departed Odysseus was left alone with the king and queen.

> ***The queen asked him who he was and whence he came and recognizing the clothes that he wore as those which her maidens and herself had made, asked from whom he received those garments. He told them and of his residence in Calypso's isle and his departure thence; of the wreck of his raft, his escape by swimming and of the help afforded by their daughter, Princess Nausicaa. The parents heard approvingly and the king offered Odysseus an estate and a position of honour if he wished to remain in Scheria. However, if his guest preferred to return to his homeland, Alcinous promised a swift ship would be furnished to that purpose.***
>
> ***Now when the child of morning, rosy-fingered Dawn appeared, Alcinous and Odysseus both rose and Alcinous led the way to the Phaeacian place of assembly that was near the ships. There they sat down side by side on a seat of polished stone. Athena took the form of one of Alcinous' servants and went round the town in order to help Odysseus get home. She went up to the citizens, man-by-man and said,***
>
> ***"Aldermen and town councillors of the Phaeacians, come to the assembly place, each of you, and listen to the stranger who has just come off a long voyage to the house of King Alcinous; he looks like an immortal god."***
>
> ***With these words she made them all want to come and they flocked to the assembly place till seats and standing room were alike crowded. Everyone was struck with the appearance of Odysseus, for Athena had beautified him about the head and shoulders, making him look taller and stouter than he really was, that he might impress the Phaeacians favourably as being a very remarkable man and might come off well in the many trials of skill to which they would challenge him. Then, when they were got together, Alcinous spoke,***
>
> ***"Hear me, aldermen and town councilors of the Phaeacians, that I may speak even as I am minded. This stranger, whoever he may be, has found his way to my house from somewhere or other, either East or West. He wants an escort and wishes to have the matter settled. Let us then get one ready for him, as we have done for others before him; indeed, no-one who ever yet came to my house has been able to complain of me for not speeding him on his way soon enough."***

Alcinous invites one and all to his palace where they can feast and hear the bard Demodocus sing ***'for there is no bard like him whatever he may***

choose to sing about.'

> ***Alcinous then led the way and the others followed after, while a servant went to fetch Demodocus. The fifty-two picked oarsmen went to the seashore as they had been told and when they got there they drew the ship into the water, got her mast and sails inside her, bound the oars to the thole-pins with twisted thongs of leather, all in due course and spread the white sails aloft.***

Once they had the ship fitted out, the fifty-two oarsmen joined the palace feast with the other guests. Demodocus, who is blind, has been seated with his harp, bread and wine. As the gathered men eat, the minstrel begins to sing about the feats of the heroes in the Trojan War and of the quarrel between Odysseus and Achilles:

> ***"Here was the beginning of the evil that by the will of Jove*** (Zeus) ***fell both upon Danaans and Trojans." Thus sang the bard, but Odysseus drew his purple mantle over his head and covered his face, for he was ashamed to let the Phaeacians see that he was weeping. When the bard left off singing he wiped the tears from his eyes, uncovered his face and taking his cup, made a drink-offering to the gods; but when the Phaeacians pressed Demodocus to sing further, for they delighted in his lays, Odysseus again drew his mantle over his head and wept bitterly*. (Note 52)**

Odysseus drew his purple mantle over his head

Seated beside Odysseus, Alcinous is the only one to notice his weeping and dejected state. He orders the minstrel to cease his song and announces that it is time to hold athletic games that will include boxing, wrestling, broad-jumping, a footrace and discus throwing. Melancholic and with so much on his mind, Odysseus is somewhat reluctant to participate in sporting events. His hesitation prompts Euryalus, who is one of the Phaeacians' most celebrated athletes, to reproach Odysseus for his lack of sporting prowess.

> ***Euryalus reviled him outright and said, "I gather, then, that you are unskilled in any of the many sports that men generally delight in. I suppose you are one of those grasping traders that go about in ships as captains or merchants, and who think of nothing but their outward freights and homeward cargoes. There does not seem to be much of the athlete about you."***

Angered by the impertinence of this challenge, Odysseus picks up the heaviest discus and hurls it much farther than any of the previous contestants. He then boldly dares the young contenders to try to best him in any athletic contest whatsoever and in particular archery, claiming he had no living equal in that sport. Odysseus' utter confidence stuns the crowd into awed silence and Alcinous apologizes for his affront to Odysseus' dignity. Lightening the mood, Alcinous continues:

> ***"We are not particularly remarkable for our boxing, nor yet as wrestlers, but we are singularly fleet of foot and are most excellent sailors. We are also extremely fond of good dinners, music, and dancing; and we very much like frequent changes of linen, warm baths and good beds, so now, please, some of you who are the best dancers set about dancing, that our guest on his return home may be able to tell his friends how much we surpass all other nations as sailors, runners, dancers and minstrels."***
>
> ***Thus did Alcinous speak and the others, all of them, applauded his proposal and sent their servants to fetch presents.***

Heeding Alcinous' request, Euryalus apologises for his insult to Odysseus saying:

> ***"I will give the stranger all the satisfaction you require. He shall have my sword, which is all of bronze, apart from its silver hilt. I will also give him the scabbard of newly sawn ivory. It will be worth a great deal to him."***

Euryalus' presentation of a finely wrought, silver-hilted sword encased within an ivory scabbard is another indication that Scheria lay somewhere near Spain, as that country has long been renowned for such craftsmanship.

> ***Meanwhile, Arête brought a magnificent chest from her own room and inside it she stored all the beautiful presents of gold and raiment that the Phaeacians had bestowed. Later, when the servants had done washing and anointing Odysseus with oil and had given him a clean cloak and shirt, he left the bathroom and went to join the guests who were sitting over their wine. Lovely Nausicaa stood by one of the bearing-posts supporting the roof of the cloister and admired him as she saw him pass. "Farewell stranger," said she, "do not forget me when you are safe at home again, for it is to me first that you owe a ransom for having saved your life."***

Beginning where he had left off the previous night, the bard continued the tale of the Trojan War. Once again Odysseus began to weep until ***'his cheeks were wet with tears'***. Odysseus' distress causes King Alcinous to rise and address the court:

> ***"Aldermen and town councillors of the Phaeacians, let Demodocus cease his song, for there are those present who do not seem to like it. From the moment that we had done supper and Demodocus began to sing, our guest has been all the time groaning and lamenting. He is evidently in great trouble; so let the bard leave off that we may all enjoy ourselves, hosts and guest alike."***

Alcinous then addressed Odysseus directly, asking him about his travels and the country of his origin so that one of his ships may shape their purpose accordingly and take him there:

> ***"For the Phaeacians have no pilots; their vessels have no rudders as those of other nations have, but the ships themselves understand what it is that we are thinking about and want."***
>
> ***"Still do I remember hearing my father say that Neptune was angry with us for being too easy-going in the matter of providing people with escort. He said that one of these days he would destroy a ship of***

> ***ours as it was returning from having escorted someone and bury our city under a high mountain. This is what my father used to say, but whether the god will carry out his threat or not is a matter that he will decide for himself."***
>
> ***"And now, tell me and tell me true. Where have you been wandering and in what countries have you travelled? Tell us of the peoples themselves and of their cities. Who were hostile, savage and uncivilised and who, on the other hand, hospitable and humane? Tell us also why you are made so unhappy on hearing about the return of the Argive Danaans from Troy. The gods arranged all this and sent them their misfortunes in order that future generations might have something to sing about."***

Odysseus Relates His Tale

Odysseus then recited the long saga of his astonishing Odyssey, describing his crossing of oceans from west to east and of the many strange lands he had visited.

When disguised as a helpful maiden, Athena had informed Odysseus that ***'many important men'*** were seated at the court of King Alcinous. These worldly and wise Phaeacians were quite capable of assimilating the various references and navigational aspects of Odysseus' voyages. The Phaeacians' ability to comprehend his amazing feat is perhaps alluded to in Homer's claim that they were ***'a sea-faring folk'*** who:

> ***... pride themselves on their masts, oars and ships in which they travel far over the sea ... they know all the cities and countries in the world and can traverse the sea just as well even when it is covered in mist and cloud, so that there is no danger of being wrecked or coming to harm.***

Odysseus' testimony of having sailed into the east and returned from the west could only be interpreted as a circumnavigation of the world! The enormity of accomplishing such a feat would explain why King Alcinous was more than happy to bestow upon Odysseus not only the highest honours, but also:

> ***'more magnificent presents of bronze, gold, and raiment then he would have brought back from Troy'***

Although it is conjecture that Homer's Phaeacians were associated with the legendary city of Tartessus, it remains a fact that the Phoenicians established the port of Gades less than 20 kilometres from the submerged ruins of Tartessos. In that newly created port, the Phoenicians erected and dedicated a temple to Hercules in honour of his circumnavigation of the world.

The French Benedictine scholar Antoine Calmet (1672 - 1757) tells us:

> *There is not therefore room for doubting that Hercules of Gades or someone of his descendants, or at least someone of the Phoenicians who had the same name, made an excursion beyond the Strait of Gibraltar, for they say of Hercules that by him the whole circuit of the globe was traversed by sea passage. To him Diodorus even attributed the foundation of the city Alecta in Septimaniæ. Certain however, it is, that Diodorus speaks of a Hercules who sailed round the world and who founded the city of Lecta in Septimania: but no writer has pointed out its situation.*

The 19th century Mexican scholar, Paul Felix Cabrera, further relates that the so-called Hercules of Gades had lived at the same time as Odysseus:

> *The other voyage in the Atlantic spoken of by Calmet is attributed to Hercules, who is the supposed author of the Gaditanian columns (Pillars of Hercules) and whom Galleo ranks as contemporary with Moses and chief of the Canaanites who left Palestine on the invasion of Joshua.* (1160 B.C.?) *This hero had the surname Magusanus, derived from the Chaldean word Gouz, signifying to scratch, and by metaphor to pass, from which root, ships and fords of rivers are called Megizze in the Chaldaic idiom. Of his sea voyages there existed a vestige in the town of West Kappell in the island of Walcherene (Netherlands). It was the painting of a ship and her captain who was represented at an advanced age, the forepart of his head bald and his face tanned by the sun. He was worshipped as a deity at a temple in the same town and sacrifices according to the Phoenician rites were offered to him. There were many other heroes of this name but no writer has decided whether to Magusanus or one of his descendants, or whether to a Phoenician distinguished by the same appellation, are we to attribute the navigation of the Atlantic. Certain, however it is, that Diodorus speaks of a Hercules who sailed round the world and founded the city of Lecta in Septimania.* **(xxxi)**

(xxxi) Cabrera, Paul Felix *Teatro Ritico Americano*

Author of the book *Gateway to Atlantis,* Andrew Collins states that he was astounded when he read Calmet's reference to Hercules and his 'round the world' voyage:

> *What Cabrera is here implying is that Hercules circumnavigated the world and on that journey founded 'the city of Lecta in a place called Septimania'. In the knowledge that Hercules was considered by certain classical writers to have sailed to the islands of Hesperides, which I identify with the Greater Antilles, I wondered whether Septimania might have been synonymous with one of these islands. The name itself seemed important, for in Latin septi means seven or a seven-fold division, while mania has echoes of manes or manium, meaning 'ghosts', 'shades of the dead', 'the lower world' or 'bodily remains'. It is from this same Latin root that we derive the English word 'mania', as in madness. Thus Septimania might be translated as meaning the seven-fold place of ghosts or shades of the dead.*

I agree with Collins' translation of *septimania* as meaning 'seven-fold place of ghosts' or 'shades of the dead'. However, I hasten to add that the Phoenicians' reference to Hercules and his 'round the world' voyage may have been inspired by Odysseus' account of his voyages to the Phaeacians. I tend to identify Septimania's 'seven-fold place of ghosts' or 'shades of the dead' with Peru (the Land of the Cimmerians) for it was there that Odysseus entered 'Hades' and consulted with the 'ghosts of the dead'.

Magellan's Voyage A.D. 1520

Situated at the mouth of the Guadalquivir River, the Spanish port of Sanlucar de Barrameda lies opposite the legendary city of Gades. Christopher Columbus' ship, the *Santa Maria,* began its epic voyage to the Americas from Sanlucar and twenty-seven years later, the first historically recognized ship to circumnavigate the world set sail from these very same docks. Named *Victoria*, the ship was one of five under the command of the Portuguese explorer Ferdinand Magellan. Manned by a multi-national crew of Spanish, Portuguese, Italian, French, English and German sailors, Magellan's fleet departed Sanlucar on August 10th, 1519. Of the 265 crewmen who began the journey, a mere eighteen men survived to complete the circumnavigation. Magellan himself was mortally wounded in the Philippines on April 27th, 1521 (his 42nd birthday). Perhaps the most remarkable feat of Magellan's voyage was his ability to navigate his way into the Pacific Ocean by way of the slender strait that bears his name. Magellan appears to have had prior knowledge that there were two ways of crossing between the Atlantic and Pacific Oceans. One was to slowly edge through a very narrow strait; the other was to risk the treacherous waters of the Horn. From the chronicles of one of the crew, Italian Antonio Pigafetta, we read:

If we had not found this strait, the captain-general had decided to go as far as seventy-five degrees towards the Antarctic Pole.

Author Gavin Menzies elaborates upon why Magellan chose the first option and persisted on for 27 days and over 373 miles through such a narrow passage:

The fact that they were 'setting course to the fifty-second degree' indicates that Magellan knew that at 52 degrees he would find the strait that was later to bear his name, linking the Atlantic with the Pacific. His fleet reached the dark and forbidding region on October 19, 1520. By that stage, Magellan and his crew were in a wretched state. Howling gales battered the ships and blizzards obscured both the passage ahead and the rocky islands surrounding them. He had problems finding an anchorage, many of his sailors were dying of scurvy, and he had succeeded in quelling a mutiny only by the brutal expedient of hanging or drawing and quartering the leaders. Now mutiny was again in the air. ***'This strait was a circular place surrounded by mountains...'*** *and to most of those in the ships it seemed there was no way out from it to enter the said Pacific sea.*

> *Magellan could not persuade his men that it was safe to go onward through the strait, so he ordered his critics to put their reasons in writing for either continuing or returning to Spain. He read their opinions aloud, then, taking a sacred oath on Saint James, whose insignia he wore upon his cloak, he solemnly swore to his men that* ***'there was another Strait which led out [to the Pacific] saying that he knew it well and had seen it in a marine chart of the King of Portugal, which a great pilot and sailor named Martin of Bohemia [Martin Behain] had made'.***
>
> *Magellan was telling the truth, though not the whole truth. The existence of the strait leading from the Atlantic to the Pacific was well known both to the King of Spain and Magellan before he set sail. He took with him on the voyage a marine chart that showed the strait and the Pacific Ocean beyond it. The contract he had signed with the king specified the aims and terms of the voyage – to set sail westwards for the Spice Islands and a share of the profits each was to enjoy. Magellan wanted knowledge of this strait to be restricted to himself alone so as to prevent others from following in his wake and claiming a share of the riches of those lands. But the King of Spain was in no position to grant Magellan's request, for the Portuguese held the master chart.* **(xxxii)**

According to Gavin Menzies, a fleet of Chinese junks had previously mapped the waters of South America and somehow the kings of Portugal and Spain had acquired a copy of this map. Magellan certainly had prior knowledge of the straits but a more feasible explanation would be that the inhabitants of southern Spain and Portugal had inherited their maps and sea knowledge from their 'forefathers', the Phaeacians. When Odysseus had addressed the court of King Alcinous, he described in detail the various aspects of his remarkable voyage, including his difficult passage through the 'straits' of Scylla and Charybidis. It is an odd coincidence that Columbus and Magellan should have launched their voyages from the Spanish port of Sanlucar de Barrameda for, as we now know, Sanlucar lies in very close proximity to where the legendary port of Tartessos is thought to have existed. Did the Phaeacians originally inhabit Tartessus? Magellan definitely knew of South America's Tierra del Fuego region. Someone had previously mapped those forbidding waters. If it was not the Chinese or an earlier Portuguese expedition, then Odysseus remains the most likely source.

(xxxii) Menzies, Gavin *1421 - The Year China Discovered the World* Bantam Books, London

Odysseus Departs Scheria and Returns to Ithaca

Thus Odysseus related the long tale of his adventures and the audience was enthralled by the charm of his story. Presently Alcinous began to speak, "Odysseus," said he, "now that you have reached my house I doubt not you will get home without further misadventure no matter how much you have suffered in the past. To you others, however, who come here night after night to drink my choicest wine and listen to my bard, I would insist as follows. Our guest has already packed up the clothes, wrought gold and other valuables that you have brought for his acceptance; let us now present him further with a large tripod and a cauldron." Everyone approved of this and then they went home to bed in their own abodes. When the child of morning, rosy-fingered Dawn appeared, they hurried down to the ship.

That night the Phaecians sacrificed a bull in honour of Zeus and feasted yet again. After they had made drink-offerings to the blessed gods that live in heaven, Odysseus offered a toast to Queen Arête:

"Farewell, queen," said he, "henceforward and forever, till age and death, the common lot of mankind, lay their hands upon you. I now take my leave; be happy in this house with your children, your people and with king Alcinous."

As he spoke he crossed the threshold and Alcinous sent a man to conduct him to the seashore and his ship. Arête also sent some maidservants with him - one with a clean shirt and cloak, another to carry his strongbox and a third with corn and wine. When they got to the waterside the crew took these things and put them on board, with all the meat and drink. For Odysseus, they spread a rug and a linen sheet on deck that he might sleep soundly in the stern of the ship. Then he too went on board and lay down without a word.

The crew took every man his place and loosed the hawser from the pierced stone to which it had been bound. Thereon, when they began rowing out to sea, Odysseus fell into a deep, sweet and almost deathlike slumber. The ship bounded forward the way a four-in-hand chariot flies over the course when the horses feel the whip. Her prow curved as if it were the neck of a stallion and a great wave of dark blue water seethed in her wake. She held steadily on her course and even a falcon, swiftest of all birds, could not have kept pace with her.

> ***Thus, she cut her way through the water, carrying one who was as cunning as the gods but was now sleeping peacefully, forgetful of all that he had suffered both on the field of battle and by the waves of the weary sea.* (Note 53)**

Homer's reference to the prow of a Phaeacian ship being ***'curved as it were the neck of a stallion'*** may be yet another indication that the Phaeacian kingdom lay somewhere in the vicinity of ancient Spain. Writing in the 5th century B.C., Herodotus reports in his *Histories* that the mariners of southern Spain had the head of a horse carved upon the prows of their ships.

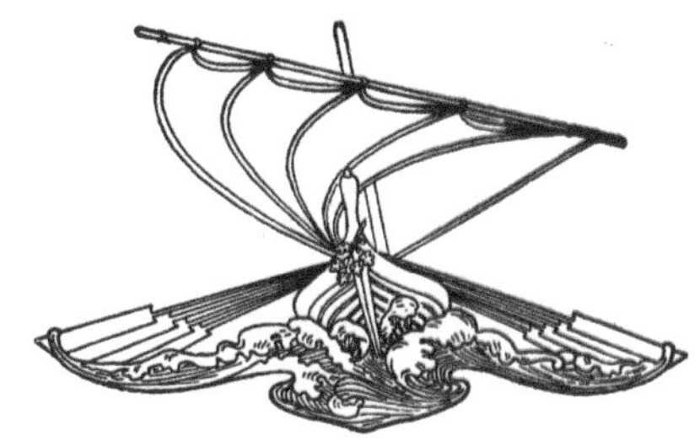

Chapter 12

ISLE OF ITHACA
(The Aegean)

Soundly asleep aboard a sleek Phaeacian ship, Odysseus was swiftly transported over the sea to his island home of Ithaca.

> ***When the bright star that heralds the approach of dawn began to show, the ship drew near to land. Now there is in Ithaca a haven of the old merman Phorcys, which lies between two points that break the line of the sea and shut the harbour in. These shelter it from the storms of wind and sea that rage outside, so that, when once within it, a ship may lie without being even moored. At the head of this harbour there is a large olive tree and at no great distance, a fine overarching cavern sacred to the nymphs who are called Naiads.***

Not wishing to disturb Odysseus' deep slumber, the Phaeacians carried their passenger ashore and laid him gently on the sand. Beside his sleeping body they placed the gifts that had been presented to him by King Alcinous and Queen Arête.

Nearby was a sea-cavern that had:

> ***... two entrances, one facing North by which mortals can go down into the cave, while the other Southern one is more mysterious; mortals cannot possibly get in by it, it is the way taken by the gods.***

Located at the foot of Mount Neritin, the sea-cave was said to be the abode of Phorcys, a primeval merman who had been venerated on the island of Ithaca from time immemorial.

Homer's description of Phorcys' sacred cavern serves to remind us that Odysseus' long odyssey began within a similar sea-cave. We may recall that during his time in Egypt, a stranded Odysseus had sought the advice of the seal-god Proteus. The seal-god had prophesied that Odysseus would eventually gain the treasures he so eagerly sought, but would first have to pay homage to all the gods that inhabited the world's ancient realms. It is most significant that Odysseus should once again find himself within the precincts of a sacred, coastal cave.

Phorcys (Phorcus)

A member of the ancient Titan pantheon, Phorcys the Intrepid was a son of the sea-god Pontus and the earth-goddess Gaea. Wedded to his sister Ceto, Phorcys sired unusual offspring including the three snake-haired mermaids called Gorgons and their sisters the Granae ('old ones') who were born into the world with white hair.

In other writings, Homer refers to Phorcys as ***'the old merman who rules the waves'***. He also wrote that Phorcys had a nymph/naiad daughter named Thoosh who wed Poseidon and gave birth to the monstrous Cyclops, Polyphemus. According to Homer, old Phorcys was the father-in-law of Poseidon and therefore grandfather to the same Cyclops that Odysseus had blinded during the earlier stages of his odyssey.

On learning that the Phaeacians had delivered Odysseus safely back to Ithaca, Poseidon became enraged and stormed off to visit his brother Zeus. Standing obdurately before the Olympic pantheon, Poseidon demanded that at a time best suited to him, he should be allowed to punish the arrogant Phaeacians. The assembly of Gods unanimously agreed with Poseidon who then swore a bitter oath that he would destroy the Phaeacian kingdom by sinking it beneath the waves.

There may be another reason for Poseidon's unrelenting animosity towards Odysseus. With the completion of his long voyages, Odysseus had achieved the first circumnavigation of the world. The '***limitless and immeasurable deep***' had been unofficially encircled and 'chartered'. As a consequence, Poseidon's power was now somewhat diminished. His daunting and seemingly 'limitless' ocean realms would never again be quite so mysterious and forbidding.

Phorcys' Sea Cave

Upon awaking, Odysseus was disoriented and did not at first recognise his native island. It was not until the goddess Athena appeared and informed him that his journey was complete did he realise that he was indeed, finally home. The ***'goddess of wisdom'*** then led Odysseus to a deep recess within Phorcys' Cave and there he stored the treasures bestowed by the Phaeacian nobles. The custom of depositing offerings at sacred sanctuaries such as caves and grottos was widespread in the ancient Greek world.

In the year A.D. 1932, a British archaeologist working in a shrine-cave on Ithaca's Polis Bay found the fragments of an ancient three-legged cauldron of the type in use during Odysseus' time. Although this tripod shaped vessel cannot be proven to be the very same one Odysseus had secreted, its discovery does provide us with an example of the sort of offerings that were deposited within such caves.

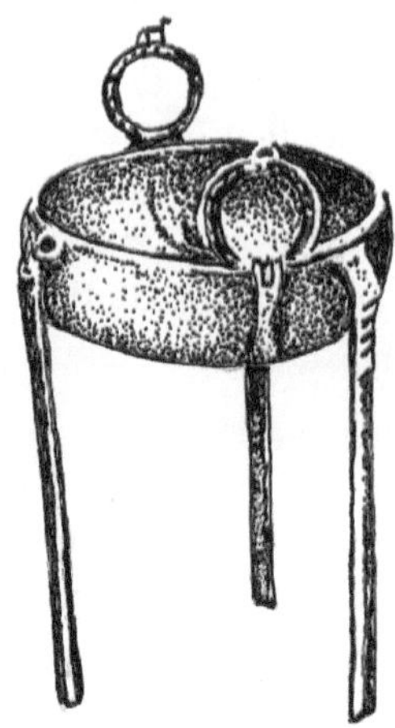

Artist's impression of the three-legged cauldron found near Polis Bay

Island of Kefalonia

No remnant of Odysseus' palatial home on the island of Ithaca has as yet been unearthed and this has led some scholars to dispute that such a grandiose residence ever existed. The general consensus of opinion among today's researchers is that Odysseus' stately residence was more likely to be located on the neighbouring island of Kefalonia. **(Note 54)**

In A.D. 1991, Greek archaeologists working on Kefalonia discovered a large tomb in the hills outside Poros. Housing at least 72 persons within its stone niches, the tomb, which dates to 1300 B.C., is the largest of its type yet found in northeast Greece. Excavation of the site revealed gold jewellry and seals incised onto precious stones that indicate the tomb was used to bury kings, or at least citizens of high rank. Included among the hoard of jewels was a gold broach that matches the exact description of one worn by Odysseus. In Book X1X of *The Odyssey*, Homer tells us that

Odysseus' mantle was fastened with a gold broach, displaying '***a dog holding a spotted fawn between his forepaws and watching it as it lay panting upon the ground'***. **(Note 55)**

Greek archaeologists have also discovered sections of ancient walls that extend up into the hills well beyond Poros. These walls encompass both the village and a steep adjoining hill, connoting that the site once served as an acropolis (hilltop fortress).

Melissani Sea Cave

Homer's description of cave-dwelling nymphs who '***weave their robes of sea purple, very curious to see'*** has certain affinities with Kefalonia's famous Melissani sea-cave. When the sun's rays shine directly down through its rooftop opening, they highlight the lapping waters of the interior, creating a myriad of purple-blue hues. Homer's account of a sacred sea-cavern having dual entranceways correlates with the Melissani cave in that it also has two entrances; one an opening in its vertex and the second, a subterranean water channel.

> ***There are mixing bowls within it and wine-jars of stone and beehives there.***

The reference Homer makes to bees living in Phorcys' sea-cave again finds resonance with the Melissani cave as its name, *melissani,* means honey-gatherer or honeybee.

Rising to 1630 metres, Kefalonia's Mount Ainos (Enos) is the tallest peak in the Ionian mountain chain. During Mycenaean times, the uppermost regions of this rugged mountain were dedicated to Zeus. Although Homer states that Odysseus concealed his Phaeacian treasures at the foot of Ithaca's Mount Neritum, we should note that Kefalonia's Mount Ainos would have been a more suitable place for Zeus to witness the concluding chapter of Odysseus' ordeal. **(Note 54)**

The Pig Herder

Having sealed the entrance to the mysterious sea-cave with a large boulder, Athena and Odysseus sat themselves down beneath a sacred olive tree. The goddess of wisdom then devised a plan so that Odysseus might take revenge on the suitors who had taken up residence in his palace.

She firstly advised Odysseus to avoid his palatial home for the time being and instead make his way to the hut of a humble pig-herder named Eumaeus. Transfigured by Athena into the guise of a lowly ragged beggar, Odysseus follows a path to the far side of the island. In the meantime, Athena (who is now playing a pivotal role in the unfolding events) subtly persuades Odysseus' son, Telemachus, to also pay a visit to the pig-herder's hut.

An Oxford University poet-laureate and august translator of the Ancient Classics, Robert Graves informs us that Phorcys' name pertains to the Latin word *porcus* (pig). In their respective books, *The White Goddess* and *The Mythic Image*, Robert Graves and Joseph Campbell investigated the widespread pig symbology evidenced in World mythologies. According to their writings, both primitive and advanced cultures attached great importance to the pig. From as far north as the Orkney Islands (*ork* is the Irish word for pig) and extending to Ireland, Greece, Egypt, and even to the Oceanic Islands of the Pacific, pig rituals were enacted and these ceremonies were usually associated with the mysteries of the Underworld.

In his disguise, Odysseus is unrecognised by the pig-herder Eumaeus, who was one time faithful servant during Odysseus' childhood. Odysseus tells him that he is an old Cretan sea-trader down on his luck. The pig-herder takes pity on the ragged beggar and invites him to spend the night. The next day, Odysseus' son Telemachus visits the pig-herder's hut as bidden by Athena. At first Telemachus does not recognize his father and so Athena transforms Odysseus back into his true form. The startled Telemachus throws his arms around his father's neck and they both break down and weep. When they regain their composure, Odysseus takes counsel with his beloved son and presents his plan for revenge.

> ***Now therefore return home early tomorrow morning and go about among the suitors as before. Later on the swineherd will bring me to the city disguised as a miserable old beggar. If you see them ill treating me, steel your heart against my sufferings. Even though they drag me feet foremost out of the house, or throw things at me, look on and do nothing beyond gently trying to make them behave reasonably. However, they will not listen to you, for the day of their reckoning is at hand.***

With the exception of a sword and spear for their own personal use, Odysseus advises his son to conceal all the armories that are in his house. He also reminds Telemachus not to let anyone know that he has returned home, neither his grandfather nor any of the servants, not even Penelope herself.

The Beggar in the Palace

Despite an altercation with a fellow beggar who had been blocking the entranceway, Odysseus finally entered his palatial home. Penelope did not recognize her disguised husband and after a short conversation with him, assigned her faithful maid, Eurycleia, the task of washing his feet. As she was bathing what she thought were the feet of a beggar, the aged Eurycleia noticed a distinctive scar above Odysseus' knee and instantly discerned her master's presence. In his youth, a savage boar had suddenly confronted Odysseus during a hunting expedition on Mount Parnassus. He managed to kill the beast with his spear but not before the boar had ***'ripped him above the knee with a gash that tore deep, though it did not reach the bone.'*** The memory of that pig's goring signaled a warning to Odysseus that a similarly ferocious and cunning foe was residing in his palace.

Taking advantage of Odysseus' protracted absence the princes from neighbouring precincts had thoroughly entrenched themselves in his palace. Whenever the occasion suited they would gorge themselves like pigs at Odysseus' once-noble table. In their ardent desire to usurp both Odysseus' home and his virtuous wife, the princes constantly badgered Penelope with insinuations that her husband was either long-dead or else had no intention of ever returning to her.

In regal response, Penelope informed the suitors that their marriage proposals would not be considered until she had completed a large and complex tapestry. Endeavoring to forestall such a loathsome prospect, Penelope spent the long hours of night unraveling the threads she had woven during the day. Over the many years of her husband's absence Penelope had remained faithful and resolute in maintaining the large household. Despite her efforts, the wealth of her estranged husband's estates was all but exhausted.

Overwhelmed with grief and the understanding that Odysseus was now unlikely to return to her, Penelope sorrowfully resigned herself to the fact that she would eventually have to choose one of the princes. Amid the tears of her dilemma, Penelope witnessed an apparition of Athena. The goddess instructed her to firstly fetch Odysseus' Great Bow from its storage chamber and present it to the suitors saying, ***'whosoever is able to string the mighty Bow, draw it and release an arrow to its target, would be a worthy husband'***.

Penelope fetches Odysseus' bow

Athena concluded her discourse with the advice that the appropriate time for this archery contest would be the feast day of the archer-god, Apollo.

In his trilogy *The Masks of God - Occidental Mythology*, Professor Joseph Campbell comments on the lunar-solar aspects of this episode:

> *Odysseus returned to Ithaca 'just at the rising of that brightest star which heralds the light of the Daughter of Dawn'. He rejoined his wife 'on the twentieth year'; i.e., as soon as the nineteenth was complete. He came at the new moon, on the day which the Athenians called 'Old-and-New'; when one month is waning and the next rising up. But this new moon was also the day of the Apollo Feast, or Solstice Festival of the Sun, and the time was winter.*

The Great Bow

Odysseus quietly entered the great hall of his palace dressed as a vagabond. Humble rags covered broad shoulders that had once been draped in a royal cloak. His humble presence occasioned loud outbursts of derision from the suitors who were attempting to string his Great Bow. Having curbed his anger at their insolence, the wily Odysseus invited further ridicule by requesting that he might try his arm at stringing the bow. Accepting the Great Bow from Eumaeus the swine-herder, Odysseus twisted it this way and that, testing for signs of worm infestation and then:

> ***... as easily as a musician who knows his lyre, Odysseus strings the Great Bow without effort or haste.***

Reunited with his trusty bow, Odysseus turned slowly to face a long trench within which twelve battle-axes had been placed in a single row. As if to mark the significance of the moment, there came a bellowing thunderclap sent from Zeus. Odysseus then picked up an arrow that had being lying on a table beside him:

> ***... and he laid it on the centrepiece of the bow and drew the notch of the arrow and the string toward him, still seated on his stool. When he had taken aim he let fly and his arrow pierced every one of the handle-holds of the axes from the first onwards till it had gone right through them and out into the courtyard.***

The release of the arrow through the rings of the twelve, sacred battle axes marked the mystical culmination of Odysseus' epic voyage.

When Odysseus first began his long odyssey, the Egyptian seal-god Proteus had warned him that he:

> ***... could not return to his homeland until he had offered holy hecatombs to the immortal gods that reign in Hades.***

Odysseus had indeed offered hecatombs to the immortal gods of Hades. Over the course of his 'round the world' voyage, Odysseus also passed through the realms of all the immortal gods. This is symbolically demonstrated when he fires an arrow through the rings of twelve sacred axes. The twelve axes represent the twelve *'Immortal Gods'* of the Greek Pantheon, otherwise known as the Zodiac (Greek: 'circle of animals'). **(Note 56)**

The Cosmic Archer

The mythological origin of the Cosmic Archer can be traced back to Paleolithic times when man had little choice but to hunt for his food. Having patiently stalked a herd of wild animals, the hunter had only one chance to make his kill. The slightest sound or change of wind direction could cause the herd to stampede. It was a tense and risky business. If the hunter misfired then his entire tribe would go hungry. Naturally, a tribe's most successful hunters would have been held in high regard while some may have achieved a legendary status. Neolithic tales of heroic feats were originally related around campfires and handed down over the ages. The ancient Mesopotamians later inscribed these stories onto clay tablets, thus we have knowledge of primeval hunters such as Adapa, Gilgamesh and the vengeful Ninurta whose Greek equivalent was Orion the Giant. **(Note 57)**

Ninurta slays his enemies

The Aryan Legacy

Robert Graves suggests that Odysseus' Achaean ancestors had entered Greece c.1900 B.C. According to Graves, these fierce 'warrior-farmers' were a branch of Indo-Europeans who revered a male trinity of gods. The trinity was akin to the ancient Hindu deities: Mitra, Varuna and Indra who respectively correspond to the Classical Greek gods: Apollo, Cronos and Hades. Another branch of the Indo-European family is theorised to have migrated onto the Indian subcontinent c.1700 - 1300 B.C. A subject of continual debate, this massive migration into the northeast of India is arguably referred to as 'the Aryan Invasion'.

Rudra/Siva: The Vengeful Beggar-God

It is thought that the Aryans introduced into India a set of scriptures called the Vedas. One of the most important of the Vedic gods was Rudra the Divine Archer. Known as 'the roaring one', God of Storms and the Lord of Time and Death, Rudra had to be implored to refrain from inadvertently slaying or injuring anyone during an uncontrollable wrath. The mythic attributes of Rudra were eventually integrated with those of Siva, a Hindu god sacred to the Dravidians who were the original inhabitants of the Indian subcontinent. To this day, Siva is honoured as an ascetic beggar; his imagery brings to mind Homer's description of 'Odysseus in rags'. Acknowledged as Lord of the Universe and Begetter of all Creation, Siva is both instigator and terminator of mankind's progressive cycles.

The vengeance of Odysseus

Having delivered his 'cosmic arrow', Odysseus immediately stood up to confront the astonished suitors. Discarding his beggar's guise he sprang forthwith up onto the threshold. Clutching a quiver laden with ***'winged'*** arrows he looked down upon the suitors and thundered:

> ***"Dogs, did you think that I would not come back from Troy? You have wasted my substance, have forced my women servants to lie with you and have wooed my wife while I was still living. You have feared neither God nor man and now you shall die."***

In unabated rage Odysseus then commenced to slaughter the suitors. E.V. Rieu's translation of *The Odyssey* vividly describes the fury of Odysseus' wrath:

> ***They lay in heaps in the blood and dust, like fish that the fishermen have dragged out of the grey surf to lie in masses on the sand gasping for the salt seawater till the bright sun ends their lives.***
>
> ***She (his old nursemaid) found Odysseus among the corpses of the fallen, spattered with blood and filth like a lion when he comes from feeding and with the blood dripping from his breast and jaws on either side, a fearsome spectacle. That was how Odysseus looked with the gore thick on his legs and arms.***

Homer's gruesome description of bloody revenge may have been based upon legendary accounts of the terrible bloodletting that occurred during the period of the Dorian invasions. It might also be noted that at about this same period in history, c.1225 - 1125 B.C., one or more enormous earthquakes struck the Mediterranean region. The extreme violence of these quakes was intense enough to decimate many of the eastern Mediterranean's largest citadels, including: Mycenae; Hattusas, the Hittite capital and Jericho, the world's oldest city.

'*... the walls of Jericho came tumbling down'*. (Joshua 5:1)

Mycenaean Migrations

The ancient peoples did not regard these devastating catastrophes as geological events but instead interpreted them as manifestations of their gods' displeasure. The upheaval and movement of nations at this time in history was of an unprecedented magnitude. **(Note 58)**

Dorian hordes streamed down from the north into Greece, their iron weapons quite literally shattering the bronze-made armaments of the Mycenaeans. With invincible force, the Dorians crushed and enslaved the 'faithless' Mycenaeans, condemning them to a period of cultural darkness that lasted some six hundred years. Because the Dorians were lacking in both naval fleets and seamanship, many of the once-proud Mycenaeans were able to escape to the nearby islands of Crete, Rhodes and Cyprus. In less than twenty-five years, two-thirds of the Mycenaean population had sought refuge abroad.

Ionian Refuge

The majority of the Mycenaeans who fled the Greek mainland made their way to the Ionian coast of western Turkey. The Anatolian cities of Miletus and Ephesus had long been the domain of the 'mother-goddess' Cybele. In her role as the protective mother-goddess, Cybele conferred sanctuary to the Ionian, Achaean, Car and Aeolian tribes of the formerly all-powerful Mycenaean Empire. In light of these tumultuous times, it is doubtful that the now reunited Odysseus and Penelope would have remained in Dorian-dominated Greece. If they, like so many of their compatriots, had sought refuge in the Anatolian city of Miletus, then Odysseus would certainly have had the opportunity to inform its citizens about a distant and opulent port city he had once visited on the Atlantic seaboard (Scheria/southern Spain). Although this is highly conjectural, it might give explanation to Irish Chronicles that record the arrival of a seafaring race called the Milesians. Having set out from Anatolia, the Milesians are reported to have migrated to Ireland via Crete, North Africa and Spain, c.900 B.C. **(Note 59)**

The Philistines

Various other seafaring tribes of the currently defunct Mycenaean Empire sought sanctuary along the Ancient Near East's biblical shores of Canaan. Phoenician harbours such as those at Sidon and Tyre made it possible for them to recoup and resume their lucrative trading ventures.

Called Philistines by the Hebrews, these fierce Mycenaean migrants quickly became renowned not only for their military prowess, but also for their architectural and metalworking skills. The mastery of the art of metallurgy is clearly illustrated in the biblical account of young King David's slaying of the Philistine giant, Goliath. The fearsome Goliath is described as being attired in:

> *... a helmet of bronze and a breastplate of mail ... graves of bronze on his legs and also a shield of bronze.*

The ancient Israelites claimed that the Mycenaeans/Philistines were ungodly because they did not practice the rite of circumcision. However, Achaeans such as Odysseus may well have been treated as exceptions. It was previously noted (see Introduction) that Egyptian scribes at the time of the Sea Peoples' invasions of the Nile Delta, c.1221 – 1187 B.C., had recorded how the captured Achaeans were unique among the Aegean sea-peoples in that they were circumcised.

Solomon

The biblical King David fought numerous battles against the well-armoured Philistines but it was not until his son Solomon became ruler that a relative peace was established. The ever-wise Solomon employed the Philistines as mercenaries and one might suppose that circumcised Achaeans, such as Odysseus, were perhaps accepted as being members of a 'lost branch' of the Hebrew tribes.

The Bible also recounts that sometime during the period 960 - 930 B.C., the astute King Solomon formed a maritime alliance with King Hiram of Phoenicia. Together these two kings assembled a mighty fleet of ships that sailed westwards from the Red Sea to the land of Tarshish and also eastwards to the mythical land of Ophir.

Tarshish

Jeremiah 10:9
Silver spread into plates is brought from Tarsish and gold from Uphaz, the work of the workman, and of the hands of the founder: blue and purple is their clothing: they are all the work of cunning men.

Book of Kings 10:22
The king had a fleet of ships from Tarshish at sea along with the ships of Hiram. Once every three years it returned carrying gold, silver and ivory, and apes and baboons.

Ophir

Book of Kings 8: 26-28
And King Solomon made a navy of ships in Ezion-geber, which is beside Eloth, on the shore of the Red Sea. And Hiram sent in the navy his servants and shipmen that had knowledge of the sea, with the servants of Solomon, and they came to Ophir and fetched from thence gold, four hundred and twenty talents (around 700 kilos).

In *Chronicles 2* it is said that the round voyage to Ophir took three years to complete so Ophir obviously lay a great distance from the shores of the Red Sea. The Jewish historian, Josephus, understood Ophir to be in the vicinity of India, while other historians have located it further eastward. A jungle mountain in Malaya was once called Ophir and another Mount Ophir can be found in the Pasemah highlands of Sumatra. In present-day times, these two regions both support profitable gold mines and so might qualify as being possible 'Ophirs'.

Despite claims that Ophir refers to either India or S.E. Asia, the late American archaeologist and adventurer Gene Savoy remained adamant that Ophir was synonymous with Peru. According to Savoy's research, the etymology of the words, *o-phir* and *pir-u*, is 'land of fire'. During a 1966 expedition to Peru's Utcubamba Valley, Savoy came across a cliff face displaying two extraordinary petroglyphs. He recognized the smaller marking as synonymous with the Babylonian hieroglyph for 'ship'. The second glyph also indicated a sea-going ship, one that had a high vertical prow and a marking of the Egyptian hieroglyphic sign for 'God', which read *ni-ther* ('he of the tree'). Savoy claimed that an identical ancient pictograph is incised upon a rock in Israel.

Shortly after Savoy discovered the enigmatic glyph in Peru, archaeologists working at the ancient port site of Tel Qasile in Israel unearthed a pottery shard that bears this message in Phoenician-Hebrew:

Gold of Ophir, the possession of Beth-Horon, thirty shekels

The inscription, which dates to the time of Solomon, had apparently denoted a cache of gold that was stored in the hold of a Phoenician merchant ship.

Ancient 'Glyph of Ophir' found in both Israel and Peru

In 1986 Gene Savoy located and named the Chacapapoya ruins of Gran Vilaya. In a nearby cave he found three engraved stone tablets, each of which weighed several tons and measured about 6 x 10 feet or 2 x 3 metres. Savoy identified the engraved script as ancient Phoenician-Hebrew and presented the following interpretation:

We have sailed across the big ocean and then travelled up this huge river (the Amazon) and we then traded for gold with these people and are going back to our home now.

According to Savoy, King Solomon's gold-seeking expeditions had made their way to the highlands of Peru via the upper reaches of the Amazon River. To this day, Brazilians continue to refer to this particular stretch of the Amazon as the Solimões River. If Savoy's hypothesis proves to be correct, then perhaps it is also possible that King Solomon and King Hiram's Phoenician sailors had deciphered the allegorical content of Odysseus' sea voyages and consequently employed this information when setting sail for South America.

Odysseus and Penelope/Helen - Their Final Years

The eventual fates of Odysseus and Penelope/Helen remain a mystery. The various authors who lived in the centuries prior to Christ have left us with a plethora of conflicting versions. The validity of those various reports is questionable and Homer's somewhat cryptic commentary of events is the most widely accepted.

Odysseus and Penelope reunited

Homer's Version

According to Homer, the blind seer, Tiresias, had accurately predicted Odysseus' eventual fate:

> ***"When you get home you will take your revenge on these suitors. After you have killed them by force or fraud in your own house, you must take a well-made oar and carry it on and on until you come to a country where the people have never heard the sea and do not even mix salt with their food; nor do they know anything about ships and oars that are as wings of a ship. I will give you this certain token that cannot escape your notice. A wayfarer will meet you and say it must be a winnowing shovel that you have got upon your shoulder; on hearing this you must fix the oar in the ground and sacrifice a ram, a bull and a boar to Poseidon. Then go home and offer hecatombs to all the gods in heaven one after the other."***

Tiresias' prediction that Odysseus would eventually return home and take his revenge upon the suitors is straightforward. The prophecy foretelling how Odysseus would carry an oar upon his shoulder and later imbed it into the earth is rather more puzzling. The final words of Tiresias' augury were:

> ***"As for yourself, death shall come to you from the sea and your life shall ebb away very gently when you are full of years and in peace of mind and your people shall bless you. All that I have said will come true."*** **(Note 60)**

The Telegony

The Telegony is a now 'lost' ancient Greek tale that was one of the 'Epic Cycles' forming the *'Trojan Cycle'*. The story of *The Telegony* comes chronologically after that of *The Odyssey*, and is the final episode in the said 'Epic Cycle'. The date of *The Telegony's* authorship is uncertain. Kyrene, the native city of Eugamon (the purported author), was founded in 631 B.C. but the story may have been in existence prior to Eugamon's rendition.

The Telegony comprises two distinct episodes: Odysseus' voyage to Thresprotia and the story of Telegonos. In the current critical editions only two lines of the poem's original text survive. For its storyline we are almost entirely dependant on the summarised 'cyclic epics' contained in the *Chrestomatheia*, which has been attributed to the 5th century A.D. philosopher, Proclus Diadochos. A scant few other references also give indications as to the poem's narrative.

The Telegony opens in the period following Odysseus' return home to Ithaca. Penelope's dead suitors are buried and Odysseus has decided to make a voyage to Elis. On arrival, he meets a mysterious figure called Polyxenos who entertains him and gifts a special mixing bowl depicting the story of Trophonios. Odysseus returns to Ithaca and then sails on to Threspotia (the westerly Greek mainland). There, Odysseus reputedly has an affair with the Thesprotian queen, Callidike, who bears him a son called Polypoites. Odysseus fights for the Thesprotians in a war against the neighboring Brygoi in which the gods also participate. His paramour Callidike is killed during the battle and Odysseus subsequently returns to Ithaca. **(Note 61)**

Meanwhile, it transpires that Circe of Aeaea, whom Odysseus previously partnered, had bore him a son named Telegonos (meaning born far away). On the goddess Athena's advice, Circe tells Telegonos that he is the son of Odysseus. Before sending him off in search of his father, Circe presents Telegonos with a remarkable spear for his self-protection. Forged by the smith-god Hephaestus, the spear is tipped with the poisonous barb of a stingray. As fate would have it, a storm forces Telegonos onto the island of Ithaca. Not realizing that he has landed on his father's home isle, Telegonos unwittingly begins to steal Odysseus' cattle. When Odysseus comes to defend his property, he and Telegonus fight. Telegonus kills Odysseus with his unusual spear, thereby fulfilling Teiresias' prophecy that death would come to Odysseus from 'out of the sea' (the poisonous stingray barb). As Odysseus lies there dying, he and Telegonos at last recognize one another and Telegonos bitterly laments his mistake. In the aftermath Telegonos escorts Penelope and her son Telemachus back to Aeaea where Circe bestows immortality upon both of them. Circe marries Telemachus and Telegonos weds Penelope.

A variant of this tale is found in Sophocles' *Odysseus Akanthoplex*. Having found out from an oracle that he is doomed to be killed by his son, Odysseus assumes that it is Telemachus and promptly exiles him to a neighboring island. When Telegonos arrives in Ithaca, he approaches Odysseus' palace but the sentries do not permit him entry and a commotion ensues. Odysseus, thinking Telemachus has returned, rushes into the fray.

In the midst of the skirmish, Telegonos kills Odysseus. According to Roman mythology, Telegonos became the founder of Tusculum, a city southeast of Rome. Sometimes he is also said to be the founder of Praeneste (modern Palestrina), a city in the same region.

Apollodorus

The ancient mythographer Apollodorus, not only reported the slaying of Odysseus by Telegonos but also wrote other versions, quite unrelated to Telegonos. According to Apollodorus' *Epitome* 7: 38 - 40, Penelope was unfaithful to Odysseus' during his long absence:

> *38: But some say that Penelope was seduced by Antinous and sent away by Odysseus to her father Icarius and that when she came to Mantinea in Arcadia she bore Pan to Hermes.*
>
> *39: However others say that she met her end at the hands of Odysseus himself, on account of Amphinomus who had allegedly seduced her.*
>
> *40: And there are some who say that Odysseus, being accused by the kinfolk of the slain suitors, submitted the case to the judgment of Neptolemus, king of the islands off Epirus. Neoptolemus, thinking to get possession of Cephallenia if Odysseus was put out of the way, condemned him to exile. Odysseus went on to Aetolia where he married the daughter of Thoas, and leaving a son, Leontophonus, whom he had by her, died in old age*

Plutarch

Plutarch's *Quaest Graec* concurs with Apollodorus' account of Odysseus' exile. According to Plutarch, the kinsmen of the slain suitors rose in revolt against Odysseus; but Neptolemus, having being invited by both parties to act as arbiter, sentenced Odysseus to banishment as punishment for the bloodshed he had occasioned. The sentence obliged Odysseus to withdraw not only from Ithaca, but also from Cephallenia and Zacyntrhus and in compliance, he retired to Italy. Nepolemus also condemned the friends and relatives of the suitors, ordering them to pay an annual compensation to Odysseus for the damage they had done to his property.

Summary

Homer related that Odysseus' death would ***'come from the sea'*** and it would be a gentle death occurring when Odysseus was ***'full of years'***. The writings of Apollodorus and Plutarch both accord with Homer so we might safely dismiss the violent death versions that are found in Eugamon's *Telegony* and Sophocles *Odysseus Akanthoplex*. The claim in *Telegony* that Penelope and her son Telemachus sailed to Aeaea whereupon Circe wed Telemachus and Penelope wed Telegonosis is clearly erroneous. Although it is quite possible that an aged Penelope returned to her father's home in Arkadia, reports that she '*bore Pan to Hermes*' during her time there are also specious. **(xxxii)**

The Greek writer Pausanias visited Arkadia in the 2nd century A.D. and in his *Description of Greece*, Book VIII, he makes mention of a local tradition which has Penelope spending her final years in that region:

> *On the right of the road is a high mound of earth. It is said to be the grave of Penelope, but the account of her in the poem called Thesprotis is not in agreement with the saying. For in it the poet says that when Odysseus returned from Troy he had a son Ptoliporthes by Penelope. But the Mantinean story about Penelope says that Odysseus convicted her of bringing paramours to his home and having been cast out by him, went away at first to Lacedaemon, but afterwards she removed from Sparta to Mantineia, where she died.*

Helen and Menelaus

The eventual fates of Helen and Menelaus are also in dispute. Pausanias' *Description of Greece*, Book XIX, presents two different endings for the pair:

> *The name of Therapne is derived from the daughter of Lelex and it is in the temple of Menelaus that Menelasus and Helen were buried. The account of the Rhodians is different. They say that when Menelaus was dead and Orestes still a wanderer, Helen was driven out by Nicostratus and Megapenthes and came to Rhodes where she had a friend in Polyxo. The wife of Tiepolemus, Polyxo they recount, was an Argive by*

(xxxii) Pseudo-Apollodorus, *Bibliotheca E7. 39.* Herodotus, *Histories 2* *descent and when she was married to Tiepolemus, shared his flight to Rhodes. At the time she was queen of the island and had been left with an orphaned boy. They say that Polyxo desired to avenge the death of Tiepolemus on Helen (now that she had her in her power). So she sent handmaidens dressed up as furies against her when she was bathing. They seized Helen and hanged her from a tree and on account of this, the Rhodians maintain a sanctuary called Helen of the Tree.*

APPENDIX

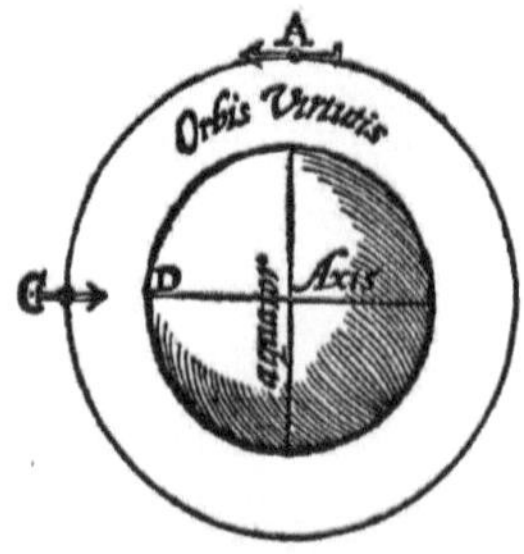

A Spherical Earth

Although it was evident to Odysseus that he had circumnavigated the world, he would have found it very difficult to describe such an incredible achievement to his fellow Greeks. The wise and learned men who attended the court of the Phaeacian King Alcinous (c.1130) may well have grasped the concept of a spherical Earth, but it was not until the 7th century B.C. that the first written theories were recorded.

Thales of Miletus (c. 625 - 546 B.C.)

Thales' writings are no longer in existence but there are good reasons to accept that he had envisaged the Earth as spherical. Scholars such as Aristotle (Cael. 297 b25-298 a8), Cicero (Rep. I.XIII.22) and Aëtius II.9-10; III.10; and III.10) all attributed Thales with knowledge of a spherical Earth.

Isaiah

Writing in the 6th century B.C, the biblical prophet Isaiah describes his God thus:

> *It is He who sits above the circle of the Earth, and its inhabitants are like grasshoppers.* Isaiah 40:22

When Isaiah wrote this verse he used the Hebrew word *khug* to describe the shape of the Earth. The common English translation of the word *khug* is circle, but a more literal translation would be 'sphere'.

Pythagoras (c.582 - 507 B.C.)

The first person in the western world to espouse the theory of a spherical Earth was the Greek mathematician and philosopher, Pythagoras. After completing the prerequisite rites for admission, Pythagoras enrolled into an Egyptian temple school at Diospolis. A dedicated student, he adopted many of the priestly traditions including a commitment to purity, the refusal to wear clothes made from animal skins and an adherance to secrecy. These precepts were later passed on to the students in his school of arcane knowledge. A master mathematician and a mystic, Pythagoras discovered that the pitch of a taut string varies exactly in inverse proportion to its length. He therefore taught that all things in Heaven and Earth are arranged in numerical proportion. The basic proportions of Plato's acoustical harmony are revealed in the architectural design of Greeks temples, and indeed these ratios may be found in all the sacred buildings of the ancient world.

Plato (427 - 347 B.C.)

Having studied Pythagorean mathematics in southern Italy, Plato returned to Athens and established his own school wherein he proclaimed that the Earth was a sphere. If man could soar high above the clouds wrote Plato, Earth would resemble *'a ball made of twelve pieces of leather, variegated, a patchwork of colours'*.

Aristotle (384 - 321 B.C.)

Born 43 years after Plato, Aristotle wrote the following account:

> *Again, our observations of the stars make it evident, not only that the Earth is circular, but that it is a circle of great size. For quite a small change of position to south or north causes a manifest alteration of the horizon. There is much change, (I mean, in the stars which are overhead), as one moves northward or southward. Indeed there are some stars seen in Egypt and in the neighborhood of Cyprus that are not seen in the northerly regions. Hence one should not be too sure of the incredibility of the view of those who conceive that there is continuity between the parts about the Pillars of Hercules and the parts about India, and that in this way the ocean is one.* **(xxxiii)**

(xxxiii) Aristotle, *On the Heavens* Book II Chapter 14

Aristotle offered three proofs that the Earth is a globe: (1) ships leaving port disappear over the horizon; (2) as one travels to the south, stars that are not visible in Greece appear above the southern horizon; and (3) during an eclipse, the Earth's shadow on the moon is visibly curved.

Aristarchus of Samos (310 - 230 B.C.)

Astronomer, mathematician and at one time, head of Alexandria's famed library, Aristarchus of Samos presented the first known heliocentric concept of our solar system. Aristarchus' concept was not well received by his contemporaries and incredibly, it was not until A.D. 1543 that Copernicus was able to revive and successfully introduce the theory of a heliocentric solar system.

Aristarchus of Samothrace (c.220 - 143 B.C.)

During the first millennium B.C., *The Odyssey* had undergone a series of rewritings. In an effort to correct the many discrepancies that were appearing in these revised editions, Aristarchus of Samothrace took it upon himself to rewrite the entire classic. As the elected head of Alexandria's esteemed library, Aristarchus was able to access the various versions of *The Odyssey* that had accumulated there over the centuries. These miscellaneous accounts of *The Odyssey*, along with 40,000 other invaluable manuscripts, were unfortunately destroyed when Julius Caesar ordered the burning of Alexandria's wharves in the year 47 B.C.

Eratosthenes (c.276 - 194 B.C.)

A successor to Aristarchus of Samos and a good friend of Archimedes, Eratostenes made several important contributions to the studies of mathematics, astronomy and geography. By measuring the sun's angle of elevation at noon in Alexandria, Eratostenes was able to calculate that the Earth's circumference was 250,000 stradia. Despite the fact that no-one knows whether Eratostenes' stradia equalled the length of a Roman, Greek or Egyptian stadia, he is neverless credited with being accurate to within 70 miles in his estimation of the Earth's circumference. Noted for having coined the word geography, Eratosthenes is also acknowledged for drawing a map of the entire world. His writings suggested that the seas of the Earth were connected, that Africa might be circumnavigated and that India could be reached by sailing westward from Spain.

Crates of Mallus (2nd Century B.C.)

Regarded to be one of the most important grammarians of the Classical Age, Crates of Mallus (nickname: *Homerikos*) was also a gifted geographer and it was in this capacity that he is acclaimed for constructing the first model of a terrestrial globe. Believed to be 10 feet (3 metres) in diameter, Crates' globe was put on display c.150 B.C. at Pergamum, an ancient town in Asia Minor. Determined to present a plausible account of Odysseus' wanderings, Crates had long engrossed himself in an extensive study of *The Odyssey* (c.169 B.C.). Crates' fervent endeavours to unravel the mysterious journeys of Odysseus were apparently successful, for shortly after he had completed his studies he proclaimed Homer to be the 'Father of Geography' and credited him with knowledge of a spherical Earth.

Reconstruction of Crates' globe 150 B.C.

Strabo (64 B.C. - A.D. 24)

The belief in a spherical Earth was current at the time of Christ:

However, we may show summarily that the Earth is spherical, from the consideration that all things however distant tend to its centre and that every body is attracted towards its centre of gravity. This is more distinctly proved from observations of the sea and sky, for here the evidence of the senses and common observation is alone requisite. The convexity of the sea is a further proof of this to those who have sailed; for they cannot perceive lights at a distance when placed at the same level as their eyes, but if raised on high, they at once become perceptible to vision, though at the same time further removed. So, when the eye is raised, it sees what before was utterly imperceptible. Homer speaks of this when he says: ***'Lifted up on the vast wave he quickly beheld afar...'*** *(The Odyssey,* Chapter V: 393). *Sailors, as they approach their destination behold the shore continually raising itself to their view; objects which had at first seemed low, begin to elevate themselves. Our gnomons also, are among other things, evidence of the revolution of the heavenly bodies and common sense at once shows us, that if the depth of the Earth were infinite, such a revolution could not take place.*

Strabo, *Geography* Book 1 Chapter 20

Citing Posidonius of Rhodes (135 B.C. - 51 B.C.), who was a renowned expert on geographical matters, Strabo further notes:

> *... of the more recent measurements we prefer those which diminish the size of the Earth, such as that adopted by Posidonius which is about 180,000 stadia.*
>
> Strabo, *Geography* Book 2 Chapter 2:2

Continuing his appraisal of Posidonius, Strabo adds:

> *Posidonius supposes that the length of the inhabited Earth is about 70,00 stadia, being the half of the whole circle on which it is taken; so that, says he, starting from the west, one might, aided by a continual east wind, reach India in so many thousand stadia.*
>
> Strabo, *Geography* Book 2 Chapter 3:6

For reasons he does not explain, Strabo reduced Eratosthenes' estimation of the Earth's circumference from 250,000 stadia to 180,000 stadia. He also states that a little less then half of that distance (70,000 stadia) was the direct westerly distance to India. Commenting further Strabo writes:

> *We have now traced on a spherical surface the area in which we say the inhabited world is situated; and the man who would most closely approximate the truth by constructed figures must necessarily take for the Earth a globe like that of Crates and lay off on it the quadrilateral and within the quadrilateral put down the map of the inhabited world.*
>
> Strabo, *Geography* Book 2 Chapter 5:10

> *For Crates, following the mere form of mathematical demonstration, says that the torrid zone is 'occupied' by Oceanus and that on both sides of this zone are the temperate zones, the one being on our side, while the other is on the other side of it. Now, just as these Ethiopians on our side of Oceanus, who face the south throughout the whole length of the inhabited land, are called the most remote of the one group of peoples, since they dwell on the shores of Oceanus, so too, Crates thinks, we must conceive that on the other side of Oceanus also there are certain Ethiopians, the most remote of the other group of peoples in the temperate zone, since they dwell on the shores of this same*

> *Oceanus; and they are in two groups and are 'sundered in twain' by Oceanus.*
>
> Strabo, *Geography* Book 1 Chapter 2:24

Claudius Ptolemy (active A.D. 127 - 151)

In the year A.D. 150, a resident of Alexandria named Claudius Ptolemy, produced a hefty eight-volume tome entitled *Geographia.* Ptolemy's *Geographia* located the countries of Serica and Sinae (China) as lying beyond the island of Taprobane (Sri Lanka,) and the Aurea Chersonesus (South East Asian peninsula).

Ptolemy also devised and provided instructions on how to create maps of the whole inhabited world (*Oikoumen*). In the second part of *Geographia* he provided the necessary topographic lists and captions for his map. Ptolemy's *Oikoumen* spanned 180 degrees of longitude (from the Canary Islands in the Atlantic Ocean to China), and about 81 degrees of latitude (from the Arctic to deep Africa). Although Ptolemy was instrumental in creating the first 'accurate' maps of the inhabited world, he also remained aware that he had mapped but one quarter of the globe.

Was the original manuscript of *The Odyssey* written by a woman?

Having translated *The Odyssey* in the latter part of the 19th century, Samuel Butler noted how the epic often reflected a feminine perspective. Butler's perceptions led him to conclude that the original transcript of *The Odyssey* had been 'written by the hand of a woman'. Butler's ardent belief in his theory led him to devote an entire book to the subject. Entitled *The Authoress of the Odyssey*, he contended that *The Odyssey:*

> *... was demonstrably written from one single neighbourhood and hence presumably by one person only and that it was written certainly before 750 B.C., in all probability before 1000 B.C.*

If Butler is correct in presuming that *The Odyssey* was composed as early as 1000 B.C., we might further suppose that there once existed an original draft, recorded in either an Egyptian or Phoenician script. As members of Mycenaean aristocracy, Helen and Penelope may have been tutored to read and write in these neighboring languages. The Greek writers Stesichorus, Euripides and Herodotus unanimously agreed that Helen had spent many years in Egypt and that being the case, she would have, as a matter of course, become conversant in the Egyptian language. Although she was unlikely to have mastered hieroglyphics, Helen could nevertheless have employed Egyptian scribes to record the events of her husband's voyages. Likewise, Penelope may also have, at a later stage in her life, narrated to a scribe an account of Odysseus' journeys.

Helen/Penelope

As far as I am aware, no other scholar of *The Odyssey* has suggested that Helen and Penelope might be one in the same person. We know that:

1) Both were beautiful women who attracted long lists of suitors.

2) Both women were renowned as skilled weavers whose husbands had embarked on long voyages after the fall of Troy.

3) Both are said to have spent their final years on the Peloponnesus.

One may also ponder how Penelope could possibly have known the secrets of Helen's heart when she proclaimed:

> ***Nay, not even Argive Helen, daughter of Zeus, would have lain with a stranger and taken him for a lover had she known that the warlike sons of the Achaeans would bring her home again to her own dear country. Howsoever, it was not the god that set her upon this shameful deed; nor ever did she lay up in her heart the thought of this folly.***

Homer may well have been aware of these similitudes, but for the sake of a 'good story' chose to present the beautiful and lonely queens as two separate identities. I think that perhaps Homer (and countless other scholars since) simply failed to completely unravel this vital ingredient in *The Odyssey*. An explanation for Homer's confusion may be found in the ancient Greek concept of the 'Triple Goddess'. The adherents of this ancient ideology believed a woman's existence evolves through three distinct phases. A separate patron-goddess was assigned to each stage and corresponded to the months of September, October and November.

1) Hestia (Virgo), the youthful virgin
2) Aphrodite (Libra), the fruitful seductress
3) Athena (Scorpio), the wise matron

A youthful Helen exemplifies Hestia, the virgin protectress of Olympia but in her elopement with Paris she displays the attributes of Aphrodite. When an aging Penelope can no longer discourage her suitors, it is Athena, the goddess of wisdom, who suggests that she should organize an archery

The Triple Goddess. Iraq Museum

contest. Athena's role becomes paramount as *The Odyssey* draws towards its conclusion and it is she who presides over the final scenes.

The ancient Greek concept of the 'triple goddess' also attracted the attention of novelist and scholar Robert Graves. In the introduction to his book *Greek Myths,* he informs us that:

The moon's three phases of new, full and old recalled the matriarch's three phases of maiden, nubile woman and crone. Then, since the sun's annual course similarly recalled the rise and decline of her physical powers - spring a maiden, summer a nymph, winter a crone – the goddess became identified with seasonal changes in animal and plant life; and thus with Mother Earth who, at the beginning of the vegetative year, produces only leaves and buds, then flowers and fruits and at last ceases to bear.

She could later be conceived as yet another triad: the maiden of the upper air, the nymph of the Earth or Sea, and the crone of the Underworld – typified respectively by Selene, Aphrodite and Hecate.

> *These mystical analogues fostered the sacredness of the number three, and the Moon-goddess became enlarged to nine when each of the three persons – maiden, nymph and crone – appeared in triad to demonstrate her divinity. Her devotees never quite forgot that there were not three goddess, but one goddess; though, by Classical times, Arcadian Stymphalus was one of the few remaining shrines where they all bore the same name: Hera.*

Bettany Hughes' *Helen of Troy* offers the following commentary regarding Helen's divinity:

> *Divinities are also often described as shining or radiant. There are two possibilities here: the first is that Helen is being remembered as 'quasi-divine' because she was illustrious in life; the second that she was a mortal character being used as a foil for an idea about divinity. Time again when we read about Helen, we are told she glows with a white, bright luminosity."And Helen, the radiance of women, answered Priam," says Homer. She wears cloaks that shimmer. It has been suggested that her name derives from an Indo-European root, 'svarana', meaning 'the starry one' or 'the shining one', which gives us the Greek word 'elene' that can mean a torch or light. See Skutsch (1987), 188-93. Homer often talks about Helen as 'Argive Helen'. The obvious interpretation is that she was a representative of the Greeks (also known as Argives) or a woman whose influence resonated through the Argive plain, but there is also the possibility that the bard is playing on words. In the Greek language 'arguros' first appears as a word in Homer's Iliad where it means silver or silvery.*

The silvery moon is synonymous with the 'triple goddess'. The goddesses Hestia, Aphrodite, Athena, Selene and Hekcate were individually and collectively associated with the moon. The shining, lunar aspect of the 'triple goddess' is also personified in the image of a faithfully celibate Penelope, who, as she weaves and unweaves her tapestry, enacts the waxing and waning of the silvery moon.

NOTES

Introduction

Note 1

Helen in Egypt

The Odyssey Book 4: Line 106 -

> ***Polybus lived in Egyptian Thebes, which is the richest city in the whole world; he gave Menelaus two baths of pure silver, two tripods and ten talents of gold; besides all this, his wife gave Helen some beautiful presents, to wit, a golden staff and a silver box that ran on wheels, with a gold band round the top of it. Phylo now placed this by her side, full of fine spun yarn, and a distaff charged with violet colored wool was laid upon the top of it.***

The Egyptian Polybus' presentation to Helen of a magnificent spindle draws parallels to Odysseus' wife Penelope, who is more readily recognised as being the 'queen at her loom'.

> ***She (Penelope) set up a great tambour frame in her room, and began work on an enormous piece of fine needlework - whereon we could see her working on a great web all day long, but at night she would unpick the stitches again by torchlight.***
>
> Homer, *The Odyssey* Book 2: Line 84

Stesichorus c.600 B.C.

In one of his earlier compositions the Sicilian poet Stesichorus wrote about how Helen's father, Tyndarius, sacrificed to the gods but neglected Aphrodite. In anger, Aphrodite cursed the daughters of Tyndarius to be *'married twice and thrice and be husband deserters'*.

Socrates reports that Helen struck Stesichorus blind for having written such blasphemy about her. Apparently Stesichorus then came to understand the truth and wrote a new poem called *The Palinode*, meaning 'song-reversed'. The revised poem sought to restore Helen to her former dignity as a Spartan goddess. In *The Palinode*, Stesichorus questions Homer's authority by claiming that it was an imaginary Helen who was carried to Troy. Stesichorus asserts that the real Helen never deserted her husband but was sent to Egypt where the noble pharaoh Proteus became her minder. Apparently Stesichorus' *Palinode* succeeded in placating Helen, for his sight was restored shortly after he completed his writings.

Euripides c.420 B.C.

The Greek dramatist Euripides also experienced a radical change of opinion in regards to Helen. Writing in the fourth century B.C., Euripides composed a play that he simply entitled *Helen.* Set in a period seventeen years after the fall of Troy, the play takes place on Egypt's Isle of Pharos. Like Stesichorus before him, Euripides claimed that Helen had never set foot in Troy, but instead spent the prime of her life in Egypt. He maintained that the Helen who had eloped to Troy with Paris was merely a phantom figure created by Aphrodite. Euripides' account of Helen in Egypt differs somewhat from that of Stesichorus. In the Euripides' version, the good Pharaoh Proteus is dead, and his evil son, Theokyminos, has ascended to the throne. The central theme of Euripides' play is of Helen's dilemma in reuniting with her long lost husband who, having wandered about the Mediterranean suddenly reappears in Egypt alone and destitute. During her husband's long absence Helen has become betrothed to Theokminos. In order to extricate herself from a desperate situation, Helen pretends that her returned husband is her brother. Biblical scholars will recognize a somewhat similar scenario in *Genesis* 12:14-20, wherein it is written that Abraham and his wife Sarah present themselves as brother and sister to a courting Egyptian pharoah.

Euripides' portrayal of Helen as being a faithful wife to Menelaus is echoed in Homer's representation of Penelope patiently awaiting the return of Odysseus. Both women are described as gifted weavers whose beauty attracts the attention of numerous rich suitors. Homer has evidently assigned to each the various traditional motifs associated with a faithful queen awaiting the return of her seafaring husband.

Note 2

Helen and Paris in Egypt (Herodotus, *Histories* Book II)

CXIII. When I inquired of the priests, they told me that this was the story of Helen. After carrying off Helen from Sparta, Alexandrus (Paris) *sailed away for his own country; violent winds caught him in the Aegean and drove him into the Egyptian sea; and from there (as the wind did not let up) he came to Egypt, to the mouth of the Nile called the Canopic mouth, and to the Salters.*

Now there was (and still is) on the coast a temple of Heracles (Hercules)*; if a servant of any man takes refuge there and is branded with certain marks, delivering himself to the god, he may not be touched. This law continues today the same as it has always been from the first. Hearing the temple law, some of Alexandrus'* (Paris) *servants ran away from him, threw themselves on the mercy of the god and brought an accusation against Alexandrus meaning to injure him, telling the whole story of Helen and the wrong done to Menelaus. They laid this accusation before the priests and the warden of the Nile mouth whose name was Thronis.*

CXIV. When Thronis heard it; he sent this message the quickest way to Proteus at Memphis:

"A stranger has come, a Trojan, who has committed an impiety in Hellas (Greece). *After defrauding his guest-friend, he has come bringing the man's wife and a very great deal of wealth, driven to your country by the wind. Are we to let him sail away untouched, or are we to take away what he has come with?" Proteus sent back this message:*

"Whoever this is, I want to know what he has to say."

CXV. Hearing this, Thronis seized Alexandrus (Paris) *and detained his ships. He then bought Alexandus, Helen and the suppliants to Memphis. When all had arrived, Proteus asked Alexandrus who he was and whence he sailed; Alexandrus told him his lineage, the name of his country and about his voyage. Then Proteus asked him where he had got Helen. When Alexandrus was evasive in his story and did not tell the truth, the men who had taken refuge in the temple confuted him and related the whole story of the wrong. Finally, Proteus declared the following judgment to them saying:*

> *"If I had not made it a point never to kill a stranger who has been caught by the wind and driven to my coasts, I would have punished you on behalf of the Greek noble, you most vile man. You committed the gravest impiety after you had had your guest-friend's hospitality; you had your guest-friend's wife. And as if this were not enough, you got her to fly with you and went off with her. And not just with her, either, but you plundered your guest-friend's wealth and brought it too. Now then, since I make a point not to kill strangers, I shall not let you take away this woman and the wealth but shall watch them for the Greek stranger until he comes and takes them away; but as for you and your sailors, I warn you to leave my country for another within three days and if you do not, I will declare war on you."*
>
> *CXVI. This, said the priests, was how Helen came to Proteus. And in my opinion, Homer knew this story too; but seeing that it was not as well suited to epic poetry as the tale of which he made use, he rejected it, showing that he knew of it.* **(i)**

I agree with Herodotus' claim that Homer was well aware of this Egyptian legend. It shares the same basic ingredients as the Menelaus version. A seafaring prince is beset by storms and arrives at the mouth of the Nile River. Left destitute, he is advised or ordered by the Egyptian pharaoh/deity Proteus to depart Egypt. Homer tells us that both Menelaus and Odysseus finally returned home with an ample amount of treasure. Strabo partly confirms this in his *Geography 1.2.31*:

> *They who assert that Menelaus went by sea to Ethiopia, tell us he directed his course past Cadiz into the Indian Ocean; with which, say they, the long duration of his wanderings agrees, since he did not arrive there until the eighth year. Others say that he passed through the isthmus that enters the Arabian Gulf; and others again, through one of the canals. At the same time the idea of this circumnavigation, owes its origin to Crates, is not necessary; we do not mean it was impossible, (for the wanderings of Odysseus are not impossible). But neither the mathematical hypothesis, not yet the duration of the wandering, require such an explanation; for he was both retarded against his will by accidents in the voyage, as by [the tempest] which he narrates five only of his sixty ships survived; and also by voluntary delays for the sake of amassing wealth. Nestor says [of him]. Thus he, provision gathering as he went, and gold abundant, roam'd to distant lands.*

(i) Herodotus, *Histories* Book II Chapters 113-116

It might also be noted that all three princes, Alexdandrus (Paris), Menelaus and Odysseus are recorded to have at one time been a suitor of the same beautiful Helen who, according to the Greek writer Euripides, had spent 17 years in Egypt awaiting the return of her lost sea-faring consort.

List of Helen's Suitors

Odysseus, son of Laertes

Ajax, son of Oileus

Agapenor, son of Ancaeus

Ajax and Teucer, sons of Telamon

Amphilochus, son Amphiaraus

Amphimachus, son of Nestor

Diomedes, son of Tydeus

Elephenor, son of Chalcodon

Eumelus, son of Admetus

Eurypylus, son of Euaemon

Idomeneus, son of Deucalion

Leitus, son of Alector

Leonteus, son of Coronus

Meges, son of Phyleus

Menelaus, son of Pleisthenes or Atreus

Menestheus, son of Peteos

Paris (Alexandros), son of Priam

List of Penelopes's Suitors

Odysseus, son of Laertes

Aegyptius, aged lord in Ithaca

Agelaus, son of Damastor, suiter from Ithaca

Amphimedon, son of Menanus, suiter from Ithaca

Amphinomus, son of Nisus; suitor from Dulichium

Antinous, son of Eupeithes; leader of the suitors

Ctesippus, son of Polytherses; suitor from Same

Eupeithes, a lord in Ithaca

Eurymachus, son of Polybus; suitor in Ithaca

Halitherses, son of Mastor; seer and prophet

Irus, town beggar

Leiocritus, son of Evenor; suitor from Ithaca

Leiodes, son of Oenops; soothsayer for the suitors

Noemon, son of Phromius; ship owner;

Chapter 1

Odysseus in Egypt

Note 3

Proteus

The Greek female equivalent of Proteus was the sea nymph Thetis. In order to evade her future husband Peleus, Thetis took on the form of a horse, bird, fish etc. Peleus managed to keep his clasp of Thetis and eventually she conceded to wed him. Robert Graves further informs us that the 'dance of the fifty Nerieds at Thetis' wedding can be traced back to the ancient European legend of *selkies* who were said to discard their sealskins under a full moon.

The persona of a sea king who guarded secret knowledge may have survived over the ages to resurface as the inspiration for Pellas, the 'Fisher King' of Arthurian legend. According to Medieval French writers, Pellas safeguarded both the Holy Grail (Sangreal) and the Sacred Lance of Destiny at a seaside castle called Carbonet. Two rampant lions protected the entranceway to this four-quartered castle and only the purest of heart could gain entry into the mystical citadel. Sought after by King Arthur's Knights of the Round Table, the Holy Grail was believed to be the 'silver' chalice used by Christ at the Last Supper. Mediaeval alchemists were of the belief that the metal silver contained metaphysical properties that enabled the deflection of evil. Consequently the knights of romantic fable encased themselves in protective silver armor and wielded silver lances to slay dragons. As previously mentioned, the etymology of the word silver can be traced to the old English *'seol for'* (seal fur), an apt term to describe Proteus, the old seal king of the silver moon.

Note 4

The Egyptian Sun God

Depending upon whether it was rising, at its zenith, setting, or traversing the underworld, the sun was variously identified with the solar gods, Atum, Ra, Amun Ra and Horus.

Atum

The sum of all existence, Atum rose in radiant splendour from the bosom of the Cosmic Ocean at dawn to become Ra.

Ra

During the hours of daylight Ra rode across the heavens in his Sun Boat.

Amun Ra

The ram-headed Amun Ra sat enthroned in the Sun Boat as it journeyed through the underworld of night.

Horus

The falcon-headed Horus was considered to be a personification of the sun. Under the name of Ra Harakhte, he later reigned symbolically over all Egypt.

The Underworld

In regards to an afterlife, the ancient Egyptians held similar views to those of the Greeks who believed that when a person died, one's soul faced the challenge of traversing an Underworld river called the Styx. To successfully cross over the Styx, one needed to employ the services of the ancient ferryman Charon. For a nominal fee he would transport one's soul across the river. The northern European concept of the 'afterlife voyage' involved a giant solar horse. During the course of the day the giant horse was envisioned as drawing the 'Chariot of the Sun' across the heavens. As night descended, the horse transformed itself into a swan that glided its way over an Underworld lake. It was the shrewd Odysseus who devised a plan to end the ten-year siege of Troy with the gift of a most curious, giant wooden horse. The totemic imagery of a giant horse indicates that Odysseus was versed in the northern European concept of 'solar-voyaging'

Trundholm sun chariot c.1000 B.C., National Museum Denmark

Note 5

Remains of Punt Ships Discovered in Egypt

In December 2004, Kathryn Bard, a CAS Associate Professor of Archaeology at Boston University, and her former student Chen Sian Lim discovered an ancient man-made cave while excavating at Wadi Gawasis on Egypt's Red Sea coast.

Promptly joined by renowned Italian archaeologist Rodolfo Fattovien, the team uncovered a rectangular entranceway to yet another cave. Constructed with cedar beams and blocks of limestone (which originally served as ship anchors), the entranceway led into a huge network of rooms where an assortment of nautical items including ropes, a wooden bowl and mesh bag were unearthed.

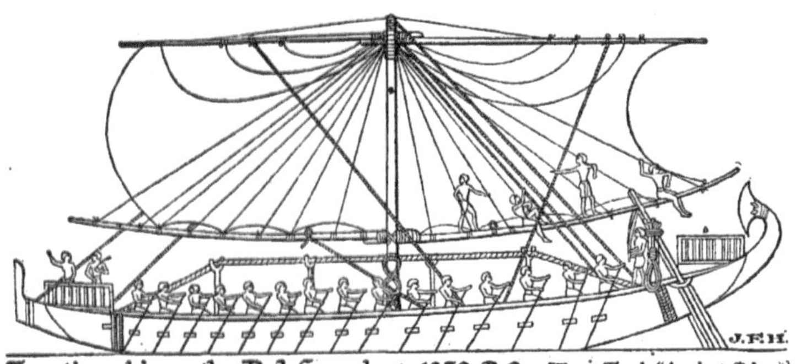

Egyptian ship on the Red Sea, about 1250 B.C. [From Torr's "Ancient Ships."]

Two curved cedar planks were also found and what were possibly the steering oars from a 21-metre (70 feet) long ship that had once participated in Queen Hatshepsut's 15th century B.C. naval expedition to Punt. Several very worn stelae were discovered in niches outside the second cave. However, one stele has been remarkably well preserved due to it having been left face down in the sand. Bearing the cartouche of Amenemhat III, the stele records how two expeditions were launched to Punt and Bia Punt during the period c.1800 B.C. Bard had selected the Wadi Gawasis site because an Egyptian archaeologist, working in the 1970's, had identified it as the likely location of Saaw, an ancient seaport that had been recorded in texts as the departure point for expeditions to Punt. The find has excited archaeologists worldwide and Bard is certain that at least one other cave exists. Limited to the six weeks between semesters each winter, Bard estimates that there are years of work to be carried out in the area.

Note 6

Egypt's Ancient Canals

Many students of Homer's *Odyssey* are unaware that ancient canals once connected the Mediterranean to the Red Sea. The Greek teacher Aristotle (3rd century B.C.) wrote:

> *One of the kings tried to dig a canal to it* (the Red Sea). *For it would be of no little advantage to them if this whole region was accessible to navigation: Sesostris is said to be the first of the ancient kings to have attempted the work.* **(ii)**

The Greek historian Strabo (64 B.C. - A.D. 24) reports:

> *There is another canal which empties into the Red Sea and the Arabian Gulf near the city Arisnoe, a city which some call Cleopatris. The canal was first cut by Sesostris* (1880-1935 B.C.). **(iii)**

Pliny's *Natural history* (c.A.D.78) concurs with Aristotle and Strabo:

> *This project was originally conceived by Sesostris, King of Egypt.* **(iv)**

Rock inscriptions found near Sehel by de Morgan in 1894 indicate that Pharaoh Senusret III (1878 - 1843 B.C.) had successfully engineered a west-east canal through the Wadi Tumilat. This canal is thought to have joined the Nile to the Red Sea thus enabling a direct trade with Punt. During the time of the Hykos invasion (c.1786 - 1567 B.C.), this initial canal all but disappeared by way of the shifting sands. Two hundred years later, Amenhotep III (c.1391 – 1351 B.C.) re-constructed a similar canal system which having diverged from the Nile near Bubastis, then continued along the Wadi Tumilat to Heroopolis near Pithom, a port at the head of the Heroopolite Gulf (the Bitter Lakes of today). According to an inscription on the temple at Karnak, these canals were in constant use throughout the reigns of Seti I (c.1305 - 1279 B.C.), and his son Rameses II (c.1279 - 1213 B.C.).

(ii) Aristotle, *Meteorologica* 1:15:25-30.
(iii) Strabo, *Geography* 17:1:25.
(iv) Pliny, *Natural History* 6:33:165

Other records written during their reigns announce that Egypt at that time was receiving ships coming not only from the Indus, Insia and Arabia, but also from Phoenicia, Crete, Greece, the Adriatic and the Black Sea littoral.

Rediscovery of the Ancient Canals

Shortly after the 1967 Arab/Israeli War, Israeli geologists began to study aerial photographs of the Nile Delta. Scanning the landscape, they noted clear vestiges of two ancient canals that are estimated to have predated the Suez Canal by as much as 4,000 years. Beginning at Pelusium, the so-called Eastern Canal runs south for 22 kilometres before veering sharply towards the coastal port city of Ismailia. This Red Sea canal route may have formed the basis of a canal system that was later attributed to the Persian conqueror Darius.

Wind and sand have covered over much of the canal's original course. Geologists Itamar Perath, Amihai Sneh and Tuvia Weissbrod believe the canal was split into two directions; one branch following the great east-west depression called the Wadi Tumilat to link up with the Nile, while the other continued a course southwards into the Red Sea. The Israeli geologists believe that the depth of the old waterway ranged between two to three metres. Despite the estimated shallowness of these canals, they would nevertheless have been sufficiently deep enough to ferry Odysseus' fleet of Greek ships.

Chapter 3

Land of the Lotus Eaters

(Sri Lanka)

Note 7

Aphrodite

If Odysseus had in fact been ***'wind-driven'*** to the exotic island of Sri Lanka, he would have soon comprehended that the local goddess, Parvati, was worshipped there in the form of a smooth fertility-stone called a '*Yoni*'.

Odysseus' observation of the Sri Lankan natives venerating the '*Yoni*' may have prompted him to compare their island with Cyprus where a similar veneration of female sexuality was practiced c.1160 B.C.

According to Asia Shepsut's *Journey of the Priestess,* the Cypriot devotees of Aphrodite honoured the goddess's sexual power in a ritual involving a polished black stone that was housed within the inner sanctum of her temple at Paphos.

Note 8

Yapahuwa

An ancient fortress and one time capital of Sri Lanka, Yapahuwa is situated about 90 miles from the present capital, Colombo. Carved from a massive rock that rises abruptly to a height of 90 metres (300 feet), Yapahuwa is surrounded by moats, has ramparts and features an ornamental stairway. Recent excavations of Yapahuwa indicate that its kingdom had established diplomatic ties with China during the 13th century A.D. and furthermore, their diplomatic relationship may have been inaugurated as early as 1,000 B.C. Excavating Yapahuwa in December,

2002 an archaeological team headed by Dr. Senarath Dissanayake reports as follows:

> *We found a number of new pebbles at last year's excavations. There were 24 new stones. Also some strong evidence was gathered from the six acres of flat land on the Yapahuwa Rock. It has pre-historic (from 1000 B.C. to 500 B.C.) or early historic (from 500 B.C. to 200 A.D.) human settlements and is the earliest such settlement to be found on the rock. Furthermore, the evidence reveals that it was not a rural settlement but a somewhat urban type of settlement.*
>
> *www.lankalibrary.com.geo/yapahuwa.htm*

Emperor Wu

Written during the Han Dynasty, a Chinese document reports that in the year 140 B.C., the illustrious Emperor Wu led an expedition of ships on a voyage to India. Accompanied by numerous court officials, Wu set out from the old capital Ch'ang An in northern China. The fleet at first sailed 3,000 miles south. Having passed through the straits of Malacca, the fleet continued on across 1,200 miles of open sea to Huang-Chih, an ancient port that modern Chinese scholars have identified as Conjeveram (which is near Madras, S.E. India). Having safely anchored their ships, the Emperor's cargo of gold and silk was then exchanged for precious gems, pearls and rock crystal. With their new cargoes stored and secured, the fleet returned home via the same route.

It seems probable that a China-India sea-route long existed prior to Wu's expedition. It is doubtful that a Chinese Emperor and his royal attendants would have risked lives and riches on such an ambitious voyage if similar expeditions had not preceded them.

Note 9
The Helas

Integral to the Hela culture were the ocean going vessels that enabled them to trade with other South East Asian communities. Hela kings were purported to have sent sea-borne armies to Indonesia and Burma to assist them in protecting their lands from invading hordes.

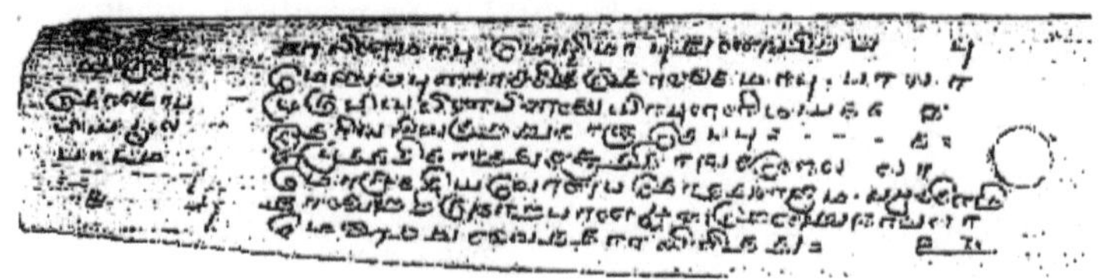

Sinhala *ola* (palm leaf) writing c.500 B.C.

500 B.C.
Led by a king called Vijaya, Hindus from the mainland of India conquered the Island of Heladiva c.500 B.C. King Vijaya's Sinha (lion) Clan soon dominated Hela culture and the Helas were thence known as the Sinha-Hela or Sinhelase. The Hela nation was subsequently divided into four main tribes which all spoke one language (Hela Basa). Due to there being four main Hela tribes, the island became known at that time as Sivuhela (*Sivu*: meaning four), or by the shorter version, Sihela. The four Hela tribes were Yakka, Nagha, Asura and Raksha.

Note 10

The Lotus

The earliest representation of the lotus in art is found incorporated among the flowers adorning the head of a mother-goddess statue (c.3000 B.C.) that was unearthed at Mohenjo-Daro in the Indus Valley.

In Hindu 'creation' mythology, the spirit of the Supreme Being is often personified as a golden lotus, serenely afloat upon a gentle ocean. The sacred lotus is believed to have been the creative catalyst of our universe; from its petals came the mountains, hills, valleys and rivers. The lotus-born, creator-god Brahma is sometimes depicted as issuing from the navel of the Supreme Being, Vishnu. As an incarnation of Vishnu, Buddha is also associated with the lotus.

Note 11

Odysseus might well have been apprehensive to sail further eastward into an uncharted ocean, but the seafaring natives who abode in the Land of the Lotus-Eaters probably allayed his fears. These mariners would have informed Odysseus that the summit of Sri Pada (Adam's Peak) could be seen from as far away as three days' sailing. When the Arab traveller Ibn Battutu sailed to Sri Lanka in 1344 A.D., he recorded how he had noticed smoke rising from the island nine days before he made landfall. Batutu's report indicates that he may have witnessed smoke spiralling from a fire beacon that was maintained atop of Sri Pada. The fire beacon method of guiding ships ashore was probably employed by native seafarers throughout S.E. Asia.

Antique map displaying Sri Pada (Adam's Peak)

Chapter 4

Land of the Cyclopes

(South East Asia)

Note 12

Greek Rituals in Indonesia

A foremost authority on world mythology, Professor Joseph Campbell informs us that:

> *The Indonesian myth of Satine, Rabia and Hainuwele carries not only every major theme associated with the ancient Greek myth of Demeter, Hekate and Persephone, but is remarkable in the similarities of minute details. The number of these details is too great to have been the consequence of either chance or of what Sir James G. Frazer has plausibly called "the effect of similar causes acting on the similar constitution of the human mind in different countries and under different skies."*
>
> *At the heart of both Greek and Indonesian myths, there is a trinity of goddesses identified with local food plants, the pig, the underworld and the moon, whose rites ensure both a growth of plants and a passage of the soul to the land of the dead. In both, the marriage of the maiden goddess or Dema is equivalent to her death and is imaged as a descent into the earth that is followed by her metamorphosis into food.*

In Indonesia the maiden becomes the yam and in classical Greece she is the grain or sheaf of wheat. Human sacrifice was prevalent in both Pre-Homeric Greece and Indonesia. The Greek myth reflects a less brutal method of appeasement and thanksgiving. The Greek Festival of Thesmophoria survived from early times and was exclusively for women. It expresses the grief of Demeter, whose daughter Persephone was abducted by Hades into the Underworld, and her subsequent joy upon obtaining Persephone's release (helped by Hekate, a moon- goddess) even though it was only for a part of the yearly cycle. During the first day of this festival, suckling pigs were thrown, presumably alive, into an underground chamber called a *megara* where they were left to rot for a year, the bones from the previous year being carried up to the Earth again and placed on the altar. Figurines of serpents and human beings made from flour and wheat were also thrown into the 'chasm' at this time. Many snakes lived within the chamber, consuming much of what was thrown into it and so a 'rattling din' was made to scare them off before the women could draw up the remains.

Professor Campbell continues:

> *... the Greek and Indonesian myths examined have revealed not only a shared body of ritualized motifs but also signs of a shared past, an earlier stratum of their common story, in which a snake and not a pig played the animal part. And in fact that (one way or another) the two cycles were not merely linked remotely by a long tenuous thread, but established on a broad, common base is made evident by a baffling series of further likenesses. For example, in both mythologies the numbers 3 and 9 were prominent. We know also that in the Greek rites of the goddess – and of her dead and resurrecting daughter Persephone, as well as of her dead and resurrected grandson Dionysus – the choral chant, the boom of the drum and the hum of the bullroarer were used just as in the rites of the cannibals of Indonesia.*
>
> *We recognize the labyrinth theme in both traditions, associated with the Underworld and rendered in the figure of a spiral: in Greece, as well as Indonesia, choral dances were performed in this pattern. The reference in the Indonesian myth to Ameta's desire to prepare a drink for himself from the blossoms of the coco palm suggests a relationship of wine or intoxication to the cult of the maiden–plant–animal complex that would correspond nicely with the formula in the archaic Mediterranean culture. And finally, is not the figure of Demeter, at the time of her departure in wrath from Olympus, bearing in each hand a long staff–like torch, comparable to Satene standing at the labyrinthine gate, telling the people of the mythological age that she is about to leave them, and holding in each hand an arm of hainuwele? There can be no doubt that the two mythologies are derived from a single base. The fact was recognized some time ago by the classical scholar, Carl Kerenyi and his argument has been supported since by Professor Jenson, the ethnologist chiefly responsible for the collection of the Indonesian material.*

Joseph Campbell, *The Masks of God - Primitive Mythology* p.183, Viking Press N.Y. 1959

Note 13

Antonio Galvano's *Discoveries of the World* continues his account of ancient geography:

> *It may have been that Malacca and China, as Ptolemy sets forth, extended beyond the line to the south; Malacca might have joined the land called Jentana with the islands of Bitam, Banca and Salistres; likewise China might be united with the Lucones, Boneo, Lequeuo, Mindanao and others. Some are of opinion that Sumatra joined with Java across what is now the Straits of Sunda; and that Java also joined with the islands of Bali, Anjave, Cambava, Solor, Hogalcao, Maulva, Vintara, Rosalaguin and others in that range; all of which are so near as to appear continuous when seen from a small distance. They are still so near together that in passing through the channels which divide them, the boughs of the trees on each side may be touched by the hands. It is not long since several of the islands of Banda (in the east), were drowned by the sea overflowing them. In China, about 180 miles of firm land are said to have become a lake. All these things are to be considered as coming within the limits of probability, especially when we take into account what has been related of similar events by Ptolemy and others.*

Chapter 5

Kingdom of Aeolus

(Shang China)

Note 14

World View According to Homer

The Homeric conception of the world represented as a flat circular disc of land surrounded by a continuous ocean-stream remained a popular notion in the Greek world even after many philosophers and scientists had accepted the theory of the sphericity of the earth enunciated by the Pythagoreans and subjected to theoretical proof by Aristotle. In this interpretation the world is like a plateau on the top of a mountain; inside this, close to the surface of the Earth, lays the House of Hades, the realm of Death, and beneath it Tartarus, the realm of Eternal Darkness. The plateau of the earth is surrounded by Oceanus, the world river, and from its periphery arises the fixed dome of the sky. The sun, the moon and the stars rise from the waters at the edge of the dome, move in an arc above the Earth and then sink again into the sea to complete their course beneath the Oceanus. The atmosphere above the mountain of the Earth is thick with clouds and mist but higher up is the clear AEther with its starry ceiling.

Siebold, James *Ancient Maps*

Note 15

Shang-Olmec Connection

In his book entitled *Origin of the Olmec Civilization,* linguistics Professor Mike Xu, proposes that the Olmec civilization of Mesoamerica was strongly influenced by a group of Shang Chinese refugees who fled across the Pacific Ocean c.1150 B.C. According to Professor Xu, the beginning of the Olmec civilization coincides with the ending of China's Shang Dynasty (namely King Wu's attack and defeat of King Zhou). Professor Xu states that notable scholars such as Ekholm (1964), Heine-Geldern (1972), (Needham (1985), and Shao (1998), have all presented evidences of the many cultural coincidences that exist between Shang China and ancient Mexico. (see also Campbell's *The Mythic Image*)

Comparison of Shang and Olmec Symbols

During the years 1994 - 97, Professor Xu made drawings of the markings he found on various Olmec artifacts and presented these drawings to China's leading experts on ancient writing. The majority of learned men agreed that they closely resemble the characters used in Chinese oracular bone writings and bronze inscriptions. Commenting on Professor Xu's findings, Claire Lui of *Sinorama Magazine,* Taiwan 1997 writes:

> *As long ago as the 1920s and '30s, several scholars pointed out numerous points of similarity between the cultures of China's Shang and Zhou dynasties and those of Mesoamerica. For instance, the structure of the temples on top of Maya pyramids can be compared with that of Chinese ancestral temples and the feathered serpent spirit worshipped in Mesoamerica is similar to the various human-headed, snake-bodied spirits such as Fu Xi and Nu Wa, which were known to the early Chinese. Even more striking is the traditional love of jade shared by peoples on both sides of the Pacific and practices such as placing a jade bead or jade cicada in the mouth of the dead, or even painting jade corpse-amulets with the life-giving color of cinnabar.*
>
> *In China, some people have also inferred from ancient records that the Chinese discovered America. For instance, the Liang Shu (History of the Liang) from the 7th century A.D. mentions that in the Southern Dynasties period a monk named Huishen crossed the ocean and*

discovered a land named 'Fusang', which Liang Qichao (1873 - 1929) believed to be today's Mexico. Others have tried to match the places described in the legends of the 'Shan Hai Jing' (Classic of Mountains and Seas) with individual locations in the Americas.

It has also been claimed that from Olmec statues it appears that they had the custom of manipulating children's skull bones into a more pointed shape, which was a practice also seen among tribes in northeastern China. In Xu's view, both peoples venerated their ancestors, practiced human sacrifice and worshipped the sun and rain spirits. Furthermore, the Olmec worshipped the cougar, the eagle and the snake, while the Chinese regarded the tiger as a symbol of strength, the people of the Shang used birds as clan totems, and wasn't the dragon, which Chinese people venerate, also derived from the snake? In terms of astronomy, the settlements excavated at La Venta are arranged facing eight degrees west of north, while Shang sites face five degrees east of north. What is remarkable about that?

In one of his articles Mike Xu writes that the 'eight degrees' and 'five degrees' are actually with reference to the magnetic north indicated by compasses, and not the true North Pole. Thus both actually face true north. He believes that for both peoples to have known how to determine true north as long ago as 1200 B.C. is no coincidence. The time of the rise of the Olmec civilization coincides with the fall of the Shang dynasty and there are a number of similarities between the two cultures. On this basis, Xu boldly infers that some 5,000 people from the Shang Dynasty sailed across the Pacific on bamboo rafts and landed in western Mexico; later, they gradually spread to the central regions and built up a civilization of art, religion, architecture, agriculture and trade. Xu has even written a historical drama, 'Fallen Grace', which describes how the lost people of Shang may have crossed the sea.

Chapter 6

Land of the Laestrygones

(Polynesian Samoa)

Note 16

Lapita Pottery

So far no skeletons or other human remains have been found in any early Lapita site, so it is difficult to be certain who these people were, or exactly where they came from. In fact the question of their origins - and their descendants - is one of the most contentious subjects in Pacific anthropology. We believe, however, that there is overwhelming evidence to show that the descendants of the Lapita people can be firmly identified as the islanders we now call Polynesians. That being so, we can make a reasonable hypothesis about where the Lapita people came from, when they entered the Pacific and how they laid the foundations for the last great colonization of that ocean.

The available evidence strongly suggests that around 4,000 years ago pottery-making people from eastern Indonesia or the Philippines – or perhaps the coast of Asia itself – began to move eastwards. Just why they migrated is not yet clear, but given the population growth and economic changes in that region, following the introduction of rice agriculture and the spread of metallurgy, it would not be surprising if some groups had been displaced. This would be especially true of people who according to the evidence in the Lapita sites, did not grow rice or use metals (although in other ways they were quite sophisticated, having stone adzes, shell tools and some domesticated plants and animals).

In a very rapid expansion the Lapita people island-hopped past New Guinea and into the southwest Pacific. Besides their undoubted skills as pottery-makers, the Lapita people were skilled boat-builders and deep-water sailors. This capacity enabled them to move out through the Melanesian islands quite rapidly, as their habitation sites show. Their skills seem to have impressed the Melanesians, because in some areas the local people adopted the Lapita terms for sailing, navigation and so on. (We know this because their expressions were in a language quite unrelated to the Melanesian languages; what the Lapita people spoke was one of a group of related languages called Austronesia, widely used in Southeast Asia.)

Sailing on past the outer, settled islands of Melanesia, the Lapita navigators began to find and establish themselves on new and uninhabited islands – New Caledonia, Vanuatu (New Hebrides) and Fiji. Then they went further east, crossing large open gaps to settle the Tongan islands by 3,000 years ago, and Samoa soon after. In less than 1,000 years they had pushed more than 5,000 kilometres out into the Pacific Ocean from their base in Southeast Asia. By this time the Lapita people had left Melanesians far behind and were well and truly on their own. And over the next 1,000 years a new culture evolved from those Lapita pioneers – the culture of Polynesia.

In Tonga and Samoa today the origins of the Polynesians are easy to see. The people there are clearly Asian – mongoloid, with flat faces, straight black hair, light skin colour and the epicanthic eye-fold; all features which as we described earlier, evolved in northern Asia as a response to the environments of the ice ages.'

Alan Thorne and Robert Raymond, *Man on the Rim* Angus and Robertson Sydney 1989

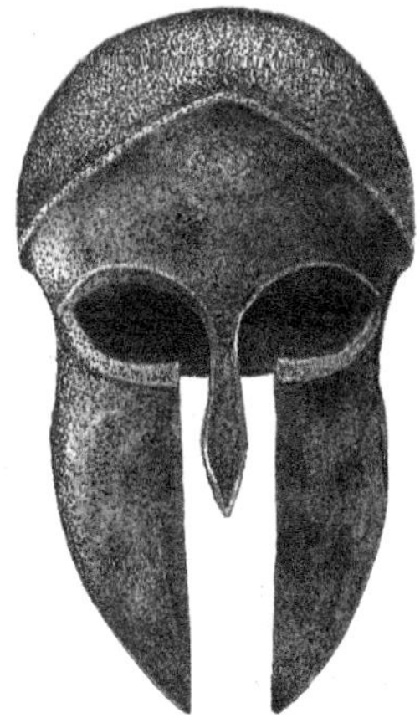

Mycenaean helmet c.1100 B.C.

Lapita pottery c. 1100 B.C.

Chapter 7

Circe's Realm of Aeaea

(Central America)

Note 17

The phrase ***'fierce heat of sun'*** is from Butcher and Lang's translation of *The Odyssey,* London 1879. Notes from a Spanish expedition that had landed on the Yucatan peninsula around A.D. 1510 reported that the Mayan Indians had referred to their homeland as *'the land of turkey and deer'*. Upon his arrival in Aeaea, Odysseus had killed a stag with his spear.

Note 18

In Book 1: Chapter 21 of his *Geography*, Strabo criticizes Odysseus for his lack of geographical knowledge:

> *For one should not, on the one hand, be so ignorant of the Heavens and the position of the Earth as to be alarmed when he comes to countries in which some of the celestial phenomena that are familiar to everybody have changed, and to exclaim:*
>
> ***'Neither West know we, nor East, where rises or where sets the all-enlightening sun.'***
>
> *Still, we do not expect that they* (Odysseus and his crew) *should be such thorough masters of the subject as to know what stars rise and set together for the different quarters of the earth; those which have the same meridian line, the elevation of the poles, the signs which are in the zenith, with all the various phenomena which differ as well in appearance as reality with the variations of the horizon and arctic circle.*
>
> *Those who, through carelessness and ignorance, are not familiar with the globe and the circles traced upon it, some parallel to each*

other, some at right angles to the former, others, again, in an oblique direction; nor yet with the position of the tropics equator, and zodiac, (that circle through which the sun travels in his course, and by which we reckon the changes of season and the winds), such persons we caution against the perusal of our work. For if a man is neither properly acquainted with these things, nor with the variations of the horizon and arctic circle, and such similar elements of mathematics, how can he comprehend the matters treated of here?

So those who have written the works entitled 'On Ports', and 'Voyages Round the World', have performed their task imperfectly, since they have omitted to supply the requisite information from mathematics and astronomy.

It is interesting to note Strabo's reference to an ancient book entitled *Voyages Round the World*. One might wonder just how many 'voyages round the world' had been accomplished at the time of Strabo's writing (c.A.D. 7 - 15).

Note 19

Teopantecuanitlan (Place of the Jaguar Temple)

We cannot dismiss the possibility that Odysseus came ashore in Acapulco Bay. If Odysseus and his crew had trekked 80 kilometres inland along the then present mountaintrails, they would have arrived at Teopantecuanitlan.

Situated at the convergence of the Amacuzac and Balsas rivers, the archaeological site of Teopantecuanitlan represents an unexpectedly early development of complex society in that region. Occupied from 1400 to 500 B.C., Teopantecuanitlan was the focal centre for an area that included Oxtotitlan, Juxtlalahuaca, Xochipala, Zumpango del Rio, and Chilpancingo.

Art and Architecture

The site's settlement largely consisted of residential compounds characterized by four structures arranged around a shared courtyard plaza. The structures themselves were made of perishable materials built over stone basal foundations. Imported shell and obsidian artifacts, as well as Olmec-influenced ceramic wares, have been found in association with and inside the residential groups. These artifacts provide material evidence that the Teopantecuanitlan community was a part of an interregional trade network that linked the Gulf Coast with the highlands of Central Mexico. **(a)**

Sunken Patio

In addition to the residential areas, Teopantecuanitlan is notable for its monumental architecture, art, and agricultural terraces, in particular one of the first civil-ceremonial structures in all of Mesoamerica, El Recinto (the enclosure), also known as the Sunken Patio, constructed during Phase II (between 1000 and 800 BCE). The Sunken Patio is so-named because it is 2 metres (7 feet) below the natural ground level, built on a base of yellow clay, dressed with travertine blocks.

Four large, nearly identical, monumental travertine blocks adorn the east and west sides of the Sunken Patio. These blocks are carved to resemble anthropomorphic creatures, most likely were jaguars, with almond-shaped eyes and down-turned mouths. In fact, it is these 3 to 5 ton monuments that are referred to in archaeologist Guadalupe Martinez Donjuán's name for the site, Teopantecuanitlan, Nahuatl for 'place of the temple of the jaguar' **(b)**. *According to Martinez Donjuán, these sculptures are situated so as to mark the equinoxes or solstices, and they 'symbolized the opposing forces that ruled the world'* **(c)**.

The back of one of these monuments, Monument 2, contains symbols that Martinez Donjuán interprets as '10 Flower'. If his interpretation is correct, then this would be the oldest Mesoamerican calendar date yet discovered.

This site also contains two ball courts. One miniature ball court is located within the Sunken Patio itself **(d)**, *while the other lies 900 metres to the northeast. At one end of the smaller ball court there is an adobe sweat bath. This sweat bath was most likely used as a social bonding environment for the developing Teopantecuanitlan elite.*

Teopantecuanitlan is also home to the oldest known Mesoamerican dam. This dam was constructed around 1200 BCE and built of rough uncut rocks. This dam relied on gravity to bring water to the agricultural land. Canals, or channels, made of large flat stone slabs are also present in Teopantecuanitlan. The lining of these canals was of benefit to the domestication of plants by means of irrigation. These canals prevented erosion damage, loss of water also acted as a sewer.

This site is also the first known within Mesoamerica to utilize the architectural feature known as a corbelled vault. This vault allowed for high ceilings without the use of trapezoidal cut stone. These corbelled vaults were used in ancient structures such as the tombs of the elite and in temples.

Teopantecuanitlan society was not egalitarian — otherwise such monumental structures would not have been built. There was a leader in place to oversee the building of these structures as well as instruct the laborers and ensure that all the necessary resources were available.

(a) Reilly, p.756. **(b)** Malmström, p.1 and **(c)** Martinez Donjuán differentiate the four monuments into two pairs, with either a bird-beak or feline-like 'orifice'. Other researchers in this field do not make this distinction. **(d)** Due to its very small size and placement within the sunken patio, Martinez Donjuán considers this to be a symbolic, rather than actual ball court.

Coe, Michael (1994), *Mexico: From the Olmecs to the Aztecs*, 4th edition, Thames & Hudson, NY

Diehl, Richard A. (2004) *The Olmecs: America's First Civilization*, Thames & Hudson, New York

Evans, Susan Toby (2004) *Ancient Mexico & Central America: Archaeology and Cultural History*, Thames & Hudson, New York

Reilly, F. K., (2000), *Tlacozotitlán (Guerrero, Mexico)* in Evans, Susan Toby, *Archaeology of Ancient Mexico and Central America*, Taylor & Francis

Malmström, V. H., *A Survey of Teopantecuanitlan, Guerrero, Mexico*

Martinez Donjuan, Guadalupe (2000), *Teopantecuanitlan*, in *The Oxford Encyclopedia of Mesoamerican Cultures*, Carraso, David ed., Oxford University Press

Martinez Donjuan, Guadalupe (1986), *Teopantecuanitlan*, in *Arqueologia y Etnohistoria del Estado de Guerrero*, Roberto Cervantes-Delgado ed., Instituto de Antropologia e Historia of Mexico, pp 55-80

Note 20

Circe's Aeaea (surrounded by water)

During his reconnaissance of Circe's realm, Odysseus is reported to have ascended to a high point and reported that the land was surrounded by water. Odysseus' observation concurs with Mesoamerican folklore which states that this land was called Cemanabuac, meaning ***'land surrounded by water'***. It is also possible that having ***'climbed to a point of vantage'*** somewhere on the narrow isthmus of Central America, Odysseus may have in fact sighted the Caribbean Sea. If this were the case, it would have been reasonable for him to assume that the land was surrounded by water. In the year 1572 A.D. Sir Francis Drake made a very similar reconnaissance. He however, had moored his galleon near Nobre de Dios on the Caribbean side of the isthmus, close to the entrance of the Panama Canal. Having trekked inland Drake scaled a high tree whereupon he made his first sighting of the Pacific Ocean.

Note 21

Emperor Yao

The renowned American archaeologist and epigrapher Sylvanus Griswold Morley (1883 - 1948) noted that one of the Maya 'long count' calendar records he had found at Palenque referred to the year 2358 B.C. Having previously considered the apparent similarities that exist between Ancient Chinese and Olmec cultures, it is a remarkable coincidence that the Mayan 'long count' date of 2358 B.C. should coincide with the enthronement year of the legendary Chinese Emperor Yao. According to legend, Yao became ruler when he was 20 years old and died at the age of 119. His throne was then occupied by the great Shun to whom Yao had earlier presented his two daughters in marriage. Often extolled as being the morally perfect sage-king, Yao's benevolence and diligence served as a model to future Chinese monarchs and emperors. The early Chinese often spoke of the emperors Yao, Shun and Yu as historical figures. Contemporary historians believe they may represent the chiefs of allied tribes who had established a unified and hierarchical system of government during the transition period to a patriarchal feudal society. The initial chapters of the Chinese *Book of History* deal with the exploits of Yao, Shun, and Yu.

Note 22

Votan

Doctor Paul Felix Cabrera's *Teatro Critico Americano* firstly acknowledges Bishop Nurez de la Vega's historic references to the demigod Votan. It then presents a description of a valuable memoir communicated to him by Don Ramon Ordonez y Aguiar:

> *The memoir in his possession consists of five or six folios of common quarto paper, written in ordinary characters in the Tzendal language, an evident proof of its having been copied from the original in hieroglyphics, shortly after the conquest.*
>
> *At the top of the first leaf, the two continents are painted in different colours, in two small squares, placed parallel to each other in the angles: the one representing Europe, Asia and Africa, is marked with two large SS; upon the upper arms of two bars drawn from the opposite angles of each square, forming the point of union in the centre; that which indicates America has two SS placed horizontally on the bars but I am not certain whether upon the upper or lower bars but I believe upon the latter. When speaking of the places he had visited on the old continent he marks them on the margin of each chapter with an upright S and those of America with a horizontal S. Between these squares stand the title of his history: 'Proof that I am Culebra' (a snake).*
>
> *With this title he proves in the body of his work, that he is Culebra, because he is Chivim. He states that he had conducted seven families from Valum Votan to this continent and assigned lands to them. Being the third of the Votans, he was determined to travel until he arrived at the root of heaven. In order to discover his relations (the Culebras) and make himself known to them, he made four voyages to Chivim (which is expressed by repeating four times from Valum Votan to Valum Chivim, from Valum Chivim to Valum Votan). He arrived in Spain and went to Rome; he saw the great House of God building; he went by the road that his brethren the Culebras had bored; he marked it and passed by the houses of the thirteen Culebras.*
>
> Ramon Ordoñez y Aguiar, *Probanza de Votan*

Ramon Ordoñez y Aguiar's memorized recital of the Votan legend is somewhat difficult to interpret. Aguiar claims that Votan made a total of four voyages between Europe and Central America. On one of these journeys he arrived in Spain and then proceeded on to Rome where *'he saw the great House of God building'*. This claim vaguely informs us that one of his voyages occurred sometime during either the Roman Empire or later Christian era.

Roman-style head c.A.D. 20 excavated near Mexico City

The Discovery of a Roman Sculpture Near Mexico City

In 1933, archaeologist José García Payón discovered a small, sculpted head at a burial site in Calixtlahuaca, about 60 kilometres west of Mexico City. The burial site was beneath two undisturbed, cemented floors that antedated the destruction of Calixtlahuaca by the Aztecs in A.D. 1510. In 1961, the Austrian anthropologist Robert Heine-Geldern examined the head and declared that it derived 'unquestionably' from the Hellenistic-Roman school of art. He found that its distinctive naturalism suggested it could date to c.A.D. 200. The identification of the head as Roman work has been further confirmed by Bernard Andreae, Director Emeritus of the German Institute of Archaeology in Rome. In Andreae's *Domenici*, he also pronounces the sculpted head to be:

> *... without any doubt Roman and the lab analysis has confirmed that it is ancient. The stylistic examination tells us more precisely that it is a Roman work from around the 2nd century A.D. and the hairstyle and the shape of the beard present the typical traits of the Severian Emperors' period [193-235 A.D.].*

It is also feasible that the Votan voyages occurred c.500 B.C - 250 B.C. as this is the period in which Cathaginian mariners such as Hanno were making their daring voyages.

> *Moreover, Hanno the Libyan started out from Cathage and passed the Pillars of Hercules and sailed into the outer Ocean, with Libya on his port side and he sailed on towards the east, five-and-thirty days all told. But when at last he turned southward, he fell in with every sort of difficulty - the want of water, blazing heat and fiery streams running into the sea.*
>
> Arrian, *The Anabasis of Alexander* VIII (Indica)

In section 30 of his *Diocesan Constitution*, Nunez de la Vega writes:

> *Votan is the third gentile placed in the calendar. He wrote an historical tract in the Indian idiom wherein he mentions by name, the people with whom and places where he had been.*

La Vega's statement that '*Votan is the third gentile placed in the calendar*' may imply that he was the third in a series of 'white' avatar teachers who came from the Mediterranean. Is it possible that the first Votan was Odysseus and that the subsequent visits of Votan occurred at intervals of 394 years? The Maya refer to these 394 year time periods as *Baktums*.

Votan 1	1158 B.C.	Greeks? (Odysseus)
Votan 2	764 B.C.	Phoenicians?
Votan 3	370 B.C.	Carthaginians?
Votan 4	24 A.D.	Romans?

The bearded Aztec deity Yacatecuhtli (long nose) was patron god of commerce and merchant travellers

Note 23

The Seri (Naga Serpent People)

Renowned for their fierce attacks upon early Spanish settlers, the Seri people of Mexico's Tiburon Island survive today as an impoverished people. The Seri proclaim that their ancestors (protected by their sacred totems) had migrated to the Gulf of California on balsa rafts. To this day the Seri people continue the custom of painting sacred totems upon their cheeks. Unchanged by modern society, Seri 'chanters' relate that they were originally called Nagas, a race of 'serpent-people' who had lived long before the time of 'The Deluge' in a mighty ocean kingdom.

The folkloric traditions of the Seri concur with Hindu teachings which claim that the earliest inhabitants of India and Sri Lanka were also a snake worshipping people called Nagas. According to L. Taylor Hansen's, *He Walked the Americas,* the Seri who survived the 'great flood' had fled south to a land called 'Snows of the Southland' (South America?) where they built cities above giant caverns and called themselves 'Men of the Mountains'. After many ages, a northern army had swept down and burned the cities. The Seri 'serpent-people' fled through the caverns to their waiting ships and thence began another series of migrations.

The Seri report of a northern army sweeping down upon the mountainous Southland concurs with an Aztec legend that tells how their war god, Huitzilopochtli, had decapitated his warrior-sister and attacked her brothers who were called Centzon Huitznahua ('The Four Hundred Southerners').

Seri legend also tells of Tlazoma 'The Miracle Worker' (Odysseus?) who came to them in a 'canoe driven by wind power'. When the 'miracle worker' stepped ashore at dawn, the Seri were amazed at his long white toga, gleaming red hair and eyes the colour of the deep-sea.

Chapter 8

Land of the Cimmerians

(Coast of Peru)

Note 24

Origin of Cotton in South America

The Spanish conquerors of the Aztec and Inca empires were astonished to see natives attired in 'Mediterranean-styled' garments made of cotton.

A study into the genetics of cotton plants from all over the world by Hutchinson, Silow and Stephens (published 1947), shows that the wild cotton indigenous to the New World is short napped and cannot be used for spinning or weaving. All wild cotton has 13 chromosomes. In the Americas these chromosomes are short in size, while those of the cotton plants in the Middle Eastern Old World are long.

The 1947 research demonstrated that cotton cloth uncovered in archaeological excavations of Pre-Inca Peruvian tombs was produced from a man-made, hybrid strain of cotton. This cotton had 26 chromosomes: 13 short ones of the wild South American variety and 13 long chromosomes from a Middle Eastern strain.

The finding posed a huge botanical problem. How did the Indians of Mexico and Peru obtain the 'large 13 chromosome' species of cotton typical of the Old World and then cultivate it into cotton that could be spun to produce a fabric 'which exhibited the finest of mesh, and decorative patterns that were unsurpassed anywhere'?

There are only two possible explanations. The first is that ancient unknown seafarers intentionally introduced the Old World species to the Pre-Columbian natives. This is not a popular theory with mainstream academia. More widely accepted is the 'Drift Theory', which suggests that the seeds of the long-napped Middle Eastern cotton plant floated across the Atlantic Ocean to the then unknown New World.

In response to the 'Drift Theory', Thor Heyerdahl pointed out that:

> *One must postulate that Indians were standing on the beach when the seeds of the Old World cotton drifted ashore; they then recognized them for what they were, planted them and hurried to find some wild American cotton to cross with them. After successfully developing a hybrid with long lint, they next invented a ceramic spindle whorl identical to that of the Middle East with which to produce thread; with hundreds of yards of thread, they then invented the loom and started producing Mediterranean–type loincloths and cloaks - in the warmest parts of America where clothing was least required.*

Heyerdahl, Thor *Early Man and the Ocean* Doubleday & Co. 1979

Note 25

Sumerian Bowl

The Fuete Magna Bowl displays Sumerian cuneiform writing

Found in the region of Peru's Lake Titicaca, a ceremonial bowl incised with Mesopotamian cuneiform writing has caused many archaeologists to re-evaluate their knowledge of ancient sea voyages. Named after the place where it was found, the 'Fuente Magna' bowl has been dated to 2000 B.C. and is but one of a number of 'Sumerian-type' artifacts that have recently come to light.

Note 26

Large Peruvian Rafts

Inca raft A.D.1526

In A.D.1526, a Spanish sea captain named Bartolomeo Ruiz was sailing south from the Panamanian isthmus in order to explore the coast of the Equator. To his astonishment, he suddenly saw another vessel travelling north towards him. It was a large raft described as being roughly equal in size to Ruiz's caravel but much less maneuverable. He had little difficulty in overpowering the twenty native men and women on board. With the casual cruelty for which the Spanish of that period were notorious, eleven Indians were thrown overboard, five were taken prisoner and four were left with the raft after it had been thoroughly examined. The raft was made of balsa - the lightest wood in the forests of South America. Composed of nine logs, the longest of which was placed in the middle, it had progressively shorter ones on either side, which gave the craft a prow at one end. At right angles to the logs and raised several inches above them, was a deck made of slender canes which remained dry while the logs beneath were permanently awash. Indeed, there was no attempt to prevent water from running between them. Both logs and canes were held in place by lengths of henequen rope, not unlike hemp. The raft was an excellent load carrier. The Spanish estimated that it had a capacity of thirty-six tons. They were equally impressed with the rigging that 'carried masts and yards of very fine wood and cotton sails in the same shape and manner as our own ships'.

Ralling, Christopher *The Kon Tiki Man* p.97 BBC Books London 1990

Note 27

The Sun God - 'Apu Inti'

The Incas constructed numerous 'Temples of the Sun' wherein they placed discs of beaten gold. Considered to be the 'teardrops' of the sun-god Apu Inti, gold was fashioned into countless artifacts, many of which featured a golden 'man-god'. Thus began the legend of El Dorado - the 'Golden Man'. The Inca people thought of their emperor as a living god placed on Earth by the sun-god Inti, from whom they were all descended. To this day, the Festival of the Sun (*Inti Raymi*) is celebrated during the midwinter solstice.

Note 28

The Introduction of Agriculture and Irrigation

In the wake of Odysseus' surmised visit to Peru, improved methods of irrigation became commonplace (c.1150 B.C.). From that time hence the coastal Paloma people increased in stature. Although the general health of the Paloma improved, the pressure of their increased numbers upon the natural resources caused the local environment to deteriorate. Abandoning their ancient coastal settlements, the Paloma resettled in the nearby Chilca Valley where they began an intensive agricultural program utilising simple canals and other water control systems to irrigate their gardens. Many centuries later, these early agricultural practices had developed into massive communal irrigation systems. Huge ceremonial complexes were erected and these monumental constructions soon dwarfed the original buildings at El Paraiso.

Note 29

Tiwanaku Pottery

Shortly after being informed that local natives on Lake Titicaca's Pariti Island had discovered notable Classic Period, Tiwanaku ceramics, archaeologists from the University of Helsinki visited the island and confiscated them. The 'recovery' of the high quality ceramic ware led to a series of excavations that were carried out in August 2004. Digging in the vicinity of an ancient ceremonial site, the team stumbled upon a deep pit full of intentionally broken Classic Period, Tiwanaku ceramics. Archaeologist Antti Korpisaari reports:

> *The dig contained approximately 300 kilograms of deliberately broken ritual ceramics, which, according to radiocarbon dating, had been buried sometime between A.D. 900 - 1050. Some twenty vessels have been preserved intact. The objects can be equated to the best china of royal households or to sacramental communion vessels. By comparing decorative details, such as clothing, headgear, jewellry and even facial characteristics, to others found in the highland areas, we can actually start drawing conclusions about the ethnic identities of the people who lived here at the time. The discovery provides new information on the relationship between the Inca and Tiwanaku cultures.*

One of the exquisite pottery pieces displays the head of a 'white' native. The tattooed and protruding face displays elongated, pierced ears and is crowned with a small hat.

Note 30

South American Legends of 'White Visitors'

Compiled by the son of an Inca princess in the 17th century A.D., *The Royal Commentaries of the Inca* record how the natives of Ecuador had received white-skinned visitors in the ancient past. The bearded, giant white men had arrived from the Pacific Ocean by boat. '*Their hair hung down to their shoulders and they had eyes as big as saucers'*. Clad in animal skins, the visitors had introduced advanced methods of house building and sinking wells. Curious legends of a white, bearded race of people also exists in the region of Lake Titicaca in Bolivia. According to Bolivian folklore, the descendants of an ancient race of white people were responsible for the construction of age-old megalithic temples. Bolivian folklore also relates the tale of a mysterious group of 'white people' who were annihilated by natives arriving from Ecuador at a later date.

In his *Chronicles of Peru*, the Spanish historian Pedro de Cieza de León, (A.D. 1520-54) recorded a local tradition that tells of giants coming ashore about 75 kilometres south of Lima:

> *As there is in Peru a story of some giants who landed on the coast at the point of Santa Elena, in the vicinity of the city of Puerto Viejo.*

Note 31

Mummies With Red Hair

The ancient Peruvians echoed the ancient Egyptians in their treatment of the dead. They utilised some of the same general mummification techniques, such as the removal of the viscera, embalming and providing possessions of value for the spirit's journey into the next world. The custom of interring the dead with valuable objects has of course attracted numerous tomb robbers. The recent discovery of a plundered tomb in Peru has revealed that certain ancient Peruvians had auburn or ash-blonde hair. Prior to this find, reports of fair-haired natives by Spanish Conquistadors were regarded as exaggerative.

Note 32

Egyptian Symbolism

The jackal-god Anubis (Tutankhamun's tomb, 1323 B.C.)

Pre-Columbian vase motif, Peru

Papyrus of Hunefer c.1285 B.C

To this present day the native peoples of the Yucatan, Central America and the northern coasts of Peru and Chile continue to decorate their paintings, sculptures and woven crafts with 'royal spirals' and 'stepped-thrones'. Denoting divinity, the 'royal spiral' and 'stepped-throne' motifs are clearly depicted on the Egyptian 'Papyrus of Hunefer' which was created in the Nineteenth Dynasty c.1200 B.C. (see illustrations p.270)

Note 33

The Oruro Tablet

Discovered in Oruro, Bolivia, the stone tablet pictured below displays Cretan-type symbols that may have possibly been carved by Odysseus or one of his crewmen.

According to the eminent linguist, Dr. Clyde Winters:

> *This tablet is very interesting to me. After a cursory examination of the tablet, it appears that the personage on the right side of the tablet seems to have a headdress similar to that worn by the People of the Sea or Hittites, when they attacked Egypt around 1200 B.C. I cannot read the characters on the tablet, but they appear to be Linear B, signs similar to the writing of the Greek-speaking people of Crete. Again, this is my opinion and I welcome the observation of other people on the forum. If this tablet is authentic, it indicates that in addition to the Sumerians in ancient South America, Indo-European speaking people also began to arrive here at least by 1200 B.C.*

(www.world-mysteries.com/sar-8.htm)

Note 34

El Dorado Fables

Many members of expeditions have lost their lives combing the jungles of the Amazon for fabled 'cities of gold'. When the Spanish and Portuguese first arrived in South America in search of gold, they encountered persistent, intriguing legends, such as those of 'El Dorado' and the lost city of 'Ma-Noa'. The description given to Francisco López by Indians at the time of the conquest of Peru, contained elements that would appeal to any treasure hunter:

> *Ma-Noa is an island in a great salt lake. All the serving dishes for the palace are made of pure gold and silver. And even the most insignificant things are made of silver and copper. In the middle of the island stands a temple dedicated to the sun. Around the building there are statues of gold, which represent giants* ('white gods'). *There are also trees of gold* (maple) *and silver* (silver fir?).

The native description of 'Ma Noa' oddly fits that of Minoan Crete. Archaeologist Arthur Evans coined the word Minoa to describe the ancient civilization he discovered on Crete. Is it possible that Mediterranean sailors in their attempt to describe the treasure-laden island of Crete to the natives of Brazil had created the legend of Manoa? Early explorers such as Sir Walter Raleigh went in earnest search of Manoa and even in this present day, treasure-hunting adventurers continue to scour the Amazon in hope of finding this fabled kingdom.

Note 35

Labyrinths

According to Charles Berlitz's *Mysteries From Forgotten Worlds*, a Pre-Columbian labyrinth design found in Ecuador corresponds with labyrinth designs that '*appear throughout the Mediterranean*', and are '*especially centered in the Minoan civilization of ancient Crete*'. In Greek legend, the labyrinth was literally 'the cage' for the 'man-bull' Minotaur. In the tomb labyrinths of ancient Egypt, the maze was allegorically connected with the wanderings of the soul after death.

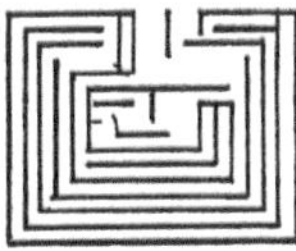

Pre-Columbian labyrinth, Ecuador **Cretan coin**

Note 36

Sirens

The name 'Siren' derives from a Greek root-word meaning 'to attach or bind' and this illustrates the role the Sirens played in Greek mythology. In primitive times the Sirens had been the daughters of the river-god Achelous and according to various authors, their number was two, three, four or eight.

The names of the Sirens describe their 'charming' ability:

Molpe (the songstress)

Peisinore (the persuasive)

Thelxepeia (of words that enchant)

Aglaophonos (of the brilliant voice)

There are different explanations for their 'bird' bodies. A common belief is that they were originally the maiden-companions of Persephone and had witnessed her abduction and ravishment by Hades, the god of the Underworld. At their request Zeus had provided them with wings so that they could fly in pursuit of Hades. This particular version of the Sirens' origin might explain why Odysseus identified them in what he perceived to be the realm of Hades (Peru). Ancient Greek mariners sailing along a foreign coastline inhabited by mysterious, primitive tribes might well have thought of the female natives as Sirens.

At the time of Odysseus, the peoples of the Chilean and Argentinean regions were likely to have been adorned with feathers. The haunting sounds of eerie flute trills may have compounded a fear that female Sirens could lure them ashore. When visiting these waters in the 19th century A.D., the English naturalist Charles Darwin reported that local natives had shouted to him from a canoe. Expressing his aloof disdain of their appearance he wrote:

> *Viewing such men, one can hardly make oneself believe that they are fellow creatures and inhabitants of the same world. We often try to imagine what pleasures in life some of the lower animals can enjoy. How much more reasonably the same questions may be asked concerning these barbarians.*

Illustration of a Patagonian native by French explorer Jules Dumont d'Urville A.D. 1840

Chapter 9

Land of Helios

(Coasts of Argentina and Brazil)

Note 37

Helios

> *Every morning Helios emerged in the East from a swamp formed by the river-ocean in the far-off land of the Ethiopians. To his golden chariot, which Hephaestus had fashioned, the Horae harnessed the winged horses. They were of dazzling white; their nostrils breathed forth flame and their names were Lampon, Phaethon, Chronos, Aethon, Bronte, Pyroeis, Eous and Phlegon. The god then took the reins and climbed the vault of heaven. Drawn in his swift chariot, he sheds light on gods and men alike; the formidable flash of his eyes pierces his golden helmet; sparkling rays glint from his breast; his brilliant helmet gives forth a dazzling splendor; his body is draped in shining gauze whipped by the wind. At midday Helios reached the highest point of his course and began to descend towards the West, arriving at the end of the day in the land of the Hesperides where he seemed to plunge into the Ocean. In reality, there he found a barque or a golden cup, made by Hephaestus, in which his mother, wife and children were awaiting him. He would sail all night and in the morning regain his point of departure. Again it was said that his horses rested on the islands of the Blessed, at the western extremity of the Earth, where they browsed on a magic herb.* New Larousse Encyclopedia of Mythology

The sun-god Helios had numerous wives, including the nymph Rhode who bore him seven sons called 'Heliads' and one daughter named Electryone. The Heliads were distinguished for their intelligence and credited with the division of the day into hours and perfecting the art of shipbuilding. Helios also married Clymene, the Queen of the Ethiopians who in contrast, bore him seven daughters and one son, who was named Phaeton. Helios is traditionally associated with the Ethiopians and it was from Ethiopia that the sun-god was said to begin his daily journey.

Citing the Greek historian Ephorus (c.400 B.C.), Strabo tells us that some of the Ethiopians '*penetrated into the extreme west*'. Although the 'extreme west' is generally interpreted to imply Morocco, one might also suggest that it could possibly refer to the Caribbean.

But there is another ancient tradition related by Ephorus, which Homer had probably fallen in with. He tells us it is reported by the Tartessians (of Southern Spain), that some of the Ethiopians, on their arrival in Libya, penetrated into the extreme west and settled down there, while the rest occupied the greater part of the sea-coast. In support of this statement he quotes a passage from Homer: 'The Ethiopians, the farthest removed of men, separated into two divisions'.

Strabo, *Geography* Chapter 2: 26

Note 38

The Paraiba Stone

Located on Brazil's Cape of Sao Roque, the town of Joao Pessoa (formally called Paraiba) is renowned for the discovery of a mysterious stone that might well have provided proof that Mediterranean mariners had found their way to Brazil two thousand years before Christopher Columbus.

The stone is said to have broken into four pieces shortly after its discovery in September 1872. Although the four pieces subsequently disappeared, copies of the stone's intricate inscription have been retained and preserved. A detailed study of the Paraiba Stone's markings was made by the German scholar, Lienhardt Delekat who documented them in his book entitled *Phonizier in Amarika* (Bonn, 1969). Delekat believes that the Brazilian inscription was written in ancient Tyro-Sidonian, which he dated to the 6th century B.C. His interpretation reads as follows:

We are children of Canaan, from the city of Sidon. We are a nation of traders. Our ship is beached on this far-off mountainous coast and we want to make sacrifice to the gods and goddesses. In the 19th year of Irmas' reign, we set sail from Ezlon Geber across the Red Sea, with ten ships. We have been sailing now for two years and we have sailed all around this land, both hot and far from the lands of Baal (cold). Twelve men and three women have arrived here.. Ten of the women have died on another coast, because they had sinned. May the gods and goddesses be favourable towards us.

After studying interpretations made by other scholars including Netto, Schlottmann, Gordon and Sudhoff, Delekat came to the conclusion that the 'lost mariners' had reached Brazil via the Pacific Ocean. According to Delekat, their claim of having sailed south of the Bering Strait and south of Cape Horn (cold zones), as well as sailing between the two hot zones, indicates that they had voyaged across the Pacific Ocean. If Delekat is correct in his findings, then it would certainly add plausibility to the possibility that Odysseus could have made a very similar voyage 600 years prior to the unfortunate Phoenicians.

Note 39

Typhon: The Cyclonic God

Typhoon, the Chinese word for a tropical storm, is derived from the Neolithic European deity, Typhon. Mythographers identify Typhon with the Egyptian god, Seth, who was represented as the epitome of evil. In cross-referencing apparently disparate ancient myths, I discovered that the father of Typhon was the Pre-Egyptian whirlwind demon, Typhoeus. Originally a hundred-headed Gigante, Typhoeus became the mythopoeia of the Greek god, Zeus.

Zeus fighting with Typhon

Chapter 10

Calypso's Isle of Ogygia

(The Caribbean)

Note 40

The Goddess Ca

The Greek words *charisma* and *katharos*, meaning pure, best describe the primeval moon-goddess Ca. The ancients believed the moon to be the ruler of feminine emotions and a legacy of this credo can be found in the ancient words:

cardia (Greek: the heart)
carus (Latin: dear)
caru (Old English: care)
carim (Gaelic: I love)

The goddess **Ca** was universally revered by our ancestors who saw her as a 'controller of destinies', particularly those associated with death and the seasons. To the ancients of Ireland she was ***Cailleach Bheare***, the immortal, ancient mountain-mother who controlled the season of winter. In the Hindu religion we find her as **Ka**li, a goddess of retribution who governs the **Ka**rmic Wheel of Life (Sanskrit: ***Cakra***: wheel). The ancient Ainu of Japan were a Caucasian people who venerated the Mother Nature spirit as **Ka**moi. In the Shinto religion, 'the way of nature' is referred to as ***Kami,*** hence the 'divine' wind is called ***Kami-kazi***. In ancient Egypt, an individual's soul was called their **Ka**. An association with the **Ka**'s travelling across the waters of the Underworld may be reflected in the universal use of the prefix 'ca' in words describing sea vessels:

Canoe: native boat
Cayik: Turkish long boat
Caraba: Spanish for boat
Carh: Gaelic word for boat
Karfi: Old Norse term for boat
Caravel: Spanish ship

Note 41

In his essay *Human Lymphocyte Antigens*, James. L Guthrie presents numerous evidences to support the theory of Trans-Atlantic voyages c.3000 - 1500 B.C.:

> *On the basis of stone points, axes, pottery and other evidence, Kennedy (1971) connected the Caribbean with other Pan-Atlantic cultures of 3000 - 1500 B.C. Focusing on pottery, he listed six traits, such as coil-building, that are typical of Atlantic Europe, Northwest Africa, Middle America, the Caribbean and southeastern North America. He said that southeastern check-stamped wares (2000 B.C.) are identical to those of Morocco; that the red slip technique came from northwestern Africa or southern Spain about 2500 B.C.; that rockering reached Ecuador by 2000 B.C., and so forth. According to Kennedy, many traits of the European Late Neolithic period derive from predynastic Egypt, being preserved by Berbers, Maltese, and others, then being transmitted to the Caribbean, southeastern North America and eventually to the Pacific Coast, where numbers increased owing to better conditions. He called this era one of the greatest periods of voyaging in man's history, describing the Bell Beaker people as an aggressive industrial culture marked by exceptional mobility by land and sea. Much other evidence supports this view, especially the findings of Chadwick (1971) and Alcina Franch (1985) and many previous publications. Chadwick put such elements of the Beaker complex as stirrup-spout pottery, as early as 2000 B.C. at Tlatilco (Central Mexico) and Kotosh (Peru), but he also thought there had been a second Pan-Atlantic wave at about 500 B.C. Alcina's study of stamp seals led him to conclude that they had reached Middle America about 1500 B.C. from the Canary Islands.*

Note 42

Britomartis/Brigit/Briganta

The legend of Ino/Leucothea is somewhat similar to the sad plight of the Cretan maiden, Britomartis. Rather than succumb to King Minos' relentless pursuit, Britomartis had cast herself into the 'turbulent sea'.

The numerous fish-tailed images of Britomartis that have been found throughout the island of Crete give testament to the legend that the maiden not only survived her ocean plunge, but continued swimming across the seas until she arrived (or returned) to the shores of Ireland where she was venerated as Brigit (Briganta, Brighia).

> *In remote times her followers, the Brigantes, held festivals in her honour, mounting a statue of the goddess into a processional boat (brigatine) that they then conveyed ceremoniously across the countryside.*

Denning, *Magical Philosophy* III p.166

Chapter 11

Scheria: Land of the Phaeacians

(Southern Spain)

Note 43

Sacred Peninsulas

Nausicaa's description of her Phaeacian land as ***'jutting into the surrounding sea'*** might identify it as being located on a 'sacred peninsula'. Strabo's writings tell us that the Greeks recognised various promontories as being symbolic 'Pillars of Hercules'. Temples dedicated to Hercules were generally located at the coastal tip of these land spits. Although the temples were usually erected to mark the extents of Hercules' legendary travels, they might also have been built on even older sites that had long been considered sacred because they were remnants of lands that had been submerged by the ocean. The ancients who lived on the coasts of Portugal, France, Britain and Ireland retained legends of a sunken kingdom. In each of these countries there also exists a so-called 'sacred peninsula' whose headland points to a region in the ocean where there once existed a land of villages and people: Lyonesse, Lethowstow, Cantreys of Dyfed, Ile Verde and 'Y's.

The Sacred Peninsula of Lusitania

Presently called Cape Saint Vincent, the 'sacred peninsula' of Lusitania in Portugal is the most westerly point of Europe. According to Strabo, Lusitania's peninsular lay about one day's sailing from Gades. His estimation however, contradicts that of his predecessor, Eratosthenes (276 BC - 194 B.C.), who claimed that the 'sacred promontory' was five sailing days from Gades. (Strabo, *Geography*, Book 3:1)

It is possible that Eratosthenes identified the 'sacred peninsula' with either Land's End in Cornwall or the western tip of Brittany. According to Cornish folklore, the now submerged land of Lethowstow once joined Land's End to the Scilly Isles. The many towns that are said to have once existed on this land were suddenly submerged at an unknown date. On the opposite side of the English Channel, Breton traditions tell of the once fabulous kingdom of 'Y's which is also reputed to have vanished beneath the ocean's waves. Commenting on the Sacred Promontory, the geographer Artemidorus (c.100 B.C.) wrote:

> *The Sacred Promontory compares to a ship; three little islands, each having a small harbour, contribute to give it this form; the former island resembling the beak of the ship and the two latter, the beams on each side of the ship's bows. There is no temple of Hercules shown there, as Ephorus falsely states, nor yet any altar [to him] nor to any other divinity; but in many parts there are three or four stones placed together which are turned by all travellers who arrive there in accordance with a certain local custom. It is not lawful to offer sacrifice there, nor yet to approach the place during the night for it is said that this is when the gods take up their abode at the place.*

Artemidorus' reference to the Sacred Promontory as having three islands suggests that he is perhaps describing the Scilly Isles. 'Turning stones' were a feature of southern England's megalithic culture. Located along ley lines, 'holy rocks' (*carreck sans*) such as Cheesering in Cornwall, are rumoured to vibrate and mutter at night. Traditional Cornish superstition states that if you can spend the night at Cheesering you will see the top stone turn three times at sunrise.

Originally drawn in the 2nd century A.D., Ptolemy's map of Ireland displays yet another sacred promontory. Located off Wexford and serving as a first point of contact for ships arriving to Ireland, the promontory may have at some time in history formed a land bridge to Wales. The locals who live on the Welsh side of the 'land bridge' retain the legend of the lost city of Cantrey. According to their traditions, 16 towns were destroyed when a tsunami overwhelmed an ancient sea wall.

Remnants of land bridges between the British Isles and mainland Europe were in existence until c.6000 B.C. It stands to reason that the people who inhabited the coastal regions had at various times experienced catastrophic inundations of their lands. In all probability, they began to erect megalithic monuments in order to placate the destructive sea-gods. This may explain why the majority of Europe's megalithic sites are located in close proximity to the coast and particularly on 'sacred peninsulas'. It seems that the Phaeacians also practiced such customs.

Note 44

Sea Peoples

The Egyptian priest who first informed Plato about the legend of Atlantis also spoke of the armies of Atlantis (c.9000 B.C.) and how they had once gathered together in an attempt:

> ... *to enslave by one single onslaught both your country* (Greece), *ours* (Egypt) *and the whole of the territory within the Straits* (the Mediterranean).

The Egyptian and Greek civilizations were not in existence 9000 B.C. The scenario described to Plato was more likely based on the mysterious Sea Peoples' invasions of the Nile Delta which occurred 1227 - 1207 B.C. This time period also coincides with the Trojan War that has been variously dated from 1250 B.C. (*Herodotus*) to 1209 B.C. (*the Parian Marble*). It might also be suggested that among the 'sea peoples' who attacked Egypt were clans who had come from as far away as Spain. Listing the sea captains who fought against Troy, Homer writes of:

> *Halizones, Odius and Epistrophus who were captains from far distant Alybe, where is the birthplace of silver*. (*The Iliad,* Chapter 2: 845)

Scholars such as Eustathius have identified Alybe with the Spanish port of Calpe (Gibraltar). The fact that Spain has long been regarded as the 'birthplace' of silver mining supports the suggestion that sea captains who fought against Troy had come from far distant Spain. Alybe was situated close to the sophisticated El Argar culture that flourished in southern Spain c.1800 - 1300 B.C. The Argarians mined bronze, silver and gold, which they skillfully crafted into weapons and jewellry. Cultural exchanges between the Iberians of El Argar and the Mycenaeans of Greece are pronounced. Abandoning the European megalithic tradition of multiple burials, the Argarians adopted the Mycenaean practice of interring the ashes of their deceased in large jars or *pithoi*, while the Hellenes adopted the Iberian custom of constructing round tombs (*tholos*).

Scholarship continues to debate the identity of the nations that comprised the Sea Peoples' armada. It seems quite probable that the Myceneans (Peleset?), the Danaans of Greece (Denyen?) and the Etruscans (Tursha/Tyrhenians?) were among those involved. I might suggest that the horn-helmeted Sherdens (the main protagonists?), originated from Eastern

Europe. The Egyptian *Great Karnak Inscription* recognises the various tribes constituting the Sea Peoples as:

> *Akawasha, Terusha, Lukka, Sherden, Shekekesh, northerners who came fron all lands.*

Theban scribes further identified the invaders as:

> *... Peleset, Tjeker, Shekelesh, Denyen and Weshesh, united lands. They laid their hands upon the lands to the very circuit of the Earth, their hearts confident and trusting: 'Our plans will succeed!'*

Relief sculpture on the walls of Egypt's Medinet Habu temple displays the remarkable diversity of the Sea Peoples

Distaining any culture other than their own, the Sea Peoples erected new settlements directly over the ashes of the coastal settlements they conquered. When excavating the structures above the charred ruins, archaeologists found numerous artifacts including brooches and amber beads, as well as drinking cups and knives that are akin to those unearthed in central Germany c.1800 - 1600 B.C. Bronze weapons and ceramic vessels of a distinctly Italic style have also been uncovered.

Note 45

Azores-Gibraltar Fault Line

> *Swath-bathymetry and acoustic-backscatter data from the southwest Iberian margin, which hosts the present-day boundary between the European and African plates, reveal the surficial expression of several*

fault structures 100 km offshore of Portugal. The location and dimension of these newly identified structures agree with the modelled source suggested for the A.D. 1755 Lisbon earthquake and tsunami, possibly the most destructive event in Western Europe during historical time. These fault escarpments and deformed seafloor sediments associated with a cluster of shallow seismicity suggest that these thrusts are active and may pose a significant earthquake and tsunami hazard to the coasts of Portugal, Spain, and Morocco.

(International Commission for the Scientific Exploration of the Mediterranean Sea Congress)

Note 46

The Larousse Encyclopedia of Mythology informs us that the name Titan probably derives from the Cretan word for king. It is also thought that Titan extends from the Greek *teino* meaning 'I strain', as the Titans, according to Hesiod's *Theogony, 'strained in insolence and did a deed for which they would be punished afterwards'.*

Other scholars such as Jane Ellen Harrison assert that the word Titan comes from the Greek τιτανος, signifying white earth, clay or gypsum, and that the Titans were referred to as 'white clay men' because they covered themselves in white clay or gypsum dust during their rituals.

Note 47

Giants of Britain

The British Isles abound in legends of giants. The creation of landforms such as the Giant's Causeway, Ireland and the island of Saint Michael's Mount in Cornwall are said to be the handiwork work of ancient giants. The Greek geographer Eratosthene wrote of an Isle of Kerne (Britain) that lay beyond the Pillars of Hercules. (See Strabo, *Geography* Chapter 3: 2) Today we recognise Kerne as the Cerne Abbas Giant ('Cerne the White Giant') whose image can still be clearly seen on a Dorset hillside. Another giant figure called The Long Man of Wilmington is found on Windover Hill near Wilmington in Sussex. Other famous giants of the British Isles include Bran who waded across the Irish Sea; Dagda, whose club was so large that it needed eight men to carry it and Gogmagog, who was defeated by the Trojan Brutus when he arrived in Britain c.1200 B.C. In a certain legend, Stonehenge was purportedly constructed so that it might record 'the Giants' Dance'. The folk term 'Giants' Dance' possibly relates to the Precession of the Equinox.

Cerne Abbas Giant, Dorset

Hu

Perhaps the most renowned giant of megalithic Britain was Hu. According to Gertrude Jobes' *Encyclopedia of Mythology:*

> *Hu was a British oak and sun deity; the elementary and primitive all-pervading God of gentleness and the first of three chieftains who obtained dominion over Britain. He established himself not by bloodshed and war, but by justice and peace. He killed a dragon and caused the cessation of disastrous floods; he federated the people into tribes and introduced civil government; he taught them the art of agriculture and was the first on British soil to draw a furrow with a plough. He introduced letters, literature and history. He appears to be identical with the Guernsey Hou; with the Welsh Hu Gadarn and with the Welsh Llew (Lleu).*

Hu might also be recognized as the:

Turkic	Hu	Viking	Hugi
Egyptain	Shu	Chinese	Huang-Ti
Babylonian	Huwara	Inca	Hua
Iberian	El Hu or Huelva	Aztec	Huemae

Note 48

Tartessus

In Robert Graves' *White Goddess* we read that the Aegean word *Tar* meant west or dying sun:

> *Tartessus on the Atlantic was the most westerly Aegean trading station - Tarraco was the port on the extreme west of the Mediterranean and Tarrha, the chief port of western Crete. The duplication 'tar-tar', meaning 'the far, far west' has evidently given Tartara, 'the land of the dead', its name.*

As the Ionic Greek word *tesseres* means four, the word Tartessus might imply the existence of four cities or four races of man that abode in the far west. The symbolic 'four' concept is also found in the Greek legend of the Hesperides. The four Hesperides - Aruthsae, Angle, Erythia and Hespia - were said to inhabit a land that was located beyond the Pillars of Hercules (Mediterranean), at the extreme western limits of the world.

The four Hesperides

Tarshish

Biblical scholars identify Tartessus with the mysterious land of Tarshish:

> *Silver spread into plates is brought from Tarshish and gold from Uphaz, the work of the workman and of the hands of the founder: blue and purple is their clothing: they are all the work of cunning men.* Jeremiah 10: 9

The kings of Tarshish and of distant shores will bring tribute to him. Psalm 72:10

Tarshish was thy merchant by reason of the multitude of all kind of riches; with silver, iron, tin, and lead, they traded in thy fairs. Ezekiel 27:12

The ships of Tarshish did sing of thee in thy market: and thou was replenished, and made very glorious in the midst of the seas. Ezekiel 27:25

Sheba, and Dedan, and the merchants of Tarshish, with all the young lions thereof, shall say unto thee, Art thou come to take a spoil? Hast thou gathered thy company to take a prey? To carry away silver and gold, to takeaway cattle and goods, to take a great spoil. Ezekiel 38:13

Note 49

Origin of the Phaeacians

Although the early Romans had studied Etruscan literature, scarce remnants exist today, having been destroyed by the Early Christians who deemed them pagan. The sanctimonious behavior of the Early Church has resulted in the absence of direct historical records and what little remains of their writing is yet to be deciphered by modern scholars. However, on the northern Aegean island of Lemnos, archaeologists have found inscriptions written in a language that is remarkably similar to Etruscan. Lemnos and the nearby islands of Imbros and Lesbos lie in close proximity to the legendary city of Troy and are traditionally associated with maritime peoples called Tyrsenians or Tyrrhenians. Scholars of the Classical Period were of the belief that the Tyrrhenians were one in the same people as the Etruscans. The Greek historian Herodotus (c.500 B.C.) was certain that the Etruscans had originated from Lydia in Asia Minor. According to his writings, a group of Lydians had once fled Lydia and having sailed:

... past many lands they came to Umbria in Italy where they built cities and still live to this day, changing their name from Lydians to Tyrrhenians after the king's son Tyrrhenus who had led them.

Also writing in the fifth century B.C., the Greek historian, Hellanicus of Lesbos, mentioned a group of Pelasgians who upon their arrival in Italy changed their name to Tyrrhenians. Dionysius of Halicarnassus (c.100 B.C.) agreed that the Etruscans were a branch of the Pelasgians but he insisted that they had subsequently been absorbed into Tyrrhenia. He also remained adamant that the original Etruscans were not from Lydia:

> *... for they do not use the same language as the latter, nor can it be alleged that, though they no longer speak a similar tongue, they still retain some other indications of their mother country.*

Note 50

The Seafaring Serpent

The blue-eyed, blonde seafarers variously called Danaids, Danuna, Danae, Danyen and Danaoi, probably originated from the Danube delta region of Bulgaria (Thrace). The Danaans are reported to have entered Greece from Bulgaria via Troy and the Aegean. Their initial settlement was at Argolis in the Peloponnesus c.2100 B.C. These 'Greek' Danaans are thought to have retained links with the Tyrhennians and Trojans of the northern Aegean. According to Professor Michael Sakellariou's *Prehistory and Protohistory*, the Indo-European root word *danu* implies water or river, and Greek myth credits Danaos and his daughters with the discovery of springs and the construction of wells: *'Danaos made Argos well-watered where previously it had been waterless'*. When the mythological Cadmus invaded Greece from the East (c.1500 B.C.?), he reportedly slew the Danaan dragon/serpent that stood guard over the sacred spring waters of Delphi.

Hindu mythology names Danu as a goddess and mother of the dragon Urta, as well as a group of daemons that were associated with springs. Danu was also the Mother Goddess of the Tuatha de Danaan of Ireland. It is generally accepted that the name Tuatha de Danaan translates as *'people of Danaan'* or simply *'the people'*. The Indo-European etymology of Danu is perhaps *da* (thunder) and *nu* (daughter). The goddess Danu might then be recognized as the daughter of Da, the god of thunder or Dag-da meaning the 'good god' of thunder. Danu's Greek equivalent would be Athena, the daughter the 'good god' of thunder, Zeus.

The Seafaring Centaurs

The fact that ancient Irish and Aeolic Greek dialects share certain similarities prompts me to suggest that the warlike Centaurs may have emerged from Ireland c.1900 B.C. In his *Greek Myths*, Graves suggests the name Centaur is derived from *centuria* meaning *'war-band of one hundred'*. This title may also allude to the Centaurs' ability to man ships with a crew of 100 oarsmen. Bestowed with a navigational knowledge of the heavens by Chiron, the Centaurs also had a fearsome reputation for being drunken brawlers and rapists. The giant-sized Centaurs claimed to have descended from an ancestral father called Ixion. According to Pindar's *Pythian Odesii* (33 - 89), Zeus had once invited Ixion to feast at his table on Mount Olympus. During the supper, the ungrateful Ixion became inebriated and at night's end he attempted to ravish Zeus' wife, the goddess Hera. As punishment for his loutish behavior, Zeus condemned Ixion to be eternally chained to a fiery (solar?) wheel that *'rolled without cease through the sky'*. (See: Apd.Ep.1.20; Dio.4.69.1, 4.69.5, 4.70.1, 4.12.6; Ov.Met.12.210, 12.504; Pin.Pyth.2.21ff. - 2.44ff.)

Underlying this ancient legend is a possible historical account of huge Abante or Alba 'sea peoples' forcing their culture, or lack of it, upon the Pelasgians of ancient Greece. The uncouth Centaurs were probably the same *'herd of cattle'* that Hercules is said to have driven from Erytheia (Ireland?) to Mycenae (Greece).

Amalgamation of the Serpent and Centaur

Sometime around the year 1628 B.C., the volcanic island of Santorini exploded with such force that large rocks from its crater were flung as far away as the Black Sea. Millions of tonnes of molten ash were spewed 23 kilometres up into the sky and destructive tsunami waves devastated the coastal settlements of the Aegean. Charles Pellegrino's book *Unearthing Atlantis* provides us with a chilling description of the tsunami's power.

> *On the west cost of Turkey, just north of the island of Rhodes, is a small body of water whose shoreline is like an ever-narrowing funnel. Its open mouth faces west, toward Thera and anyone living behind that mouth might just as well have been a flea located in the throat of a cannon. As the shock wave surged east between increasingly confined shorelines, the waters piled higher and higher until at last they became a foaming white mountain eight hundred feet tall. The wave*

penetrated thirty miles inland, in the general direction of Mount Ararat and when it receded it dislodged house-sized boulders, scoured the soil and carved out channelled scablands. Elsewhere, on a strip of Turkish coast only ninety miles north of the funnel, the wave seems to have risen barely twenty feet high. Tsunamis are like that – capricious.

In order to avoid the bedlam of a devastated Aegean, the surviving Pelasgian clans of Danaans and Centaurs may have amalgamated and sailed to the western extents of the Mediterranean or beyond to the Atlantic seaboard of southern Spain. It is also possible that others returned to their original homeland of Ireland. The Irish Annals record the return to Ireland of a seafaring people called the Fir Bolg who are said to have spent 230 years in Greece.

Note 51

Irish Centaurs?

Typically related in a series of symbolic 'threes', the Irish Annals tell of ancient sea migrations between Ireland and Greece. In the long distant past, a seafaring race called the Nemedians are said to have arrived in Ireland from Greece. Led by three Nemedian chiefs, the Nemedian sea-warriors went to battle against Ireland's primitive Fomorians. Despite a crushing defeat at the hands of the Fomorians, the Nemedians survived and three generations on they divided into three groups. One group reached the Northern Isles and became the ancestors of a people called the Tuatha de Danaan, the second group settled in Britain, while a third are said to have sailed to Greece whereupon they became enslaved for a period of 230 years.

Semeon went in the lands of the Greeks. His progeny increased there till they amounted to thousands. Slavery was imposed upon them by the Greeks; they had to carry clay upon rough mountains so that they became flowery plains. Thereafter they were weary of their servitude and they went in flight, five thousand strong, and made them ships of their bags: [or, as the Quire of Druim Snechta says, they stole the Greeks' for coming therein]. Thereafter they came again into Ireland, their land of origin.

Leabhar Gabhála (The Irish Book of Invasions)

Having constructed ships made of leather (coracles), the enslaved immigrants escaped from Greece and on their arrival in Ireland were called Fir Bolg ('men of the bag'). During the Fir Bolg's long absence from Ireland, their ancient 'brothers', the Tuatha de Danaan, had been dwelling in the Isles of the North where it is said they were taught the arts of magic. The Tuatha de Danaan subsequently returned and took control of Ireland and when the Fir Bolg reappeared they were deemed inferior and assigned the task of constructing ring-forts called *raths*.

Cambridge Conference

In July 1997, many of the world's leading archaeologists, geologists and astronomers gathered together at Britain's Cambridge University. The object of their meeting was to share the evidences indicating how meteorite impacts and massive volcanic eruptions have at certain times in history resulted in major upheavals for mankind. Among the many excellent papers presented to the conference was one written by Mike Baille of Queen's University, Belfast. Baillie's tree-ring analysis of Irish bog oaks revealed that a very significant narrowing of tree-rings occurred around the years 2345 B.C., 1628 B.C. and 1159 B.C. Baillie identified tephra from Iceland's Hekla 4 volcano (c.2310 - 20 B.C.), Santorini's Stroggilí volcano in the Aegean (c.1670 - 1530 B.C.), and again Iceland's Hekla 3 (1120 - 30 B.C.) as the likely cause for the narrowing of the tree-rings. Volcanoes occur quite regularly, but every five hundred years or so, one erupts with an enormous explosive Index of VEI 6. These 'colossal' eruptions have a displacement volume of between 10 and 100 KS, which makes them capable of spewing plumes of ash 25 kilometres into the atmosphere. In the aftermath of such eruptions, skies darken, crops fail and massive migrations of people occur. According to Baillie, this is what happened in the year 2345 B.C. which he describes as:

> *... a classic marker date, i.e. a date which will show up on a regular basis in studies of various kinds.*

The 2345 B.C. time frame correlates with the simultaneous, sudden endings of the Akkadian Empire in Mesopotamia, the Old Kingdom in Egypt, the Indus Valley civilization, the Hongshan Culture in China, as well as the Early Bronze Age kingdoms of Israel, Anatolia and Greece.

A series of upheavals also occurred throughout the Mediterranean during the periods 1628 - 1550 B.C. and 1150 - 1120 B.C. The highly evolved Irish peoples who inhabited the Boyne River region c.2800 - 1500 B.C. must have also fallen victim to these 'world-wide' upheavals. In search of 'greener pastures', migrations across the Irish Sea by certain clans aboard their *curraghs* (skin boats) would have undoubtedly occurred. Having spent a lifetime analysing and interpreting the Greek myths, the esteemed scholar and poet Robert Graves made numerous references to the many cultural and mythological connections that once existed between Ireland and ancient Greece.

The Irish Book of Leinster (A.D. 1150) and *The Book of Invasions* (*Leabhar Gabhála* or *Lebor Gabala Erren* c.A.D. 1090) confirm Graves' view. Compiled from oral traditions, these Irish Annals report that at a very early stage of Ireland's history, clans of seafarers had migrated to and from the land of ancient Greece.

One of these ancient migrations could include the arrival into Greece of the archaeologically termed Abantes peoples (c.2300 B.C.). It might be noted that the longhaired Abantes lived in regions that are mythically associated with the Centaurs. Might the brawling Centaurs (Abantes?) of ancient Greece have originated from the British Isles? If we accept the mythological account of Hercules' Tenth Labour, then yes, perhaps they did! One of the Twelve Labours assigned to Hercules was to herd together the cattle of the mysterious three-headed Geryon and drive them all the way from Erytheia to Mycenae in Greece. The three-headed Geryon's abode in Erytheia was an island (Ireland?) located somewhere beyond the Pillars of Hercules (the Atlantic). In various Greek myths (i.e. Hermes' stealing the cattle of Apollo), the term 'cattle' is often used as an analogy for tribes of people. This is probably the case here, for Hercules could hardly have driven a herd of cattle across the ocean from Erytheia.

The Aeolians

Did the Aeolians of Greece originate from ancient Eire? The Aeolian people formed one of the three great divisions of Hellenic genetic stock. Their dialect is recognised as the oldest form of Hellenic speech and was spoken in Boeotia, a region of Central Greece, as well as on the island of Lesbos and in other Greek colonies. According to Herbert Smyth's *Greek Grammar*, par. 656:

The Aeolic dialect made extensive use of the so-called athematic verb conjugation, i.e the conjugation ending in -mi. The same is found in Irish where this selection has been generalised, i.e -im.

Notes from Robert Graves' *The Greek Myths* (1955) inform us about the Aeolians' arrival into Greece.

43.1 The Ionians and Aeolians, the first two waves of patriarchal Hellenes to invade Greece, were persuaded by the Hellads already there to worship the triple-goddess and change their social customs accordingly becoming Greeks (graikoi, worshippers of the Grey Goddess, or Crone).

45.2 It seems that late in the second millennium B.C. the seafaring Aeolians, who had agreed to worship the pre-Hellenic moon goddess as their ancestress and protectress, became tributary to the Zeus-worshipping Achaeans and were forced to accept the Olympian religion.

We might also note that the legendary Aeolian harp of ancient Greece is comparable with the emblematic harp displayed in Ireland's coat of arms.

Similarities in Greek and Irish Mythology

Set within the precincts of the ancient Greek town of Calydon, the tale of the Calydonian boar hunt begins in the court of Oeneus, king of Calydonia. When Oeneus omitted offerings to Artemis, the goddess sent a huge boar to ravage his kingdom. King Oeneus then invited all of the heroes of Greece to help him slay the wild boar and after a difficult battle a local hero named Meleager finally killed the beast. We might note that Meleager is a son of Aeolus, the ancestral father of the harp playing Aeolians.

This legend may have had its origins in an earlier Irish legend. The Irish legend does not tell who killed the wild boar, Orc Triathth, but it is revealed that the beast had in his possession the maiden Brigit, a daughter of the thunder-god Dagda.

A somewhat similar tale is found in the Welsh *O'Mabinogion.* In this version a once great king becomes enchanted into the shape of a savage boar named Twrch Trwyth. In this guise the former King begins to create havoc among the inhabitants of Ireland and Britain. The hero responsible for the demise of this wild boar is none other than King Arthur. Together with his knights, he drives the monstrous beast into the Irish Sea

.

It was also in the guise of a wild boar, that the Irish hero Finn Mac Cool killed handsome Diarmuid, the lover of the beautiful Grainne. A parallel tale is found in Greek mythology where it is reported that Apollo, disguised as a wild boar, kills the handsome Adonis.

Caledonians of Scotland

The Romans who conquered Britain recognised the peoples who dwelt north of Hadrian's Wall as being Caledonians ('hard tough people'). The Romans' possible identification of the northern British Caledonians with the Calydonians of Epirus in Greece indicates that both tribes were, if not one in the same stock, closely related.

The Scots, who according to the 9th century monk Nennius, had '*arrived in Ireland from Spain*' (c.900 B.C.?) were allied to the northern British Caledonians. Having inhabited Ireland for some 400 years, the Scots had migrated to the northern regions of Britain (c.500 B.C). Renowned for their strict adherence to ancient traditions, the Scots are noted for wearing distinctly 'un-Celtic' kilts. I suspect that the Scots' kilt-wearing custom was adopted during their long sojourn in Greece. According to Robert Graves' *The White Goddess* p.132:

> *Scota, who has been confused in Irish legend with the ancestor of the Cottians, is apparently Scotia ('the Dark One'), a well-known Greek title of the Sea-Goddess of Cyprus. The Milesians would naturally have brought the cult of the Sea-Goddess and her son Hercules with them to Ireland and there would have found the necessary stone-altars already in place.*

Note 52

The Trojans

It is quite plausible that Trojans were included among the ***'many important men'*** who attended King Alcinous' royal court. The Roman writers Livy and Aneas tell us that after the Trojan War, the Etruscans (Phaeacians) allied themselves with the Trojans. The dating and location of the Trojan War remains a contentious issue. Certain scholars are of the opinion that a series of conflicts between the Greeks and the Trojans occurred long before the time of Odysseus (1180 - 1100 B.C.?). This claim agrees with the histories of the ancient Greeks who placed the Trojan War variously in the 14th, 13th and 12th centuries B.C. (Eratosthenes 1184 B.C., the Parian Marble 1209/8 B.C., Herodotus c.1250 B.C. and Douri 1334/3 B.C.)

The premise here is not to deny that Odysseus fought against the Trojans as a young man, but to suggest that the Trojans in the court of King Alcinous were perhaps descendants of Trojans who had fought in earlier 'Trojan Wars'. According to Carpenter's *Folktale, Fiction and Saga in the Homeric Epos* (1946):

> *... there seems to have been some doubt in the minds of the Greeks as to where exactly Troy was located. In the Iliad, the word most commonly used for the city of the Trojans is not 'Troy' but 'Ilion'. It is possible that Troy was not the name of a town at all, but rather the name of an area or district inhabited by the Trojans.*

The Greeks clearly had a legend about a war against the Trojans but there is disagreement as to the site of Troy. Livy's *History of Rome* (59 B.C. - 17 A.D.) tells of a Trojan leader named Antenor who having survived the destruction of Troy, sailed into the farthest part of the Adriatic. He was accompanied by a number of Enetians who had been driven from Paphlagonia (Asia Minor) by revolution and the loss of their King Pylaemenes:

> *The combined force of Enetians and Trojans defeated the Euganei who dwelt between the Sea and the Alps and occupied their land (the region of Venice). The place where they disembarked was called Troy and the name was extended to the surrounding district; the whole nation was called Veniti. Similar misfortunes led to Aeneas becoming a wanderer but the Fates were preparing a higher destiny for him. He first visited*

Macedonia and then was carried down to Sicily in quest of a settlement; from Sicily he directed his course to the Laurentian territory (Italy). *Here, too, the name of Troy is found. There the Trojans disembarked and as their almost infinite wanderings had left them nothing but their arms and their ships, they began to plunder the neighbourhood.*

Livy, *History of Rome*

The Aeneid

A complete account of Aeneas' journeys is found in the Virgil's *Aeneid.* Composed c.30 B.C., the mytho-historical *Aeneid* tells the epic tale of a Trojan named Aeneas. Having survived the Trojan War, Aeneas and his comrades are said to have sailed away in search of a new homeland. Their seven years' voyage took them by way of Thrace, Delos and Crete, onwards to Sicily and Carthage, and eventually to the Tiber River in Italy. When Aeneas encountered opposition from one of the local tribes he allied his army with the Etruscans and together they won a great victory. Aeneas then founded a dynasty of kings called Alba Longas (tall whites). According to Roman legend, Aeneas' son Ascanius settled along the shores of Lake Albano. This legend may have credibility as Etruscan-styled tombs dating to 1100 B.C. have been discovered there. Other tales of Trojan migration and colonization are related in the legend of Aeneas' great grandson Brutus.

Compiled from the early oral traditions of British history as recorded in Gildas' *De Excidio Brittaniae et Conquestu* (c.542 A.D.) and Nennius' *Historia Brittonum* (c.822 A.D.), Milton's *History of Britain* (A.D. 1670) relates the tale of Britain's supposed first king. According to Milton he was a Trojan leader named Brutus. Granted the command of a fleet of 340 ships, Brutus had set sail from the Aegean. After some encounters on the African coast he came to the Tyrrhenian Sea where:

> ... *he happens to find the race of those Trojans, who with Antenor came into Italy; and Corineus, a man much famed, was their chief: though by surer authors it be reported, that those Trojans with Antenor were seated on the other side of Italy, on the Adriatic, not the Tyrrhene shore.*

Joining forces with Antenor and Corineus, Brutus and his fellow Trojans passed through the straits of Gibraltar and thence onwards to the mouth of the Ligeris River in Aquitaine. Having sacked and burnt the towns of Gaul, the combined Trojan armies subsequently set their sights on Albion (Britain). Brutus landed at Totes in Cornwall and after a short struggle with local 'giants', he was victorious and subsequently handed over control of the region to his ally, Corineus.

Brutus is said to have gone on to establish the town of London as his place of rulership and having conquered most of the land, he named it Britain after himself.

Strabo

The Greek geographer Starbo informs us that in the years following the Trojan War, the Trojans:

> *... wandered over the face of the whole Earth. For at the conclusion of the war both the Greeks and Barbarians found themselves deprived, the one of their livelihood at home, the other of the fruits of their expedition; so that when Troy was overthrown, the victors and still more the vanquished, who had survived the conflict, were compelled by want to a life of piracy; and we learn that they became the founders of many cities along the sea-coast beyond Greece, besides several inland settlements.*
>
> Strabo, *Geography* Book III: 2.

Note 53

The Phaeacians

The Phaeacians boasted of the swiftness of their ships and how it would take but one night to deliver Odysseus to his island home of Ithaca. This idle claim was taken literally by later Greek writers who identified Scheria with Corfu. Although it takes only one day to sail to Corfu from Ithaca and granted the island was considered sacred to the Phaeacians, it never was nor could be the Phaeacian island of Scheria. Odysseus was an Achaean prince and his fleet of ships had been gathered from the islands that neighboured Ithaca. He would surely have been aware of an island as large as Corfu, especially if it hosted a kingdom as opulent as that of the Phaeacians'. The identification of Corfu with Scheria is partly due to an ancient tradition that associates sickle-shaped Corfu with the sickle that supposedly castrated Ouranos (Uranus), the 'godfather' of the Phaeacians.

> *Next to Bolina, Akhaia, a cape juts out into the sea, and it is told how Kronos* (Saturn) *threw into the sea here the sickle with which he mutilated his father Ouranos* (Uranus). *For this reason they call the cape Drepanon* (sickle).
>
> *Pausanias:* 7.23.4

> *In the Keranian Sea fronting the Ionian Straits there is a rich and spacious island, under the soil of which is said to be the sickle used by Kronos to castrate his father Ouranos. From this reaping hook the island takes its name Drepane* (sickle) - *the sacred nurse of the Phaiakians* (Phaeacians) *who by the same token trace their ancestry to Ouranos.*
>
> Apollonius Rhodius (c.250 B.C.) *Argonautica* Book IV Line 9

Strabo identified the Phaeacians with the mystical seafarers called Telkines:

> *They (the Telkhines) were the first to work iron and brass and in fact fabricated the scythe for Kronos.*

NOTES

Chapter 12

Isle of Ithaca

(Homeshores)

Note 54

Published in 2005, a book entitled *Odysseus Unbound* challenges the long-held notion that Odysseus' palace was located on the modern-day island of Ithaca. Author Robert Bittlestone argues that the geographical position of 'modern' Ithaca does not comply with Homer's description of the island as lying *'furthest to sea'*. In other words, Homer is stating that Ithaca is the western-most island of the Ionian group.

I am Odysseus, Laertes' son, world-famed
For stratagems, my name has reached the heavens.
Bright Ithaca is my home; it has a mountain,
Leaf-quivering Neriton, far visible.
Around are many islands, close to each other,
Doulichion and Same and wooded Zacynthos.
Ithaca itself lies low, furthest to sea
Towards dusk; the rest, apart, face down and sun.

The Odyssey Chapter 9: 19-26

Bittlestone proposes that the island of Kefalonia once incorporated two separate islands and that one of these islands was the original Ithaca. According to his hypothesis, a catastrophic earthquake occurred about 3,000 years ago. Massive landslides were triggered and material from these avalanches filled the narrow sea channel that was in existence at the time of Odysseus. In the autumn of 2006, Bittlestone set about the task of proving his theory. With colleagues James Diggle, Professor of Greek and Latin at Cambridge University and John Underhill, Professor of Geology at Edinburgh University, Bittlestone set up a geophysical expedition on the shallow strip of land that connects Kekalonia to the Paliki peninsula. The British-led team drilled a borehole down past the current sea level to a depth of 122 metres (400ft). Core samples taken from various depths have revealed only loose aggregations of rock. Commenting on these initial drillings Professor Underhill explains:

> *Crucially, we didn't hit limestone bedrock, which means the theory still holds. The second key thing we have found is that the landslide and rockfall debris of the right type extends to at least 40m below the surface and vitally, scanning electron microscopy undertaken at the Academy of Sciences in Sophia shows that it contains Holocene microfossils – it is in the right time frame.*

Although the team does not have exact dates, the rockfall debris is young enough to support their theory. Microscopic marine fossils caught up in the sediments are consistent with the impact of a catastrophic landslide that would have ejected a large volume of water out of the channel and saturated the infill material. Data acquired during an undersea seismic survey have shown what appears to be a buried channel exactly where it would be expected and the analysis of sea level rise and fall in the region matches the timing of the valley's submergence and relative uplift. The surface of the surrounding landscape also displays ancient roads that have been suddenly interrupted by landslides and major rockfalls, providing further evidence that the region was subjected to a destructive Bronze Age earthquake.

Note 55

> ***Odysseus wore a mantle of purple wool, double-lined and fastened by a gold brooch with two catches for the pin. On the face of this there was a device that showed a dog holding a spotted fawn between his forepaws. The dog was watching and strangling the fawn that was struggling convulsively to escape. Everyone marvelled at the way in which these things had been done in gold.***

Note 56

The Twelve Planetary Realms

The episode in which Odysseus is said to have fired an arrow through the handle-rings of twelve sacred axes is obviously suffused in metaphorical imagery. As Professor Joseph Campbell writes in his *Occidental Mythology*:

> *The solar hero having thus demonstrated his passage of the twelve signs and his lordship of the palace, proceeded masterfully to the shooting down of the suitors.*

I agree with Professor Campbell's interpretation of the twelve axe rings as being representative of the twelve planetary houses. According to the ancient Greeks, each of the twelve houses was governed by one of the twelve Olympian gods. Beginning his odyssey at the most distant sphere ruled by Dis (Pluto), Odysseus continued to transit the various domains until he eventually arrived at the realm of the sun-god Apollo/Helios. The following is a summarised interpretation of the twelve realms traversed by Odysseus.

Pluto: Dis

Traits: Sexuality, Destruction, Jealousy, Endings, New Beginnings

The raping and pillaging of cities fell under the jurisdiction of the god Dis/Pluto. Odysseus' sacking of both the Trojan and Cicone cities was attributed to the influence of this Underworld deity. When Odysseus had completed his attack upon the Cicones, he invoked Pluto to release the souls of his dead comrades. Pluto may also be recognized in the form of the ancient, cave-dwelling Proteus. Caves were thought to be a domain of

Pluto and it was within Proteus' cave that Odysseus was advised to begin a journey whereby he might pay homage to the 'everlasting gods'.

Neptune: Poseidon

Traits: Dreams, Drugs, Mimicry, Duplicity

After experiencing a violent hurricane, Odysseus' ship was swept into unknown waters. Odysseus was hopelessly lost in the open sea for a period of nine days but eventually came ashore in a land whose inhabitants were under the influence of a drug obtained from the lotus flower. With much persuasion and some force, Odysseus managed to extract his crew from this somnolent place and together they continued sailing into the vastness until they reached the Land of the Cyclopes. Described as being the son of Poseidon/Neptune, the duplicitous Cyclops trapped Odysseus and his men within his cave. In order to escape their predicament, Odysseus in turn tricked the Cyclops by offering wine and then blinding him with the thrust of a burning shaft of wood into his single eye.

Uranus

Traits: Deviation, Kindness, Friendliness, Unpredictability

Having been accused of deception by the blinded Cyclops, Odysseus departed the monster's realm and sailed to a land that was described as ***'floating upon the sea'***. There he met with King Aeolus, ***'the Keeper of the Four Winds'***.

King Aeolus treated Odysseus with great hospitality and after a pleasant stay he set sail on good terms. However Odysseus' attempt to return home via a northern route above Asia reveals how utterly disoriented he really was. The release of the 'four winds' by his disobedient crewmen necessitated Odysseus' return to the Kingdom of Aeolia. King Aeolus' complete reversal of attitude towards him typifies the nature of Uranus.

Saturn: Cronos

Traits: Cruelty, Tenacity, Cold-heartedness

Having been treated with contempt for his inability to find his way homeward, a despairing Odysseus had little option but to continue his journey towards the rising sun. After numerous days of laborious rowing, Odysseus came to the Land of the Laestrygonians. The main body of his fleet sailed into what appeared to be an idyllic cove. Odysseus however, was suspicious of this land-locked harbour and decided instead to moor his ship in the open sea. The native Laestrygonians soon began hurling huge stones at the fleet. All the vessels that had anchored in the harbour were destroyed and the surviving crewmen fell prey to the cannibalistic Laestrygonians. The practice of cannibalism identifies the Laestrygonians with the god Cronos/Saturn who 'devours his own children'.

Jupiter: Zeus

Traits: Extravagance, Benevolence, Optimism, Self-indulgence

With both grief for their slain companions and elation at their own escape, the crew of Odysseus' lone ship pursued their course eastward until they arrived at the Land of Aeaea where Circe, a 'daughter of the sun' dwelt. Circe's opulent abode and her ability to tame wild animals associate her with the god Jupiter.

With a magical brew Circe had ensnared Odysseus' unsuspecting men and turned them into pigs. The sorceress offered Odysseus the same enchanted potion hoping to also consign him to the pigsty with his crew. Forewarned, Odysseus drew his sword and rushed at her with 'fury on his countenance'. Circe fell to her knees and begged for mercy. Odysseus then extracted a solemn oath from her that she would forthwith release his companions and practice no further harm against him or them. Circe was as good as her word. The men were restored to their human shapes and the rest of the crew was summoned from the shore. They were subsequently all magnificently entertained day after day. It seemed that Odysseus had forgotten all about his native land and was reconciled to an inglorious life of ease, pleasure and self-indulgence.

Mars

Traits: Pioneering Spirit, Action, Bloodthirstiness

Mastering his dread, Odysseus boarded his sleek ship and careened across the deep ocean with the north wind behind him to arrive in the misty realm of the Cimmerians. Immediately upon landing, he dug a trench and then sacrificed a young ram and a black ewe as Circe had bidden. With the fresh blood flowing into the trench, Odysseus summoned the ghost of the blind Theban seer, Teiresias. Circe had advised him that while he was waiting for Teiresias to manifest, he should drive off with his sword the many other ghosts who would be drawn to the blood:

> ***… then I drew back and sheathed my sword, whereupon, when he had drank the blood, Teiresias began his prophecy.***

Waxing Moon

Traits: Memory, Sentimentality, Shrewdness, Impressionability

Lashed to the mast of his ship and with his crew's ears filled with bees' wax, Odysseus had been able to listen to the bewitching Sirens who promised to reveal their ***'knowledge of all the future happenings on Earth'***. The Sirens' beautiful songs had been meant to lure Odysseus' ship onto the jagged rocks but it glided past unharmed. When eventually his vessel had ***'come to the limits of the World; to the deep flowing Ocean'*** it encountered the fearsome Scylla and Charybdis, 'daughters of Earth and Oceanus', who had been made monstrous by jealous adversaries.

Earth: Gaea

Traits: Virginal, Natural, Critical, Warlike

Lampetia and Phaethusa, the virginal daughters of Helios, tended their father's flocks and herds in Thrinacia. Odysseus and his crew had come ashore on the strict understanding that they did not 'violate' or interfere with Helios' 'cattle of the sun'. Despite Odysseus' dire warnings, his starving men went about slaughtering and feasting upon the cattle.

Waning Moon

Traits: Unforgiving, Moodiness, Tenacity

Not long after departing Thrinacia in the Land of Helios, Odysseus' ship was destroyed by a typhoon and his entire crew drowned.

Venus: Aphrodite

Traits: Harmony, Beauty, Gentleness, Social Grace

The sea-nymph Calypso is described as singing sweetly within a beautiful abode that would have ***'filled a god from Heaven with wonder and delight'***.

The shipwrecked Odysseus was kindly received by Calypso. She entertained him most graciously for many years and having become enamored of him, pleaded with the gods to allow him to stay with her on the island forever. Calypso's wish was to offer Odysseus immortality.

Mercury: Hermes

Traits: Swiftness, Travel, Commerce, Disguise, Communication

It was the 'fleet-footed' Mercury who visited Calypso and delivered Jupiter's directive that she must allow Odysseus to continue his journey homeward. Aided by the downcast Calypso's advice, he set about constructing a sea-worthy vessel and then once more put out into the open sea. Odysseus was shipwrecked yet again but with great difficulty he managed to swim onto the shores of Scheria, a land inhabited by the Phaeacians. The mercurial Phaeacians were said to have ***'knowledge of all the peoples who inhabit the world'***. Disguised within a mist that the goddess Athena had spread around him, Odysseus entered into a great hall where the Phaeacian chiefs and senators were pouring libations to the god Mercury. At the request of the Phaeacians, Odysseus stood proudly and recounted all the adventures that had befallen him since his departure from Troy. The next day Odysseus was presented with gifts and once aboard a swift Phaeacian ship, he fell immediately into in a 'death-like' slumber and was delivered safely to Ithaca. Finally realising that he was at last on home soil, Odysseus and Athena hermetically sealed his Phaeacian gifts within a cave that had dual entranceways. One portal represented the way of mortals, the other, the way of the gods.

Sun: Apollo

Traits: Royalty, Dignity, Drama, Bravery

On the Feast Day of the sun-god Apollo, Odysseus entered his own royal palace in the guise of a beggar. After accepting the challenge to string his Great Bow, Odysseus fired an arrow through the 'rings' of twelve sacred axes. Upon achieving this remarkable feat, he and his son Telemachus took up arms and like 'rampaging lions', massacred the proud suitors.

Note 57

Ninurta

The first mythologies to be written down were recorded on clay tablets by the ancient peoples of Mesopotamia and it is there that we find references to ancient hunters such as Adapa, Gilgamesh and Ninurta. Akin to the ancient Greek giant Orion, the Sumerian giant Ninurta is a somewhat more complex character. Ninurta was sometimes perceived as an avatar-god who incarnated at various epochs. Ningirsu, the blessed son of the Virgin Goddess is an example.

The Three Mystical Steps

The Hindus of India appear to have adopted the manifold aspect of Ninurta and applied it to their god Vishnu. According to the Hindu religion, the avatar-god Vishnu incarnates upon the Earth whenever it is in spiritual decline. To date, Vishnu has apparently manifested in human form on nine separate occasions. At his tenth, which is yet to occur, Vishnu is expected to destroy all the powers of evil.

Sacred Hindu writings such as the *Rig Veda* and *Bhagavata* state that during one of his earthly incarnations Vishnu challenged his evil counterpart Bali to a cosmic contest. The basis of this contest was a wager in which Bali would grant Vishnu rulership of all the land that he could stride over within three steps. When Bali readily accepted the wager, Vishnu immediately transformed himself into a cosmic giant (Ninurta?) and in three strides encircled the entire Earth. One school of Hinduism suggests that the three steps represent Vishnu's final three incarnations. (See: W.Wilkins, *Hindu Mythology* p.130)

The Stepped-Throne of Egypt

The triple incarnation concept might also be recognized in the hieroglyphic throne symbology of ancient Egypt. Certain images of the goddess Isis, whose name means 'throne', depict her with a 'three- stepped throne' motif hovering above her head. Pharaohs (god-kings) seated upon

three-stepped thrones are often displayed in Egyptian art. The enthroned Pharaohs were considered to be at one with the godhead and as such, their 'word' was considered to be divinely inspired.

North American Indian Lore

The three stars of the Orion's Belt constellation form the basis of various North American Indian myths. The *Madrid Codex* records that the Maya associated the three stars of Orion's Belt with a turtle that is described as bringing *'the three hearthstones of creation on his back as he descends from heaven'*. The three stars represented the Underworld, Earth and Heaven.

Note 58

Natural Catastrophes During Bronze Age Civilizations:
(Archaeological, geological, astronomical and cultural perspectives:)

Invited by SIS (Society for Interdisciplinary Studies) to present a paper on the above subject, Mike Baillie of Queens University, Belfast wrote:

> *In 1988 the observation was made that narrowest-ring events in Irish sub-fossil oak chronologies appeared to line up with large acidities in the Greenland ice records from Camp Century and Dye 3. Three of the events, at tree-ring ages 2345 B.C., 1628 B.C. and 1159 B.C. turned out to be of particular interest as they contributed to debates on the Hekla 4 eruption in Iceland, dated to 2310 B.C. (plus or minus 20 years), Santorini in the Aegean, dated to circa 1670 - 1530 B.C. and possibly, Hekla 3, linked by Hammer and colleagues to their 1120 B.C. (plus or minus 30 years) acid layer. It quickly became apparent, most notably through comments from Kevin Pang that the two later events might relate in some way to the start and end of the Chinese Shang dynasty. It is equally of interest that the Egyptian New Kingdom traditionally spans the approximate range 1570 to 1080 BC. So the question arose whether these two volcano-related events could have caused widespread dynastic change. In order to proceed with this debate it is necessary to attempt to get a better handle on the nature of the effects. The paper will look at information from American and Fennoscandian tree-ring records and make some attempt to define the*

nature of the 1628 BC and 1159 BC events; are they truly abrupt, as would be expected with volcanoes, or are they imposed on pre-existing downturns? Existing evidence suggests that the latter may be the case. If this is correct, it seems appropriate to ask what might have caused the downturns. This question leads logically to the speculation that loading of the atmosphere from space might be a significant factor in the environmental downturns.

One of the most fascinating aspects of Baillie's work is his linking of the period 1159 - 1120 B.C. to a particular eruption of Iceland's Mount Hekla volcano. Other archaeologists in Scotland and Northern Ireland support Baillie's findings. They report that sometime around this same period, the population of Northern Britain was suddenly reduced by more than 90 percent, probably due to the eruption of Mount Hekla which spewed an estimated 12 cubic kilometres of volcanic dust into the stratosphere.

According to David Keys of *The Independent* (August 1988):

The catastrophe was so sudden and severe that it appears to have forced hundreds of thousands of people to leave their upland homes to seek a new life in the already inhabited valleys and lowlands. Widespread warfare would have followed and in the latter half of the twelfth century B.C., valley settlements start to be fortified. As populations competed for food, conflict would have spread and large numbers of displaced people would have exerted pressure to neighbouring tribes. There may have been a 'domino effect' over a considerable period, with each displaced group displacing its neighbours. In general, in northern Britain the tribal 'dominoes' would have tended to fall in a southerly direction – the direction in which most agriculturally viable land existed.

The southerly migration of agricultural tribes at that time may well explain the swift arrival of the Dorians into Greece c.1130 B.C.

Note 59

The Milesians of Irish legend are said to have originated in Greece early in the second millennium B.C. and to have taken many generations to reach Ireland after wandering about the Mediterranean. The Milesians of Greek legend claimed descent from Miletus, a son of

Apollo, who emigrated from Crete to Caria in very early times and built the city of Miletus; there was another city of the same name in Crete. The Irish Milesians similarly claimed to have visited Crete and to have gone thence to Syria and thence by way of Carenia in Asia Minor to Gaetulia in North Africa, Baelduno or Baelo, a port near Cadiz and Breagdun or Brigantium (now Compostella) in north-western Spain. Among their ancestors were Gadel - perhaps a deity of the river Gadylum on the southern coast of the Black Sea near Trebizond; 'Niulus or Neolus of Argos'; Cecrops of Athens; and 'Scota, daughter of the king of Egypt'. If this account has any sense, it refers to a westward migration from the Aegean to Spain in the late thirteenth century B.C. when, as we have seen, a wave of Indo-Europeans from the north, among them the Dorian Greeks, was slowly displacing the Mycenaean 'Peoples of the Sea' from Greece, the Aegean islands and Asia Minor.

Robert Graves, *The White Goddess* p.131

Note 60

Did Odysseus Make a Return Voyage to the Caribbean?

According to Dante's twenty-sixth canto of *The Inferno*, Odysseus (Ulysses) did not remain long on his home shores of Ithaca. Driven by *'the restless itch to rove'*, he felt compelled to leave his beloved wife, his aged father and his son and set forth once more:

> *... on the deep and open sea with a single ship and that little band of comrades who even then had not deserted me.*

There is no Greek or Roman antecedent for Dante's story so it is assumed that he either invented it or had access to a work unknown to other writers of his time. Dante, recounting Odysseus' journey through Hell, introduces him as one of the '*Fraudulent Counsellors*' who inhabit the *'Eighth Circle'*. This was a place of punishment set aside for those who had injured others through their duplicity. According to Dante, cunning Odysseus had been condemned to Hell for devising the 'Trojan Horse' - a strategy that resulted in the destruction of Troy. Odysseus and his crew begin a second Odyssey by sailing westward across the Mediterranean. With Africa on their left and the coast of Spain to their right, they soon find themselves staring at the foreboding and seemingly limitless Atlantic Ocean. Addressing his crew, Odysseus proclaims:

> *Brothers, you who have passed through a hundred thousand perils to reach this place, do not deny yourselves this last exploit. Here lies a chance to learn what lies in this unknown world on the far side of the sun where no people dwell.*

Odysseus tells his men that they had not been born to live in brutish ignorance but rather, for the pursuit of knowledge and excellence; and so they put their shoulders to their oars and eagerly go forward into the unplumbed ocean that stretches before them. The course Odysseus steers takes them towards Brazil. They pass the Equator and gradually the familiar stars of the northern sky slip below the horizon. Sailing onwards beneath foreign constellations, a mountain begins to appear, "*dark in the distance*", [says Odysseus] "*and so lofty and so steep, I have never seen its like before.*" It is, as Dante explains later in his epic poem, the 'Mountain of Purgatory', however Odysseus is completely ignorant of this. Having sighted the mysterious land, Odysseus and his crew rejoice and blithely continue towards it. All of a sudden a fierce storm forms over the land and advances towards them. The ship is caught by whirlwinds and spun around three times. The fourth spin proves fatal; the ship's stern shoots up, its prow sinks and the sea closes over Odysseus and his men. Odysseus never reaches the 'Isle of Purgatory'. Instead, Dante has Odysseus destined to burn eternally among his fellow tricksters in Hell's 'Eighth Circle'.

Note 61

Chaonians, Thesprotians and Molossians

The Telegony relates how the Thesprotian queen, Callidike, met her death whilst fighting a neighbouring tribe called the Brygoi (Brigantes). It has been well documented that during times of war, Celtic queens such as Boudicca and her female compatriots would join with men in battle. Other Celtic-like traits such as the veneration of oak trees in association with the thunder god Dagda (Zeus) and his son Lugh (Apollo) are recognised in the customs of certain tribes who inhabited the coastal regions of Epirus (western Greece). Plutarch informs us that three principal tribes, namely the Chaonians, Thesprotians and Molossians, emerged from Epirus in western Greece.

According to Strabo, the Chaonians initially ruled over Epirus while the Thesprotians and Molossians dominated at a later date. Perhaps Strabo's statement is implying that the Chaonians were the original inhabitants and that the Thesprotians and Molossians arrived subsequently.

Certain Greek myths maintain that the sun-god Apollo had once travelled to Greece upon the back of a dolphin. Couched in allegorical terms, this claim quite possibly alludes to the arrival of the Bronze Age seafarers from Britain who venerated Apollo.

Commenting on the founding of Delphi in his *Descriptions of Greece,* Pausanias writes:

> *Boeo, a native woman who composed a hymn for the Delphians, said that the oracle was established for the god Apollon by comers from the Hyperboreans* (British Isles). *Olen* (a semi-legendary poet) *and others said that he was the first to prophesy and the first to chant the hexameter oracles.*

According to Pindar's *Olympic Odes,* the Hyperboreans were renowned for providing Olympia with sacred laurel trees. Of Hercules and his establishment of the first Olympic Games, Pinder writes:

> *For the Hyperborean folk, Apollon's servants, he so persuaded with fair words for the all-hospitable grove of Zeus. His loyal heart begged for the tree to make shade for all men to share; and for brave deeds of valorous spirits, a crown.*

The first century historian, Diodorus Siculus, describes the Hyperboreans of Ancient Britain thus:

> *They worship Apollo above all other gods because they daily sing songs in praise of this god and ascribe to him the highest honours. They say that these inhabitants demean themselves as if they were priests of Apollo who have there a stately grove and renowned Temple of a circular form* (Stonehenge?)*, beautified with many rich gifts. And that there is a city likewise consecrated to this god, whose citizens are most of them harpers who, playing upon the harp, chaunt sacred hymns to Apollo in the Temple, setting forth his glorious acts. The Hyperboreans use their own natural language; but of long and ancient time have a special kindness for the Grecians; and more especially for the Athenians and the Delians. Some of the Grecians passed over to the Hyperboreans and left behind them divers presents (gifts dedicated to*

the gods) inscribed with Greek characters; and that Abaris formerly travelled thence to Greece and renewed the ancient league of friendship with the Delians.

Included among the ranks of Chaonians, Thesprotians and Molossians were *prostates* (protectors), *demiourgoi* (creators), *synarchontes* (co-rulers) and *hieromnemones* (those invested with sacred memory). The title 'hieromnemones' is possibly synonymous with the ancient Druidic practice of memorising vast tracts of their history that are related in an oral tradition. Examples of recited histories can be found in the Irish *Book of Invasions* (*Lebor Gabala Erenn*). Usually narrated in series of three, *The Book of Invasions* claims that three hundred years after 'the flood', an ancient hero named Partholan (a descendant of Noah's son Japheth), settled in Ireland with his three sons and their people. This remarkable claim brings to mind Plutarch's report of Molossian history, which states:

Deucalion and Pyrrha, (the Greek equivalents of Noah and his wife) *having set up the worship of Zeus at Dodina, settled there among the Molossians.*

Evidence of religious activity incorporating a sacred oak dating back to the second millennium B.C. has been detected at Dodona, Greece. Like their counterparts in the British Isles, the worshippers at Dodona believed they could hear their future being whispered in the wind as it rustled through the leaves of holy oak trees.

Perhaps the oldest and certainly one of the most famous sanctuaries in Greece was that of Dodona where Zeus was revered in the oracular oak. Thus when ancient Greek kings claimed to be descended from Zeus and even to bear his name, we may reasonably suppose that they also attempted to exercise his divine functions by making thunder and rain for the good of their people or the terror and confusion of their foes. In this respect the legend of Salmoneus probably reflects the pretensions of a whole class of petty sovereigns who reigned of old, each over his little canton, in the oak-clad highlands of Greece. Like their kinsmen the Irish kings, they were expected to be a source of fertility to the land and of fecundity to the cattle; and how could they fulfill these expectations better than by acting the part of their kinsman Zeus, the great god of the oak, the thunder, and the rain? They personified him, apparently, just as the Italian kings personified Jupiter.

James Frazer, *The Golden Bough* Chapter XV p.159

The Molossians were renowned for the huge, vicious hounds that were used by shepherds to guard their flocks. The ancient Irish also bred hounds for the protection of their stock and deployment in war. Regular references to these huge Irish wolfhounds being trained for dogfighting are found in the ancient Irish Sagas. Their astonishing size, speed and intelligence made them ideal animals for hunting boars and wolves. The hounds were perhaps overly efficient, for the boar and wolf are now extinct in Ireland.

BIBLIOGRAPHY

Allen, Richard Hinckley
1963 ***Star Names: Their Lore and Meaning*** New York: Dover Press: Reprint of 1899 edition.

Ancient Records of Egypt
(1962) Five volumes, New York: Russell & Russell, Inc.

Beaglehole, Professor J.C.
1979 ***The Life of Captain James Cook*** Stanford University Press.

Berlitz, Charles
1972 ***Mysteries from Forgotten Worlds*** London: Souvenir Press.

Bittlestone, Robert
2005 ***Odysseus Unbound*** Cambridge University Press.

Bingham, Hiram
1915 ***Types of Machu Picchu Pottery*** The American Anthropologist.

Bostock & Riley
1855 ***The Natural History***, ***Pliny the Elder*** London.

Brinton, Daniel G
1882 ***American Hero-Myths.***

Brockesmith, Peter
1980 ***Legends of the Lost*** *(The Unexplained),* London: Orbis Pub. Co.

Buck, Sir Peter
1938/75 ***Vikings at Sunset*** Christchurch: Whitcombe&Tombs.

Bulfinch, Thomas
1981 ***Myths of Greece and Rome*** Middlesex England: Penguin Books.

Burn, A.R.
1965 ***The Penguin History of Greece*** London: Penguin.

Butcher, S.H.
1974 ***The Complete Works of Homer***. New York: Modern Library.

Butler, Samuel
1967 ***The Authoress of the Odyssey*** Chicago: University of Chicago Press.

Cabrera, Paul Felix
1822 ***Teatro Critico Americano*** translated, London.

Cabrera, Paul Felix & Rio, Antonio de
1822 ***Accounts Regarding the Maya*** London: Henry Berthoud.

Campbell, Joseph
1974 ***The Mythic Image*** Princeton: Princeton University Press.
1976 ***The Masks of God*** *(Primitive Mythology, Occidental Mythology, Oriental Mythology)* Middlesex England: Penguin Books.
1983-9 ***Historical Atlas of World Mythology*** New York: Harper & Row.

Carpenter, Rhys
1946 ***Folktale, Fiction and Saga in the Homeric Epos*** Berkeley and Los Angeles.

Cavalli-Sforza, L. Luca, Paolo Menozzi and Alberto Piazza
1994 ***History and Geography of Human Genes***. Princeton: Princeton University Press.

Cavalli-Sforza, L. Luca, Alberto Piazza, Paolo Menozzi and Joanna Mountain
1988 ***Reconstruction of Human Evolution***: *Bringing together Genetic, Archaeological, and Linguistic Data* The National Academy of Sciences USA 85:6002-06.
1989 ***Genetic and Linguistic Evolution*** Science 244(4909): 1128-29.

Christopoulos, George A. (editor-in-chief)
1974 ***Prehistory and Protohistory*** Athens; London: Ekdotike Athenon; Heinemann Educational.

Clavigero, Francesco S.
1721 - 1787 ***History of Mexico*** 1787 London, 1804 Philadelphia.

Collins, Andrew
2000 ***Gateway to Atlantis*** London: Headline.

Cottrell, Leonard and Davidson, Marshall B.
1962 ***Horizon Book of Lost Worlds*** New York: American Heritage Pub. Co. Inc.

Cribb, J. (editor)
1986 ***Money: from cowrie shells to credit cards*** London: British Museum Publications.

Diehl, Richard A.
2004 ***The Olmecs Americas First Civilisation***. N.Y. Thames & Hudson.

Doumas, Christo G.
1983 ***Thera: Pompeii of the Ancient Aegean,*** Excavations at Akrotiri 1967-1979 London: Thames & Hudson.

Dryden, John
1997 ***Virgil's 'Aeneid'*** Translated by John Dryden and F. M. Keener, Editor, Penguin.

Durdin-Robertson, Lawrence
1990 ***The Year of the Goddess*** London: The Aquarian Press.

Ekholm, Susanna M.
1969 ***Mound 30a and the Early Pre-classic Ceramic Sequence of Izapa, Chiapas, Mexico*** Papers of the New World Archaeological Foundation No. 25 Provo, UT: Brigham Young University, Ford James
1969 ***A Comparison of Formative cultures in the Americas.***

Emboden, William
1979 ***Narcotic Plants*** London: Macmillan Pub. Co.

Evans-Wentz, W.Y.
1966 ***The Fairy-Faith in Celtic Countries*** New York: University Books Inc.

Fell, Barry
America B.C. New York: Pocket Books.

Fix, William R.
1979 ***Star Maps*** London: Jonathon-James Books, Octopus Books Ltd.

Foster, Mary Le Cron
1999 ***The Transoceanic Trail: Proto-Pelagian*** Penguin Books ***Language Phylum, Pre-Columbiana*** 1: 88-113.

Frazer, James
1922 ***The Golden Bough*** London: Penguin Books

Gracia, Eulalia, Danobeitia, Juanuo, Verges, Jaume
Geological Journal The Geological Society of America.

Graves, Robert
1955 ***The Greek Myths*** (Complete Edition) London: Penguin Books.
1961 ***The White Goddess*** London: Faber and Faber Ltd.

Grumble, Sir Arthur
1972 ***Migrations, Myth and Magic from the Gilbert Islands*** London: John Murray.

Guthrie, James L.
2001 ***Human Lymphocyte Antigens***: *Apparent Afro-Asiatic, Southern Asian & European HLAs in Indigenous American Populations* New England: Antiquities Research Association.
http:/www.neara.org/Guthrie/lymphocyteantigens01.htm

Guirard, Felix (Editor)
1960 ***Larousse Encyclopedia of Mythology*** New York: Prometheus Press.
1959 London: Batchworth Press Limited.

Hapgood, Charles
1966 ***Maps of Ancient Sea Kings*** Philadelphia: Chilton Book Company.

Hancock, Graham
1995 ***Fingerprints of the Gods*** New York: Three Rivers Press.

Hansen, L. Taylor
1980 ***He Walked The Americas*** Amherst Press.

Harbison, Peter
1922. ***Prolegomena to the Study of Greek Religion*** Cambridge: Cambridge University Press.

Henderson, Joseph L., and Maud Oakes.
1971 ***The Wisdom of the Serpent*** New York: Collier Books.

Herodotus
1968 ***The Histories*** (Translated by Aubrey de Selincourt) Baltimore, U.S.A.: Harmondsworth, England.
Ringwood, Victoria, Australia: Penguin Books.

Heine-Geldern, Robert
1972 ***American Metallurgy and the Old World*** in ***Early Chinese Art and its Possible Influence in the Pacific Basin*** (editor) Noel Barnard pp. 787 - 822 New York: Intercultural Arts Press.

Heine-Geldern, Robert and Gordon F. Ekholm
1951 ***Significant Parallels in the Symbolic Arts of Southern Asia and Middle America***: *The Civilizations of Ancient America* (editor) Sol Tax, International Congress of Americanists Chicago: University of Chicago Press.

Hesiod
1973 ***Theogony*** Translated by Dorothea Wender in *Hesiod and Theognis* Baltimore U.S.A; Harmondsworth, U.K.; Ringwood Aust.ralia: Penguin Books.

Heyerdahl, Thor
1953 ***American Indians in the Pacific*** - *The Theory behind the Kon-Tiki Expedition* London: George Allen and Unwin.
1978 ***Early Man and the Ocean*** - *The beginnings of Navigation and Seaborne Civilisations* London: Allen and Unwin.

Heyerdahl, Thor and Ralling, Christopher
1990 ***The Kon-Tiki Man*** London: BBC Books.

Houston, Jean
1992 ***The Hero and the Goddess*** New York: The Aquarian Press.

Hunt, Ben W.
1954 ***Indian Craft and Lore*** New York: Simon and Schuster.

Hughes, Bettany
2005 ***Helen of Troy*** London: Johnathan Cape.

Huyghe, Rene
1962 ***Larousse Encyclopedia of Pre-Historic and Ancient Art*** London: Paul Hamlyn Pub. Co.

Ibarra, Grasso and Dick, Edgar
1954 ***Grupos y cronología de las influencias surasiáticas y oceánicas en la América indígena***. Acta Asiática 1(2): 13-35.
1961 ***Hachas planas con agujeros posteriores de tipo oceánio, en la Bolivia prehispánica*** Journal of Austronesian Studies 2(2): 45-49.
1967 ***Introducción a la americanista, crítica, y teoría*** Cochabamba: Editorial Universitaria, Universidad Mayor de San Simón
1969 ***La imitación de objetos metálicos en otros materiales por pueblosprecolombinos que no trabajaban los metales*** International

Congress ofAmericanists 38: 79-84
1982 ***América en la prehistoria mundial: Difusión greco-fenicia*** BuenosAires: Tipográfica Editoria Argentina.*

Ions, Veronica
1987 ***The World's Mythology in Colour*** London: Hamlyn Publishing Group Ltd.

Jairazbhoy, R. A.
1974 ***Ancient Egyptians and Chinese in America*** London: Prior.

Jobes, Gertrude
1962 ***Dictionary of Mythology, Folklore and Symbols*** New York: Scarecrow Press Inc.

Kennedy, Robert A.
1971 ***A Transatlantic Stimulus Hypothesis for Mesoamerica and the Caribbean, Circa 3500 to 2000 B.C.*** *Man Across the Sea: Problems of Pre-Columbian Contacts* (editors) Carroll L. Riley, J. Charles Kelly, Campbell W. Pennington and Robert L. Rands pp. 266-74 Austin: University of Texas Press.

Kingsborough, Lord
1885 ***Antiquities of Mexico*** London.

Knappert, Jan
1995 ***Indian Mythology*** London: Diamond Books.

Koch, John T
2010 ***Celtic from the West*** London: Oxford Books.
Celtic from the West Chapter 9: Paradigm Shift? Interpreting Tartessian as Celtic.

Landa, Bishop Diego de
1566 ***Relación de las cosas de Yucatan*** English translation by William Gates (1937) entitled ***Yucatan Before and After the Conquest*** Baltimore: The Maya Society of Baltimore reprinted in 1978 New York: Dover Publications.

1982 ***New World Cotton as a Clue to the Polynesian Past*** in ***Oceanic Studies: Essays in Honor of Aarne A. Koskinen*** (editor) Jukka Siikala, pp. 179-92 Transactions of the Finnish Anthropological Society 11 Helsinki.

Lathrap, Donald W.
1973 ***The Antiquity and Importance of Long-Distance Trade Relationships in the Moist Tropics of Pre-Columbian South America*** *World Archaeology* 5(2): 170-86.

Lindblom, Gerhard
1927 ***The Use of Stilts, Especially in Africa and America*** Smärre Meddelanden 3. Stockholm: Riksmuseets Etnographiska Avdelning.

Leach, Maria (Ed), and Fried, Jerome (Assoc. Ed.)
Funk and Wagnalls Standard Dictionary of Folklore, Mythology and Legend New York: Harper & Row Publishers.

Lloyd, Christopher
1957 ***Sir Francis Drake*** London: Faber and Faber.

Malmström, V. H.
1997 ***Cycles of the Sun, Mysteries of the Moon: The Calendar in Mesoamerican Civilization*** University of Texas Press.
1998 ***A Survey of Teopantecuanitlan, Guerrero, Mexico***.

McIntyre, Michael
1979 ***South-East Asia*** London: B.B.C. Books.

Mead, G.R.S.
1949 ***Thrice Greatest Hermes*** Three volumes, London: John M. Watkins.

Morley, S.G., Brainered, G.W. and Sharer, R.J.
1983 ***The Ancient Maya*** Stanford: Stanford University Press.

Muller, Max
1969 ***The Vedas*** Varanasi: Indological Book House.

Murray, Margaret
The Splendour That Was Egypt

Needham, Joseph
1985 ***Trans-Pacific Echoes***, p. 30 Sahagun, Fray Bernardino de 1950-1969. ***The Florentine Codex: General Story of the Things of New Spain*** (Editor) Arthur J.O. Anderson and Charles Dibble 12 vols. Sante Fe NewMexico: School of American Research and University of Utah.

Pellegrino, Charles
1991 ***Unearthing Atlantis*** Random House.
Porphry, on the Cave of the Nymphs in the Thirteenth Book of the Odyssey Translated by Thomas Taylor 1917 London: John M. Watkins.

Radhakrishnan, S. (translator and editor)
1953 ***The Principal Upanishads*** New York: Harper and Brothers.

Rolleston, T.W.
1995 ***Celtic Myths and Legends*** London: Gresham Publishing.

Schele, Linda, and Freidel, David
1990 ***A Forest of Kings*: *The Untold Story of the Ancient Maya*** New York: William Morrow and Company.

Shao, Paul
1998 ***China and Pacific Basin Art and Architectural Styles - Pre-Columbian*** 1(1): 37-5.

Smart, Ninian
1969 ***The Religious Experience of Mankind*** London: Collins Pub. Co.

Soustelle, J.
1985 ***The Olmecs*: The *Oldest Civilization in Mexico*** Translated by H. R. Lane.

Sorenson, John L. and Raish, Martin H.
1996 ***Pre-Columbian Contact with the Americas Across the Ocean*** Provo: Research Press (1st edition 1990).

Stewart, Joe D.
1974 ***Mesoamerican and Eurasian Calendars*** Calgary: University of Calgary Press.

Taylor, Colin
1991 ***The Native Americans*** London: Salamanda Books.

Stillwell, Richard; MacDonald, William L. and McAllister, Marian Holland (editors)
1976 ***The Princeton Encyclopedia of Classical Sites*** Princeton: Princeton University Press.

Stoneman, Richard
1991 ***Greek Mythology*** London: The Aquarian Press.

Taylor, Colin
1991 ***The Native Americans*** London: Salamanda Books.

Stillwell, Richard; MacDonald, William L. and McAllister, Marian Holland (editors)
1976 ***The Princeton Encyclopedia of Classical Sites*** Princeton: Princeton University Press.

The Times Atlas of World History.
1986 London: Times Books.

Torquemada, Juan de
1723 ***Monarchia Indiana*** Madrid.

Waldman, Carl
1992 ***Encyclopedia of Native American Tribes*** New York: Facts on File Publications.

Vega, Nuñez de la
1702 ***Constituciones Diocesanas, Prologo*** Rome.

Verlag, Scherz
1969 ***The Seven Wonders of the World*** London: Weidenfeld and Nicolson Ltd.

Wadler, Arnold
2006. ***One Language***. Lindisfarne Books

Westwood, Jennifer (ed.).
1987 ***The Atlas of Mysterious Places*** London: Guild Publishing.

Wilkins, W.J.
1972 ***Hindu Mythology*** *(Vedic and Puranic)*
Delhi: J.K. Ahuja Delhi Bookstore.

Von Winning, Hasso
1989.***Trans-Pacific Contacts with Mexico*** - *A Review of Recent Research* Circum-Pacific Prehistory Conference, Seattle; *Prehistoric Trans-Pacific Contacts* Pullman: Washington State University.

Wiercinski, A.
1972 ***Inter-and-Intrapopulational Racial Differentiation of Tlatilco, Cerro de Las Mesas, Teothuacan, Monte Alban and Yucatan Maya*** XXX1X Congreso International de Americanistas, Lima 1970, Vol. 1, pp. 231-252.

Wiercinski, A. & Jairazbhoy, R.A.
1975. ***The New Diffusionist***, 5 (18), 5.

Wilbert, Johannes
1978 ***Navigators of the Winter Sun***; *The Sea in the Pre-ColumbianWorld.*

Winters, C.A.
1997 ***Olmec Writing*** http://geocities.com/olmec982000/olwrit.htm
1977. ***The influence of the Manade Scripts on American Ancient Writing Systems*** Bulletin de l'IFAN, t.39, Ser.B Number 2, 405-431.
1979. ***Manding Writing in the New World*** Part 1 Journal of African Civilization 1 (1), 81-97.
1981/1982 ***Mexico's Black Heritage*** - *The Black Collegian* pp. 76-82.
1983 ***The Ancient Manding Script*** I. Sertima (editor).
Blacks in Science: Ancient and Modern (ed.) I. Sertima pp. 208-214 London: Transaction Books.
1984 ***Blacks in Ancient America - Colorlines*** 3(2): 27-28.
1984 ***Africans Found First American Civilization*** African Monitor.
1986 ***The Migration Routes of the Proto-Mande*** The Mankind Quarterly 27 (1): 77-96. *
1997 ***The Decipherment of Olmec Writing*** Paper presented at the 74th Meeting of the Central States Anthropolo.

Wuthenau, Alexander von
1975 ***Unexpected Faces in Ancient America, 1500 B.C. - A.D. 1500: The Historical Testimony of Pre-Columbian Artists*** New York: Crown Publishers.

1978 ***World Mythology;*** *Encyclopedia of World Mythology* London: Peerage Books.

Xu, Mike H.
1996 ***Origin of the Olmec Civilization*** University of Central Oklahoma Press.

WEB PAGES

Human Lymphocyte Antigens
Apparent Afro-Asiatic, Southern Asian, &European HLA's in Indigenous American Populations
Guthrie James L.
http://www.neara.org/Guthrie/lymphocyteantigens01.htm

Helen in Egypt
Euripides
http://clasics.mit.edu/euripides/helen.html

The Conflicting Views Regarding Helen
Katie Desker
http://wwwperseus.tufts.edu/classes/KOp.html

Sea peoples raid on Nile Delta
http://en.wikipedia.org/wiki/Sea_Peoples

Land of Punt
http://en.wikipedia.org/wiki/Land of Punt.

Archaeologists discover ancient ships in Egypt
Stoddard, Tim (2004).
http://www.bu.edu/bridge/archive/2005/0318/archaeologisthhtml

Solomon's Ships in South America
http://www.cristobalcolondeibiza.com/2eng/2eng00.htm

Yahuwa - The Chinese Connection
Gamage Anjana
http://www.lankalibrary.com/geo/yapahuwa.htm

Dionysus and Kalaragama Parallel Mystery Cults
Patrick Harrigan
http://www.xlweb.com/heritage/skanda/dionysus.htm

Polynesian Origins and Migrations
AhChing, Peter Leiatua
http://polynesianlineage.tripod.com/polynesians/

TransPacific contacts?
Mike XU
http://www.chinese.tcu.edu/www_chinese3_tcu_edu.htm

Polynesian Pathways.
Peter Marsh
http://www.users.on.net/~mkfenn/page4.htm

Mysterious Strangers. New findings about the First Americans
Graham Hancock (1997)
http://w.w.w.grahamhancock.com/features/strangers-pl.htm

Early Monumental Architecture on the Peruvian Coast
James Q Jacobs (2001)
http://www.jqjacobs.net/andes/coast.html

Ancient Sumerians in Peru
http://www.world-mysteries.com/sar_8.htm
http://www.geocities.com/Tokyo/Bay/7051/poko2.htm

Islands of the Sun and Moon
http://www.perurail.com/Pages/History/hstrylktiticaca1.htm

The Andean explorer's foundation and ocean sailing club
http://www.aefosc.org/newsite/index.php?con=expeditions_grandophir_about

Brazil's Pedra da Gavea
Becari Luiza
http://www.viewzone.com/gavea.html

Same
http://www.earth-history.com/Atlantis/Donnelly/donnelly-atlantis-3-3.htm

Taino Caves
http://www.flmnh.ufl.edu/jca/Beekeretal.pdf

Anguilla's Fountain Cave
http://web.ai/stamps/fountain/

Taino History
http://www.hartfordhwp.com/archives/41/013.html

Taino Megaliths
http://www.nyboricua.com/boricua.htm

WEB PAGES

Cuba versus Hispaniola
http://andrewcollins.com/page/articles/cabrera.htm
Ancient Maps

James Siebold
http://www.henrydavis.com/MAPS/Ancient%20Web%20Pages/AncientL.htm

Phoenician Origins of Britons and Scots
Waddle. L.A.
1924. Williams & Norgate.
http://w.w.w.jrbooksonline.com/pob-ch13.htl

SIS Cambridge Conference
Natural Catastrophes during Bronze Age Civilizations: Archaeological, Geological, Astronomical and Cultural Perspectives.
http://www.meteor.co.nz/nov97_1.html

Sunken city discovered near Gibralter
http://212:58.240.35/l/hi/world/europe/3227295.stm

The Geography of Strabo
http://penelope.uchicago.edu/Thayer/E/Roman/Texts/Strab/1A*.html

The Geological Society of America
http://www.geosociety.org/

Eruption of Thera
Richard Shand
http://www.mystae.com/restricted/streams/thera/thera.html

Island of Ithaca
www.odysseus-unbound.org.

INDEX

www.ingramcontent.com/pod-product-compliance
Lightning Source LLC
Chambersburg PA
CBHW031957040826
48979CB00043B/1688/J

* 9 7 8 0 6 4 6 9 1 7 7 3 3 *